Nuyorican Feminist Performance

Nuyorican Feminist Performance

FROM THE CAFÉ TO HIP HOP THEATER

Patricia Herrera

University of Michigan Press
Ann Arbor

Published in the United States of America by the
University of Michigan Press
Manufactured in the United States of America
Printed on acid-free paper

A CIP catalog record for this book is available from the British Library.

First published July 2020

Library of Congress Cataloging-in-Publication Data

Names: Herrera, Patricia, 1974– author.
Title: Nuyorican feminist performance : from the cafe to hip hop theater / Patricia Herrera.
Description: Ann Arbor : University of Michigan Press, 2020. | Includes bibliographical references and index.
Identifiers: LCCN 2020004734 (print) | LCCN 2020004735 (ebook) | ISBN 9780472074488 (hardcover) | ISBN 9780472054480 (paperback) | ISBN 9780472126767 (ebook)
Subjects: LCSH: American literature—Puerto Rican authors—History and criticism. | American literature—Women authors—History and criticism. | American literature—20th century—History and criticism. | American literature—New York (State)—New York—History and criticism. | Arts, Puerto Rican—New York (State)—New York. | Arts, American—New York (State)—New York. | Puerto Ricans—New York (State)--New York—Intellectual life. | Puerto Ricans in literature. | Nuyorican Poets Cafe.
Classification: LCC PS153.P83 H475 2020 (print) | LCC PS153.P83 (ebook) | DDC 810.9/9287089684295—dc23
LC record available at https://lccn.loc.gov/2020004734
LC ebook record available at https://lccn.loc.gov/2020004735

To mamí and papí for their strength and resilience.
And for the amores de mi vida—my husband, Rider, and children, Aurelio, Adelina, and Adrián—who remind me every day to live boldly, passionately, and authentically.

Contents

Acknowledgments ix

Prologue 1

CHAPTER 1. Practicing a Feminist Nuyorican Aesthetic: We Are All Honorary Nuyoricans 8

CHAPTER 2. Gendering the Genealogies of the Nuyorican Aesthetic: The Young Lords, Neorican Seminar, and Nuyorican Poets Café 20

CHAPTER 3. The Founding Mothers of the Nuyorican Poets Café 48

CHAPTER 4. Masculinity in Hip Hop, Spoken Word, and Slam Poetry 73

CHAPTER 5. "It Was Definitely a Family Affair": La Bruja's *Boogie Rican Boulevard* 84

CHAPTER 6. Performing Afro-Latinidad: Nilaja Sun's *La Nubia Latina* and *Black and Blue* 101

CHAPTER 7. A Hip Hop Feminist Approach to Aya de León's *Thieves in the Temple* 118

CHAPTER 8. Beyond the Tangible: Performing Spirituality in Nuyorican Performances and Hip Hop Theater 138

Epilogue 163

Notes 171
Bibliography 209
Index 227

Digital materials related to this title can be found on the Fulcrum platform via the following citable URL: https://doi.org/10.3998/mpub.6710954

Acknowledgments

While working on this book, I gave birth to three amazing children. I've witnessed my children turn from infants to teenagers alongside the epic germination and development of this project. Just as the process of birthing and raising my children demanded a network of supporters, the birth of this book benefited from the critical generosity and intellectual and emotional support of many mentors, colleagues, and friends, who read, commented, discussed, and re-read my work and cheered me on. It has been many years in the making and I want to thank those most essential to its completion.

This project was first conceived during my time at the CUNY Graduate Center, which granted me institutional support throughout my graduate career. During his time at the Graduate Center, Marvin McAllister directed me in an independent study, which led to the initial stages of a dissertation proposal. His relentless assistance, professionalism, honesty, and collegiality are qualities that I truly admire and aspire to. My deepest thanks to members of my dissertation committee. Each one was instrumental to the development of this project. I am indebted to Jane Bowers for believing in me and showing me how to put words on paper with strength, clarity, and joy, and for the intimate intellectual and personal relationship; Juan Flores for thinking about my future; Gloria Waldman for a sharp eye to perfection; David Savran for theoretically pushing me; and Diana Taylor, whom I met many years ago as an undergraduate at Dartmouth College, and originally inspired me to work on Latinx theater and performance, and has continued to advise and encourage me. The interest, enthusiasm, and critical response of Jill Dolan in the early days of my project reminded me of the importance of weaving love and justice in my scholarly work. Biggest thanks to the many Graduate Center friends who contributed to the inception of this project or served as great support, such as Ramón Rivera-Servera, Dalia Bosiouny, Milton Loayza, Sharon Green, Jennifer Parker-Starbuck, Josh Abrams, and Lynette Gibson, who helped me think through the organization of the dissertation and read several drafts of the first chapter.

I never imagined that in the midst of trying to finish this book my dear mentor Juan Flores would transition to the spirit world. In one of our many conversations he asked me why I, an Ecua-American, was so drawn to the works of Nuyorican poets and performers. I was used to people confusing me as Puerto Rican, but I was never asked why I studied Nuyorican culture. His question made me reflect and acknowledge the intricate and intersectional paths I have walked to land in the work of Nuyorican poetry and performance. Juan, our many conversations firmly grounded me. I share with you some of my journey as a means of honoring and acknowledging the invisible labor of many in and out of academia that have helped me to wake up day in and day out with a sense of clarity of who I am and the path I must take. From my parents to my neighbors, they have all played a role.

It was at Dartmouth College, of all places, that I learned about what it means to be Latina and the works of Nuyorican artists. Growing up in Crown Heights, Brooklyn in the mid-seventies, then a poverty-ridden area, suffering from high rates of unemployment, crime rate, and adolescent delinquency, I did not think much of being poor or Latina. I lived a block away from Medgar Evers College and a few blocks down from the Hasidic community. Those who lived on my side of the neighborhood—a mostly Caribbean and African American hub of cultural activities—never hung out on the other side where the Hasidic community lived. While I visited Ecuador each summer until I was sixteen, my daily cultural references were mostly Puerto Rican and Caribbean. My mother did not learn how to cook until she came to New York, where she learned from her Puerto Rican friends. She would frequently say, "We eat Puerto Rican." My dad's obsession with listening to Puerto Rican salseros Tito Puente, Hector Lavoe, Frankie Ruiz, and Ismael Rivera every Friday night and all day Saturday while he cleaned the house, taught me how to feel salsa and merengue in my hips. Sadly, my cumbia skills need a lot of work compared to my Ecuadorian peers.

At the time, for the most part the Ecuadorian community was centralized in Queens. For Brooklynites, this was quite a trek, so my family were never there, unless we were visiting my cousins for special occasions. My best friend since kindergarten is Puerto Rican, and her family took me in as their daughter. They have a large family, so weekends, celebrations, and conversations were rooted in Puerto Rican cultural practices.

Upon hearing about my personal experiences and scholarly interests, Juan Flores declared I was an honorary Nuyorican. I was touched to hear this from him. A few months later, I witnessed Sandra María Esteves bestow those same words on audience members at Berkshire Community College, and somehow, her words weighed heavier on me. With great hesitation, I considered Esteves's invitation. Putting on that honorary badge, I slowly realized that her benevolent act went beyond merely blessing the crowd as Nuyoricans.

As a first-generation student, I knew little about what I was getting into when I accepted Dartmouth College's offer. Dartmouth was nothing like Crown Heights, Brooklyn. The campus was out in the boondocks. Everything was well-kept, pristine, and affluent, nothing like the apartment buildings or row houses in Crown Heights. I had never experienced so much open area, snow, or bitter cold in my life. With only Latinxs comprising only three percent of Dartmouth students, I quickly connected with organizations catering to students of color, such as the Afro-American Society and La Alianza Latina, as well as the theater groups the Black Underground Theatre & Arts Association and Nuestras Voces. I spent many nights with a pint of Ben and Jerry's Ice Cream, conversing with other students of color about how to navigate Dartmouth as a first-generation Latinx New Yorker.

The activism of my peers—along with the radical scholarly and creative works that professors such as Diana Taylor, Silvia Spitta, and Agnes I. Lugo-Ortiz exposed me to—politically awakened me and gave me tools to contextualize, theorize, and analyze Latinx cultural production. These professors arranged campus visits with scholars and artists that included Cherríe Moraga, Dolores Prida, Carmelita Tropicana, Coco Fusco, Tiffany Ana López, Roberto Gutiérrez Varea, José Esteban Muñoz, Guillermo Gómez-Peña, and Super Barrio Gómez. Each in their own way, Taylor, Spitta, and Lugo-Ortiz pointed me to the Nuyoricans and social justice art. The Nuyorican experience on the page and the stage was one that captivated me. I was drawn to the strategies of affirming cultural identity, resisting social injustice, and creating alternative ways of knowing and being. I devoted my graduate work to learning about Nuyorican poetry and performance, and quickly noticed that the Nuyorican narrative centered on male players and questioned the role of women in the field.

I later returned to Dartmouth as a César Chávez Dissertation Fellow in 2006–7 and met Laura Edmondson, Mary Coffey, and Francine A'Ness, who graciously provided me critical feedback, unconditional support, and more importantly, friendship. The Latin American, Latino, and Caribbean Studies program warmly welcomed me and made sure I had everything I needed to ensure that I was always productive and happy. Similarly, the theater department and the faculty were very enthusiastic and supportive. During my residency, I had numerous and continuous dialogue with the colleagues and friends who helped shape this project, among them Lourdes Gutiérrez-Nájera, Ana Merino, Sylvia Spitta, and Israel Reyes. I am eternally grateful to Heidi Stark and Erica Still, who were also dissertation fellows and made this writing process so much more enjoyable in the wee hours of the night. Their careful reading, thoughtful suggestions and remarks, and daily support contributed to the first iterations of this book.

Special thanks to the library staff at Dartmouth College Library; the Center for Puerto Rican Studies at Hunter College, especially Miguel Valladeras, Jorge Matos, Félix Rivera, and Pedro Juan Hernández; New York Public Library for the Performing Arts, especially Annemarie van Roessel and Doug Reside; The Public Theater, especially Andrew Kircher, Rachel London, and Avita Delerme; and the University of Richmond for their generous time, diligent resourcefulness, and institutional support.

I am grateful for the friends and colleagues who have been part of my intellectual communities, reading and/or listening to the early and not-so-good drafts of this project. Patricia Ybarra, Ramón Rivera-Servera, and Brandi Wilkins Catanes engaged with an early iteration of this project and generously provided me with guidance on the argument, organization, and my voice in this book. My longstanding writing group with Bedelia Richards and Eric Grollman have been my beacon of light. Thank you for the many hugs and words of encouragement, for the pointed feedback, and the many nudges to forge forward when everything seemed impossible. Immense gratitude to the continuous support of my co-conspirator, of now over a decade, Laura Browder, who has shown me how to dream big. Marci McMahon has been an incredible writing partner, helping me to keep my eyes on the prize and challenging me to be bold with my work. My deep appreciation to Laura Holliday, Badia Sahar Ahad, Annemarie Pérez, Nicole Maurantonio, Erika Damer, and Ernesto Semán for offering insightful feedback and asking hard questions about my project on many occasions. I am much obliged to Wilson Valentín-Escobar and Lawrence La Fountain-Stokes for their critical feedback, substantial guidance, and unwavering support. And to Jaime Carrero's family, Nestor Otero and George Malave for allowing me to share their poetry, art, and photography to the world.

Since 2013, Dorothy Mosby, Madeline Pérez, and I have been checking in on a weekly basis, sharing our progress and hardships. I am forever grateful for their continuous attention to accountability, self-care, productivity, resilience, and joy. Our accountability circle resulted from our participation in the National Center for Faculty Development & Diversity and for that I must give a big shout out to Kerry Ann Rockquemore.

Humongous thank you to Alberto Sandoval, Jorge Huerta, Roxannne Willis, Mariela Méndez, Mari Lee Mifsud, Kathleen Skerrett, Dorothy Holland, Lázaro Lima, Amy Lee Au, Martha Merritt, Ellen Sayles and the wonderful people of the Bonner Center for Civic Engagement, including Amy Howard, Sylvia Gale, Terry Dolson, Kimberly Dean-Anderson and Alexandra Byrum, who served as emotional support, offered advice, and uplifted my spirits as I chugged along. Over the span of twenty years, I have shared my work at the annual conferences of the American Society for Theatre Research and Association of Theatre in Higher Education and am honored to call them my intellectual homes.

This book would not have come into complete fruition without the tremendous support of LeAnn Fields for her persistence, thoughtfulness, and spirit of generosity as well as the University of Michigan Press team, especially Anna Pohlod and Mary Hashman. I am indebted to the anonymous readers for graciously providing me with generative, constructive feedback.

My deepest thanks to the *performeras*, Sandra María Esteves, Amina Muñoz, Caridad de la Luz, Nilaja Sun, and Aya de León, who were extremely generous and patient with me. And the *mujeres*, *madres*, and *curanderas* who helped me along the way: Miriam Colón, Maricruz Badia, Irene Lara, Laura Jiménez, Jennifer Ayala, Maria Figueroa, Esperanza Martell, Dayara Marte, and the many *guerrilleras* that sustained and maintained Casa Atabex Aché.

More than a decade ago, I met an amazing woman. I was fortunate to benefit from her mentorship, friendship, patience, faith, and strength. My deepest gratitude to you, Tiffany Ana López, for holding my hand, believing in me and my work from the very beginning, and witnessing my ups and downs.

Finally to my familia for their unconditional love, in particular my husband Rider, my firstborn Aurelio, and my daughter Adelina Babbit for patiently living with my struggles and allowing me to finish this book, spending many hours that would otherwise have been our time together. You are my light and inspiration. To my parents, Francisca and Victor Herrera, who gave me the tools to resist and persevere, as well as my in-laws, Nikki, Harold, and all the Babbits who cheered me along the way. To my soul sisters Alicia Díaz, Laura Jiménez, and Jeanette Pérez for the endless times they listened, counseled, hugged, and invigorated me both spiritually and intellectually. To my theater familia: Amarelys Pérez for godmothering my children and teaching me to believe in the magic of *teatro*, and José and Jennifer Garcia-Fleming for a critical and artistic drive.

Words cannot express the gratitude I feel for all of you who had faith and supported me along the way in the throes of this project. May you hear this shout out of appreciation and it may reverberate now and forever, for I am eternally grateful. With all my heart, *muchísimas gracias*.

Prologue

MY INITIATION TO HIP HOP theater occurred in 2001, when Rubí Theater Company, Inc., an intergenerational ensemble of mostly Latinx artists, writers, and educators, presented *Imagine the Angels of Bread* at the second New York City Hip-Hop Theater Festival.[1] The company, cofounded by Alicia Díaz, Jennifer Fleming, José Joaquín Garcia, Amarelys Pérez, and myself, transformed Martín Espada's book of poems into a hip hop theater concert, fusing modern dance, bomba, and popping and locking, while grooving to an orchestra of beatbox, stand-up bass, Puerto Rican cuatro, and Cuban tres. The time that we spent together creating and developing new works laid the foundation for this book. The intersection of feminism, social justice, and spiritual activism that characterizes the work of Nuyorican and hip hop performeras came into sharper focus time and time again as Rubí sought an aesthetic and language that would express the nuances of who we were with all our flaws, desires, and aspirations, and of how we wanted to be in the world.

As both a member of the company and a graduate student, I navigated between producing community theater and writing about the importance of it. Grappling with my positionality and learning how to bridge the two worlds, I worked to heed bell hooks's call to see the reality of the multiple centers and margins.[2] I write from the perspective of a Latina, community-based theater practitioner, scholar, and informed insider, who is—at times—an uninformed outsider engaging with various margins and different centers. This mode of seeing the world more holistically is useful in appreciating the intersecting margins and centers of the creative and scholarly disciplinary practices with which this study engages.

Rubí Theater Company produced and performed original works by individuals within the company and other Latinxs living in the United States. We also mentored and promoted emergent Latinx artists, ranging from playwrights to choreographers to hip hop dancers to rappers and singers. Although we came from different places (Puerto Rico, Dominican Republic, Brazil, Columbia, Ecuador, Mexico, and New York) and from all walks of life, we were all hungry to discover new ways of understanding and affirming our places in the larger social fabric of New York City and our nation. We worked with teenage artists to create art that would be socially relevant to a future generation, and our work was energized with the beauty of poetry, hip hop language—both physical and verbal—and the dynamism of our Latinx urban culture. Our work brought to the surface issues of colonialism, slavery, racism, immigration, environmental injustice, education inequities, poverty, gender discrimination, and other conditions and experiences that threatened the survival and existence of our communities. We were practicing what Jorge Huerta has called "necessary theater"; there was an urgency in performing our stories not only because we wanted to proclaim our very existence, but because we wanted to assure the future and livelihood of the next generation, who stood side by side with us creating theater.

I was three years out of college when I actually began to seriously put into practice Cherríe Moraga and Gloria Anzaldúa's "theory in the flesh," that "the physical realities of our lives—our skin color, the land or concrete we grew up on, our sexual longings—all fuse to create a politics born out of necessity."[3] As farmers plow the soil to plant seeds, Rubí's creative practice and process prepared our bodies to listen, feel, and express the daily triumphs and struggles of our fellow company members and Latinx communities. Drawing from a variety of Afrodiasporic performance traditions, we used our bodies—our experiences of flesh and blood—to collectively produce knowledge that would help us understand our social place in the larger context of America, fight for social justice, and heal from the trauma of a variety of social oppressions.

Rubí's collective art-making processes and practices, which incorporated meditation, yoga, martial arts, traditional and social dancing (bomba, salsa, and break dancing), beatboxing, rapping, circle work, and techniques from Boal's Theatre of the Oppressed, as well as spiritual cleansing practices, all worked toward healing and justice. The result of our work was ultimately "fleshing spirit and spiriting flesh," a theory and practice of spiritual activism offered by Elisa Facio and Irene Lara that builds on the work of Moraga and Anzaldúa, the radical foremothers of Latinx feminism.

We never positioned our work as spiritual, but it absolutely stemmed from a place of learning how to deeply know ourselves and one another's worldview. We attempted with body, mind, and spirit to comprehend the interrelationships among members in the ensemble—and beyond.[4] We did not ever call our work Nuyorican or hip hop theater, but by virtue of putting into practice urban-based, intergenerational, social justice–oriented, Afro-Latinx diasporic expressions, we inevitably wove into our work Nuyorican and hip hop expressions. We were making sense of our place in society, putting care into how we relate to each other, and finding ways to use our collective knowledge to make a more equitable place, practices which, as Inés Hernández-Avila asserts, make up one's spirituality.[5]

In the process of creating original plays and theatrical adaptations of Nuyorican works such as Martín Espada's book of poetry *Imagine the Angels of Bread* and Nicholasa Mohr's collection of stories *El Bronx Remembered*, we collectively birthed hope, empathy, compassion, trust, joy, and love, necessary medicine for combating social injustices. When theater is used in such a manner it ripples out from the confines of the stage, touching the spirits of people.[6] Audience members carry this bit of medicine with them in their everyday lives, hopefully spreading it to others. The teenagers that collaborated with us are now adults creating their own art that works toward making this world a better place. And so, I came to this book project as both scholar and practitioner, one whose theater work was shaped by necessary expressions of resistance and survival rooted in Nuyorican and hip hop culture as well as feminism—the intersecting subjects of this volume.

This book challenges the masculinist narrative of the Nuyorican poetry and theater scene in the 1970s and contextualizes the work of women influenced by the Nuyorican Poets Café. The performances of the Nuyorican Poets were crucial interventions in their time, and they remain influential to this day. The Nuyorican Poets Café, founded in the early 1970s by Miguel Algarín, Miguel Piñero, Pedro Pietri, and Sandra María Esteves, among others, was in its various locations a central gathering place for artists to reimagine community, and it was central to the emergence of the Nuyorican movement, a cultural revolution led largely by artists.[7] The café was vital in the formation of a Nuyorican aesthetic through art, poetry, theater, and performance. When places that nurtured the voices of Nuyoricans and Latinxs were few, the café served as a creative, cultural, and political refuge for artists to create and share their work.[8]

Nuyoricans were members of a generation born near the end of World War II who were deeply impacted by Operation Bootstrap.[9] Introduced by Luis Muñoz Marín, governor of Puerto Rico from 1949 to 1965, this stimulus program offered North American companies tax incentives to develop manufacturing plants and tourism on the island, thus transforming the agrarian Puerto Rican economy into an industrial one. While Operation Bootstrap generated new jobs, the high unemployment rates in Puerto Rico continued to push people to seek employment on the mainland, which gave rise to a great influx of Puerto Rican migrants in the 1940s and 1950s, particularly to New York City.[10] The children of these immigrants—the generation that came of age in the 1960s, who were shaped by this great period of migration and industrialization and who distinctly positioned themselves as New York Puerto Ricans—came to call themselves Nuyoricans.

It was this generation of Nuyorican artists, educators, activists, intellectuals, students, and blue-collar workers that incited the Nuyorican movement, a social revolution linked to the international liberation and anticolonial movements. El Nuevo Despertar (the New Awakening), as this period was called, created a form of radicalism geared toward reforming civil society. Artists were at the forefront of this social movement, and they participated in antiwar protests, civil rights demonstrations, and local grassroots initiatives to rehabilitate the inner city. Most importantly, they worked to put the community in control of public resources dedicated to urban renewal and antipoverty initiatives. The founding members of the café used poetry, visual art, and performance to articulate and document their lived experiences of poverty, unemployment, undereducation, and inhumane living conditions. Artists practicing a Nuyorican aesthetic were not making art for art's sake. Rather, they were socially and politically invested in the improvement of Puerto Rican, Latinx, and other underrepresented communities. This critical base still influences contemporary poetry, literature, visual art, and theater, and it informs artists today who still practice a Nuyorican aesthetic.

Although the Nuyorican Poets Café and its contemporaries were committed to social equity, women's contributions to the 1970s Nuyorican poetry and theater scene have tended to go unrecognized. The café's male vanguard emphasized equality across culture, race, ethnicity, and class, but gender equality was not necessarily a central concern of the group. Consequently, as with some other social movements of the time, the leaders tended to discount women as equal partners. Not surprisingly, histories of the café's performances and other scholarship on the café has mostly focused on its male participants. The café's publicity material, for instance, often featured only male poets.

A flier with hand-drawn accent marks, copied askew on cheap paper, publicized the performance of the Nuyorican Poets on August 18, 1975. This performance, part of *The Poets of the City* event, was produced by Joseph Papp's New York Shakespeare Festival, which during the summer months offered free theater in Central Park's Delacorte Theater. Fliers such as this one often serve as the sole documentation of these events, as Nuyorican performances of the period were often not reviewed.

Without ephemera like *The Poets of the City* flier and program, this moment of public cultural production and exchange by the Nuyorican Poets would be erased from twentieth-century theater history, only remembered by those who attended the performance. Yet even as Nuyorican performances have been omitted from American theater histories, within the narrative of Nuyorican history so have female cultural producers and their contributions been elided. The flier features all the male poets, but it does not feature Sandra María Esteves, a female Nuyorican poet who performed with them that night; the official program for the performance lists Esteves last. This flier not only documents a performance, it records how women were erased and rendered silent in the historical narrative of the Nuyorican Poets Café. The male poets of the café, prominent in the flier, have also predominated the history of the café and become ingrained as part of the popular thought and culture on the Nuyorican Poets. My realization of the stunning absence of Nuyoriqueñas as cultural producers in these accounts of the café inspired me to examine how women practice a Nuyorican feminist aesthetic.[11]

Nuyorican Feminist Performances attempts to break the glaring absence of and deafening silence around women in Nuyorican performance history. The book brings women to the forefront by tracing the feminist work of Nuyorican performeras, female performing poets, spoken word artists, and hip hop theater practitioners who use performances as a vehicle for social change. Nuyorican women have used a variety of expressive modalities to raise consciousness, generate collective knowledge-making forums, and cultivate healing practices. The recounting of Nuyorican history is incomplete without realizing that this history is in need of collective documentation. The work that follows thus is not meant to be an exhaustive overview of the women and feminist practices of the Nuyorican poetry movement, but rather an initial engagement with a topic that is part of a collective history that deserves more scholarly attention. More than simply raising the issue of gender inequality and unacknowledged sexism in the movement, I explore

Figure 1. Flier from 1975 performance in Central Park. Clockwise from top: Lucky Cienfuegos, Miguel Piñero, and Miguel Algarín. Sandra María Esteves, who also took part in the performance, is missing from the photo. Courtesy Billy Rose Theatre Division, New York Public Library.

the social and cultural contexts from which these artists emerged and offer close readings of works by performeras that have remained in the periphery of Nuyorican cultural productions then and now to understand their feminist performance practices.[12] Examining the development of a Nuyorican feminist aesthetic throughout time recalibrates the feminist narrative of Nuyorican history and allows for a deeper understanding of the significant role of women in the spoken word and hip hop theater world.

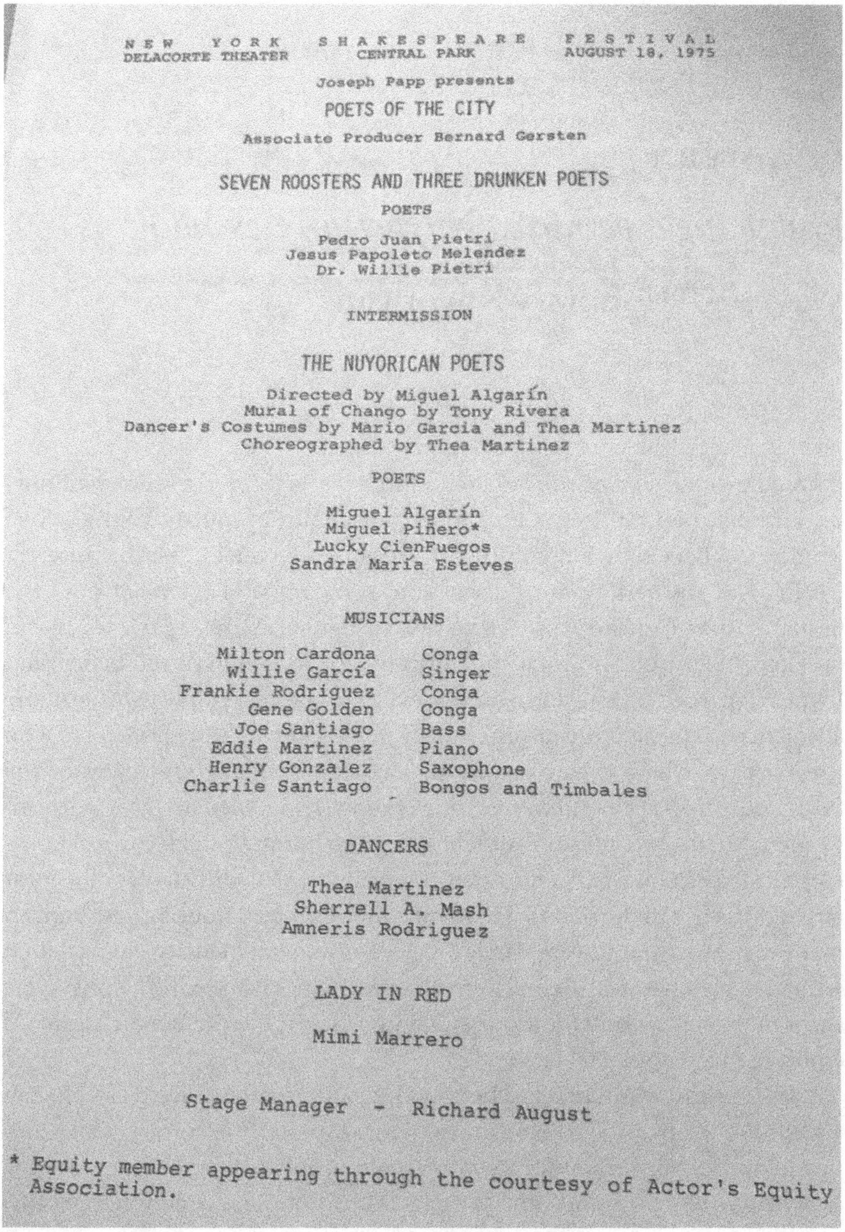

N E W Y O R K S H A K E S P E A R E F E S T I V A L
DELACORTE THEATER CENTRAL PARK AUGUST 18, 1975

Joseph Papp presents

POETS OF THE CITY

Associate Producer Bernard Gersten

SEVEN ROOSTERS AND THREE DRUNKEN POETS

POETS

Pedro Juan Pietri
Jesus Papoleto Melendez
Dr. Willie Pietri

INTERMISSION

THE NUYORICAN POETS

Directed by Miguel Algarín
Mural of Chango by Tony Rivera
Dancer's Costumes by Mario Garcia and Thea Martinez
Choreographed by Thea Martinez

POETS

Miguel Algarín
Miguel Piñero*
Lucky CienFuegos
Sandra María Esteves

MUSICIANS

Milton Cardona	Conga
Willie García	Singer
Frankie Rodriguez	Conga
Gene Golden	Conga
Joe Santiago	Bass
Eddie Martinez	Piano
Henry Gonzalez	Saxophone
Charlie Santiago	Bongos and Timbales

DANCERS

Thea Martinez
Sherrell A. Mash
Amneris Rodriguez

LADY IN RED

Mimi Marrero

Stage Manager - Richard August

* Equity member appearing through the courtesy of Actor's Equity Association.

Figure 2. Program from *Poets of the City*, including Lucky Cienfuegos, Miguel Piñero, Miguel Algarín, and Sandra María Esteves. Courtesy Billy Rose Theatre Division, New York Public Library.

CHAPTER 1

Practicing a Feminist Nuyorican Aesthetic

We Are All Honorary Nuyoricans

ON NOVEMBER 30, 2006, I watched Sandra María Esteves, a renowned Nuyorican poet, perform her poetry to a small group of mostly young, white women at Berkshire Community College in Pittsfield, Massachusetts.[1] During the postperformance discussion, someone asked, "What does the term 'Nuyorican' mean?" Esteves waved her right arm like a magic wand and declared, "You are all honorary Nuyoricans." I, too, was in the audience, and I was astonished at Esteves's willingness to invite individuals without any allegiance to the Nuyorican community to wear the label, regardless of who they were or where they came from. The universalizing ideologies of the first- and second-wave feminist movements had failed to give voice to women of color—could the audience use this honorary badge to acknowledge the experiences of Nuyorican women and the Nuyorican community at large?[2] Esteves's invitation to assume the identity of an honorary Nuyorican made me somewhat uneasy. First, my Ecua-American identity did not align with the geographical definition of Nuyorican, and second, I felt some accountability if problems arose in having a largely white female audience embrace this ethnoracial term.

Yet Esteves's willingness to bestow this honorary label needs to be seen within a Nuyorican aesthetic that puts into practice intersectional feminism. Intersectional feminism was born out of the need to differentiate the experiences of women of color. White feminists of the second wave lacked a framework to examine how race, class, and ethnicity can shape both one's gender identity and the feminist movement. The notion of intersectionality, as conceived by Kimberlé Crenshaw, suggests that sexist oppression is not just about gender; it involves multiple and intersecting forms of marginalization and oppression.[3] While Esteves was not intimately involved with the feminist movement, she was influenced by third-wave feminism. Feminist leaders of the mid-1970s—such as Gloria Anzaldúa, bell hooks, Chela Sandoval, Cherríe Moraga, Audre Lorde, and Maxine Hong Kingston—called for alternative subjectivities and laid the foundation for third-wave feminism in the late 1980s.

It is during this same period that Esteves puts into practice a Nuyorican intersectional feminist aesthetic to create her poetry, visual art, and performance. Three decades later, she continues to practice intersectional feminism, creating more inclusive expressive spaces that challenge and expand the boundaries of nationalism, gender, and citizenship. While gender is the shared axis of identification among the women in the auditorium, when Esteves provides a snapshot of her life through poetry she asserts her experiences as a Nuyorican woman distinct from the white women sitting in the audience. Her cultural references may seem foreign to her audience, but Esteves prompts them to feel like a part of something greater than themselves, transcending ethnic heritage, mastery of language, and cultural knowledge, to experience life in the skins of Nuyoricans, especially Nuyorican women.

Esteves's invitation invokes her own intersecting ethnic identities, as someone of both Puerto Rican and Dominican descent.[4] She attests to this multiplicity in "Puerto Rican Discovery #3 Not Neither":

Being *Puertorriqueña-Dominicana*
Borinqueña-Quisqueyana
Taina Africana
Born in the Bronx, not really *jībara*
Not really *hablando bien*
But yet, not *Gringa* either
Pero ni portorra, pero si portorra too
Pero ni qué what am I? *Y qué soy?*

Being Puerto Rican Dominican
Born in the Bronx, not really a traditional Puerto Rican
Not really speaking well
But yet, not Gringa either
But not Puerto Rican, yet also Puerto Rican
But then, what am I?[5]

In the poem, Esteves challenges the nationalistic principles that attempts to locate an authentic Nuyorican identity in Puerto Rico and New York and highlights the shared histories of colonialism among Puerto Rico, Hispaniola, Cuba, and other Caribbean islands. Her choice to embrace the term Nuyorican places her work far beyond a project of the Puerto Rican diaspora, encompassing a more complex, hybrid, and fluid notion of what it means to be Nuyorican. A similar intersectional feminist approach lies at the heart of the work of Nuyorican performeras in this book. Mediated by poetry and performance, the intersectional feminist consciousness that Nuyorican performeras practice sets in motion a vision of the radical self as part of a collective social body, inviting the audience to be allies by participating in the production and circulation of Nuyorican cultural knowledge.

Steering the flow of empowerment from the self to the collective is a coalition-building strategy by which Nuyorican performeras like Esteves move beyond the performing space to generate empathy and solidarity among individuals with various social histories. Before performing her opening piece "Poem for Closet Poets," Esteves takes the audience back to when she was a child in a Catholic school where speaking Spanish was forbidden. She confesses that she lived in the closet of silence—silence about her artistry, her worries, and her desires. Initially, she used painting—a nonverbal mode of expression—to make sense of her reality. She came to poetry because it helped her transform the experience of living in silence into public testimony. Esteves's words hold immense power as she shares her transformation from fear to belief in herself. In her soft but far-reaching voice, she asserts:

> This is a poem for women who write
> Who use powerful metaphors
> To describe our common victimization
> This is a call, a plea a song of your poetry
> A request to believe in the power of your voice
> There is need for your vision in a common sharing. . . .
>
> This is a poem that demands your attention
> That solicits your cooperation
> That begs to know itself through the mirror of you
> Defining itself by breaking out of chains
> Tearing down walls where our voices were sealed

Don't hide but share what you know
Don't fear, but believe
Discover the you within, bring her out
To stand on her own within the world.[6]

Seamlessly moving between relating her personal experiences and performing her poetry, she encourages other women to overcome silence, to combat feelings of alienation, to attain autonomy and self-determination, and to find the poet within themselves. Her urgent message to break the silence is neither loud in volume nor invasive; rather, her melodic voice is soothing, reassuring, and hopeful. Esteves uses this poem as a way of "daring" the women in the audience "to scream through silence" and write, because these acts "tear down walls where [their] voices [are] sealed."[7] Esteves practices a Nuyorican intersectional feminist aesthetic by shining a light on the structural oppressions that silence women, especially Nuyorican women, and that prevent them from sharing their truth.

Poets like Esteves and her contemporaries do not rely solely on the printed text but use it as a blueprint to perform. The excerpts of their poetry printed in this book privilege the written word, but lost in translation is the sound of the poetry and the physicality that comes with performing their work. As contemporary American poet Billy Collins has observed, "The poet's role is more about composing for the ears rather than writing to capture the reading eye."[8] When poets perform, they add meaning to their work acoustically; so as close readers and listeners, we need to understand the meanings created when the poet makes choices about speed, rhythm, tempo, beat, tone, inflection, and pause. With this in mind, this book considers what performances performeras generate, how they do it, what it means, and what becomes of their doing.[9] Writing about performance is challenging; the written text cannot fully capture Esteves's presentation style, the musical echoes of salsa, hip hop, jazz, or blues in the work of La Bruja and Aya de León, or the emotional intensity of Mariposa (María Teresa Fernández). Additionally, witnessing a performance inevitably alters the ways that viewers hear, read, and understand the poem later, both on and off the page. Performance and the performing body play a crucial role in the artistic process, making the term *performeras* perfectly suited for these women.

Since the performance of the live body is an integral site of inquiry, I cannot speak to the "liveness" of performances that occurred in the 1970s. Instead I have turned to archival materials, the scripts and reviews of the artists' performances that document the live bodies, which allow me to think through the potentialities of performance. Building on the work of Amelia Jones and Andrew Stephenson, who offer alternative models for reading and understanding the visual in their anthology *Performing the Body/Performing the Text* (1999), I consider the production of visual art, its viewing, and its embodied reception as performative processes. The processes of reading, interpreting, and interacting are performative acts. I seek the meanings beyond the frozen images, contextualizing the corporeal enactments on the page and their relationships to the stage and to life itself. Taken together, these components are part of a larger performance, one that makes female bodies highly visible. Considering these ontological and epistemological uses of performance allows for close readings of the interplay among the living body, textuality, visuality, history, efficacy, memory, and potentiality.

LATINX AND HIP HOP SCHOLARSHIP THAT PAVED THE WAY

While scholarship in the field of Latinx theater and performance studies and the corpus of work on artistic productions of, about, and by the Puerto Rican diaspora have grown exponentially, the contributions of Nuyorican women in the poetry, hip hop, and theater scene remain in the shadows.[10] *Nuyorican Feminist Performance* is the first to examine in depth the aesthetic and intersectional feminist work of Nuyorican performeras, foregrounding their work from the 1970s to 2000s, and closely analyzing how it articulates notions of culture, identity, gender, citizenship, and belonging. This book offers points of entry for understanding the interventions of performeras and the way that their work in the 1970s carved avenues for contemporary Latinx artists to reimagine both the self and community. Their intersectional feminism challenged the masculinist, nationalist historical narratives of the Nuyorican movement and the Poets Café, and it greatly impacted the spoken word and hip hop theater scene. This book thus engages the broader implications of the intersectional feminist consciousness enacted by Nuyorican performeras whose work radicalized the female self and mobilized the collective social body.

Nuyorican Feminist Performance takes an interdisciplinary approach that is as much infused with scholarship of theater, performance, hip hop, Latinx, and women's studies as it is by the quotidian practices of activism.[11] It draws on the groundbreaking scholarship of Arcadio Díaz-Quiñones, Efraín

Barradas, Juan Flores, and Frances R. Aparicio, offering diasporic and transnational approaches to understanding Nuyorican cultural productions with attention to Afrodiasporic music and performance practices. The scholarly commitment to Nuyorican literature by Eugene Mohr and Lisa Sánchez González provided me with a foundation to theorize Nuyorican poetry and performance.[12] Frances Negrón-Muntaner's and Arlene Dávila's attention to how the politics of culture, identity, and representation play out locally and globally in a variety of institutional settings including museums, shopping malls, mass media, and industries of contemporary culture pushed me to think more broadly about how Nuyorican performeras straddle multiple landscapes from popular culture to quotidian life to theater and performance.[13] Accordingly, the generative work of Lawrence La Fountain-Stokes on the centrality of Nuyorican queer productions and migration historicizes and theorizes the critical intervention of artists who were making sense of how their migration experiences were profoundly impacted by misogynistic, sexist, and homophobic practices. Urayoán Noel's foundational study *In Visible Movement*, released as I was finishing work on this manuscript, laid the groundwork for examining Nuyorican poetry as rooted in a practice of embodiment.[14] *Nuyorican Feminist Performance* continues the conversation staged by these notable scholars and scholarly works and significantly expands prior discussions by closely examining the production of Nuyorican feminist performeras from 1970s to the early 2000s through the lens of theater and performance studies.[15] The foundational works of theater and performance scholars Jorge Huerta, Alberto Sandoval-Sánchez, David Román, José Esteban Muñoz, Alicia Arrizón, and Tiffany Ana López helped establish the field of US Latinx theater and performance studies by expanding the concepts of Latinidad, mestizaje, and queering. These efforts in turn gave rise to the provocative works of Patricia Ybarra, Jon D. Rossini, Ramón H. Rivera-Servera, and Marci McMahon, all of whom were integral to the evolution of this book.[16]

HIP HOP THEATER, HIP HOP FEMINISM, AND NUYORICAN HIP HOP FEMINIST PERFORMANCES

The development of a Nuyorican aesthetic must be understood through two intersecting diasporas: Puerto Rican and African-based, including Afro-Caribbean. As such, there are points of contact with African-based and African American vernacular traditions and expressions as well as African American communities.[17] The marriage of hip hop and Nuyorican performance is thus a major component of this book. In the same ways that Esteves brought the intersectional feminist perspective into the Nuyorican movement, contemporary performeras of the 1990s and 2000s addressed issues of misogyny and patriarchy by engaging with the Afrodiasporic art form of hip hop. Like Esteves, contemporary performeras La Bruja, Nilaja Sun, Mariposa, and Aya de León articulate in their work their intersectional experiences as women, Afro-Latinas, working-class subjects, and artists, all challenged by colonial power. As women working within hip hop—a male-dominated art form—La Bruja, Mariposa, Sun, and de León engender a feminist perspective that expands the boundaries of Nuyorican performance, hip hop, and theater.

While there are many books on hip hop, there are few that engage with hip hop theater. The increasing visibility of hip hop theater demands that scholars use a different set of tools to not only analyze and understand the plays, but also to critically examine the intersectional feminist approaches practiced by Nuyorican performeras. Scholars need to do more theorizing of the women in hip hop theater and their contributions. Many hip hop scholars—such as Tricia Rose, Houston Baker, Robin D. G. Kelley, and Todd Boyd—acknowledge the presence of Latinxs in the hip hop world, but only a few works, like Juan Flores's landmark *From Bomba to Hip-Hop* (2000) and Raquel Z. Rivera's *New York Ricans from the Hip Hop Zone* (2003), fully explore their participation. Daniel Banks's *Say Word! Voices from Hip Hop Theater* (2011) and Kim Euell and Robert Alexander's *Plays from the Boom Box Galaxy* (2009) are the only two anthologies that historicize hip hop theater and solely showcase hip hop plays. Prior to these volumes, Harry J. Elam Jr. and Robert Alexander featured three hip hop plays in the coedited anthology *The Fire This Time* (2004). Additionally, in the coedited anthology *Black Cultural Traffic* (2005), Elam and Kennell Jackson also included several analytical essays on global hip hop, hip hop fashion, and hip hop films. Baba Israel moves in this direction with *Remixing the Ritual* (2008), which examines the process of creating his solo hip hop theater show *Boom Bap Meditations*.

To understand the various Nuyorican feminist practices deployed by the post-1970s generation of performeras, after Esteves, it is crucial not only to grasp the impact of hip hop theater, but also to theorize feminist approaches to it. Like Esteves, contemporary performeras La Bruja, Nilaja Sun, Mariposa, and Aya de León practice Nuyorican feminism, but they differ from her in that they are part of the hip hop generation and engage with a hip hop feminist aesthetic. Nuyorican, Black, and hip hop feminisms work to dismantle misogyny, sexism, and patriarchy, but generational differences between women and girls shape how each group engages with feminism.[18] Largely influenced by the civil rights and Black Power movements, third-wave feminism does not exactly address women's place in the hip hop generation. While hip hop feminism falls within the realm of third-wave feminism, it necessitates different historical and theoretical frameworks. The Civil Rights Act of 1964—as Aisha S. Durham and Bakari Kitwani argue—distinctly marks the experiences of the hip hop generation, loosely defined as people of color born between 1965 and 1984.[19] People of this generation are the beneficiaries of legalized enfranchisement, yet their experiences of this historical achievement remain elusive. The hip hop generation experienced a set of unprecedented social injustices, including class warfare, police brutality, gangs, drugs, and racial animosity.[20] In contrast to the generation of the 1960s and 1970s, who experienced constant invisibility brought about by systems of segregation, the hip hop generation grapples with a new racism, one that makes difference visible, yet also erases it.[21] The popularity of hip hop makes Blackness desirable, yet the stereotypical representations of Black people as gang members, welfare queens, drug dealers, and teen mothers practically erase them from the citizenry. Thus, the hip hop generation is simultaneously the most loved and the most hated in popular culture.

Hip hop feminism thus was born out of a need to understand the cultural, social, and political conditions that afflict women of the hip hop generation. The fact that hip hop feminism engages with hip hop—a cultural phenomenon that tends to put a Black masculinist perspective on a pedestal—is incommensurable with the theory and praxis of Black feminisms.[22] However, as Whitney A. Peoples demonstrates, it is important to understand the connections between generations of Black feminism during the three waves. One of the first authors to self-identify as a hip hop feminist, Joan Morgan, in her book *When Chickenheads Come Home to Roost* (1999) coins the phrase "fucking with the gray," an instrumental feminist theoretical framework that ignited the entire hip hop feminism movement.[23] Grappling with the lived contradiction of loving an art form that sexually objectifies and debases Black women and desiring the "in-yo-face testosterone" that creates that same objectification is what she calls hip hop feminism, "a feminism brave enough to fuck with the grays."[24]

Contemporary Nuyorican hip hop performeras La Bruja, Nilaja Sun, Mariposa, and Aya de León, I posit, "fuck with the grays." They deal with the incongruities of hip hop culture by going beyond critiques of misogyny, acknowledging the institutions that proliferate hypersexualized representations of women, and addressing the complicity of women in their own objectification. Messing with the grays means considering notions of sexual agency, which can be taboo, and offering a women-centric worldview that values the realities of the hip hop generation's women. The ability of contemporary performeras to navigate this "grayness" demands a set of tools different from those used to understand first- and second-wave feminism. According to Shani Jamila, "as women of the hip-hop generation we need a feminist consciousness that allows us to examine how representations and images can be simultaneously empowering and problematic."[25] Hers is the call for a new feminism that incited Black feminist scholars such as Gwendolyn D. Pough and Aisha S. Durham to consider what happens when hip hop and feminism are in dialogue with each other. Durham defines this feminism as "a sociocultural, intellectual, and political movement grounded in the situated knowledge of women of color from the broader hip hop or the U.S. post–civil rights generation who recognize culture as a pivotal site for political intervention to challenge, resist, and mobilize collectives to dismantle systems of exploitation."[26] Women of color have been integral to hip hop culture, but they have not received appropriate attention for their participation and contributions. Building on Morgan's ideas about hip hop feminism, Pough contends in *Check It While I Wreck It* (2004) that Black women rappers, for instance, have influenced styles and techniques by bringing a feminist stance that disrupts—or *wrecks*—misogynistic representations of Black women in their music.

La Bruja, Nilaja Sun, Aya de León, and Mariposa not only navigate the muddy waters of a hip hop culture; they use strategies that wreck this culture's masculinist practices. The works of these performeras go beyond flat representations to create living messages. Through their bodies, they restore the protest traditions of the 1960s and 1970s, deploy the artistic traditions of the Nuyorican Poets Café, and engage with hip hop to express themselves as women involved in social action, always resisting. Their artistic creations blend the political and the personal, and these performeras use spiritual foundations on which they can document, reflect, contest, and reimagine their lives as women, Latinas, and citizens.

OVERVIEW OF CHAPTERS

To fully grasp the works of these performeras, chapter 2 traces the masculinist-centric ethos of early Nuyorican cultural forms that led to the birth of the café and the formalization of a Nuyorican aesthetic. Drawing from the protest traditions of the Puerto Rican Nationalist Party and Young Lords, the poetry and drawings of Jaime Carrero in *Notes of Neorican Seminar* (1972), and the performance poetry traditions of the Nuyorican Poets Café, I examine how women have been virtually erased from Nuyorican history. Similar to the Young Lords, the café made a commitment to social equity, yet this commitment existed alongside a troubling history of gender politics; the masculinist ethos of these organizations excluded women and women's concerns in a civil rights–inspired community movement for social justice. The founders of the Nuyorican Poets Café imported some of the Puerto Rican Nationalist Party's and Young Lords' strategies into forming the café by appealing to its community on the frontlines of performance, print, and visual culture. These practices, however, stemmed from a masculinist ideology.

The masculinist ethos of the Young Lords and the café made it difficult for women to thrive in the Nuyorican scene of the 1970s. Thus, chapter 3 spotlights the work of performeras such as Sandra María Esteves, Martita Morales, Luz Rodriguez, and Amina Muñoz who contributed to the formation of the café. A major goal of my work is to rethink Nuyorican performance along gendered lines. To date, scholarship about the café summarizes the male artists involved, but the contributions made by women remain underexplored. I use the term *performeras* to establish the existence of a Latina consciousness within the Nuyorican aesthetic. This term uniquely positions these women as artists who use performance to problematize notions of class, ethnicity, race, and gender.

We cannot examine the work of these performeras in a literary vacuum. We must see their work as part of a continuous Nuyorican aesthetic, with a sharper eye toward giving women voice and agency. In preparation for the close readings of contemporary performeras—specifically La Bruja (the Witch), Mariposa (Butterfly), Nilaja Sun, and Aya de León—who continue to practice a Nuyorican aesthetic with a hip hop sensibility, chapter 4 provides the cultural and historical contexts for understanding their works.

From there, the next three chapters build on the foundational work forged by Nuyorican founding mothers to analyze the works of contemporary performeras. Inspired and mentored by founders of the Nuyorican Poets Café, La Bruja, Mariposa, de León, and Sun infuse their poetry and solo pieces with a Nuyorican and hip hop aesthetic. By incorporating hip hop into their works, they align with the struggles, experiences, and traditions of African Americans. For example, La Bruja samples popular salsa and hip hop songs to generate a "flow, layering, and fragmentation" that correlates with her experiences of displacement, transformation, and recuperation of self.[27] The presence of hip hop in the work of these performeras points to the shared histories of dispersal and fragmentation of the Afrodiaspora.[28] They "fuck with the grays" by creating cross-pollinated hip hop montages—poems that transmute into monologues, vignettes, or solo performance—to express their individual identities as women born and raised in places like the South Bronx, the Lower East Side, Los Angeles, and San Francisco, and their communal identity as Nuyorican women.

I begin chapter 5 by paying close attention to La Bruja's *Boogie Rican Boulevard* (1996) and her rap songs "Pollito Chicken" and "For Witch It Stands." The chapter argues that La Bruja practices hip hop feminism by performing women-centered familial networks as a mechanism of claiming kinship ties not only to Puerto Rico, but also to the greater Puerto Rican family—biological or not—on the mainland and beyond.

Drawing on two solo performances by Nilaja Sun—*La Nubia Latina* (1999) and *Black and Blue* (2001)—chapter 6 explores how Sun draws from both a Nuyorican feminist and a hip hop aesthetic to problematize notions of Blackness and Latinidad, as well as to reflect on her Afro-Latina identity. Her works reenact her lived experiences as an Afro-Latina, encountering multiple and intersecting racial histories of oppression.

Like Sun, Aya de León engages with the performativity of Blackness and Latinidad. What sets her work apart, however, is her performance of whiteness and commodification. Chapter 7, which focuses on her *Thieves in the Temple* (2004), studies racial stereotyping and capitalistic co-optation of hip hop. By performing the consumption of hip hop, León not only underscores how media packages hip hop as a good that consumers purchase, but also shows how women straddle between acts of complicity and empowerment.

Finally, in chapter 8, I examine spiritual performances as another feminist practice within the Nuyorican hip hop performance aesthetic. Drawing from the theories of Latina feminists Gloria Anzaldúa, Cherríe Moraga, and Laura Pérez, this chapter argues that the spiritual discourse used by Esteves—along with hip hop performeras like La Bruja, Mariposa, and Aya de León—is central to consciousness-raising and political mobilization. Performeras invite audience members to participate in different types of ritual healing, and the audiences both witness and enact the rituals. This process offers individuals and communities the hope and sustenance needed for citizenship.

Similar to Yolanda Broyles-González's work in *El Teatro Campesino: Theater in the Chicano Movement* (1994), in which she argues against a hegemonic narrative of Chicano theater, I offer a nuanced reading of the many ways that performeras struggled for personal and communal equality. The Nuyorican movement had a commitment to racial and ethnic equality. However, the founding mothers of the café experienced contradictions within the discourses around equality, colonial liberation, and social change and the sexism that they encountered both in and out of the Nuyorican art scene. Focusing our attention on the works of performeras of the 1970s allows us to more fully understand the feminist contributions that they made to the development of a Nuyorican aesthetic. This historical narrative contextualizes the emergence of a Nuyorican feminist aesthetic, opening an avenue to understanding the ways that this aesthetic interacted with hip hop theater in the 1990s.

As a participant in the Nuyorican movement, Esteves has created artistic works that value individuals and communities in all their differences and diversities. Like many Nuyorican female artists working in the 1970s, she wanted Puerto Rican women to be acknowledged for making significant contributions to all facets of life in New York City. As you read these pages, remember that Esteves desires nothing more than for you to feel as if you are a part of the Nuyorican community. It is her profound faith in the power of poetry and performance based on the flesh and blood that has inspired me to write about the poets, performers, theater practitioners, artists, educators, and activists who practice a Nuyorican feminist aesthetic.

CHAPTER 2

Gendering the Genealogies of the Nuyorican Aesthetic

The Young Lords, Neorican Seminar, and Nuyorican Poets Café

PUERTO RICAN ACTIVISTS, artists, and poets living in New York City who participated in the Nuyorican movement served as cultural agents challenging racial and economic injustices. However, gender injustice was strikingly absent from their critiques. A gendered analysis of early Nuyorican cultural forms and organizations reveals the masculinist ethos that has excluded women and women's concerns in a civil rights-inspired community movement for social justice. Foundational events such as Neorican Seminar, and organizations such as the Young Lords and the Nuyorican Poets Café, turned to a masculinist, body-centered performance aesthetics to express the Nuyorican experience, which undoubtedly influenced Nuyoriqueñas. Drawing from the protest traditions of the Puerto Rican Nationalist Party and the Young Lords, visual representations of embodiment in Jaime Carrero's *Notes of Neorican Seminar,* and poetry performance traditions of the Nuyorican Poets Café, this chapter seeks to map the masculinist-centric ethos of early Nuyorican cultural forms.

WOMEN-LED REVOLTS, BOUNDED BY A MASCULINIST NARRATIVE

"Mickey" Melendez, a member of the Young Lords, recalls how posters of revolutionary heroes—including Pedro Albizu Campos, Ramón Emeterio

Betances, Malcolm X, Ho Chi Minh, Mao Tse-tung, Frantz Fanon, Che Guevara, and the Black Panthers—covered the storefront and walls of the Young Lords' office.[1] Their images demonstrate how the Young Lords connected themselves to a complex network of international leaders, mostly men, who were both radical and inspirational to the group.[2] A captivating lithographic poster of Albizu Campos created by Antonio Martorell was among the many images that the Young Lords displayed in their headquarters.[3] In *Pedro Albizu Campos* (1969), Martorell depicts key moments of dissent—organized by the women who formed El Partido Nacionalista (the Puerto Rican Nationalist Party), an independence-seeking political party against the United States' domination of Puerto Rico.[4]

With three superimposed images of Albizu Campos, gradually decreasing in size, Martorell positions him as the leading figure in the Puerto Rican Nationalist Party. Even when depicted behind bars, as shown in the third and smallest drawing, Albizu Campos is the central force. He wears his signature attire, a black suit with a bow tie. Above his head, the poster reads: "PARA QUITARNOS LA PATRIA PRIMERO TIENEN QUE QUITARNOS LA VIDA" (in order to take our nation first they have to take our lives). His right arm is slightly raised, as if he is holding up a power fist.

Martorell inscribes on Campos's right arm images of two historic revolts led by women from the Puerto Rican Nationalist Party: El Grito de Jayuya (the 1950 Jayuya Revolt) in Puerto Rico and the 1954 attack on the US House of Representatives. The bodies on his arm, however, are depicted as a mass of protestors, without acknowledging the women who led the resistances. On October 30, 1950, Blanca Canales—who organized the Daughters of Freedom, the women's branch of the Puerto Rican Nationalist Party—led nationalists to the town square of Jayuya, raised the Puerto Rican flag, and gave a speech that declared Puerto Rico a free republic. El Grito de Jayuya, as it was called, marked the moment when the Nationalist Party took control of the town for three days, before the US National Guard attacked. Four years later, on March 1, 1954, Lolita Lebrón led Irving Flores Rodriguez, Andrés Figueroa Cordero, and Rafael Cancel Miranda—all members of the Nationalist Party—in the attack on the US House of Representatives. She wrapped herself in the Puerto Rican flag and opened fire in the House gallery. As a result, Lebrón was incarcerated and remained in prison for twenty-five years, until President Carter issued pardons to members of the group.

Martorell artistically documents these two revolutionary moments in which the Puerto Rican Nationalist Party led the resistance against colonial

Figure 3. Poster by Antonio Martorell featuring a portrait of Pedro Albizu Campos and commemorating *El Grito de Jayuya* (the Jayuya Revolt) in Puerto Rico and the 1954 attack on the House of Representatives, led by female nationalist Blanca Canales and Lolita Lebrón, respectively. Reprinted in *Palante* (the Young Lords Party's newsletter) 2.3 (1970): 35. Courtesy Center for Puerto Rican Studies Library and Archives, Hunter College, CUNY.

mandates that stripped Puerto Ricans of their freedoms. La Ley de la Mordaza (the Gag Law of 1948) and the McCarran Act of 1950 criminalized any public advocacy related to the independence of Puerto Rico and outlawed the raising of the Puerto Rican flag.[5] Citizens understood that if Puerto Ricans resisted or enacted nationalistic performances supporting the independence of Puerto Rico, the consequence would be life in prison or death. While these laws triggered several nationalist uprisings, both on the island and on the mainland, the history of Puerto Rican activism was repressed, resulting in a historical amnesia that altered the national identity of many Puerto Ricans. Martorell's *Pedro Albizu Campos* incites viewers of the 1970s to remember the history of resistance during the 1950s.

Yet the image, even as it attempts to break from the repression of the 1950s, is tightly bound by a masculinist narrative. There is no visual representation of the women who led these revolts. The body of Albizu Campos, as opposed to the body of Blanca Canales or of Lolita Lebrón, becomes the terrain on which to document these women-led revolts.[6] In eliding these female activists from this history, Martorell propagates a nationalist discourse that is constructed and represented predominantly by men. Even though female leaders were central and pivotal to leading this resistance, Martorell's remembering of this history is tightly bound by a masculinist representation.

In an attempt to commemorate the spirit of revolution of the Puerto Rican Nationalist Party, the Young Lords circulated this image in their newsletter, *Palante*; posted it throughout their headquarters; and provided political educational classes about these leaders. While the Young Lords' visual, literary, and performance styles of protest were inspired by women-led revolutionary acts of El Partido Nacionalista, such as those of Blanca Canales and Lolita Lebrón, Albizu Campos became the iconic figure of the organization. By disseminating an image that renders invisible the activism of Blanca Canales and Lolita Lebrón, the Young Lords positioned women as inconsequential and normalized masculinist constructions in nationalist discourses, a practice that was present from its inception.

PROTEST, PERFORMANCE, AND THE VISUAL CULTURE OF THE YOUNG LORDS

Like many nationalist movements of the seventies, the Young Lords were primarily focused on addressing racial and ethnic oppression while also eliding the intersectionality of identity and, more specifically, the voices of women and the issues that they confronted. Modeled after the Black Panther Party and other social liberation movements, the Young Lords' vision was to serve Puerto Ricans and other underrepresented communities and prevent them from disenfranchisement on the mainland.[7]

On July 26, 1969, during a rally at Tompkins Square Park, a group of Puerto Rican and Nuyorican college student activists announced the formation of the Young Lords Party to the entire Lower East Side community.[8] Felipe Luciano inaugurated the Young Lords Party by performing his poem "Jíbaro, My Pretty Nigger." His performance asserted how the Young Lords' political agenda intersected with both the Puerto Rican and Black communities.[9] From its inception, the Young Lords Party put forth a racial justice platform that acknowledged the shared histories of Black people and Latinx. Yet the Young Lords bound their call for racial solidarity with masculinist ideologies.

In publicly performing this poem, Luciano, an Afro–Puerto Rican man, embodied the intersecting histories of Puerto Ricans and African Americans, and the painful legacy of racism. His public presentation illustrates how the Young Lords enacted their political strategy through poetry and performance, what Urayoán Noel calls "embodied counterpolitics," "min[ing] the body as a site of political articulation while simultaneously testing its limits."[10] In his deep baritone voice, Luciano proclaimed,

> . . . .
> Jíbaro, my pretty nigger
> Father of my yearning for the soil,
> The land,
> The earth of my people.
> . . . .
> Jíbaro, my pretty nigger.
> Sweating bullets of blood and bedbugs,
> Swaying slowly to the softly strummed strains of a five String guitar
> Remembering ancient empires
> Of sun gods and black spirits and things that were once
> So simple.
> . . . .
> Jíbaro, did you know you my nigger?
> I love the curve of your brow,

The slant of your baby's eyes,
The calves of your woman dancing;
I dig you!
You can't hide.

I ride with you on subways.
I touch shoulders with you in dances.
I make crazy love to your daughter.
Yea, you my cold nigger man.
And I love you cause you're mine.

And I'll never let you go.
And I'll never let you go.
(You mine nigger!)
And I'll never let you go.
Forget about self.
We're together now.
And I'll never let go!
Uh, Uh.
Never, nigger.[11]

Luciano affirms shared historical and political tensions between the archetypal figures of the *jíbaro* and the nigger. Both terms have been used pejoratively and laudatorily. Born out of white racism, nigger is a historically derogative name for Black people that has been reclaimed by some as a term of endearment or as an establishment of brotherhood and sisterhood. While the term *jíbaro* is often used to uphold Puerto Rico culture, it can also be used to refer to poor Puerto Rican laborers and farmers as backward and unsophisticated. As a Black and Puerto Rican man, Luciano belonged to both communities, sometimes one at the expense of the other. The embodiment of this poem exemplifies how affinities between the Black and Latinx communities were developed and strengthened. Luciano's use of "Jíbaro, my pretty nigger" traces his African, Taíno, and Puerto Rican lineages. By extension, he invites community members with similar histories to create alliances for future resistance.

While Luciano proposes a strategy of collectivity for racial solidarity, he also imbues this strategy with a masculinist agenda. His poem directly speaks to men as he proclaims that the land is the "Father of [his] yearning for the soil." The few times that he mentions Black women in his poem, he portrays them as dancing bodies or sexual instruments, as when he says, "The calves of your woman dancing" and "I make crazy love to your daughter." Unbeknownst to him, his poetic performance not only inaugurated the Young Lords, but also cohered the Nuyorican aesthetic with an Afrodiasporic, masculinist focus.

The Young Lords' visual iconography and performance traditions spotlight the male performing body as an essential component of their aesthetic. Luciano's inaugural poem set the tone for paying attention to the dialogic relationship between the text and the performing male body. The film *El Pueblo Se Levanta* (1971), which documents the takeover of the Hispanic Methodist Church in El Barrio (East Harlem) on December 7, 1969, and the images that the Young Lords displayed at their headquarters to inspire and educate themselves and their community offer a direct look at how the Young Lords engaged with visual culture and a performance tradition that centered on the male body.

The film documents how the Young Lords used a body-centered aesthetic—Noel's embodied counterpolitics—as a strategy to invoke Puerto Rican empowerment, coalition, and social action. The Lords tried to address the congregation about starting a free breakfast program, but the church's minister had planted undercover police officers in the congregation. These cops beat and arrested some of the Lords. Two weeks later, the Lords took over the church's facilities for eleven days, after which the police evicted them. While their occupation was brief, they received attention from the national media and exposed the institutional abuses that residents of El Barrio experienced.

As the film documents, the Lords hung a large banner, "La iglesia del pueblo" (the People's Church) to assert the victory of occupying the church. At the entrance of the church two armed male Lords protected their newly occupied space. The militant dress code—field jacket, combat boots, purple beret, handmade button of the Puerto Rican map or the words "Tengo Puerto Rico en mi corazón" (I have Puerto Rico in my heart)—and a raised power fist visually incited community mobilization. During their eleven-day occupation, the Lords organized clothing drives, breakfast programs, political education, a day care center, free health programs, and nightly entertainment.

The Young Lords also created a performance space at the Hispanic Methodist Church, and people created theatrical vignettes, performed poetry, sang, and danced to "Qué bonita bandera" (What a Beautiful Flag), written by Pepe and Flora Flores, to affirm their self-determination and liberation. Pedro Pietri, one of the founding poets of the Nuyorican Poets Café, who was raised in this church, participated in the takeover.[12] He debuted his signature poems, "Puerto Rican Obituary" and "Suicide Note of a Cockroach in a Low Income Project," to a congregation of people committed to creating a forum for liberatory practices. Even the children responded to the atmosphere of freedom by creating a reenactment of the Young Lords' stand against systemic racism and police violence.[13] If the Lords were treated like second-class citizens outside of the People's Church, they were at least free citizens within it. This creative embodiment of the daily problems that people faced—from economic displacement to epidemic garbage, from failing schools to massive unemployment—was not just seen as a series of personal testimonies, but rather as stories connected to larger issues of colonialism and racism. The singing, the poetry reading, and the vignettes are all testaments to the ways in which visual and performance-based strategies were vital to the Young Lords movement, which stemmed from the print and visual culture implemented by Puerto Rican Nationalists. Even as the body was central to the resistance and activism of the Young Lords, they were not inclusive of all bodies but rather primarily privileged the male body.

THE YOUNG LORDS' HERSTORY

While the Young Lords' visual and performance aesthetic rendered women invisible, they played a vital role in the organization. As Iris Morales documents in *Through the Eyes of Rebel Women: The Young Lords, 1969–1976* (2016) and her coauthored foreword to *The Young Lords: A Reader*, women represented one-third of the Young Lords, and they participated in every call to action.[14] Frequently experiencing gender discrimination and confronting their male leaders with demands for equality, Young Lord women sought alternative ways to document their participation in the organization and the history of the Nuyorican movement.[15] Similar to Luciano, Morales draws on a body-centered performance aesthetic in her works; however, rather than focusing on the presence of male figures amidst women-led revolts, as in Martorell's *Pedro Albizu Campos*, she centers the women as leading agents of social change. Morales insists on reinserting women in Nuyorican history as key activists by bringing their resisting female body center stage and crediting their labor. The act of claiming women's participation and contribution repositions Blanca Canales, Lolita Lebrón, and other women in the struggle for justice as heroines, and it moves toward revising the history of the Nuyorican movement with an intersectional gender analysis.[16]

For instance, when Morales discusses the Garbage Offensive, the Young Lords' first initiative, she does not simply state that the Lords mobilized the community to act against the garbage's overflowing.[17] Instead she acknowledges the diverse bodies in action and makes evident that "[a] group of young men and women began sweeping every weekend during the summer of 1969. Among them was a young Cuban mother and university student, Sonia Ivany, one of the first women to join the Young Lords."[18] The media coverage of young men and women sweeping, stacking up garbage, and setting it on fire in the middle on the street eventually pressured the Department of Sanitation to schedule daily garbage pickups. Similarly, when Morales writes about how the Lords mobilized health teams to go door to door to conduct lead tests as a response to the high rate of lead poisoning in children, she underscores how women were central to this initiative, since mothers were more comfortable opening doors to other women.[19]

Women, as Morales demonstrates, were not only present but were putting their bodies on the frontlines and their lives at risk. When she writes about how the Lords approached the Hispanic Methodist Church congregation to start a free breakfast program and were beaten and arrested by undercover cops, Morales revises this moment by stating that five of the thirteen people arrested were women, including Elena González, Mirta González, Sonia Ivany, Denise Oliver, and Erika Sezonov.[20] It was the arrest of these thirteen men and women that led the Lords to take over the facilities two weeks later.

Morales powerfully disrupts the masculinist narrative of the Young Lords by reinserting women's bodies into the history of direct action and community mobilization. She points out how the large number of women sharing stories of gender discrimination led to the formation of the Women's Caucus in summer 1970 and the publication of *La Luchadora*, a newspaper devoted to women's issues. The Women's Caucus exposed the inherent gender oppression in the Young Lords' Thirteen-Point Program and demanded that women be supported in taking on formal leadership roles. In contrast to the poetry and images in the Young Lords' protest traditions and Jaime Carrero's *Notes of Neorican Seminar*, Morales gives body and voice to the many women who were integral to the social change and action of the Nuyorican movement. Women-centered works like Morales's not only make women visible in the print, visual, and literary culture of the Young Lords, but also document women's vital role in the making of a Nuyorican aesthetic. The history of the Nuyorican movement thus necessitates a gendered analysis that examines how masculinist practices make invisible the voices and activism of women.

THE NEO-RICAN MAN—AND THE MISSING NEO-RICAN WOMAN

The interplay between the text and the male bodies and the exclusion or reductionist representations of women literally and figuratively represented in *Notes of Neorican Seminar* (1972) offers a critical space for thinking about Neo/Nuyorican identity formation among both men and women. An analysis of the archival material on the Neorican Seminar broadens our understanding of how print and visual culture from the 1970s reinforced a Nuyorican masculinist ethos. Examining the substantial coverage of male representations throughout the Nuyorican movement offers a deeper insight into why Nuyoriqueñas created a feminist perspective. They were working within an aesthetic that forcefully promoted economic and racial equality, but that ignored concerns related to gender and sexual orientation.

The release of *Nuyorican Poetry: An Anthology of Puerto Rican Words and Feelings* (1975), coedited by café founders Miguel Algarín and Miguel Piñero, first popularized the term Nuyorican. This anthology was the first to feature the works of poets either born in or culturally connected to Puerto Rico and living in New York City. Poets used the term Nuyorican as a mode of writing, speaking, feeling, and creating identity. As Algarín puts it in the introduction of *Nuyorican Poetry*,

> The experience of Puerto Ricans on the streets of New York has caused a new language to grow: Nuyorican. Nuyoricans are a special experience in the immigration history of the city of New York. We come to the city as citizens and can retain the use of Spanish and include English. . . . The interchange between both yields new verbal possibilities, new images to deal with the stresses of living on tar and cement.[21]

As Algarín's definition suggests, the term Nuyorican means much more than "a Puerto Rican born and/or living in New York." It is a way of being—how individuals practice and embody Nuyoricanness through culture, language, and the spaces that they inhabit.

Before the term Nuyorican was popularized by Algarín and Piñero, Jaime Carrero expressed how his lived experiences encompassed both New York and Puerto Rico. In his book *Jet Neorriqueño/Neo-Rican Jetliner* (1964), a collection of Spanish and English poems, he coined the term Neo-Rican. Similar to Nuyorican, Neo-Rican expresses the ways that the colonial history between Puerto Rico and the United States has indelibly shaped the identity and experiences of many Puerto Ricans.

Originally trained as a painter and later working as a novelist, poet, and playwright, Carrero spent his formative years frequently traveling between Puerto Rico and New York. In the title poem of his 1964 collection, he captures various conversations with Puerto Rican passengers on flights from Puerto Rico to New York about their colonial identity and citizenship status. He writes:

> I was born in New York new blood.
> I was born in New York
> I'm not a Jones Act Puerto Rican
> yeah?
> I am a Neo-Rican man news flash.
> yeah?
> I known what I know no Jones Act man.
> yeah?[22]

Like Algarín and Piñero, Carrero uses his hybrid term to emphasize the making of a new identity, one "of Puerto Rican background who has been brought up in the continental United States."[23] For Carrero, the back-and-forth migration between Puerto Rico and the United States offered a new mode of identification.[24] Neo-Rican expresses access to both Puerto Rican and US citizenship.[25] The passenger in the poem speaks from the reality that, even though Puerto Ricans are Americans, they are not necessarily perceived as such. After four centuries of Spanish colonial rule, the United States gained colonial control of Puerto Rico in 1898 and since then has held it as a colonial subject.[26] Revising imperialist practices of earlier administrations, President Woodrow Wilson worked to pass the Jones Act of 1917, which granted Puerto Ricans US citizenship. However, Puerto Rico would remain an unincorporated territory, a possession of the United States. This fact meant that even though Puerto Ricans were legally Americans, they had limited citizenship rights and were still perceived as colonial subjects.[27]

Carrero explicitly differentiates Neo-Ricans from "Jones Act Puerto Rican[s]," to not only address the lasting impact of colonialism, but also create strategies to achieve liberation from colonial power. Note, however, that this poem limits the narration of colonial history to the Puerto Rican, Jones Act, or Neo-Rican man, thus setting up a pattern of exclusion in the narration of Nuyorican history.

Eight years after he published his poem "Jet Neorriqueño: Neo-Rican Jetliner," Carrero also used the term Neo-Rican as the focal point of discussion for the Neorican Seminar, a conference that he and Robert Muckley organized on April 10, 1972, at the Inter American University of Puerto Rico in San Germán. Carrero and Muckley noticed that there was a growing population of New York–educated Puerto Ricans returning to the island who were creating different linguistic and artistic forms. While Carrero witnessed the artistic expressions created by Puerto Rican students who relocated to New York and then returned to Puerto Rico, Muckley found that those same students could not be easily placed in Spanish classes with monolingual North Americans. Muckley decided to teach Spanish as an ethnic language and to develop material specifically for the Puerto Rican population who moved to New York and then returned to the island. He noticed that these people linguistically reconfigured Spanish and English to reflect their cyclic migration experience.[28]

Interested in discussing these cultural and linguistic developments, Carrero and Muckley organized the Neorican Seminar and invited guest speakers—such as Bronx Democrat Herman Badillo, columnist Juan Manuel García-Passalacqua, and members of the Young Lords—to share their views on the subject.[29] These varied perspectives offered an extremely rich and complicated understanding of Puerto Rican and Neo-/Nuyorican experiences. Muckley and Carrero documented the conference in the publication *Notes of Neorican Seminar* (1972). Among the many groups that attended this gathering, the Young Lords Party was the most visible of the radical organizations that shaped the Nuyorican movement.[30] Given that the Neorican Seminar was held in Puerto Rico, it has not necessarily been considered as part of the history of Nuyorican cultural production. To date there is no analysis on the Neorican Seminar or the documentation of this event.

Notes on Neorican Seminar, which is available at the Center for Puerto Rican Studies at Hunter College, is the only existing primary source documenting the discussions, lectures, and interviews from the conference. In this sixty-nine-page zine-like booklet, representations of Neo-Rican male

Figure 4. Illustration by Jaime Carrero humorously addressing the complexity of what it means to be Puerto Rican. From *Notes of Neorican Seminar* (1972). Center for Puerto Rican Studies Library and Archives, Hunter College, CUNY. Courtesy of Maria Dolores Carrero and the Carrero family.

bodies—in cartoon illustrations, poems, newspaper clippings, drawings, collages, one-act plays, papers, and photographs—played a major role in expressing Neo-Rican identity, politics, and history. *Notes of Neorican Seminar* is one of the first printed texts in circulation to depict Neo-/Nuyorican history. The documentation of Neorican Seminar in zine format makes this event accessible to the general public and informs readers of the political and social issues experienced by Neo-/Nuyorican through a variety of creative mediums.

Carrero explicitly states on the bottom of the front cover, "This pamphlet is not a comic book," making the claim that there are factual points to be taken seriously in the comic illustrations. In one of the comic illustrations in the zine, two men wear costumes for a Halloween party. There is a head-on view of a person dressed as Superman, and profile view of a man dressed as a Puerto Rican. Superman dons a jumpsuit with the signature logo on the front chest, a cape, a utility belt, and boots. He assumes a smug stance with his muscular torso puffed out, arms crossed, and legs planted slightly apart. Superman is unable to identify his friend's *jíbaro*-style costume—a bandana, a long-sleeved shirt tucked under a wide belt, high water pants, and ankle boots—and asks, "What are you made out to be in this Halloween Party?" His friend responds, "Why, a Puerto Rican of course!" Superman's costume is familiar because he is a popular American superhero. Yet, the man wearing a costume marking his Puerto Rican national and ethnic identity is unrecognizable. The visual and performative language of the Puerto Rican–costumed body is illegible to Superman and many other Americans.

This cartoon is emblematic of the Nuyorican movement, which registers economic, ethnic, or racial factors as sites of inclusion yet privilege the male body. As conveyed by the drawing, the politics and performance of identity are vital to understanding Puerto Rican and Nuyorican identity. Using literary and visual humor and sarcasm, Carrero positions Puerto Ricans as superheroes, challenging the normative perception of what a superhero looks like. While Carrero upholds a positive representation of Puerto Ricans, the male body—as with the iconic Superman and the Puerto Rican figures—performs a masculinist narrative.

His humor both creates distance from the social realities of Neo-/Nuyoricans and highlights some prevalent concerns about migration and identity. At the height of the 1970s, when this drawing was published, Puerto Rican radicals from both on and off the island gathered in San Germán, Puerto Rico, for the Neorican Seminar to discuss their social roles and interventions. Given the colonial status of Puerto Rico, the history of circular migration and displacement, and the place of Nuyoricans, the affirmation of Puerto Rican culture, as in the case of the costumed body with traditional Puerto Rican clothing, becomes a cultural signal. The man caught in midconversation responding, "Why, a Puerto Rican of course!" is indicative of how Puerto

Ricans are perceived as Others or excluded in the American imaginary, especially when they are claiming their cultural heritage.

Carrero extends this sarcastically humorous approach pictorially and linguistically in the cover design of *Notes of Neorican Seminar*. Like many Neo-/Nuyorican poets, Carrero stands at several junctions: at the intersection of two national spaces (Puerto Rico and the United States), between two languages (Spanish and English), and within two poetic traditions (literary and oral).[31] Caught between the islands of Puerto Rico and New York City, Carrero creates words and images that both juxtapose and fuse the Caribbean and urban worlds. He depicts residents speaking in Spanglish to demonstrate how Neo-/Nuyoricans negotiate two cultures and languages to express themselves. For example, a child holding a bat hollers, "Hey, Johni, bamos a la yarda a jugal." The Spanglishization of words like Johnny and *yard* to Johni and *yarda* and the vernacular dialects like *bamos* instead of *vamos* (let's go) and *jugal* instead of *jugar* (to play) are unique linguistic particularisms that mark the bodies on the zines as working class Neo-/Nuyoricans. The manipulation of Spanish and English reflects the dual experience of Puerto Ricans living in New York City and other metropolises. This duality helps construct a sense of home, despite the experiences of displacement, alienation, and questionable citizenship.[32]

The use of Spanglish as an alternative language affirms the formation of Neo-/Nuyorican identity. As evidenced in the Jones Act's attempt to limit the traces of Hispanic heritage on the island by making English the official language of the Puerto Rican courts and restricting the use of Spanish, Spanglish is a self-selective language-making process, as opposed to English-only mandates forbidding bilingualism.[33] Spanglish transforms both English and Spanish, refuses to be homogenized into the norms of either language, and continues to have access to both. By reconfiguring Spanish and English words, phrases, and sentences, poets generate not only a hybrid tongue, but also a hybrid identity, reflecting the experiences of Neo-/Nuyoricans. This linguistic fusion that is Spanglish is apparent not only in the works of Carrero, but in the works of the café's founding poets, and in those of more contemporary poets like La Bruja (the Witch), who originates terms like Boogie Rican, and Mariposa (Butterfly), who popularized words like DiaspoRican, to express their Puerto Rican identity.[34]

While language is a medium in which Neo-/Nuyoricans can negotiate who and where they are in relation to the rest of the American social body, it can also be an implicit tool of patriarchal power. Just as the zine cover prom-

Figure 5. Cover of *Notes of Neorican Seminar* (1972) by Jaime Carrero, comically illustrating how Puerto Ricans in New York negotiate living between two cultures and languages. Center for Puerto Rican Studies Library and Archives, Hunter College, CUNY. Courtesy of Maria Dolores Carrero and the Carrero family.

inently features men, Carrero's use of language also maintains a masculinist perspective. As the speech bubbles on the cover of *Notes of Neorican Seminar* demonstrate, "identity is presenced as language."[35] That is, Spanglish reflects the social reality of Neo-/Nuyoricans, and in this case, Spanglish maintains a masculinist perspective. Phrases such as "Hey Johni," "Hey pops," and "Hey bro" call attention to men. In this case, Neo-/Nuyorican men, and not women, create a sense of selfhood and home, and assert dominance, through the transformations of Spanish and English.

Just as language is an important component of identity-making, so too are social circumstances and individual encounters. Carrero's sarcastically humorous linguistic and pictorial representations of men address the crisis of poverty and unemployment among Puerto Ricans—both those living on the mainland and those on the island. For instance, an adult daughter smoking a cigarette yells from the window, "Hey pops, el landlord esta en el rufo esperando que tu llegues de la marqueta pa' cobrarte el bill" (Hey pops, the landlord is on the roof waiting for you to come back from the market to charge you for the bill); and a friend asks to borrow money, "Hey bro, pana. ¿Como van las cosas? Whows the family? Préstame 5 bolos. (Lend me 5 dollars)." The zine cover depicts the everyday tactics that Neo-/Nuyoricans create to overcome economic challenges. As depicted by the wide-eyed man sitting at the edge of the sidewalk, wondering, "Quien @#* am I??" (Who the @#* am I??), some find ways to beat the system by borrowing or hiding from the landlord, while others are mentally and emotionally stifled by the social and economic trauma to the point of questioning their own existence.

The few times that we see women on the cover, they are hypersexualized or dependent on the father as the provider—for example, the woman on the upper left corner asks her father about the rent—and she is depicted in a hypersexualized manner. She wears a tank top; her breasts are disproportionally large; and the shape of her nipples can be seen through the fabric. Similar to the first woman depicted on the zine, Carrero literally draws the second woman on the opposite side of the margins. She tears open the background setting of clouds and sarcastically exclaims: "¡Lo que habias estado esperando!" (What you have been waiting for!), a gesture to how the "land of milk and honey" neglected Neo-/Nuyoricans. Despite the fact that these women are not central characters on the zine cover, they offer a window into how women are represented in Nuyorican visual culture: they depend on male figures yet serve as interlocutors to reveal the harsh realities of living in America.

Throughout the entirety of *Notes on Neorican Seminar,* the interplay between the text and the body sheds light only on the male body to the exclusion of representing the bodily trauma that women have experienced. The zine moves from light and humorous to dark and serious with Carrero's poem "Neo-Rican Lesson," a four-lesson poem in English—interspersed with some Spanish—that teaches recent Puerto Rican immigrant men about the racial and ethnic discrimination that they will face in the United States. In the first lesson, Carrero advises Neo-Rican men to deny that they are Puerto Ricans. This advice comes at a huge cost, as negating one's cultural background is akin to annihilating part of oneself. Alongside his first poetic lesson, Carrero conveys the corporeal trauma of cultural disavowal by depicting a decapitated man with exposed genitalia, kneeling on a topographic map with contour lines that web around his chest. In place of the missing head, there is a photograph of a man looking into the cityscape and holding several suitcases. Typically, contour lines are found on topographic maps to indicate the elevation and shape of the terrain. In this case, the contour lines drawn on the male body underscore the ways in which migration and displacement physically impact the entire body from the shoulders to the legs. Regardless of Carrero's poetic advice, he reminds us that one's cultural identity cannot truly be hidden, as there is a sign hanging on the man's torso that reads, "A Puerto Rican."

While in the first lesson Carrero advises Neo-Ricans to disclaim their Puerto Rican identity, the second and third lessons encourage them to identify as Black men. His drawing of a fair-skinned man wearing a black mask points to the ways in which the Puerto Ricans must embrace a Black identity to acquire a sense of belonging as Americans. This image centers the politics of racial and ethnic intersectionality that was a driving force in the Nuyorican movement, but it ultimately privileges the experience of Neo-/Nuyorican men. The fourth lesson continues in this vein by warning Neo-Rican men to avoid crowds and cops. For this lesson Carrero turns to a photograph of Don Pedro Albizu Campos, leader of El Partido Nacionalista. Police tape borders the bottom of the photograph, as does an arm tied with two electrical cords. During Albizu Campos's tenure—the late 1920s and 1930s—El Partido Nacionalista drew international attention to Puerto Rico's colonial status through petitions, protests, and armed strikes against the United States. The party's militant advocacy of armed struggle increased conflict between the Partido Nacionalista and the authorities. This collage conveys how this iconic revolutionary served several prison terms on charges of seditious con-

Neo-Rican Lesson A poem by Jaime Carrero

I. Primera Lección en Inglés

Primera lección en inglés
escucha bien—
cuando vayas a caminar:
Never say Puerto Rican again.
Never say that the island is in:
within yourself.
Just say French
Peruvian
Chilean
Czech
anything else
anything else
but never, never,
open that chest
and say Puerto Rican again.

Tell me Sir, tell me something about myself:
I've met a man
just like you— a gentleman—
who said to me in Mayagüez—
loud and clear—
a gentleman, Sir—
just like you—
polite English—
not French—
the smile on the ground,
a fragile smile—
like from the corner of the mouth:
'I bet Puerto Ricans are to the intellect,
I bet, I bet,
what the Jews to the Nazis are—
. . . .
that I bet. . '

Figure 6. Jaime Carrero reveals the trauma of cultural disavowal in his poem "Neo-Rican Lessons" and illustration of a decapitated man. Reprinted in *Notes of Neorican Seminar* (1972) from the *San Juan Review.* Center for Puerto Rican Studies Library and Archives, Hunter College, CUNY. Courtesy of Maria Dolores Carrero and the Carrero family.

spiracy but continued to fight for Puerto Rico's independence from jail until his death.[36] Collectively, the poem "Neo-Rican Lesson" and the series of collages depict the traumatized Puerto Rican and Neo-/Nuyorican male body undergoing tremendous inflictions—whether pummeled into submission, compelled to disidentification, or forced into repression—to thrive in the United States.

These masculinist representations, which do the important work of documenting the formation of a Neo-/Nuyorican identity and the Nuyorican movement, are among the first images in circulation depicting Neo-/Nuyorican history. These images of the 1960s cement a masculinist Nuyorican aesthetics because they do not engage with the long legacy of Puerto Rican women as activists, economic providers, and agents shaping the migration and settlement process.

THE PRE-CAFÉ YEARS: EL PUERTO RICAN PLAYWRIGHTS'/ ACTORS' WORKSHOP AND THE YOUNG FAMILY

In 1973, four years after the Young Lords took over the Hispanic Methodist Church, the Nuyorican Poets Café opened its doors. Prior to the inception of the café, Miguel Algarín led El Puerto Rican Playwrights'/Actors' Workshop (EPRP/AW).[37] A focus on the pre-café years brings attention to the way that the history of the café—as well as Nuyorican poetry and the theater scene of the 1970s—has been canonized with only peripheral acknowledgment to the collective involvement of women.

When EPRP/AW received a working space from Joseph Papp at 4 Astor Place in 1969, its members were able to more concretely establish their creative methodologies. Like many experimental theaters of the 1960s—such as the Living Theatre, Open Theatre, and Jerzy Grotowski's Polish Laboratory Theatre—EPRP/AW advocated for collectivity and rejected traditional theater practices that emphasized plot, character, text, or directorial authority.[38] The group's concern was about fighting against social injustice, and members of EPRP/AW were personally invested in the livelihood of Nuyoricans and Latinxs.

The EPRP/AW developed a male-centered embodied counterpolitics that fought for racial, ethnic, cultural, and class inclusivity at the exclusion of women. The organizers, instructors, and most of the participants of the group were men, and the training catered to men. In his training regimen for playwrights and performers, Algarín incorporated physical activities by inviting male instructors to conduct two-hour kung fu classes. The goal was to prepare the body for the mind before they went to work on the text.[39] Rather than internalizing a script, participants were encouraged by Algarín to use sound and movement—their bodies—to generate emotions.[40] To deepen this embodied practice in the group, Algarín worked with Raymond Barry, formerly from the Open Theatre, and together they guided the mostly male playwrights and performers to look at their own stories as way of making theater.[41] The cofacilitation of physical exercises taught the actors to work collectively as an ensemble and to not simply remember and narrate their stories, but to embody the ways that systemic oppression manifests in their everyday practices as men of color. The collective art-making process and embodied counterpolitics were integral elements of the Nuyorican aesthetic; these practices, however, valued racial, ethnic, and cultural inclusivity while also privileging men.

The group worked collectively in the rehearsal space, but on paper the artistic director imposed a traditional theater hierarchy and credited the plays to single authors. This was the case with the work that was developed with Algarín, Miguel Piñero, and youths. In 1975, due to budget cuts, EPRP/AW left the space at 4 Astor Place that Papp had originally offered. By that time, Piñero's *Short Eyes*, which he wrote while in prison, had gained national recognition.[42] When Piñero was released from jail, he became part of the Family, an ensemble of former male inmates who put their passions into acting rather than reengaging in criminal activities. The Family worked with Piñero to revise the script for *Short Eyes*, which addressed the struggles of incarceration.[43] While Piñero was in negotiation with Papp about the production of *Short Eyes*, Papp invited him to EPRP/AW, and he immediately wanted to participate in the group.[44] This introduction sparked Piñero and Algarín's long friendship, which undoubtedly inspired the founding of the café.[45]

Evoking the Young Lords' protest traditions, Algarín and Piñero used the streets as their stage. Piñero, who was already experienced with the prison system and had worked with Marvin Camillo, walked around Forty-Second Street and Port Authority (then an area known for street crimes and adult movie theaters) with Algarín, recruiting delinquent youth and outcasts including young male runaways, drug users, and sex workers to join their new theater project. Many of the male youth signed up. For these young people, theater became a way to escape street life by sharing their stories. This group became known as the Young Family. The ensemble helped produce two shows: *Sideshow* (1974), which portrayed a day in the life of ghetto youths living in the Lower East Side; and *América Conga Mania* (1975), written by Lucky CienFuegos, which depicted the life of a street-hustling poet who is stabbed to death while playing cards. Both were featured at the Nuyorican Theater Festival.[46] Algarín and Piñero's invitations to these young outlaws to join the Nuyorican theater-making collective shows how inclusivity worked in this group. Their invitations complicated what it meant to be Nuyorican. They made visible those who were invisible, and they showcased the potentiality of these neglected youth. In doing this, they confronted community members with the vicious societal ills with which some Nuyoricans were forced to live.

While the collective process was integral to a Nuyorican aesthetic, Piñero or Algarín were often credited as sole authors. *Sideshow* was developed with Héctor Rodriguez, one of the actors in the Young Family, who created an improvisational exercise that incorporated a street scene he had witnessed. Like many of the members in the group, Rodriguez could not read or write, so Piñero transcribed his ideas and dramatically structured the improvised scenes. Algarín then gave the scenes a directorial touch.[47] The collective construction of this piece steered away from the common idea that one person holds authorship. As playwrights, performers, and directors, the members of the Young Family (along with Algarín and Piñero) were responsible for the production from the inception to the end. However, on paper Piñero or Algarín would receive the sole acknowledgment. In *Outlaw: The Collected Works by Miguel Piñero* (2010), for instance, Nicolás Kanellos and Jorge Iglesias credit Piñero as the sole writer of *Sideshow*. To complicate manners, "Shattering the Silences," a PBS website about minority scholars, lists Algarín and Piñero as cowriters of *Sideshow*. The Young Family narrated and acted out real-life stories that were then used for the stage.[48] Algarín and Piñero encouraged community participation in their productions, yet the masculinist practices of claiming singular authorship created a blind spot, and the failure to acknowledge the many creators of these productions erased the collective process of the Young Family. Accounting for the pre-café years reveals how the historical narrative of the Nuyorican movement has been distorted to reduce the role and participation of women. Carried over from one period to another, these masculinist practices influenced the formation of a Nuyorican aesthetic.

FORMALIZING A NUYORICAN AESTHETIC: THE BIRTH OF THE CAFÉ

The creative productivity of EPRP/AW and the Young Family inspired many poets and theater makers, yet the creative and gathering spaces were highly male gendered. Members of the EPRP/AW and the Young Family continued to meet informally, to exchange their work, and to create platforms to invite new artists. One highly frequented space was Algarín's apartment, which was often occupied until the early mornings. Eventually, the collective gained enough momentum to require a bigger and more formal space to meet. In 1975, Algarín rented Sunshine Tavern, an Irish bar that had recently gone out of business, located at 505 East Sixth Street (between Avenues A and B). This space became known as the Nuyorican Poets Café.[49] In 1978, the café moved to 236 East Third Street (between Avenues B and C). The café still stands today in that same location, but it is now managed by Daniel Gallant, who has been the executive director since 2008. Despite the collective's attempt to be inclusive, spaces like Algarín's apartment and the bars that the collective frequented were highly male gendered and not necessarily welcoming to women. Even while having a full-time job, men were able to participate in these creative exchanges, whereas women could not often attend these meetings as they had the double burden of economic and domestic labor.

Still, Algarín's decision to buy a permanent meeting space is as much a political feat as an artistic one.[50] The Lower East Side has historically been a contested terrain, and it was the home away from home for many Latinxs, immigrants, and members of other minority, poor, and working-class groups. The increasing number of Puerto Ricans migrating to the States and the economic stagnation of the 1970s were the main reasons why Irish and other European residents moved out of the Lower East Side. Faced with rising interest rates, fuel costs, and other operating expenses, some landlords committed arson as a way of salvaging what they could from unprofitable buildings. Other landlords—knowing that the foreclosure process took over five years—abandoned the maintenance of their buildings but continued to collect rent from tenants who had no other options. For Algarín, the act of reclaiming a building from abandonment for the artistic collective meant not only reversing the deterioration of the Lower East Side, but also working hand in hand with the production and visibility of Nuyorican poetry and theater.

In the introductions to his anthologies *Nuyorican Poetry* (1975) and *Aloud*

(1994), and in his essays "Nuyorican Literature" and "Volume and Value of the Breath in Poetry," Algarín identifies key components of the Nuyorican aesthetic: the oral expression of the self; the negotiation between New York/ American culture and Puerto Rican/Caribbean culture through music and language; and the transformation of the performer into a conscious cultural worker before the public. It is in these foundational works that Algarín positions men as poets; women are never mentioned, an omission that denies them the possibility of this role.

Algarín elaborates on the oration style of the Nuyorican poets in his essay "Volume and Value of the Breath in Poetry," which begins to formalize the oral and corporeal elements of the Nuyorican aesthetic. As Algarín puts it:

> When a New York street poet recites on Sixth Street and Avenue A, he cannot afford to sound pale and unengaging. . . . The poet has to get out there and project a volume that stops the crowd and concentrates it into a listening body. The success with which a poet can do this determined his reputation in the community, as a poet.[51]

Algarín trained poets to take their work to the streets, boldly projecting their voices in a declamatory style. Poet and activist Martín Espada notes that Nuyorican poets are descendants of *declamadores*, men or women renowned for their oratorical skills.[52] Taking on the style of the *declamador*, Algarín urges poets to make "open uncontrolled sound[s]" to captivate their audiences.[53] The poet can determine her effectiveness by studying whether she is fully using her voice and body when she grabs the attention of people that did not even know they were there to see her. The voice and the body are the means to articulate the experiences of Nuyoricans and to make their political rights visible.[54] Algarín insists that Nuyorican poets "carry on the oral tradition—the tradition of expressing the self in front of the tribe."[55] Just as *declamadores* voiced the social and political needs of the community in public arenas in Spain and its colonies, Algarín transforms written words into living "flesh and bone" to show audiences the struggle of working-class people, their desire for emancipation from economic and social oppression, and the actions that can and should be taken.[56]

The human voice is essential to oral practices. It is the means by which communities transmit knowledge, social and cultural values, and collective memory from one person to another, from one generation to another. In his introduction to *Nuyorican Poetry*, Algarín states:

> The poet sees his function as a troubadour. He tells the tale of the streets to the streets. The people listen. They cry, they laugh, they dance as the troubadour opens up and tunes his voice and moves his pitch and rhythm to the high tensions of "bomba" truth. Proclamations of hurt, of anger and hatred. Whirls of high-pitched singing. The voice of the street poet must amplify itself. The poet pierces the crowd with cataracts of clear, clean, precise, concrete words about the liquid, shifting latino reality around him.[57]

Like the troubadour who composes and performs lyrical poetry, the Nuyorican poet pushes the printed word off of the page, creates an oral composition, and performs it in the public arena. What the poet performs takes precedence over what the poet writes. Yet, Algarín only envisions men as poets, troubadours, or *declamadores*, denying women access to these roles.

Algarín further connects oral practices to the African diaspora by turning to bomba, a transplanted music and dance tradition of enslaved communities dating back to seventeenth-century West and Central Africa and the Caribbean. Integrating percussion, song, and dance, bomba was used to call meetings and organize slave revolts and escapes.[58] He conjures bomba to stress the elements of resistance and protest that are pertinent to the Nuyorican aesthetic. Algarín reminds poets that, since communication occurs by word of mouth, the manipulation of music and language (Spanish, English, and Spanglish) is of the utmost importance. Lastly, Algarín inserts a sense of collectivity into the oral traditions, as he envisions a gathering of the crowd in the concrete streets. His use of *concrete* calls attention to space and to the ways in which oral practices rely on an interaction with the surrounding environment.

A more salient example of the Nuyorican aesthetic in action can be seen in the film *Fried Shoes, Cooked Diamonds* (1979), directed by Constanzo Allione, which includes scenes of Algarín and Piñero performing at the Jack Kerouac School of Disembodied Poetics, Naropa Institute, in summer 1978.[59] Allen Ginsberg notes that, like the Beats, Algarín and Piñero convey their states of mind and experiences through the performance of their poetry. However, Algarín and Piñero's performance at the Naropa Institute can be distinguished from the work of the Beats in their cultural references and their collective approach. Drawing from bomba practices, they began with a choral chanting of the orishas Yemayá and Shango in a call-and-response format. This song asks these deities to descend and speak to the audience. Piñero set the rhythmic pattern of the chant with strong hand claps, and the audience then joined in. Rather than taking an individualistic approach in which each poet recites his work, Algarín and Piñero established a sense of collectivity, in which everyone partakes in composing and performing the poetry.

Musicality and language play an integral role in their performance and in the formalization of the Nuyorican aesthetic. In this event, Piñero also performed the poem "Seekin' the Cause," while intermittently singing "goodnight my love wherever you are" in doo-wop style. Though this musical element is not included in the published poem, it is a vital component of this poetic performance. His emotive singing intensifies the melancholy of absence already present in this poem. Piñero's words paint the image of a dismembered body and trace the reasons for the missing body parts. He loses his "legs in Vietnam," "his arms in Sing Sing," his "blood [that] painted the streets of the ghetto," and his "scalp on Nixon's belt," all as result of struggling with systemic oppressive forces—the military-industrial complex, prison-industrial complex, poverty, drug policies, and political corruption.[60] The a cappella aural scape that Piñero creates is soothing to the ear, but loss resonates heavily in the absence of body parts. Piñero's use of call and response and improvisational musicality root his work in an oral tradition and add extraliterary meaning to his words. The performing body breaks away from what is written on the page and plays with singing, chanting, clapping, and dancing. The work is charged with cultural, political, and personal forces—what people do from day to day, how people speak, and what they experience. He includes the music, sounds, rhythms, and beats that surround the environments that they inhabit, and he traces how they move in these spaces—while orally performing the human conditions and experiences of Nuyoricans.

Piñero transformed his social realities into artistic and political possibilities, radicalizing the role of the poet. As Algarín claims, the poet must transform himself before the public to begin healing the scars and wounds from domination. This metamorphosis occurs when spaces—like the café, or the Hispanic Methodist Church that the Young Lords took over—are created where people can freely express themselves. The poet testifies to the political repression and discriminatory injustices that he encounters in everyday life, and these are not so different from the experiences of the audience. By sharing personal life experiences, the poet not only narrates his story, but also documents the history of struggle in his community.[61] Thus, the poet becomes a community chronicler, narrating the everyday struggles of many who have gone through similar trials and tribulations to raise awareness and instigate action.[62] The articulation of the text as a performance piece facilitates the transmission, reception, and dissemination of poetry.[63] The commitment to orality—the physical acting-out of the voice and the body—invigorates a community of people who gather, reflect, and respond to the performance. Through making his experience known, the poet urges other members in the community to speak up and change their oppressive situation. After the performer leaves the stage or the urban street, the sound of his voice and the articulation of his body become part of the community's collective memory. Algarín and Piñero radicalize the role of the poet; the poet is at once artist, social critic, and political figure, one who transforms and heals the self so that the community can do the same. The oral and musical traditions of Puerto Rico are of utmost importance in understanding the Nuyorican aesthetic. Yet, Algarín solely envisions a male poet bringing into fruition this Nuyorican aesthetic, eliding the possibilities for women to be poets and even eradicating them from the oral and musical traditions of the troubadours, bomba, and Nuyorican poetry.

This chapter sheds light on how print and visual culture set the stage for a Nuyorican aesthetic that centered the male body in action, literally, figuratively, and performatively. Navigating the temporal landscapes of the 1930s to the 1970s helps us understand the different articulations of Puerto Rican and Nuyorican identity on the island and the mainland. Both the Young Lord Party and the Nuyorican Poets Café carried on the embodied protest traditions of the Puerto Rican Nationalist Party, yet the legacy of women-led acts of resistance remained backstage. The performance, visual art, and literary traditions used by the Young Lords advocated for civil rights yet privileged men. They drew from both Puerto Rican and Black cultural politics, deploying an aesthetic that ran the gamut from poetic language to revolutionary ideologies to fashion in order to call attention to the ways in which Nuyoricans, particularly men, were being systematically excluded from society. As a result, they rallied a critical mass around their social participation as Nuyoricans in the American social fabric. Like many nationalist movements, the Nuyorican movement focused on race and ethnicity, preventing intersectional activism.

The circulation of the Young Lords' tradition consequently informed the work of the Nuyorican Poets Café. The founders of the Nuyorican Poets Café saw the efficacy of appealing to the frontlines of street politics, and members imported these embodied strategies as they formed the café and developed a performance aesthetic. The café created an aesthetic that was grounded in oral practices; centered on the body; and drawn from different vanguards, including the Young Lords Party, Joseph Papp's Public Theater, the Beats, Open Theatre, and prison theater.[64] While the café and its aesthetic in its early years remained committed to justice, it often privileged men and ultimately did not acknowledge or value the participation of female poets, performers, and artists.

Yet the Nuyorican aesthetic did not go unchallenged. As demonstrated in Sandra María Esteves's performance at Berkshire Community College, she continues to practice a Nuyorican aesthetic and explicitly includes the voices and experiences of women. Performeras challenged the systemic exclusion of women by reinscribing the female perspective—and in particular, the female body—into Nuyorican history, literature, and art.

CHAPTER 3

The Founding Mothers of the Nuyorican Poets Café

DESPITE THE NUYORICAN Poets Café's marginalization of women, Sandra María Esteves and other female poets carved a Nuyorican feminist aesthetic, as documented in the landmark anthology *Nuyorican Poetry* (1975). Their poetry counters masculinist practices by using *pláticas*, a conversational style of writing and performance. By asserting women's agency in their work and by writing a history more inclusive of women, these performeras reposition women as active participants in the Nuyorican poetry movement.[1] This chapter unveils the unacknowledged sexism that was structurally embedded in the 1970s Nuyorican poetry scene and brings to the surface the contributions of women, thus creating a more inclusive narrative with which to understand the material circumstances of the past.

Drawing from a series of interviews that I conducted with Esteves and Amina Muñoz, I reposition these performeras not as *madrinas* or godmothers of the café—as they have often been called—but rather as founding mothers, who laid the foundation for Nuyorican poetry and performance. Whereas calling these performeras *madrinas* points to how they supported the café's history, repositioning them as founding mothers acknowledges not only their presence and participation in the movement, but also their significant contributions to the development of Nuyorican poetry and, as this chapter explores, Nuyorican feminism.

Here, Charlotte Canning's invitation to read performances based on lived experiences as "historiographical moments" is richly productive. Rather than reading the work of women as autobiographical or biographical, Canning urges scholars to look at the ways that performance uses the physical, gestural, and emotional processes to construct a more meaningful reading of the past. This chapter demonstrates how performeras imbued the feminist strategy of constructing history with an expansive notion of collectivity. The work of these women serves as testimonies of feminist spectators, critics, and historians who unravel how "power circulate[s] around the axis of not just gender, but of sexuality, race, and class," offering what Jill Dolan calls "a transformative politics of hope so that we can imagine, together, a better, more equitable future for us all."[2]

As I discussed in chapter 2, Algarín establishes in *Nuyorican Poetry* a Nuyorican aesthetic that includes elements of orality, performance, and performativity; collectivity; linguistic manipulation of Spanish, English, and Spanglish; and Afrodiasporic performance traditions. Influenced by the oral traditions of Puerto Rico and the United States, Algarín focuses on the vocal performance of poetry, specifically the ways in which the body and the voice of the poet worked together to enliven a written text. The poems included in this anthology protest against war, colonialism, poverty, lack of quality education or access to education, terrible living conditions, and welfare cycles that afflicted urban Puerto Ricans living in New York City. These poems, as Algarín describes, "are in the dance of the moment," engaging with relevant social and political issues of the time, "imprint[ing] a cultural presence upon the world," and documenting the survival mechanisms of the Nuyorican community.[3] Given the social inequities that the Puerto Rican community confronted in the 1970s, the publication of this anthology was extremely important, as it utilized the power of the written word and encouraged performing the poetry to expose the systemic oppression that hindered the community. Still, gender discrimination remained unacknowledged.

Algarín and Piñero asked Esteves and a few other female poets to submit their work to the *Nuyorican Poetry* anthology. While they were invited to submit, women were not actually part of the creative production or the editorial process. Muñoz explains that she never felt like a true part of the café, even though her work was included in the anthology: she "never had interpersonal relations [with Algarín]" and "never had a conversation one on one. He never gave [her] a word of advice."[4] Women were just invited to submit their work. As Yvonne Yarbro-Bejarano reminds us, "The prevalence of cultural nationalism also led to the reinscription of the heterosexual hierarchization of male/female relationships. In many organizations, male domination was the rule."[5] The curation of this anthology gave the illusion of inclusiveness, but in practice, the decision-making process was dictated by men, and women were consigned to secondary roles, thus making the Nuyorican performeras in this anthology barely visible. Of the twenty-four poets selected for inclusion in *Nuyorican Poetry*, only four were women: Sandra María Esteves, Martita Morales; Amina Muñoz; and Luz Rodriguez. Part of what makes this anthology a landmark is that it defined the term Nuyorican through poetry and positioned the poets as representing the frontline of an activist-based arts movement. Notably, with the overwhelming majority of these chosen voices being male, it also performatively defined women as occupying the margins of both Nuyorican poetry and politics. In offering an in-depth examination of how these performeras used alternative spaces to deploy a feminist positionality, this chapter disrupts or wrecks, as Gwendolyn D. Pough calls it, the masculinist narrative of Nuyorican history.

THE FEMINIST PRACTICE OF *PLÁTICAS* IN *NUYORICAN POETRY*

In her foundational essay "Poetic Discourse of the Puerto Rican Woman in the U.S." (1989), Eliana Ortega initiated new ground by critically reading the work of Nuyorican female poets featured in the anthology *Nuyorican Poetry*. Taking a cue from Ortega—who positions the female poets as the new voices of Anacaonian liberation—I suggest that these women set in motion the feminist practices of *testimoniando* (telling stories) and *platicando* (partaking in informal everyday conversations), in which women are transformative agents as opposed to passive servants.[6] While these performeras did not identify with feminism during this time, they espoused a feminist ideology. As Esteves and Muñoz share, feminism during this time was dominated by Anglo-American women and excluded women's intersectional identities. Given this reality, to identify as feminist would be considered an act of betrayal to the Nuyorican community.[7] Taken together, the poetry written by the women in *Nuyorican Poetry* was a means to share testimonies, stories that attest to the urgency with which Nuyoriqueñas struggle for survival, rather than a way to stake a claim on their work as feminist.[8]

The use of *pláticas* served as feminist interventions, carving feminist spaces for women to not only recount their memories and transmit cultural knowledge, but to also engage women in critically witnessing the lived experiences of other women. Tiffany Ana López coined the term "critical witnessing" to explain how works of art can serve as tools to engage the public in social change. In using *pláticas* as their mode of communication, Esteves and other performeras create a feminist intervention, inciting critical feminist consciousness and new understandings of the world.[9]

When Esteves stepped onto the poetry scene in 1973, she found it difficult to find her own voice and style while being surrounded by male poets like Pedro Pietri, Jesús "Papoleto" Meléndez, Lucky CienFuegos, Miguel Algarín, Miguel Piñero, and Tato Laviera, who used loud, declamatory, militant styles. It was only after someone came up to her and said that she wrote so well because she wrote like a man that she intentionally pushed herself to find her own poetic voice.[10] Muñoz also sought to find her own poetic performance style, as she shared in a personal interview: "There was all this shouting [by café poets,] and I didn't see myself as someone who's gonna just shout."[11] Likewise, and in contrast with most male Nuyorican poets, who recite with loud and strident voices, "Martita [Morales] does something else," Algarín describes. "She gets into a little conversational piece, and all of a sudden she opens up her volume and then she comes back and talks."[12] While the declamatory style dominates the work of many male poets in *Nuyorican Poetry*, the book's women—Esteves, Muñoz, Morales, and Rodriguez—focus less on volume and militancy and more on the artistry of *platicando* and *testimoniando*, a conversational style of sharing stories that cultivated revolutionary thoughts and acts.[13]

Not surprisingly, their male peers did not meet the performeras' approach of poetry as *plática* with much approval. As David Vidal writes in an early documentation of the café,

> The Nuyorican state of mind is a collective experience here, and the listeners sometimes encourage the poet by shouts of "Right On!" or "You Got it, Sister." But sometimes the poet feels his private experience is so strong and the possibilities for group understanding amid verbal outpourings so few that he may dejectedly return to his seat abruptly cutting off his reading.[14]

Immediately following this statement, Vidal includes an excerpt of Esteves's poem "Blanket Weaver," suggesting that Esteves was the poet who was left feeling dejected by her counterparts.[15] This moment captures the way that Esteves's male peers perceived her intimate conversational style as lacking power or poetic prowess. While the call for social justice was shared among the Nuyorican community, the poetic approach of the performeras was dramatically different from that of the men. The female performeras featured in

Nuyorican Poetry are in political conversation with nationalist proponents of independence like Julia de Burgos, Lolita Lebrón, and the Young Lords, but their tone and cadence steers away from confrontation and instead invites and engages in *pláticas*, intimate conversations. As such, their poetry was considered less potent because it was less authoritative in tone. On the contrary, the performeras' conversational style subverted the male Nuyorican practice of taking up space in voice and volume; instead, it cultivated a sense of intimacy around social ills that affected women, and it offered generative representations of mothers, young girls, and women. While differing drastically in voice and volume from the militant, declamatory approach formalized in *Nuyorican Poetry*, the poetry of performeras fiercely bodied forth revolutionary thoughts of freedom and social justice.

Some women, of course, have had poetic styles that were in sharp contrast to the conversational style of the female authors in *Nuyorican Poetry*. The 1940s poetry recitations by women like Julia de Burgos, for example, took on a militant and declamatory approach. Burgos wrote poetry that rallied for Puerto Rico's independence. As a member of Guajana—a 1960s Puerto Rican progressive poetry group—the poet Angelamaría Dávila defended Puerto Rican independence, criticized the bourgeois life, and called for a new sociopolitical regime. Her poetry was combative in tone and content. She "possessed a magnificent stage presence that complemented the raw forces of her verses."[16] Puerto Rican female poets from the 1960s and 1970s also took on a more militant approach. Luz María Umpierre's delivery, for instance, was very different from the conversational style of the women in the 1975 anthology. "To witness Umpierre reciting these poems," as Lawrence La Fountain-Stokes describes, "is an incredibly transformative experience, and reading them on the page barely offers a weak approximation of the strength and modulated rage expressed in her performance."[17] In the 1980s, Giannina Braschi—now a celebrated member of the Nuyorican Poets Café—began sharing her work on the Nuyorican poetry scene. While similar in themes to the work of Burgos and Dávila, Braschi's delivery style was delicate, slow placed, and serious, with a dose of humor.

REPRESENTATIONS OF LOLITA LEBRÓN

While the declamatory style dominates the work of many male poets in *Nuyorican Poetry*, Esteves, Morales, and Rodriguez put into action their approach of *platicando* and *testimoniando*. As discussed in chapter 2, Lolita Lebrón was an iconic Puerto Rican revolutionary figure that became a source of inspiration for many Nuyoricans. Just as nationalist ideologies in Burgos's poetry spoke to many Nuyoricans, so too did the moment in 1954 when Lebrón and three other nationalists took over the US House of Representatives. Lucky CienFuegos authored the protest poem "Lolita Lebrón, Recuerdo Te Mandamos." Using uppercase letters and elongating words on the page, this poem is a penetrating rally call for Lolita Lebrón's freedom: "FREEEEEE THAT SISTER / FREE THAT LOVING LOVING / LOOOOOVING SISTER / FREE THAT WOMAN / FREE THAT LOVING / LOVING WOMAN / FREE LOLITA LEBRON [*sic*]."[18] As Algarín describes it, "Lucky reaches his loudest volume, you are bound to get a street crowd. You've done another thing with that volume too. You've caused a crowd to start responding. Open uncontrolled sounds make people respond."[19] The repetition of words like *free* and *love* underscores the call for Lebrón's freedom and reminds readers that, while the United States might consider her attack to be an act of terrorism, others see her as a freedom fighter protecting Puerto Rico from the continuous repercussions of colonialism.

In contrast, Esteves's poem "For Lolita Lebron," included in her 1980 collection *Yerba Buena*, produces a contemplative space for rethinking Lebrón's nationalist labor as a pedagogical site for women and youth. Written after Lebrón's twenty-five-year imprisonment, Esteves's poem is an intimate conversation with the public about Lebrón.[20] In this poetic *plática*, Esteves positions Lebrón as an intellectual who wanted to "write us books" about her experience as a revolutionary, nationalist, and political prisoner. Esteves believes that Lebrón's life—what she calls the "brilliance from [her] waterfall"—will help us not only "to rediscover our identity," but also "to stock the young with stone."[21] Lebrón's life experiences can be a source of empowerment for youth and women. Lebrón is "Womanstrength / a mold to guide the dawn"; her "visions [and] alternatives" create "circles that touch," injecting the present generation with hope and agency.[22]

While Esteves turns to *platicando* and *testimoniando* to remember Lebrón, CienFuegos uses a protest cry to evoke her revolutionary acts. Their differing tone, volume, and style of delivery, however, do not change the political content of both poems. The poems center Lebrón and work against colonial subordination of Puerto Rico, but Esteves cultivates a conversation about how Lebrón's activism serves as a model for other women. In doing so, Esteves radicalizes Lebrón by explicitly stating how her legacy has impacted other women.

ANTONIA MARTÍNEZ: CONSUMERISM AND THE COLONIAL STRUGGLE

While Esteves's poetry takes on the form of a *plática* that produces a pedagogical site of empowerment for youth and women, Amina Muñoz uses *plática* in her poetry to signal the ways in which popular culture and history represent Puerto Rican women in particular. Muñoz takes the role of Dolan's feminist spectator as critic and uses her poetry as "a lens through which to filter the culture we consume intentionally."[23] In "welcome to san juan, oldest city in the u.s.," Muñoz layers her poem with sarcasm, highlighting the devastating consequences of the colonial relationship between the United States and Puerto Rico. Muñoz adopts advertising's conversational language, the same language that is used to sell the latest fashions and the trendiest products (such as the popular shag hairstyle that Paul McGregor created for Jane Fonda in the 1971 film *Klute*, which she references in her poem). Consumerism, as Muñoz points out, camouflages Puerto Rico's hardships and the failure of the United States to provide the better life that migrants sought.

If that were not ironic enough, Muñoz also adopts the voice of a travel agent selling Puerto Rico to tourists as an alcoholic's paradise. She writes: "let us fly you, / our Puerto Rico— / let us get drunk / with bacardi and don Q."[24] She directs her sarcasm toward politicians who use their "ultrabright smile[s]" to praise Puerto Rico for "com[ing] a long way baby," while "unemployment has risen from 15% to 25%," and "the beach has a sign / KEEP OFF / U.S. PROPERTY." Muñoz's poetry focuses on how advertisers and politicians publicly fashion the most flattering aspects of society while ignoring or covering up the less flattering sides. She "organizes the cacophony and chaos of images that come at us from multiple directions at once" in such a way that reveals the capitalist, racial, and colonial powers at work.[25]

Alongside these images of consumerism, Muñoz portrays the ways in which the spectacles of popular culture and politics insidiously surround us and distract people from seeing the violent and traumatic impact of colonialism on women. Positioning the death of another Puerto Rican heroine, Antonia Martínez, alongside the consumption of culture and material goods, Muñoz frames the struggle of colonial resistance as an ongoing process. Martínez was only nineteen years old when she was shot by the US National Guard on March 4, 1970, in Rio Piedras, Puerto Rico. Muñoz writes: "meanwhile a young student / at Rio Piedras lies on her concrete grave. / the national guard decided / she got in the way / of the 51st star of the yanqui flag."[26] Since many Puerto Rican Independentistas (members of the Independence Party) saw the presence of the Reserve Officers' Training Corps (ROTC) on the campus of the University of Puerto Rico as a symbol of colonialism, they mobilized against this US military presence. Students from the Independence Party organized marches and rallies to remove ROTC from their school, eventually setting fire to two ROTC buildings on campus.[27] Martínez stood on a nearby balcony during the bloody riots between Independentistas and the ROTC cadets. These riots started at the University of Puerto Rico, but they soon spilled into the streets of Rio Piedras. Muñoz astutely reminds her readers of the continuous resistance against colonialism when she dedicates her poem to the memory of "la querida compañera, Antonia Martínez, Nuestra lucha vencerá, Antonia" (the dear comrade, Antonia Martínez, We will overcome our struggle, Antonia).

MOTHERS, SISTERS, AND REVOLUTIONARY FIGURES

Representations of mothers, sisters, and revolutionary figures play a thematic role in the anthology *Nuyorican Poetry*. In contrast to the male poets who represent women as passive victims in their poetry, Esteves and Morales position women as agents of change. In "Ode to a Tequila Head," Esteves describes a man whom everyone in the neighborhood knows as the drunkard vagabond. When a mother walks by him, she advises her children, "DON'T BE LIKE HIM."[28] The mother in the poem is an educational agent teaching her children about the cycle of alcoholism in the community. She warns them that, if they fall into that trap, they will become destitute. This poem has a two-pronged pedagogical agenda. Esteves writes this poem as a dialogue between a mother and her children, but it also functions as a teaching moment for readers and spectators. The poet's responsibility, as Algarín proclaims, is to "teach people how to think about themselves. . . . We read our poetry not only in street corners, but in apartments, so that people can get to hear us examining ourselves."[29]

In contrast to Esteves's poem—in which the mother is positioned as an educator transmitting knowledge to her children—Pietri's "Twice a Month Is Mother's Day" and Américo Casiano's "When was the last time you saw mami smile?" each portrays a submissive, self-sacrificing mother who, as Algarín describes, "suffers and . . . is not given recognition."[30] Likewise, Jesús "Papoleto" Meléndez, in "sister, *para nuestras hermanas*," portrays a well-educated, revolutionary sister who works incessantly for the revolution and who reads Mao, Marx, Che, and Lenin—but whose destiny is that "she'll die / loving / loving you."[31] In the last sentence of the poem, the "you" refers to the man who "want[s] to lay her."[32] Pietri, Casiano, and Meléndez all place a woman as a "central role of reference," but they also relegate women to the status of passive victims or sexualized objects that need to be taken care of by men.[33]

Similar to Esteves's work, Martita Morales's "The Sounds of Sixth Street" depicts a young woman from the Lower East Side of Manhattan who is coming of age into her Afro-Latinidad and racial consciousness. As she grows older, she discovers that her parents have internalized racism, agreeing to the oppression of dark-skinned Afro–Puerto Ricans. As a child, she recalls noticing the racial difference between her parents and curiously asking, "¿Mamí, por qué tu blanca y papí tan?" (Mommy, why you white and daddy tan?).[34] When she was fifteen years old, she noticed that her father, who was racially darker, did not want her to associate with any Black people. He wanted her to consider herself white. Instead of conforming to this ideology, "she rebels / against the fact / that / her parents will not let her have a boyfriend / with an afro or *con el pelo grifo* / because he looks black / and black to them is dirty."[35] Recognizing the internal practices of racism in her household, as well as the colonial relationship between Puerto Rico and the United States, she decides to protest and fight for social equity in her school by exercising her right not to pledge allegiance to the US flag. Consequently, she gets expelled for believing that "her [Puerto Rican] flag is GOLD."[36] Despite her suspension, the reader understands that she will continue to fight because "she knows she is Right!"[37]

Morales's protagonist fiercely denounces the inequities faced by many Puerto Ricans by publicly refusing to pledge allegiance to the flag. Her actions—while not as life threatening as when Blanca Canales led the Jayuya Uprising or when Lolita Lebrón led the attack on the US House of Representatives—show a young girl's activism. Like Canales and Lebrón, she refuses to give in to American power and instead utilizes the Puerto Rican flag as a symbol of her revolutionary aspirations for independence and freedom. Two decades later, Abraham Rodriguez Jr. reexamined these issues of citizenship and dissent in his short story "Boy without a Flag" (1992), but as the title suggests, his protagonist is a young Puerto Rican boy who refuses to pledge allegiance to the flag. Nuyorican performeras like Esteves and Morales carved a space for young Nuyorican women to take center stage, modeling self-expression and various modes of communication for the generations to come.

RAISING AWARENESS ABOUT CULTURAL TABOOS

Like many feminist performers of the 1970s who raised awareness about cultural taboos, performeras featured in *Nuyorican Poetry* worked to push back on society's perceptions of menstruation and abortion. Both Esteves and Luz Rodriguez address gender issues not only as women, but as Nuyorican women. In "i look for peace great graveyard," Esteves expresses the agonizing emotions that women experience when considering an abortion. This poem is timely, as it was published two years after the US Supreme Court decided *Roe v. Wade* (1973), which made it unconstitutional for any state to ban or to regulate abortions during the first trimester of pregnancy. This decision to legalize abortion was the result of the work of the women's movement in the 1960s. Women testified about their illegal abortions in public demonstrations, and they lobbied for abortion on demand.[38]

Esteves addresses abortion by invoking the image of an unwanted child in her body. She writes: "The meat is rotting fast inside / my womb disintegrates in anal slurs." Despite the legalization of this procedure, women who had abortions often faced tremendous judgment and animosity. Esteves brings abortion into proximity with the most vulgar and denigrated part of the body—the anus—to make palpable the physical and emotional trauma that women experienced. As she describes it, even the most intimate spaces are the harshest critics: "New York spits my eye / oil dragged hummingbird, is there no peace? / sometimes i want to die i feel just die." By the end of the poem, she turns to the elements of nature as a source of grounding and healing: "trees are where I wish to live / and play the dance of chinese wind chimes / hear the ancient pipe breath / that touches my eyes to see."[39] Her poem, while she does not call it as such, cultivates Nuyorican feminist thinking. As a Nuyorican woman, Esteves makes abortion, a private issue and cultural taboo, public, and she takes a stance for the fundamental right to have an abortion.

Similar to Esteves, Rodriguez also engenders a feminist consciousness-raising in her poetry. In "i feel the eve," Rodriguez tackles the menstrual taboo by transforming menstruation from a "dirty little secret" into a desirable event. She writes, "i feel the eve / of my body / flowing through / the cycle of woman. / blood rush down / cleanse my womb. / my hair at motion, / limbs in stimulation, / effecting sensation, / submerging in love."[40] Rodriguez gives the word *eve* a double meaning. The biblical Eve was shamed and cursed with the pains of birthing as punishment for biting the apple. To counter this shame, Rodriguez uses the word *eve* to promote a body-positive attitude toward menstruation. She underscores this message by returning to the image of a woman biting an apple in the poem "Holding you." Here, biting the metaphorical apple of Eve is a joyous occasion, one on which a woman's body is admired in nature. She writes, "You smell like running through wet green grass / smelling the pureness of all that's green. . . . / diving into a rushing waterfall / biting into a crisp green apple."[41]

To write and speak openly about menstruation is to deconstruct its historical, social, and cultural reputation of fear, shame, and disgust. As such, Rodriguez inspires women to reclaim the power of their bodies.[42] Her poems serve as a formidable response to the systemic debasement and patriarchal control of all that is female, and yet like Esteves, her perspective is not solely about gender issues but about the intersections between gender, race, and ethnicity. Interestingly, her poetic themes foreshadow the leadership roles that she would later take on in the 1980s and 1990s with Latina reproductive health organizations including the Dominican Women's Development Center, Casa Atabex Ache, Latina Roundtable on Health and Reproductive Rights, and Sister Song Women of Color Reproductive Health Collective.[43]

PLATICANDO ABOUT THE YOUNG LORDS

Esteves also makes a feminist intervention by using *platicando* and *testimoniando* to explore the intersections between past and present moments. She builds her poetry and performance as conversation around the material circumstances of the past. This practice is most apparent in her 2009 performance of "Aguacero," which took place at the fortieth-anniversary celebration of the Young Lords, held at the First Spanish Methodist Church in East Harlem, the same church that the group took over in late 1969. Taking a cue from Canning, I read this performance as a historiographical moment that through Esteves's physical, gestural and emotional processes teaches spectators about the Young Lords' past and its impact on young women. Esteves invokes the living memory of the Young Lords by interweaving the social realities of the 1970s with the group's theme song, "Agua que va caer"

(Water That Goes Down), and their call to action, "¡DESPIERTA BORICUA DEFIENDE LO TUYO!" (Wake up Boricua defend what is yours!). In an earlier recording of "Agua que va caer" in the album *Patato & Totico* (1966) the strong, high voice of Totico (Eugenio Arango) resonates over the soulful drumming of Patato (Carlos Valdez) on congas. In contrast, Esteves's silvery lyrical voice holds down the rumba rhythm of "Agua Que Va Caer." Her singing is the present moment, which has been indelibly shaped by the past. Every so often, she seamlessly transitions into intimate scenarios, sharing flashes of her childhood memories.

To distinguish past from present, Esteves accentuates every new episode of her past with the refrain "growin' up." She remembers: "growin' up Puertorriqueña/Latina," "growin' up eatin' mayonnaise sandwiches," and "growing up like good little girls should."[44] Audience members chuckle, as they identify with the bittersweet memories of growing up poor, female, and Puerto Rican. Despite all the hardships, she fondly recalls that the Young Lords taught her an important lesson, "Growin' up discoverin' to stand up for our rights / Fallin' down—risin' up again / Without givin' up the fight."[45] The Young Lords equipped her with the tools to understand her culture. She was not aware "'bout Don Pedro Albizu Campos / Arturo Schomburg or Lolita Lebrón" or that she was "dancin' *bombas* and *plenas*."[46] Esteves's performance reveals how she connects her personal past and makes it part of the historical tapestry of the Young Lords, who significantly contributed to her social and political awakening.

At the same time, Esteves does not gloss over her memories of violence against women, insisting on making these personal and traumatic experiences part of her community's history and making meaning out of her culture's masculinist, racist, and colonial practices. She says:

Growin' up with sistas all around
Getting' raped by the men they love
Sistas growin' up and getting' raped
By people they loved
Not cause they deserved it
Not cause they wanted it or earned it
Just getting' raped
The way our mamas got raped
The way our ancestors got raped
The way our island gets raped

By them big hard right political ideals
By conquerors who know how to steal
Our heritage, our pride, our dignity[47]

Esteves calls attention to the pervasiveness of rape as a form of sexual, social, and colonial domination and the ways that disenfranchised communities forever carry the legacy of this violent past. Desiring to wash away the painful history, the audience sings with Esteves, "Te juro que va caer / Agua que va caer" (I swear it is going to pour / Water is going to pour). Esteves's feminist strategy of *platicando* inspirits the audience to sing along and brings the traumatic past—the histories of rape, poverty, and social negligence—into the present consciousness and shapes the community's future.

FOR TITO: *PLATICANDO* ABOUT POLICE VIOLENCE

Esteves uses her poetic style of *platicando* and *testimoniando* not only to document the role of women in the community, but also to address the death of young men to police violence and the traumatic impact on the community. She dedicates the poem "for tito" to Martín Pérez, a fellow artist who went by "Tito," and who was arrested for disorderly conduct because he was drumming in a train station. After being detained for two hours by the transit police, he was found dead in an apparent suicide. Authorities claimed that they found him hanging by his belt from the ceiling of the cell. Esteves draws on themes of love and music in her poem, which on the surface appears to describe a love affair between Tito and the poet, but a closer read reveals the love affair that Tito has with his music and the power of music as a strategy of resistance. In the introduction to this section of *Nuyorican Poetry*, Algarín describes the poem "for tito" as a declaration of love between Tito and Esteves. He states: "Sandra knows that between man and woman exists the possibility of balance. In 'for tito' she achieves a beautiful energy-giving balance."[48] The legacy of heteropatriarchy fuels Algarín's reading, as he interprets the poem's eroticism as connoting a heterosexual love affair. An examination of how Esteves engages with Tito's death in her poem illustrates how she stages feminist historiographical moments and, in so doing, reveals how Nuyoricans are negatively impacted by the systemic racism plaguing police departments.

Rather than reading this poem as a love affair between Tito and Esteves, as Algarín suggests, I redirect the focus to how Esteves depicts music as a culturally regenerative tool for individual and collective affirmation. In her opening stanza, Esteves writes, "you, macho machete / are all the fine conga rhythms / played on the street, in parties, in spring / all the beautiful vibes of *la playa sextet* / washing up against the palms in the hairs of my back / turning my blood into salsa / and filling me up inside to swell with who I am."[49] The poem—while filled with erotic overtones—explores the romantic feelings that Esteves has for Pérez's drumming and not necessarily for him. She anthropomorphizes the salsa beats, the conga rhythms, and the upbeat vibes of *la playa sextets*, and she explains how music is a fertile site for imagining the cultural power of her community. Music—already discussed—is a critically important element in Nuyorican poetry. Sometimes musicians performed alongside poets; other times poets included allusions to music in their work. Esteves paints an image of herself as possessed by Tito's music. This is most evident in the fourth stanza, where she writes:

> you, *macho soledad*
> are a unique language
> the one filling my eyes with heat for you
> growing and pounding
> with all the desire
> of your drum
> pounding with my womb
> planting seeds in the night[50]

Esteves pays homage to Tito's drumming and alludes to the powerful force of the drumbeats, which move her and fill her with joy, sensuality, and love. Police and authorities were quick to annihilate the power of an African-based cultural expression of drumming. In scripting Tito's tragic death into the current consciousness of the reader or spectator, Esteves imbues Tito's pounding drumbeats with potentiality. As she concludes, "together / we reap mystical sugarcane in the ghetto / where all the palm trees grow ripe / and rich with coconut milk."[51] Given the rampant police brutality in the 1970s, this love poem is less about imagining Martín Pérez as a lover and more about capturing how the power of the drums filled the train car with Afrodiasporic sounds, thus threatening dominant power.

Esteves continues to invoke feminist historiographical moments in two other poems dedicated to Martín Pérez in *Yerba Buena* (1980). Esteves not

Eulogy for Martín Perez

They killed you
called you slave
abused your name
sentenced you to swing by the belt
the jailhouse destiny of death

We saw it happen
just like they did it to Julio Rodan in 1970
we saw it happen again
like helpless lambs
we watched them kick your face
and break your neck
in five minutes
they claimed your fate
and forced your manhood down a gun

And now today
we look to poets for answers
and visions
and directions
for mirrors of reflection.

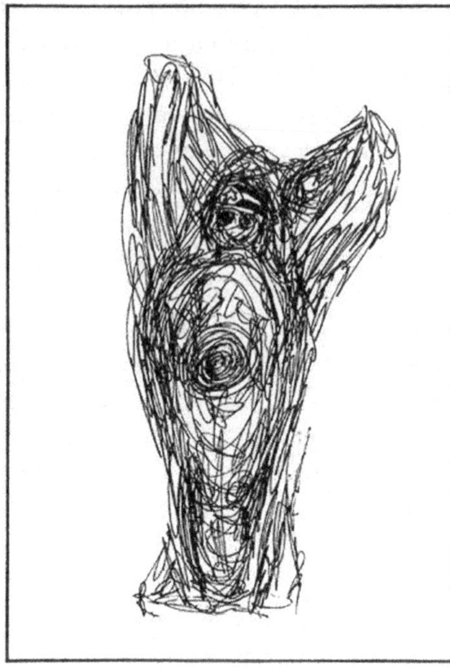

Figure 7. Sandra María Esteves commemorates the life of Martín "Tito" Pérez with her poem "Eulogy for Martín Pérez" and her angel line drawing, *Yerba Buena* (1980). Courtesy of the poet and artist.

only processes the passing of a loved one by dedicating poems to Pérez but also turns to visual representation to mourn his killing by the hands of police authorities. Alongside the poem "Eulogy for Martín Pérez," for instance, Esteves draws an angelic scribbled figure wearing a Puerto Rican bandana. She politicizes his tragic death by comparing it to similar so-called suicidal incidents. She writes: "We saw it happen / just like they did it to Julio Ro[l]dan in 1970 / we saw it happen again / like helpless lambs / we watched them kick your face / and break your neck / in five minutes / they claimed your fate / and forced your manhood down a gun" (28).

Esteves refuses to read this event as an isolated incident, and she associates Pérez's supposed suicide with slavery and the killing of Julio Roldan.[52] Like Pérez, Roldan was a Young Lord who was found dead while in detention. Esteves references numerous suicides by hanging of Black people and Puerto Ricans in precincts and jails in her poetry to underscore the intersections among history, politics, and art. Like the poem "for tito"—in which she professes the love of music that Tito created—this poem is a call for community mobilization. Esteves explains that, in response to Pérez's death, El Comité del primero de diciembre (the December First Committee) was formed, and it was named for the day of his arrest and death. The committee circulated a flier throughout the neighborhood to inform residents of Pérez's death at the hands of police.[53] Titled "Homicidio, No Suicidio" (Homicide, Not Suicide), the bilingual flier was created to inform community members that Tito was killed by the authorities, who staged his death as a suicide.[54] The flier described the history of police brutality and presumed suicides in the Twenty-Fifth Precinct. It argued that Pérez's death was not an isolated event, but rather part of a recurring manifestation of institutional violence and racism at its worst.

The flier urged individuals to come forward with any information and to write letters to congressional representatives, senators, and human rights organizations. It also provided information on an upcoming demonstration on December 9, in front of city hall in Manhattan. The flier called for the suspension of the police officers in charge of Pérez's detainment, as well as an extensive investigation into the behavior of the members of the Twenty-Fifth Precinct. The layout of this flier is simple, yet it is layered with meaning. The black and white picture of Pérez joyfully singing and drumming is a counternarrative to the typical police mug shot. A dignified image of the revolutionary icon Albizu Campos hovers above Pérez, emphasizing the recurring moments of institutionalized violence throughout history. Just as authorities staged Pérez's death as a suicide, Albizu Campos was targeted for human radiation experiments while he was an inmate.[55] Taken together, the images of Pérez and Albizu Campos point to the long history of systemic violence affecting Puerto Ricans and Nuyoricans, thus making an urgent call for justice.

While organizing protests, signing petitions, and bombarding politicians with messages are strategies that political organizations often use, the Fuerzas Armadas de Liberación Nacional Puertoriqueña (Armed Forces of National Liberation)—a clandestine Puerto Rican paramilitary organization that advocated for Puerto Rican independence—used direct action to call attention to the situation. Three days after Pérez's death, it reported that there was a dead body in an abandoned building, where its members had planted a bomb. The bomb exploded, and one police officer was severely injured and lost an eye. The organization publicly took responsibility for these actions and claimed that the bomb was a way of retaliating

HOMICIDIO, NO SUICIDIO

El primero de Diciembre de 1974 a las 10:30 pm, Martin "Tito" Perez fué arrestado por la Policía de Tránsito por "conducta desordenada". El arresto tomó lugar en la plataforma de la estación de la calle 125 en el Lexington Ave. subway. Dos horas más tarde Tito estaba muerto.

Este no es un incidente aislado dentro de la comunidad Puertorriqueña. Nosotros, el Comité del Primero de Diciembre, creemos que Tito fué asesinado y dejado ahorcado en las barras de la celda para crear un ambiente de suicidio.

El precinto 25 tiene una larga historia de brutalidades y atentados suicidios de los presos. Estas situaciones son comunes y ocurren amenudo contra Afroamericanos, Latinos, Asiaticos, y Nativoamericanos (Indios) - la comunidad del Tercer Mundo, en este caso El Barrio en East Harlem, Nueva York.

Figure 8. Flier in Spanish protesting the unexplained death of Martín "Tito" Pérez while in prison. Courtesy Sandra María Esteves.

for Pérez's brutal death, as well as avenging the countless Puerto Rican and Black people who died that year at the hands of the New York City Police Department.[56]

Esteves's poems not only deal with mourning the loss of loved ones; they also teach readers and spectators how underprivileged community members continue to die at the hands of the police. Tito represents the history of genocidal violence against Puerto Ricans. His death and the events that followed prompted Esteves to reflect on her role as a poet. If "we look to poets for answers / and visions / and directions / for mirrors of reflection," as Esteves states, then we can clearly see their contribution to social justice.[57]

THE LAWSUIT: A FEMINIST COURTROOM DRAMA

Amid the Nuyorican movement's fight for equal access to education, Sandra María Esteves addressed the gender discrimination within the Nuyorican community. In equal measure to the ways that I engage *Nuyorican Poetry* as an archive of the feminist spaces that women carved, here I turn to physical ephemera that Esteves created as feminist interventions, and in particular a flier—*The Lawsuit* flier—that Esteves circulated to protest against gender discrimination. She uses *The Lawsuit* flier to wreck the misogyny in the Nuyorican poetry and theater community during the 1970s. I sat with Esteves on the benches in uptown Manhattan across from Boricua College in 2013, nearly forty years removed from the work that she did as a young performera. As we spoke, it occurred to me that we were witnessing the results of the civil rights movement's activism in the 1960s and 1970s. Founded in 1974, at the height of the Nuyorican movement, Boricua College continues to serve the educational needs of Puerto Ricans and other Latinxs in New York City.[58] Given the context, Esteves's recollection of this period took on even more resonance.

Originally trained as a visual artist at Pratt Institute in Brooklyn, Esteves utilizes textual, visual, theatrical, and performative strategies as feminist historiographical moments to traverse the legal, artistic, and political stage. She moves personal conflicts into the realm of public history, critiques the institutions that render male figures as founders and creators, and dramatizes the ways that men and their institutions erase the presence and contributions of women. Esteves used her visual strategies to frame *The Lawsuit* flier—and the real-life lawsuit that it responded to—as a theatrical event, demonstrating the gender dynamics at play in the Nuyorican poetry and theater scene. This framing was Esteves's feminist intervention.

Engaging the foundational feminist idea that "the personal is political," Esteves placed her personal conflict with her male Nuyorican counterparts into the public sphere through the small-claims court in New York City.[59] Esteves was part of the New Rican Village, a contemporaneous venue to the Nuyorican Poets Café that was similarly important during the Nuyorican movement. Like the café, the village supported a collective of artists working in diverse media such as poetry, theater, visual art, dance, and music.[60] Esteves built the set and performed her poetry in the New Rican Village's production of *Conjunto Libre* (Free Set), which took place at the Delacorte Theater in Central Park on July 17, 1978.[61] *Conjunto Libre* was part of Joseph Papp's New York Shakespeare Festival's Summer Mobile Theater, which performed in various parks throughout the boroughs of New York.

During the play's run, Esteves received a payment of $250 for her artistic services. When the check bounced three days later, Esteves approached Eduardo Figueroa, cofounder and director of the New Rican Village, at one of the scheduled performances. Figueroa brushed aside Esteves's anger, imploring her to calm down and to get on stage because there were "important politicians in the audience." Immediately after the performance, Figueroa fired Esteves, leaving her unpaid for her artistic services.[62] Since she was the only woman on the creative team, she was "determined to make a statement," and she ended up filing charges against Figueroa and Joseph Papp, the director and producer of the Public Theater. Although Papp's Public Theater was not liable because it was a third-party administrator of the festival, Esteves included the organization "to ensure that Eddie Figueroa would show up and to humiliate him in connection to the Public Theater."[63] The arbitrator ruled in favor of Esteves. Since Figueroa admitted that there was a verbal contract between the New Rican Village and Esteves, and since the Public Theater was administering the project, they had to split the liability. Within a few days, the Public Theater paid Esteves, but to this day, she has not received a check from Figueroa or the New Rican Village for her work.

A few weeks before the court trial, Esteves created a flier that framed the lawsuit as a theatrical production. Esteves staged the lawsuit to reveal the gendered power dynamics at play in the Nuyorican poetry theater scene. Following the conventions of publicizing a theater production, she used the flier to provide the reader with a date, time, and location for the event and to

Figure 9. Drawing by Sandra María Esteves, who had filed charges against Eduardo Figueroa and Joseph Papp, the director and producer of the Public Theater. The court trial is here ironically presented as a performance titled *The Lawsuit* (1979).

make acknowledgments; and she widely publicized the production by posting it in apartment buildings, on light posts, and in bodegas around the Lower East Side. While some uninformed audience members called Esteves to make reservations, others questioned the use of the court as a performance space. Clearly, the venue did not prevent people from seeing her new work; about twenty friends and relatives attended the performance (that is, the trial). Some came to learn about Esteves's new and innovative performance space, hoping to tap into this new resource. The defendants were taken aback when they learned that Esteves created a satirical production out of the court trial. By framing the lawsuit as a performance, she also made a mockery of the court. She transcended the conventions of the courtroom by exercising her right to be there as an actress and theater director staging a performance.

While Eduardo Figueroa's action made Esteves's presence invisible, in *The Lawsuit* flier, Esteves creates a sense of being watched as she draws a pencil-thin man dressed in a suit. There is a pair of eyes on top of his U-shaped head. He stands erect, and his hands are folded like a proper gentleman, while many eyes watch him. The flier publicized the lawsuit as a performance, so that spectators could bear witness to Esteves's satirical shaming of Figueroa, a Nuyorican male figurehead, for failing to uphold notions of collectivity and for neglecting to pay her. On the bottom of the flier, Esteves includes a section of acknowledgments. She thanks the Nichiren Shoshu Academy for Buddhist Consciousness for being one of the resources that made her aware of the existing oppression that marginalized communities face.

Esteves invented the next two organizations that she names on the flier—the International People's Cultural Movement and the Holistic Center for the Advancement of Human Society. This gesture of jamming, imagining a collective, as opposed to acknowledging individuals, is Esteves's subversive strategy of writing the labor of woman and their desire for collectivity into the official history. The flier's images call attention to the performance dimensions of social institutions that uphold heteropatriarchal practices. By using the visual dimension, Esteves has complete control in creating a feminist aesthetic, as opposed to when Algarín and Piñero dominated the curatorial decisions for *Nuyorican Poetry*. She has continued throughout her career to inject a sense of collectivity into her performances.

Despite the New Rican Village's disavowal of Esteves's participation in

Figure 10. Flier advertising performance of New Rican Village's salsa performance, July 17, 1978 at the Delacorte Theatre. Designed by Néstor Otero. Courtesy of Sandra María Esteves.

Figure 11. Poster of New Rican Village performance, Summer 1978. Designed by Sandra María Esteves. Courtesy of the artist.

the New York Shakespeare Festival's Summer Mobile Theater, Esteves's experience of sexism fueled her critical engagement with the collective. Prior to creating the flier for *The Lawsuit*, Esteves designed a tour flier for the New Rican Village's band Conjunto Libre (Set Free). Esteves's flier is strikingly different from one designed by Néstor Otero for the band's New York performances.[64] On the flier for the band's performances at the Delacorte Theater, Otero—a visual artist and designer for the show—drew instruments including a guitar, a piano, a flute, a brass instrument, several different types of drums (congas, bongos, and timbales), and pairs of claves and maracas.

While Otero's design spotlights the musical vibrancy of this show, Esteves's flier—which publicized Conjunto Libre's tour—used photographs of men and women in motion. The image of the dancer moving across the page captures a sequence of movements. If we read the body from the top to bottom, we see the dancer jump in the air and extend her arms and legs to execute a jeté, and then reach sideways, extending her arms upward, and fall to the ground.

Esteves employs visual techniques to rescript both the female artists of color during the Nuyorican Movement, and their bodies in motion. *The Lawsuit* and the Conjunto Libre fliers are archival documents that visually script the ways that Esteves responded to the misogyny within the Nuyorican community. In these spaces of visuality, Esteves has complete control over the creation of a feminist aesthetic. The lawsuit, the framing of the lawsuit as a theatrical event, and the visual signs of surveillance that kept her male counterparts in check are some of Esteves's many feminist interventions.

This discussion of Esteves's work sets the stage for studying a range of performance strategies employed by Nuyorican performeras. These strategies are not the only scenes of Nuyorican expressions that exist; however, these examples serve as feminist historiographical moments, connective tissues linking the past, present, and future. Esteves strategically places her work at the juncture of visual art, poetry, theater, performance, and other artistic modalities to create a Nuyorican feminist aesthetic—both on the page and on the stage—that counters patriarchal dominance. By putting the works of Sandra María Esteves, Luz Rodriguez, Amina Muñoz, and Martita Morales center stage in this chapter, I spotlight these female poets as the founding mothers of Nuyorican poetry rather than simply godmothers, and I mark their significant roles as forebearers and pioneers of the Nuyorican poetry movement.

As illustrated in this chapter, these women counter masculinist practices by producing and performing poetry that functions as poetic *pláticas*, a conversational style of poetry that carves out feminist collective spaces, positioning women as active agents and history makers. Esteves and these other founding mothers serve as precursors to spoken word and hip hop theater as well as the work of contemporary Nuyoriqueña performeras such as La Bruja (the Witch), Mariposa (Butterfly), Nilaja Sun, and Aya de León, to whom I will turn in the next few chapters.

CHAPTER 4

Masculinity in Hip Hop, Spoken Word, and Slam Poetry

THE POPULARIZATION AND GLOBAL CIRCULATION of hip hop, spoken word, and slam poetry have embedded these art forms in mainstream culture. Black and Latina women participating in these artistic mediums, however, notoriously continue to be placed in the shadows rather than center stage. This chapter thus contextualizes the influences of hip hop, spoken word, and slam poetry to frame the close readings that follow of contemporary Nuyoriqueña performeras La Bruja (the Witch), Mariposa (Butterfly), Nilaja Sun, and Aya de León. I offer a gendered analysis that accounts for the dominant masculinist aesthetic ingrained within these minoritarian art forms.[1] This chapter positions the evolution of hip hop, spoken word, and slam poetry in dialogue with the Nuyorican aesthetic, while also documenting the exclusion or marginalization of women in these forms. Born during the height of the hip hop era, La Bruja, Mariposa, Nilaja Sun, and Aya de León are undeniably influenced by a hip hop as well as a Nuyorican performance aesthetic. As performeras—women of color navigating the poetry slam and hip hop theater scene, spaces that are often dominated by a masculinist aesthetic—they have all encountered challenges posed by gender that markedly shaped their creative works, which is the focus of the next three chapters.

THE BIRTH OF HIP HOP

Born against the backdrop of structural changes occurring in New York's South Bronx back to the 1950s, hip hop, as Suzanne Bost argues, "is by nature, contestorial, resistant, and political."[2] Robert Moses's Cross Bronx

Expressway—on which construction began in 1948—drastically affected residents' lives. The expressway was not completed until 1963, fifteen years after workers broke ground. This development led to a familiar pattern of white exodus to the suburbs. It also created a physical barrier that dissected neighborhoods; people driving from the suburbs to the city could now bypass the poor, deteriorated, and neglected communities of the Bronx. Out of sight, out of mind.

The construction of the Cross Bronx Expressway in the 1950s led directly to disinvestment by the federal government and ethnic dislocation in the South Bronx in the 1970s. Many Puerto Ricans settled in the barrios of the South Bronx and were profoundly impacted by the governmental neglect. During this time, the South Bronx had a disproportionately high concentration of poverty and unemployment. Residents experienced embattled living conditions, racial segregation, and inferior education. By the 1980s, the South Bronx had lost two-thirds of its population, and the neighborhood became world famous for urban deterioration, crime, and arson. In the 1990s—when the population of the Bronx had declined, and only the nation's poorest people still lived there—the neighborhood had one of the highest concentrations of Puerto Ricans in the city.

Amid the urban decay, the Bronx was the stomping grounds for Latinx, African American, and Afro-Caribbean youth. This group worked with musical mixes, "boogying down" to funk and disco at the block parties. This musical innovation produced the cultural and artistic phenomenon now known as hip hop—including break dancing, rapping, emceeing, and deejaying.[3] The birth of hip hop was the product of a certain set of social and political circumstances. These included Reagonomics; the digital age; an exploding prison population; and the epidemics of crack, guns, and AIDS. These factors—combined with New York City's populations of Puerto Ricans, Dominicans, Jamaicans, and working-class white people—created the hip hop art form, including speech and song, dance and display, and visual and performance art. Nuyoricans and African Americans lived as neighbors, sharing similar experiences of discrimination. Hip hop thus is a transethnic site, facilitating relationships among people from different cultural backgrounds.[4]

While hip hop originates as a form of resistance and protest, it is not free from exclusion and oppression. The hypermasculine posturing of male rappers and DJs, the unrelenting objectification of women as gold diggers, whores, and video vixens, and the representation of Black men as violent savages make hip hop an uninviting space for women to artistically flourish.[5] The prevalent misogynistic images of women in hip hop generate a masculinist aesthetic that hinders and constrains women's agency. As women from the hip hop generation, La Bruja, Mariposa, Nilaja Sun, and Aya de León encounter these masculinist adversities and—as we will see in the coming chapters—overcome them by drawing on Nuyorican and hip hop feminist aesthetics.

SPOKEN WORD AND SLAM POETRY AT THE NUYORICAN POETS CAFÉ

While the Nuyorican Poets Café and hip hop emerged in two different locations in New York City, they did so simultaneously. The 1970s—the decade during which the café opened its doors—witnessed the city's height of poverty and arson, which left buildings unoccupied and decaying on the Lower East Side. Despite the conditions, this neighborhood became New York's hottest artistic center by the 1980s. As art critics Walter Robinson and Carlo McCormick note, the Lower East Side was fertile ground because of its "unique blend of poverty, punk rock, drugs, and arson, Hell's Angels, winos, prostitutes and dilapidated housing that add up to an adventurous avant-garde setting of considerable cachet."[6] Art galleries, dance clubs, studios, and coffee shops replaced old tenement buildings, and vacant lots became the building grounds for condominiums. Ultimately, this transformation displaced the socially unwanted.

Although popular among artists, the café lacked the finances to maintain its building. The café faced plumbing and electrical problems, as well as an unsafe hole in the roof, which forced it to close its doors in 1982.[7] The city promised to renovate the building, but construction halted after builders took off the roof. The job was never finished. When Miguel Piñero died from AIDS complications on June 16, 1988, Miguel Algarín gathered artists to honor him by "spreading [his] ashes thru the Lower East Side," as Piñero had requested. Soon after, Bob Holman—who had coordinated Poetry Project readings from 1977 to 1984 and watched Marc Smith's poetry slams at Chicago's Green Mill—approached Algarín to reopen the café to host its own poetry slam. The café reopened a year later, in August 1989. This opening marked the second wave of the café, igniting the spoken word and slam poetry scene in New York City.[8]

While spoken word and poetry slam are intimately connected, they are two distinct artistic forms.[9] Spoken word is the performance of poetry and is very much in line with the Nuyorican embodied aesthetic of taking poetry off the page and bringing it to the masses. Slam poetry, on the other hand, is the competitive art of performing poetry. Unlike spoken word, slam poetry involves a contest, in which judges score the poets and their poems. While the practice of scoring was never a part of the Nuyorican aesthetic, Algarín's philosophy that a poet's skill should be determined by his ability to captivate unintended audiences worked hand in hand with the idea that slam poets had to compete for the attention of audience members, who also acted as judges. This practice is antithetical to the *plática* style of the founding mothers of the Nuyorican Poets Café, discussed in the last chapter. The elements of theatricality, spectacle, and competition in slam considerably differ from the conversational intimacy established in the poetry of Sandra María Esteves, Luz Rodriguez, Amina Muñoz, and Martita Morales.

According to the system that Smith and Holman established, the master of ceremonies of a slam would—with a keen eye toward diversity—choose three to five judges from the audience. To avoid any appearance of discrimination, these judges had to be from different races, genders, and ages. The judges scored each performance on a 0–10 scale. The highest and lowest scores were dropped from the five scores, giving each performance a rating between zero and thirty points. Like Algarín, who in the early 1970s envisioned poetry as performance, Holman set up slams as "theatrical events [and] not [as] listening booths. . . . With this is mind, it becomes clear that the popular appeal of slam poetry relie[d] on, and indeed create[d], not just an oral culture but a performative culture."[10]

As the original slam master of the Nuyorican Poets Café and the person who launched it to success on its reopening, Holman became the face of an artistic hub that had been first envisioned for Nuyorican artists. Cristin O'Keefe Aptowicz recalls that most people were under the impression that Holman, "a white, half-Jewish guy from Kentucky," was the sole founder of the Nuyorican Poets Café.[11] The slam movement began to redefine the venue, not by what it culturally stood for or represented, but by the national and international attention that it garnered and the people that it drew from all walks of life.[12] Unlike the café's first anthology, *Nuyorican Poetry* (1975, edited by Algarín and Piñero), its second anthology, *Aloud: Voices from the Nuyorican Poets Café* (1994, edited by Algarín and Holman), included poets of different nationalities, races, ages, and social backgrounds. The advent of slam poetry and spoken word performances at the café expanded the term Nuyorican from a label of identification to one of aesthetic.

While spoken word and slam poetry events attempted to create democratic and inclusive creative spaces, the café—in its early years of this second stage in its history—was still a primarily heteronormative, male-centered venue, and thus women and queer bodies were virtually absent.[13] Javon Johnson's *Killing Poetry* (2017), an ethnographic study of spoken word and poetry slam venues in Los Angles, demystifies the notion that spoken word and slam are inherently democratic and utopian art forms and instead reveals how the prevailing strains of sexism and heterosexism augment male and masculinist power. As Marc Smith, the founder of the poetry slam movement, remarked, the slam has "become a man thing."[14] This fact, however, did not prevent women and queer folks from winning slam championships and taking on the role of slam master at the Nuyorican Poets Café. Mahogany L. Browne, Karen Jaime, and Sarah Jones, among others, offered role models, mentorship, and opportunities. The café's rich, creative atmosphere inspired Caridad de la Luz to take the mic for the first time on April 3, 1996, to debut her artistic persona, La Bruja, and it also influenced Mariposa, Nilaja Sun, and Aya de León.[15] The presence of women, however, does not mean that the café or the poetry slams eschewed masculinist practices. What spoken word and slam artists must continue to do, as Johnson proposes, is keep working toward transforming venues into welcoming and safe spaces for women, queer, and gender-nonconforming communities.[16]

POPULARIZATION OF SPOKEN WORD AND SLAM POETRY

Hip hop's oral practices and traditions—from emceeing to rap battles—make it well suited to converge with the spoken word and slam poetry movements. As a proponent for the inclusion of hip hop, Holman advocates that "RAP IS POETRY—and its spoken essence is central to the popularization of poetry. Rap is taking its place, aloud, as a new poetic form, with ancient griot roots."[17] It was thus unsurprising that the hip hop mogul Russell Simmons popularized spoken word and slam poetry with the HBO series *Def Poetry Jam*, which ran for five years (2002–7) and featured La Bruja and Aya de León, among other poets. As a powerful gatekeeper in the entertainment and media industry, Simmons opened doors for many artists of color, but he also ruined the careers of many women with his pattern of sexual assault and harassment, making it difficult for women to navigate the hip hop music and entertainment industry.[18]

Simmons had already capitalized on the ingenuity of hip hop by starting his own record and clothing companies. Working with partner Rick Rubin, he founded Def Jam Records in 1984. Under Simmons and Rubin's management, this label promoted some of the major hip hop figures in the music industry, such as Kurtis Blow, the Beastie Boys, LL Cool J, Public Enemy, and Run-DMC. Simmons further expanded his hip hop empire by launching Phat Farm—a clothing company—in 1992. Phat Farm later begat Baby Phat and Run Athletics. These establishments produced what we now call hip hop fashion. He also took his vision to TV a decade before *Def Poetry Jam* aired, producing the HBO series *Def Comedy Jam* in 1992–97. The show brought Black comedians—including Bernie Mac, Chris Rock, and Martin Lawrence—to mainstream America.

With Simmons's "hip-hopification" of American media coming along, he cultivated a loyal audience that followed him when he and Stan Lathan harnessed the momentum of the slam poetry and hip hop scene in New York City. These two men created and produced *Def Poetry Jam on Broadway*, for which La Bruja auditioned.[19] The *Def Poetry Jam on Broadway* ensemble showcased a diverse group of nine wordsmiths and thespians, including African Americans, Puerto Ricans, a Jamaican, an Asian American, and an Anglo-Saxon poet. As a director, Lathan made sure that his cast "reflect[ed] a cross-section of young artists who were influenced by hip hop."[20] Additionally, most poets in *Def Poetry Jam on Broadway* had performed at the Nuyorican Poets Café, competing in the Nuyorican Grand Slam (Mayda del Valle, Staceyann Chin, and Tamika Harper [Georgia Me]), participating in the Nuyorican Poets Café Slam Team (Steve Coleman), or using the café as a space to share their poetry (Beau Sia and Lemon).

The atmosphere inside Broadway's Longacre Theatre in November 2002 was all its own, neither normal Broadway fare nor standard slam poetry scene. The slam poets were not in their intimate coffeehouse venue. The DJ—who was surrounded by crates—was far removed from the club or urban setting. He created a lively cannot-stop-your-body-from-moving-to-the-music vibe, mixing old-school funk and hip hop tunes on his turntable. Still, the majestic chandeliers seemed incongruous, hanging above the mostly young people of color. The theater was buzzing with teenagers, young adults, and young professionals of color, as opposed to out-of-town tourists or mostly white theatergoers. Hip hop sound, style, and energy already influenced music, fashion, and language; now the hip hop sensibility had found a new artistic venue, the theater. Slam poetry graced the Broadway stage, even after Harold Bloom denigrated the poetic genre as "the death of art."[21] These artistic modalities may seem displaced—or perhaps misplaced—given that the Great White Way did not recognize slam or hip hop as legitimate art forms. Yet, *Def Poetry Jam on Broadway* proved to be quite legitimate, especially after winning the 2003 Tony Award for Best Special Theatrical Event.[22]

The success of *Def Poetry Jam on Broadway* garnered hip hop theater audiences, differed from the traditional theatergoer, cutting across the divides of gender, race, class, and generation. Lathan threaded the cast's poetry together by themes, including identity, culture, and nation. Every word uttered was full of fervor and urgency. These performers made their experiences, ideas, and desires matter during a time when America was still dealing with the aftermath of September 11. During the finale, the cast collectively performed the poem "I Write America," in which they reflected on what the country means to them. Perspectives spanned from the critical to the hopeful—first heard singularly and then collectively—as they gradually began to talk over one another in a group creation.

As Jill Dolan argues, *Def Poetry Jam on Broadway* models "how radical democracy might feel, in a celebration of agency that values each individual voice in this panoply of identities and imagines them harmonizing."[23] This performance pushes a rhetoric of belonging in America by "engag[ing] the constitution of our country to stretch it wider, to let the umbrella of true citizenship cover more of its people."[24] With the sexual assault and harassment allegations that arose during the #MeToo Movement fifteen years after the show premiered, this staged democratic utopia reveals the gender discrimination that women face as they participate in predominately masculinist spaces.

THE EMERGENCE OF HIP HOP THEATER

Def Poetry Jam on Broadway arrived just as the New York Hip-Hop Theater Festival (HHTF, now known as Hi-ARTS) was preparing for its second annual presentation. That is, the hip hop theater scene had already taken root when *Def Jam* arrived on Broadway. Journalist Holly Bass was the first to coin the term *hip hop theater*, doing so in her 1999 essay "Blowing Up the Set." Bass acknowledges the dynamic array of poets, musicians, and thespians at the

1999 National Black Theatre Festival who were pushing the boundaries of theater by implementing a hip hop aesthetic. In summer 2000, Danny Hoch, Kamilah Forbes, and Clyde Valentin founded HHTF, a leading urban arts organization. The festival showcases solo and ensemble performances, including dance, performed poetry, plays, and live music. Nilaja Sun's *Black and Blue* was presented at the first HHTF, while La Bruja's *Boogie Rican Boulevard* and Aya de León's *Thieves in the Temple* were featured in the second. The festival also includes workshops that explore hip hop forms, and panels that focus on hip hop's history, evolution, and future. HHTF has inspired similar festivals in Washington, DC; Baton Rouge, Louisiana; San Francisco and Riverside, California.

Interestingly, the content, form, and style of hip hop theater echoed the aesthetic of the 1970s Nuyorican Poets Café. From making the self vulnerable as a form of communal healing to using poetry as a type of political protest, these artists used their words to carve themselves into the fabric of American history. They were also thinking about their words as an extension of the living body—so much so that most of them began creating solo works. Staceyann Chin, for instance, performed her one-woman shows *Unspeakable Things* (2000), *Hands Afire* (2001), and *Border/Clash* (2005); Mayda del Valle created *The Insecurities of an Eagle* (2002) and *Salida* (2010); Suheir Hammad performed *Blood Trinity* (2002), *ReOrientalism* (2003), and *breaking letter(s)* (2008); and Lemon Andersen performed *County of Kings: The Beautiful Struggle* (2009). These artists pushed their poetic style into the theater scene with one-person shows that reproduced a Nuyorican aesthetic of belonging.

The integration of hip hop into the theater world was not a new phenomenon. Hip hop dancers and theater companies were incorporating dramatic narratives into their pieces and expanding the conventions of hip hop and dance before the term *hip hop theater* was even coined. For instance, the Rhythm Technicians—whose members included individuals from the b-boy (break dancing) group Rock Steady Crew—created the hip hop musical *So! What Happens Now?* (1991), which was presented at Performance Space 122 (PS 122).[25] Shortly after, GhettOriginal Productions brought together Rock Steady Crew, Magnificent Force, and Rhythm Technicians to create *Jam on the Groove* (1995), presented off-Broadway at the Minetta Lane Theater.

Regional theaters also produced hip hop plays. New York's Playwrights Horizons staged Marion McClinton's *Police Boys* (1995). Reg. E. Gaines's *Bring in 'da Noise, Bring in 'da Funk* was staged at the Public Theater that same year, and in 1996 it became the first hip hop musical to make it to Broadway. New

Haven's Long Wharf Theatre and Minneapolis's Penumbra Theatre presented Michael Henry Brown's *Generations of the Dead in the Abyss of Coney Island Madness* (1996). Trinity Repertory Company of Rhode Island produced Robert Alexander's gangsta rap play *A Preface to the Alien Garden* (1998). And African Continuum Theater Company of Washington, DC, staged Kamilah Forbes and Hip Hop Theatre Junction's *Rhyme Referred* (1998), which was part of the first Hip-Hop Theater Festival in 2000.

The now defunct New WORLD Theater, founded and directed by Roberta Uno, was a theater company at the University of Massachusetts at Amherst dedicated to the works of people of color.[26] New WORLD Theater was one of the primary organizations to produce works infused with a hip hop aesthetic, including from such artists as Nilaja Sun and Mariposa. In comparison with other regional theaters, New WORLD Theater championed more inclusive seasons and programming. Founded in 1979, this company produced works that pushed against the reductive notion of multiculturalism with the goal of democratizing the arts.[27] Additionally, New WORLD Theater held a biannual Intersections Conference between 1998 and 2008, with the goal of creating networking opportunities for artists and educators and engaging with the cutting-edge aesthetics and staging of hip hop theater.[28]

Among the many conference presenters were several hip hop practitioners. New WORLD Theater offered some participants week-long residencies to get their theatrical pieces ready for production, including, among others: Danny Hoch, *Jails, Hospitals, and Hip Hop* (1999); UNIVERSES, *Slanguage* (2001, 2002) and *Eyewitness* (2003); Mariposa, *DiaspoRican Dementia* (2001); Rha Goddess, *Rha Goodness* (2001); La Bruja and Staceyann Chin, spoken word performances (2001); Nilaja Sun, *Mezclacitas/Mixtures: An Evening of 3 Solo Works* (2002); Rubí Theater Company's *Imagine the Angels of Bread* (2002); Suheir Hammad's *ReOrientalism* (2003); Marc Bamuthi, *Word Becomes Flesh* (2003); and Rickerby Hinds, *Dreamscape* (2006). I mention these plays to acknowledge that before the term *hip hop theater* was created, New WOLRD Theater under the leadership of Uno was pioneering this theatrical art form.

Just as hip hop culture constantly evolves—using new songs, new beats, new stars, and new fashion styles, hip hop theater is also shaped by the period's social and cultural conditions. By the late twentieth century, hip hop solo performance came into being. Danny Hoch wrote and performed *Some People* (1994), *Jails, Hospitals, and Hip Hop* (1998), and *Taking Over* (2008). Hip hop dancer Jonzi D successfully combined break dancing, a cappella rap, and theatrical conventions in *Lyrikal Fearta* (1995). Sarah Jones came onto the hip hop performance scene as a poet, winning the grand slam championship at the Nuyorican Poets Café in 1997, with "Your Revolution," a reworking of Gil Scott Heron's 1975 proto-rap song "The Revolution Will Not Be Televised."

"Your Revolution" and Jones's other poems evolved into monologues, eventually becoming the eight characters in her solo performance piece *Surface Transit: More Sketches of Ordinary People* (1995). Actor, rapper, playwright, spoken word artist, and vocalist Will Power fused jazz with rap and Latin rhythms and hip hop beats. In his solo work *The Gathering* (2001), he deals with the struggles of Black men in America, focusing on the places where these men gather, including the barbershop, the jazz club, the basketball court, and the street corner. The above-mentioned practitioners have all played major roles in defining hip hop theater.

WHAT IS HIP HOP THEATER?

Between 1999 and 2006, *American Theatre* magazine printed a series of articles in which practitioners ruminated about the term *hip hop theater*.[29] Several schools of thought directed conversations around this term. Performer and writer Will Power defines hip hop theater as theater that uses at least one of the four cornerstones of hip hop culture—break dancing, emceeing, deejaying, and graffiti art—to tell a story. Writer and performer Psalmayene 24's idea of hip hop theater is not just about bringing one of the four elements of hip hop into theater, but also about infusing hip hop culture with important theatrical elements, like lighting, set, sound design, playwriting, directing, and acting.[30] Psalmayene 24 envisions a symbiotic relationship between hip hop culture and theater. Finally, according to Danny Hoch, hip hop is the type of "theatre that is by, for and about the hip-hop generation, which spans roughly ages 12 through 36."[31] The age range is important to Hoch, since hip hop theater is transforming the face of the American theater community. Hoch's insight points toward hip hop's fluidity and appeal across many generations.

While some have embraced hip hop theater, others have remained ambivalent. As Jeff Chang asks, "are there limitations that are being put on artists, especially artists of color because they have to get into a 'hip-hop box?'"[32] Playwright Jorge Ignacio Cortiñas agrees, saying that "the [hip hop theater] genre always brings us back to a reactive, North American–centric, black-white bifurcation that is ill-suited to deal with the complexity of our transnational, multilingual 21st century."[33] He wants artists to avoid pigeonholing themselves into a single style, simply because it is trendy. Similarly, Mildred Ruiz, cofounder of UNIVERSES, remarks, "We come from hip-hop and poetry and our cultures, but what we do is theatre."[34] Artists have expressed concern that producers and presenters will only scout out artists using the four elements of hip hop, thereby narrowing notions of what hip hop theater could be. As Roberta Uno observes, "our theatres, however, appear at a loss as to how to consider, contextualize and support this work [hip hop theater]."[35] She describes hip hop theater as the future aesthetic, because it demands a new style of theater making, one that changes the demographics of theater artists and audiences. Uno instantiates hip hop theater as a rigorous discipline that the broader American theater fails to acknowledge. She thinks that the theater community lacks an understanding of hip hop' context—its people, history, tools, and methodology. It is with this rich intersecting history of hip hop, spoken word, and slam poetry and its masculinist practices that we need to read contemporary performeras La Bruja, Nilaja Sun, Mariposa, and Aya de León with a hip hop feminist lens.

CHAPTER 5

"It Was Definitely a Family Affair"

La Bruja's *Boogie Rican Boulevard*

USING A FEMINIST Nuyorican poetry aesthetic, Esteves paved the way for contemporary Nuyorican performeras like La Bruja, whose work widens our understanding of Nuyorican aesthetics by interweaving rap and beatboxing with other hip hop elements. I never set foot into the Nuyorican Poets Café until summer 1998, nor did I know about La Bruja (the Witch). If it were not for Dartmouth College professors—who taught me about the café in Hanover, New Hampshire—I would have never experienced this place or La Bruja's work. On that summer day, she debuted *Boogie Rican Boulevard* at the café. Three years later, I attended her off-Broadway production of *Boogie Rican Boulevard* (2001) at the Producers Club and LATEA (Latin American Theater Experiment & Associates). She then participated in the third Hip-Hop Theater Festival (2002), presenting excerpts of this solo work. After the successful run of *Boogie Rican Boulevard*, La Bruja decided to convert the show into a multiactor musical, which ran for one month in 2009 at the Puerto Rican Traveling Theater in Midtown Manhattan. Additionally, between her first and last productions of *Boogie Rican Boulevard*, La Bruja made several albums, including *The Bru* (2001), *Brujalicious* (2005), and *For Witch It Stands* (2010). She also collaborated with children's folk singer Dan Zanes on the CD *Nueva York!* (2008), for which she created a hip hop version of the Spanish-English nursery rhyme "Pollito Chicken." She gained so much popularity within the Latinx and hip hop community that not only did the café sponsor her show but so did corporations such as Red Bull, Urban Latino Media, Café Bustelo, and Hot 97. La Bruja, however, maintains her grassroots activism, while also carefully navigating the corporate world.

La Bruja's theatrical and musical performances incited my curiosity as I

Figure 12. Program from *Boogie Rican Boulevard* (2002) a solo performance written and performed by Caridad de la Luz and sponsored by Urban Latino, Café Bustelo, and Nuyorican Poets Café.

began to notice the connective tissues between Sandra María Esteves and La Bruja. I was especially excited that La Bruja was on the same album as Rubí Theater Company, which I cofounded. I was particularly intrigued by a televised discussion between Dan Zanes and La Bruja promoting *Nueva York!* and *Boogie Rican Boulevard*, as part of the program *Caught in the Act*, sponsored by the Brooklyn Independent Network.[1] Zanes began by giving *Boogie Rican Boulevard* accolades and admiring La Bruja's daughter, who joined her onstage. La Bruja responded with, "it was a family affair. It was definitely a family affair." Her comment propelled me to think about how she deploys ideas of *la familia* to ground her work. While La Bruja's inclusion of her daughter in *Boogie Rican Boulevard* made the production a family affair, the ways that she uses theater and performance to instill cultural traditions passed on to her by her family are what I find particularly instructive. This familial feel resonated with me, just as it had when I walked into the café for the first time.

Building on the call for collectivity in Nuyorican poetry aesthetics, as practiced by Esteves, La Bruja utilizes Nuyorican and hip hop aesthetics to demystify conventional notions of a nuclear family and underscore the importance of alternative familial arrangements, patterns, and networks. Her performance of *Boogie Rican Boulevard* at the Nuyorican Poets Café revealed the ways that her idea of family extends beyond biological kinship structures to include informal support networks across multiple households, including her artistic home. In *Boogie Rican Boulevard*, La Bruja draws from her family's memories and the quotidian experiences of Puerto Ricans and other Latinxs in the Boogie Down Bronx, the place where she was born and still resides. Ultimately, she functions as a cartographer, using linguistic blending as well as various performance techniques, and visual strategies to create a new map of the Americas. This map conceptualizes a space for Puerto Rican culture in the Bronx, creating a cultural sense of *familia*.

La Bruja conceptualizes family life within wider systems of economic and political structures.[2] Her characters embody both familial and familiar archetypal figures. There is Don José, a middle-aged father and former *basebol* player, who teaches his boy how to catch and that "ketchup and rice don't go together."[3] Then, there is the wannabe hip hop star Pito, who attempts to rap with chicks, but nobody notices. There is also the very pregnant teenager Cuca, who was abandoned by the father of her child. La Bruja complements these characters with her poetic words, Afro-Caribbean music, and hip hop influences, while also using photographic images of her father, homeless people, prostitutes, abandoned buildings, and neglected areas in the Bronx. In performing her story—alongside the stories of her neighbors—she treats the people and places in her community as part of her extended familial networks. Some people might be biological or chosen family, and some places might be native, foreign, or both.

Paying close attention to *Boogie Rican Boulevard*—and the rap songs "Nuyorico" (2005), "Pollito Chicken" (2008), and "For Witch It Stands" (2010)—this chapter argues that La Bruja deploys Nuyorican and hip hop aesthetics and performs a women-centric genealogy of alternative familial networks. Through this genealogy, she claims kinship ties not only to Puerto Rico but also to the greater Puerto Rican family, both on the mainland and beyond.[4] Just as the 1970s Nuyorican poets engaged with their local experiences and Afrodiasporic roots, La Bruja utilizes a variety of expressions from Puerto Ricans, Nuyoricans, and Boogie Ricans (New Yorkers from the Bronx). Infusing her work with raps, songs, and chants to distinguish her unique cultural and political reality, she experiments with different hip hop modalities while maintaining her Nuyorican aesthetic. After all, she is a part of a generation of artists influenced by both Nuyorican and hip hop aesthetics. Significantly, *La Bruja* creates different geographies of home, pushing the boundaries of Puerto Rico into the Bronx and those of the Bronx into Puerto Rico.

THE TRADITION OF *FAMILIA* IN THE CAFÉ

Influenced by the public culture of the 1960s and 1970s, the Nuyorican Poets Café functioned as an extended family, providing economic support, protection, and caretaking. La Bruja—perhaps more than any other performer affiliated with the café—has both highlighted and widened the café's definition of family and the political valences of this approach. Recall Miguel Algarín and Miguel Piñero's collective theater-making project with the Young Family, a group of outcast youth. Even the group's name redefined the traditional family, comprising blood relations. The group created kinship based on its youths' shared social experiences—such as homelessness, addiction, and prostitution—as performed in the plays *Sideshow* (1975) and *América Conga Mania* (1975). These ideas of *familia* stand in contrast with those of 1950s and 1960s television sitcoms such as *Leave It to Beaver* and *The Adventures of Ozzie and Harriet*. These shows popularized the idea of a typical American nuclear family—a white, middle-class, and heterosexual household, composed of a father, mother, and one or more children. Of course, many compositions of the nuclear family existed then—as they do now—but this typical family image often prevails.[5]

While the Young Family no longer exists, the café remains inclusive and continues to generate a sense of family. The physical architecture of the café creates an intimate atmosphere, which I experienced when entering the space for the first time in 1998 to watch *Boogie Rican Boulevard*. This intimate, vibrant, and brick-walled performance space holds up to 120 people. When I was there, candles flickered alongside the bar. About a dozen small, round tables made up the seating area—as opposed to the formal rows of seats arranged for viewing performances. For the audience, the proximity to the performance platform broke the theatrical illusion of the fourth wall. The café encouraged a cozy, home-like feel. Several audience members hugged when greeting one another. Hip hop beats played in the background. The small performance platform resembled someone's bedroom—with congas, a baseball cap, a jersey, a hoodie, a flannel shirt, and a balloon. Together, these subtle signifiers produced an upbeat, warm, and welcoming environment.

BOOGIE RICAN: WHERE THE BOOGIE DOWN AND PUERTO RICO MEET

While it is nearly impossible to replicate in writing the spatial intimacy of the café, La Bruja's opening might come close to conveying the warm relationship between the performer and the audience. A spotlight shone on La Bruja, as she grabbed the microphone and asked the audience in a conversational tone:

> Are you here to Boogie or what?
> [The audience cheered and clapped]
> Are you ready to see where the tropical paradise meets the city?
> And sandy beaches cover the concrete?
> Open your hearts
> And try not to miss a beat
> And enjoy where the Boogie Down and Puerto Rico meets
> Welcome to my world of Boogie Rican.[6]

Reminiscent of the way that café founders Algarín and Piñero created the neologism Nuyorican, La Bruja blended the words Boogie Down Bronx and Puerto Rican to produce the portmanteau Boogie Rican.

Whereas Nuyorican gained popularity in the 1970s, the nickname Boogie Down—created by South Bronx locals—did not catch on until the 1980s. The term Boogie Down hit critical mass in 1985, with the music industry's promotion of the group Boogie Down Productions. La Bruja preoccupies herself with locating the spaces and places that people inhabit—an idea that has always been central to the Nuyorican Poets Café. La Bruja's work brings attention to how Nuyoricans *imagine* and *occupy* spaces and places, rather than just *being* in a space or place. In keeping with the performance traditions of the café, La Bruja invents a new place, Boogie Rican Boulevard, to reflect her two localities, Puerto Rico and the South Bronx.

Also, like Esteves and other 1970s performeras, La Bruja incorporates a feminist aesthetic in her works. Her performances use a conversational style and encourage audience members to imagine a place for them to feel at home in the Bronx and Puerto Rico. La Bruja's warm invitation to enter Boogie Rican Boulevard situates the audience in a specific location. Despite the street's nonexistence, the street name demonstrates that Puerto Rican culture is interwoven into the fabric of the Bronx. The gestures of welcoming the audience and inviting its members to enter Boogie Rican Boulevard deepened the intimate vibe that I sensed when I first entered the café.

When La Bruja invites the audience to walk along Boogie Rican Boulevard, the audience responds with claps and hollers of "yeah, that's right girl." Just as the café renders a sense of closeness, Boogie Rican Boulevard establishes a sense of home. Taking great pride in her origins, La Bruja uses the term Boogie Rican Boulevard to underscore that her parents moved from Puerto Rico. She was born and raised and still lives in the South Bronx. La Bruja uses autobiographical moments to shape her work. She reenacts her birth story, which includes her parents meeting at a club, falling in love, and exchanging humorous comments on the day that she was born.

The reenactment of her birth story caused my naïve autobiographical realism to take over.[7] That is, I held her autobiographical work at face value, essentializing La Bruja at the center of the performance.[8] As Ellen McCracken contends, when the writer—and in this case, performer—shares firsthand accounts, "readers often forget the fictionality of the autobiographic mode, temporarily believing that they are experiencing life as it was at the time of the narrated events."[9] Leigh Gilmore coins the term *autobiographics*—instead of autobiography—to emphasize how these multiple identities can mix truth and lies.[10]

By applying Gilmore's notion of autobiographics to La Bruja, we can position her as an autobiographer performing both real and invented histories. This approach calls attention to the self and the community. She delineates her commitments to both self and community by admitting, "It does not bother me that my show is called an autobiography because I am sharing the stories of other women who do not have a chance to voice their ideas. My work is personal and in that respect, it could be looked at as autobiographical."[11] In an interview in *Urban Latino*, she explains: "I am an artist—a performance artist. I love that form of expression, and the freedom of creating another world within a world. It is just a reflection, even though it is so personal."[12] La Bruja's comment offers audience members a way to understand that her performance engages with notions of family that are both real and fictional.

Following her invitation, La Bruja situates the audience in the social fabric of Boogie Rican Boulevard, projecting slides of her father in Puerto Rico and El Morro (the historic fortress in San Juan) and juxtaposing these images with pictures of daily activities in the Bronx. She includes images of children riding their bikes and urban entrepreneurs traveling with their pushcarts, selling *piraguas* (a pyramid-shaped, flavored-ice treat) to make ends meet. La Bruja also shows a photo of the squatters camping on the streets. Below the squatters' transient homes, an ad reads, "Great job, Rudy [Giuliani]." Despite the urban rehabilitation programs introduced by the former mayor of New York, the South Bronx continues to be among the most impoverished places in America. La Bruja emphasizes the community's creativity—despite great deprivation—and she quips, "to know the spirit of the Bronx is to know the unique ways people from the Bronx express themselves." As she speaks, La Bruja projects photos of residents beautifying the South Bronx. She includes the work of graffiti artists on abandoned buildings and the adornment of trees with household items like sneakers, clothes, and toys.[13]

Together, the slides bring the long history of Puerto Rican migration to the Bronx into the present consciousness. La Bruja's work reconfigures the social imaginary of Puerto Ricans and Nuyoricans, situates her own identity, and emphasizes how Puerto Rican culture is interwoven into the cultural fabric of the South Bronx. Ultimately, La Bruja brings this fictional place into existence, producing a sense of home and *familia*. In so doing, she creates what Juan Flores refers to as "a new map of the Americas." "The Latin[x] imaginary," as Flores explains, "focuses on the lived experiences, social struggles, and historical memory of Latin[x]s, rather than just demographic analyses."[14] While the recent neologism of Latinx comes after Flores's time, I invoke it here to stress the inclusion of gender-nonconforming, genderqueer and genderfluid identities in this imaginary. Drawing from Latinx communities across ethnic, generational, and other lines, this imaginary acknowledges the shared experiences of "ongoing oppression and discrimination, racism and exploitation, closed doors and patrolled borders."[15]

A PLACE CALLED NUYORICO

La Bruja's rap song "Nuyorico" on her album *Brujalicious* (2005) deepens the intersecting Afrodiasporic practices of Nuyorican and hip hop aesthetics, as well as the cartographies of Puerto Rico and the Bronx.[16] As Lawrence La Fountain-Stokes notes, Nuyorico is a utopian concept "that riffs off the tradition of Nuyorican cultural resistance that has been a hallmark of diasporic Puerto Rican life since the late 1960s but also points toward more recent cultural developments."[17] The English translation of Puerto Rico means "a port full of riches," and La Bruja's rap lyrics reflects the cultural riches of Puerto Rico. She also describes the homeland of Nuyoricans as a place where everyone is welcomed, regardless of race or ethnicity.[18] She passionately greets listeners: "*Bienvenidos todo el mundo*. Welcome everybody to the most beautiful place in the world, Nuyorico." Infused by hip hop beats, salsa rhythms, the café's aesthetic, and invocations to El Reverendo Pedro Pietri, La Bruja's rap actualizes this place called Nuyorico.

La Bruja models how to share information about Nuyorico by concluding her rap with a conversation with her friends about this newfound place. La Bruja uses the in-your-face poetic style of open mic nights and poetry slams and communicates the urgency of inventing a street called Boogie Rican Boulevard that exists only in Nuyorico so that she can firmly root her identity in a place where the Empire State Building and El Morro coexist, and where "todos somos amigos" (we are all friends). In fact, Boogie Rican Boulevard in Nuyorico becomes her official homeland, similar to how Nuyorican artists Pedro Pietri, Eddie Figueroa, and Adál Maldonado created a sovereign state of mind through *El Puerto Rican Embassy Project* (1994).

Since passports symbolize a government's verification of identity and citizenship, Pietri, Figueroa, and Maldonado created a Puerto Rican passport for *El Puerto Rican Embassy*. They treated Puerto Rico as a sovereign state, especially for those who choose to call it home. Pietri's "El Spanglish National Anthem" was part of this project. By creating a national anthem, E. Machado Sáez Dalleo and Elena Machado Sáez remind us, "Pietri supposes a nation, a group of like-minded people who imagine themselves belonging."[19] As such, Nuyorico is—as La Fountain-Stokes demonstrates—an *embodied mindscape*, easily adjusting to change.[20] La Bruja's work uses this practice of belonging in Nuyorico. Just as passports legitimize one's citizenship status, La Bruja legitimizes Boogie Rican Boulevard—or Nuyorico—by placing herself in a space ensconced by both Puerto Rico and the Boogie Down Bronx.

Nuyorican artists of the 1970s often wrote about a dual sense of home, since they frequently moved between Puerto Rico and New York. Esteves—whose poetry book titles include *Yerba Buena* and *Tropical Rain*—has strong ties to Puerto Rico, and she understands her identity as located between here and there. As she explains in her poem "Here," "I am two parts / a person." La Bruja, however, adds a dimension of intersectionality to migration. Rather than living in between, being "two parts / a person," or standing with one leg here and another there, La Bruja anchors herself where the contours of Puerto Rico and the Bronx intersect. Boogie Rican Boulevard "ain't New York and it ain't Puerto Rico"; it has its own location, with its own coordinates.[21] This is where her body, mind, and soul reside.

La Bruja understands that the migration process includes the blending of the geographic boundaries of Puerto Rico and New York. Migration thus not only manifests in bodies moving from one place to another but also includes the cartographies of Puerto Rico and the Bronx moving onto each other. In an advertisement for the musical version of La Bruja's work, she makes this place come to life by creating a classic, green-and-white New York City street sign (figure 13). In using a street sign labeled "Boogie Rican Blvd," La Bruja spatially occupies her diasporic identity—both dispersed and intertwined within two homelands—weaving the history of Puerto Rican life into the Bronx and, by extension, into the fabric of American history.

THE PRESENCE AND ABSENCE OF A FATHER

Boogie Rican Boulevard focuses on the character of Don José, the patriarch of the household, whom La Bruja juxtaposes with Pito, the absent father figure. In direct view of the audience, La Bruja changes into Don José's costume, dressing him in a Pirates jersey and a *basebol* cap, with a pocket for a portable radio. With his Boricua English accent, Don José shares his migration story. *Basebol* was his entry to New York City—the launching ground for his professional *basebol* career, but also the nesting ground for future generations. He recalls:

> *Basebol* brought me here to New Jork City. Wheng I was your age, ju could not estop me from playing *basebol*. I could hit a ball over thee mountain. I played for my hometown of Yabucoa, Puerto Rico. We was called *los azucareros*. The sugar *papis*, check it out. *(Does hand gestures.)* You'll never know what that means!!! We were so good, they sent us here to play.[22]

Don José, who played for *los azucareros* (which he humorously translates as the "sugar *papis*") now teaches his grandson to play *basebol*. His humped back and half-bent knees suggest how time—both playing professional *basebol* and owning a bodega—has taken its toll on his body. For each pitch that Don José throws, he shares an important lesson or memory with his grandson. Playing *basebol* was a labor of love, especially since practice left him full of strawberry-sized mosquito bites. All that work paid off, however, when his manager flew *los azucareros* to New York City to play *basebol*. Don José believed that his lifelong dream of playing with Roberto Clemente would come true, but that did not happen. Instead, he stayed in New York City and started a family. Luckily, his "friend's father's cousin's uncle's brother" owned a store by Yankee Stadium, and Don José worked and lodged there. He met his wife in that bodega, and after many years, he now owns it.

When La Bruja embodies Don José's playing *basebol* with his grandson, she shows how Nuyoricans changed the cartography of New York City. Drawing on his cultural roots, Don José reconstitutes what home means to him. He inscribes Puerto Rico onto the landscape of the South Bronx through familial networks, two generations of which now reside in New York City. Toward the end of this scene, Don José remembers Latinx *basebol* icon Sammy Sosa, and he asks his grandson to reenact one of Sammy's home runs. When Don José pitches the ball, the audience hears a crowd cheering, signifying that his grandson has successfully hit a home run.

In directing his grandson to hit Sammy's home run, Don José situates embodiment as central to the transmission of knowledge. He uses this physical act of playing Sammy to encourage his grandson to remember the long history of Caribbean *basebol* players, and to communicate to his grandson that he, too, can be successful. Since La Bruja delivers José's *basebol* lessons directly to the audience—and since the grandson never appears—she invites the audience to adopt the grandson's role and to imagine themselves hitting

Sammy's home run. Thus, La Bruja attempts to actualize Don José's unattained dreams of being a baseball player.

The potency of La Bruja's work lies in the interplay between the constructed circumstances on the stage and the actual circumstances of life. La Bruja transforms in front of the audience; for example, she shoves a balloon into her oversized sweater, suggesting that she is pregnant. Because this costume change is not offstage, it breaks the illusion of the play. This fact centralizes La Bruja's point that, although she performs (fictional) characters, they are real to some members of her community. In performing Cuca, a teen poet who has become pregnant by Pito, La Bruja gestures to the related crises of teenage pregnancy and absent fathers. Although the pregnancy rates of Black and Latina teens have dropped, they are still twice as high as those of white teens.[23] In placing the issue of teenage pregnancy alongside issues of migration, masculinity, and femininity, La Bruja communicates that teen pregnancy is not an isolated issue. Pregnancy rates are related to the social circumstances of poverty and school dropout numbers, both in the Bronx and nationwide.

Many poems in the 1975 *Nuyorican Poetry* anthology and other US Puerto Rican literature point to the virtual absence of a father figure. They address how social and economic circumstances—such as war, drugs, poverty, and migration—have created a severe strain on families. As Marisel C. Moreno explains, the number of US Puerto Ricans reporting absent father figures suggests, "that the fatherless model is more reflective of prevailing family structures in the diaspora."[24] Consequently, we see more representations of Puerto Rican women heads of households. This context illuminates La Bruja's attempts to create extended familial networks.

During La Bruja's performance, the audience learns that the baby's father does not want to be a part of Cuca's and the baby's lives. The young woman's family does not support her decision to have a baby when she is not married, and they also abandon her. Her mother wants to keep her out of the public eye, so that no one will know that she is pregnant. Her brother insists that she should have an abortion. Against all odds, Cuca decides to have the child, even without the support of the father, her family, and her friends. She is determined to "find a way to deal, find a way to put up." Becoming a mother is one of the most significant decisions of a woman's life. In this case, Cuca's familial networks turn against her, leaving her to survive on her own. Her rap reveals a complex mix of emotions, including love, anger, and hope. While Cuca loves Pito, she realizes that she needs to cut him loose because her child's life is more important than his. However, she complicates this decision by considering the need for positive male role models.

La Bruja emphasizes the support that Cuca will need to raise her child by projecting a slide of her own husband, carrying their newborn child and singing, "es un pedazo de mi, un diamante" (he is a part of me, a diamond). After this moment, the mode of delivery changes. La Bruja—as Cuca—raps about the struggles of this teenager who has decided to keep her child. Her tough, staccato delivery conveys that she firmly believes that she should keep her baby. Her tough mannerism quickly changes, however, when she realizes the gravity of raising a child without no familial networks. La Bruja overlays soft instrumental beats on top of her melancholic words. The juxtaposition of the image of a father carrying his son with the story of Cuca's situation is both hopeful and overwhelming. While her son will not have a father or an immediate family, La Bruja does suggest that Cuca can create a strong network of people who can help her raise her child, her new family.

CREATING FAMILIAL NETWORKS

In 2009, La Bruja converted *Boogie Rican Boulevard* from a one-woman show to a full ensemble musical. That same year, the musical had a one-month run at the Puerto Rican Traveling Theater.[25] The musical was directed by Nuyorican actor, writer, and producer Nelson Vásquez.[26] As in her solo performance, La Bruja played all the major characters, but this time, the ties that bind came from more than a shared neighborhood. Rather, the characters' shared sense of identity was emboldened by the designation of a family name. Now, these formerly disparate characters were given a shared identity through the same last name: Pacheco. Don José Pacheco is the new patriarchal figure of the family. He owns a bodega; reminisces about his *basebol* years; and tries to make sense of his relationship with his wife (referred to as Mamá) and his three daughters, Maribella (a proud virgin and fashionista), Cuca (a teen poet, who got pregnant by Pito), and Lola (his eldest daughter, who has chosen drugs over motherhood). In performing various members of the family, La Bruja returns to family values—whether the traditional nuclear family, the modern extended family, or the single-parent household. As she states, "You need family. Without your family, you're nobody."[27]

The advertisement shown in figure 13 portrays the cast as a network of support. The cast is made up of real family members of La Bruja's as well as

Figure 13. Poster of the musical version of *Boogie Rican Boulevard* (2009), performed at the Puerto Rican Traveling Theater, includes Caridad de la Luz (aka La Bruja) as Mamá, Pito, and Don José and portrait of cast members, who play different family members.

community leaders, individuals who—in the process of bringing the story to life—illustrate the value of family and friends. Vásquez, the director, spoke to the tight bond among the cast: "The bottom line [of the musical] is, we are all family."[28] The cast included Carina de la Luz (La Bruja's daughter) as Papo (Don José's granddaughter); Alejandro Pagan (La Bruja's cousin) as Eddie; Patricia Marte (also known as Patty Dukes, and cofounder of Circa '95, an independent hip hop, music, and media group) as Patchy; RephStar (cofounder of Circa '95) as Chico; and finally, Dimitri Minucci as Johnny, an openly gay man. Even Kelson de la Luz-Vázquez, La Bruja's eleven-year-old son, worked as a production assistant.

In converting *Boogie Rican Boulevard* into a musical, La Bruja shifted from being the primary agent transmitting experiential knowledge to being the one who passes along her wisdom and sees the cast as the new agents of transmission. Here, La Bruja models a different way of mothering. As an "elder" among youth, she shows them that they can teach others about their own experiences as Puerto Ricans, Latinxs, and members of the working class. The audience witnesses this passing of experiential history from one generation to the next, from older cousin to younger cousin, and from mother to daughter.

Recall Don José, whose entry ticket to New York City was *basebol*, and his dreams for his grandson. In the solo performance of *Boogie Rican Boulevard*, there was not a physical person acting as the grandson. However, in the musical ensemble version, Carina de la Luz, La Bruja's daughter, played the role of grandchild. Don José always wanted a son or grandson, and he never got one. Consequently, he refers to his granddaughter as a boy and calls her Papo. Don José wants Papo to inherit the bodega. Papo reminds her grandfather that—even with all their ball-playing practice—she is not a boy. In fact, she has bigger dreams. While Don José passes his knowledge from one generation to another, La Bruja, who created the role of Papo, insists that her daughter not be ashamed that she is a girl. Here, the passing of experiential knowledge occurs as a constructed transaction between grandfather and granddaughter and an actual transaction between mother and daughter.

Women are important to La Bruja's work. In the solo performance of *Boogie Rican Boulevard*, the character scenes that La Bruja stages do not focus on mother figures. However, I argue that mothers and *abuelitas* (grandmothers) are central to her identity as an artist. In her televised conversation with Dan Zanes, La Bruja discussed the rap lyrics and compositional development for their song "Pollito Chicken":

> Really a connection to bilingual roots, being Nuyorican, Boogie Rican, those things. And you know, my grandmother sang ["Pollito Chicken"] to me and my mother sang that to me. My mother sang it to my daughter. I sang it to my daughter. It was definitely something that I was grateful to preserve on your album. Preserve it and then take it to the next level.[29]

Similarly, in her rap song "For Witch It Stands," she honors her *abuelita*, whom she calls ma: "From the time I was five when I learned to recite from my ma / Who herself couldn't read or even write / She was my beacon of light, she changed the course of my life." Her engagement with notions of family underscores her performance and identity. She even features her parents in "For Witch It Stands." La Bruja stands between her parents, and she jubilantly side-hugs them as they groove to the rhythm of her song. The familial representations relate to the cultural production of performance, identity, and community as conceptual forms of belonging.

La Bruja acknowledges that culture is central to her creations. The focus on mother figures epitomizes how notions of family inform her work. For example, she plays the role of an extended mother, which is most explicit in the song "Pollito Chicken." In the music video, she plays the role of a Spanish teacher, and her daughter is among the students learning a new language. She uses this moment to pass on cultural knowledge—including oral, musical, and linguistic traditions—that she inherited from her grandmother and mother. Nursery rhymes already function in this manner, but La Bruja inserts a Nuyorican and hip hop sensibility, creating a more inclusive notion of family tradition.

The song "Pollito Chicken" lies close to La Bruja's cultural and familial history. She proudly uses it to affirm her bilingual, Nuyorican, and Boogie Rican identities. She points to the continuity among four generations of women in a family—her grandmother, her mother, herself, and her daughter—to celebrate the passing on of a tradition of poetic recitation. La Bruja's mother and *abuelita* are the wellspring from which their values flow. La Bruja disseminates the traditions of recitation, music, language, and cultural values. The song has political implications that layer La Bruja's work with meaning—well beyond an innocuous nursery rhyme converted into a rap.

As discussed earlier, the United States attempted to sever Puerto Rico's cultural and linguistic traditions. According to American policy makers, the English language and other American cultural traits were innately superior, and "the Spanish language was one of the things 'wrong' with Puerto Ricans."[30] After the Spanish-American War (1898), the US colonial government established English as the language of instruction in Puerto Rico's public schools.[31] "Pollito Chicken" was a bilingual nursery rhyme used in Puerto Rican schools to teach English: "*Pollito*—chicken / *gallina*—hen / *lápiz*—pencil / *y pluma*—pen. / *Ventana*—window / *puerta*—door / *techo*—ceiling / *y piso*—floor." In Puerto Rican popular culture, this song reminds the audience of the failed project of assimilation.[32]

Renowned Puerto Rican writer Ana Lydia Vega titled her 1977 short story after the nursery song. Vega's story stirred up debate among Nuyoricans and Puerto Ricans. Suzie Bermiúdez, the protagonist, is a Nuyorican who denies her Puerto Rican identity, but she still returns to Puerto Rico on vacation.[33] Suzie's speech pattern straddles Spanish and English, but it is far from the dialectic, linguistic fusion practiced by Esteves, Algarín, and other Nuyoricans.[34] Instead, Vega abruptly inserts English into Spanish, interrupting the flow of Nuyorican language. The song "Pollito Chicken" assumes that Spanish can be easily translated to English. Vega, however, reveals the incommensurability of translating Nuyorican language. Some argue that this linguistic representation dismisses Nuyorican experience, while others argue that this linguistic style demonstrates how the English language suppresses or colonizes the Spanish language.[35]

Puerto Rican–born and New York–raised writer Nicholasa Mohr critiqued Vega for caricaturizing Nuyorican culture, language, and identity.[36] However, Mary Green posits that Vega's "Pollito Chicken" exemplifies the existing tensions, overlapping histories, and mutual experiences shared by Puerto Ricans, both on and off the island.[37] William Burgos, on the other hand, proposes that Vega set out to "remind her readers that Puerto Ricans, a colonized people, were not free." However, he explains, "choosing a Nuyorican character to represent a colonized society only perpetuated a conservative model of Puerto Rican identity, one that is grounded in the island's culture and rejects hybridity as mere schizophrenia."[38] Both the song and the short story versions of "Pollito Chicken" serve as sites to explore what it means to be a diasporic Puerto Rican.[39]

La Bruja's conversion of a bilingual nursery rhyme into a rap song offers a vision of history at the intersection of past and present. The simple lyrics—passed from one generation of women to another—allude to the vestiges of US colonial history, such as the teaching of English to Puerto Rican schoolchildren, as experienced by her *abuelita*. This harm was passed on to the next generation—her mother—who had to migrate to New York because of Operation Bootstrap. Instead of using the song to teach her granddaughter English, however, La Bruja's *abuelita* now uses it to teach her Spanish. She raps:

> My *abuelita*—that's Spanish for grandma
> She would cook and sing at the same time
> She knew my Spanish was just so, so, so, so
> She taught me this rhyme *¡Abuelita!*[40]

Following in her mother's footsteps, La Bruja uses "Pollito Chicken" to teach Spanish to English speakers. This time, however, the lyrics ride on a hip hop beat, giving the song an urban feel that resonates with many Puerto Rican immigrants in New York City. Born and raised during the genesis of hip hop, La Bruja uses rap to underscore Puerto Ricans' participation in hip hop culture and their connection to Afrodiasporic linguistic practices.[41]

Reminiscent of the Nuyorican mode of "inventing a new language, a new tradition of communication" and the hip hop aesthetic of "flow, layering, and fragmentation," La Bruja's work performs matrilineal networks that create, preserve, and circulate Nuyorican culture.[42] Like Esteves and other Nuyorican women poets, she incorporates her family history and familial networks to expand our understanding of the relationships among culture, identity, and community. La Bruja maps out geographies of home that expand notions of family from the nuclear to the extended, from the local to the transnational.

CHAPTER 6

Performing Afro-Latinidad

Nilaja Sun's *La Nubia Latina* and *Black and Blue*

IN THE SOLO WORKS *La Nubia Latina* (1996, 1999) and *Black and Blue* (2001), Nilaja Sun draws from Nuyorican feminist and hip hop aesthetics to problematize notions of Blackness and Latinidad.[1] She reenacts her lived experiences as an Afro-Latina—born to an African American father and Puerto Rican mother—and encourages the understanding of intersecting racial histories of oppression.[2] Growing up in the 1980s in the Lower East Side—a polycultural community of immigrants at the center of hip hop's genesis—Sun (like the characters that she creates) has been shaped by the same sociohistorical context from which hip hop emerged.[3] Although Sun does not explicitly employ hip hop's most notable elements—deejaying, emceeing, break dancing, and graffiti art—she cements hip hop culture by addressing the issues of the hip hop generation, such as poverty, drugs, Reaganomics, displacement, gentrification, and other postindustrial racial and class-based inequities.[4]

This chapter complicates notions of Afro-Latinidad by examining the ways that solo performer Nilaja Sun negotiates her identity onstage. The term Afro-Latinx refers to Latinxs in the United States and Latin America who are of African ancestry. These individuals choose to identify racially with Blackness and ethnically with their Latinx national origin. As Suzanne Oboler and Anani Dzidzienyo demonstrate in their introduction to the 2005 anthology *Neither Enemies nor Friends: Latinos, Blacks, Afro-Latinos*, "the experience of blackness is heterogeneous," and much remains to be studied about the "constructions and meanings of race attributed to blackness in the Americas."[5]

Like most categories of identification, the term Afro-Latinx is loaded with social, political, and historical meanings. As noted by many scholars, the transnational discourse linking Black Latin Americans and Latinxs crucially allows us to appreciate the intersections, interactions, and exchanges that exist among various diasporas.[6] That is, this term considers how bodies, ideas, beliefs, practices, and artifacts move across the Atlantic Ocean. The term Afro-Latinx encompasses the many "histories, memories, social locations, expressive cultures, social movements, political organizations, and lived experiences of peoples of African descent in Latin/o America."[7]

Like many labels of identification, Afro-Latinx occupies disparate histories, cultures, and traditions. Thus, recent scholarship avoids strict categories of identification but rather embraces the ambiguities and contradictions that complicate, critique, and expand the meanings of terms like Afro-Latinx and Latinx. In emphasizing difference, scholars have moved from relying on national and geographic boundaries to focusing on individuals' actions and feelings.[8] In this vein, identity becomes a practice. It is not who people are, but what they *do* and how they *experience* the doing that defines their identity. Because Sun focuses on the *doing*, her performances are integral sites for understanding Afro-Latinx identity, agency, and community.

For Nilaja Sun, the term Afro-Latinx alludes to an identity consciousness that embraces the experiences that are lived and embodied by individuals who are both African Americans and Latinxs. In *La Nubia Latina* and *Black and Blue*, Sun exposes the entangled diasporic histories and formations of Afro-Latinxs by infusing her body with "Africanity, Americanity, and Latinidad."[9] Sun's performances suggest that Afro-Latinidad is an embodied identity that resonates in the United States, Latin America, and Africa. She understands that she comes from three communities with distinct but overlapping sensibilities. Sun's performances create a hybrid, translocal identity, one that erases the hyphenation that separates Afro from Latinx and Latinx from Afro.[10] Remembering the history of Africa in Latin America reminds us that, like the term Latinx, Afro-Latinx is an umbrella term, one that links individuals with shared histories of displacement, migration, and exile.

For Sun to "feel Latina," she must transform her body or enact a body that is not her own. In her various solo works, she either hyperracializes with gestural signifiers of Blackness or Latinaness, or she reinvents herself in characters as disparate and imaginative as Smurfette and a roach.[11] These drastic physical alterations let her perform her diasporic identity, which connects with both her estrangement from the Black and Latinx communities and her desire for belonging. Rather than splintering her racial identity from her ethnic roots, she layers these physical mutations with her feeling of unwanted exile from both the African American and Latinx communities. Thus, her work reflects US racial politics, her intertwined diasporic identity, and the performative nature of ethnicity, race, and gender.

(WHAT DID I DO TO BE SO) BLACK AND BLUE

A brief summary of *Black and Blue* is necessary to analyze how Sun engages Nuyorican and hip hop aesthetics to complicate notions of Blackness and Latinidad.[12] In *Black and Blue*, Nilaja Sun chronicles her 1982 world premiere as Smurfette in the musical *The Smurfs Saved Their Village against the Evil Gargamel*.[13] This solo work centers on both the preparation and the creation of her blueface performance as Smurfette, demonstrating how Sun came into racial consciousness. Sun's engagement with American pop culture to narrate and question race and racism in the United States and among Latinxs is similar to the work of other Nuyorican artists. For example, Arthur Avilés and Elizabeth Marrero took up Disney's *Cinderella* (1939), MGM's *Wizard of Oz* (1950), and other familiar stories such as the Ugly Duckling, as discussed by Ramón H. Rivera-Servera and Lawrence La Fountain-Stokes. The appropriation of these popular forms offers what Rivera-Servera calls "progressive sites of interaction and even collective imaginaries" that incorporate a distinctly Afro-Latinx perspective, produced by Sun, and a queer Latinx perspective, produced by Avilés and Marrero.[14] Sun uses the popular icon Smurfette to define the structures of exclusion that separate Latinxs from Black people and vice versa.

In *Black and Blue*, Sun plays the role of several campers, including Yolanda, Angel, Keeshaw, Tyrell, and Señora Rivera Libertad, a retired mambo dancer who directs the theatrical events at the summer camp. Señora Libertad initially gives the role of Smurfette to Yolanda, the most popular girl in school—and the girl with the lightest complexion. While rehearsing, young Sun tries to teach Yolanda the choreography. Yolanda not only rejects young Sun's help, but also fails to rehearse her moves, and performs terribly. The director realizes that Yolanda is relying on her looks to get through life, even using her appearance as an excuse not to learn the choreography. Wanting to teach Yolanda a lesson, Señora Libertad decides to recast young Sun in the role of Smurfette. Sun has already learned the series of movements. The members of the group question the decision, since they do not understand how young Sun could play the role of Smurfette, mostly due to her dark complexion. Sun's experience as a thirteen-year-old camper playing Smurfette in blueface profoundly shaped her identity. Consequently, she reenacts the moments before, during, and after her Smurfette performance.

As *Black and Blue* demonstrates, summer camp can be integral to the shaping of a youth's identity. For many Latinx youth, summer camp can be both memorable and extremely traumatic. In Nicholasa Mohr's coming-of-age novel *Nilda* (1973), the title character navigates the politics of being Nuyorican when she travels with her summer camp to a greener environment. As a ten-year-old, she was content and comfortable. However, when the only other girl at camp who knows Spanish, Olga Rodriguez, hears Nilda speak with her Puerto Rican accent, she accuses her of not speaking Spanish properly and warns her to not ever speak that way again. Since they are the only two Latinas at camp, Olga creates an ethnic hierarchy that differentiates her from Nilda. She disassociates herself from a Puerto Rican like Nilda, and she establishes that her way of speaking is the code of conduct at the camp.

For many children of the Lower East Side, television was an escape from the drugs and violence in the neighborhood. By 1982, the year that Sun performed in the musical *The Smurfs Saved Their Village against the Evil Gargamel*, the Saturday-morning cartoon *The Smurfs* (1981–89) had gained national popularity. For eight years, Hanna-Barbera Productions aired it on NBC. Much like the seven dwarfs in *Snow White*, each Smurf serves an allegorical function. There is Lazy Smurf, Grouchy Smurf, Brainy Smurf, Jokey Smurf, and Farmer Smurf, to name a few. As the original story goes, Gargamel, an evil human wizard, decides to take revenge on the Smurfs by creating Smurfette, who has straight, stringy, brown hair, ugly eyelashes, and a big nose. She wears a plain white dress with white shoes. Gargamel plans to use Smurfette as a decoy to find the Smurf village, which is nearly impossible for non-Smurfs to find. Lost in the forest, Smurfette convinces the Smurfs that she needs to be rescued, or she will perish. Papa Smurf, with his sophisticated alchemy and knowledge, saves her. He transforms the "ugly" Smurfette into the charming blonde bombshell that the Smurfs admire. Each episode hinges on the Smurfs' adventures saving their village from their nemesis, Gargamel, who spends his days planning to capture and destroy the Smurfs.

While the Smurfs' village resembled a socialist commune, the campers could not translate the collective qualities of the Smurfs' society into their world, as evidenced by Sun's work.[15] The campers' performance of the popular cartoon turned into a power game of representation and visibility that revealed the discursive undercurrents of racial and gender stratification. Young Sun, for example, originally played the part of Nobody Smurf because unlike so many other campers she did not look like Jennifer Lopez, and she was, as she recalls, often forgotten. Tyrell, the thuggish boy, played Niga Smurf. Keeshaw Black, the asthmatic boy, played the part of Evil Gargamel. The given names of each camper function as racial holders. Keeshaw, Tyrell, and Nilaja (Sun's first name) are often perceived as African or African American names. Consequently, these campers were correlated with the "bad" or less important characters. Because of Nilaja's name, Yolanda called her an "African booty-scratcher" in response to Nilaja's offer to teach her the Smurfette choreography. The most popular children in the class, Angel José Rivera and Yolanda María Yvette Rey the Third—whose names ethnically marked them as having Latinx descent—played the lead roles of Papa Smurf and Smurfette. Even the name of the director, Señora Rivera Libertad, is quite fitting, since her name in English means Lady Liberty. She is the only adult with whom the campers interact, and she tries to "free" them from the racial stratification that they have replicated from the adult world around them.

The campers impose a racial order according to their Smurf names, in part because this order reflects the power relations that they have experienced in everyday life. Sun's peers often excluded her from the Latinx community, since her dark skin marked her as African American. "Race, unlike ethnicity," as feminist philosopher Linda Martín Alcoff asserts, "has historically worked through visible markers on the body, which trumps dress, speech, and cultural practices."[16] Despite her many attempts to perform Latinidad—by speaking Spanish and performing as Smurfette—Sun remains invisible to the Latinx community because her racial identity masks her ethnic identity. The blue cartoon characters let the Latinx campers embody the existing racial order and division among them, while relegating African Americans to the lowest level of the racial hierarchy. Although the shared histories of oppression—struggling to obtain social, economic, and educational opportunities—among Latinx and Black people can potentially incite alliances, a growing divide exists between these two communities of color.[17] This divide stems from the dichotomous function of race.

In contrast to the Blue Man Group, a dynamic multimedia theater company that uses the color blue to create abstract, nonhuman, and nonracial characters, Sun deploys the color blue both to interrupt the racial dichotomy of Black and white and to show how race, class, and gender intersect. Sun portrays Smurfette in blueface to expose the complicated and interlocking relationships among race, ethnicity, class, and gender. Thus, in this solo work, the color blue takes on multiple social meanings. For instance, the term *blue-collar worker* resonates, and Sun aligns it with the manual labor and the socioeconomic status of people from the Lower East Side.

The color blue carries over as a gender signifier into the world of the Smurfs, who are all male, until Gargamel creates Smurfette, the only female character with whom they ever interact. Smurfette's existence relies on how the male gaze dictates the construction of womanhood. However, the most nuanced use of blue in Sun's work is as a racial signifier. The campers are quick to practice a racial dichotomy. After Señora Rivera Libertad announces that Sun will be the new Smurfette, the campers protest. Keeshaw asks: "How is she [Sun] going to be Smurfette when she is Black? Smurfette ain't Black, am I right?" Keeshaw's comment inflects a racial hierarchy and patriarchal order to Smurfette that denies Nilaja the right to perform this character. The campers unanimously decide that Yolanda should play the role of Smurfette because her light brown complexion makes her deserving of this position. According to the campers, only a cinnamon-skinned Latina—and not Sun, a dark-skinned Latina—could embody Smurfette. The campers cannot disconnect race from Smurfette. They believe that Sun's darker complexion means that she could never embody Latinidad or whiteness. Thus, only girls like Yolanda (cinnamon-skinned Latinas) can play Smurfette.[18]

In color-coding her body blue, Sun gestures at the ability—or inability—to translate one's identity into performance. She uses the color blue not only to personify Smurfette, but also to consider how material performance functions when ideological notions of Latinidad and Blackness are revealed on stage. Sun uses dance to assert her identity, to evoke her feeling of alienation, and to articulate her desire to be accepted as a Latina by her peers. In the opening scene of *Black and Blue,* the adult Sun moves in a restricted fashion, trying to remember the movements to the instrumental reprise of the song, "(What Did I Do to Be) So Black and Blue." When she performs the dance for the musical production, she is not concerned about these specific technicalities.[19] Instead, she accents her arms and hips, energizing Smurfette's movements with such splendor that even she takes a moment to revel at her performing body. Young Sun articulates this moment of amazement: while she does not look like the other Jennifer Lopez–esque campers, she still has the ability to perform Smurfette.

The kinesthetic dancing shows Sun as a young child, learning to live in her skin, and Sun as an adult, raising consciousness about the Latinx community's internal racial inequities. The adult Sun enacts her childhood experiences to demonstrate the multiple significations of Latinidad and Blackness. By dancing the choreography of Smurfette in front of her peers, young Sun brings her female body to the center of the racial conflict. Given that the campers collectively agree that Yolanda better fits the role of Smurfette, this cartoon character becomes a medium through which Sun claims her place in Afro-Latinidad. Sun masters the movements that Yolanda should have automatically known, since she was a Latina bombshell playing Smurfette. Sun also imbues Smurfette with social and political value. This performance is her initiation not only into the world of theater, but also into the Latinx community. Dancing in blueface becomes the way that she overcomes the feelings of exclusion and lack of resources that accompany racial alienation. Although the campers imbue blue with Latinx significations, the color blue also contains other racial meanings.

When Yolanda mistakes Sun's first name, Nilaja, for Nigeria, she denigrates Sun for her Blackness. Through this slippage, Yolanda locates her own Latina identity as contingent on this act of denigration. In performing Yolanda, Sun juxtaposes the embrace of Latinidad and the rejection of Blackness to emphasize the tensions that she experiences as a person with a diasporic identity. Yolanda—with her cinnamon complexion—has the ability not only to pass as Smurfette but also to costume herself with markers of whiteness: a blonde wig, a white dress, and white heels. For Sun, this costuming is not so easy because of her dark skin.

After dancing as Smurfette, young Sun looks at the audience as at a mirror, anxiously puts on her bright blonde wig, and smears her face with blue paint. She nods with satisfaction. Then, she attentively stands by for her entrance music to begin. The instant that she hears the Smurf anthem, she merrily dances and lip-syncs:

> La, la, la, la, la, la, sing a happy song
> La, la, la, la, la, la, Smurf the whole day long
> [whistle]—Smurf along with me
> [whistle]—Simple as can be
> Next time you're feeling blue just let a smile begin
> Happy things will come to you so Smurf yourself a grin
> [Spoken by Gargamel] "Ooh, I hate Smurfs! I'll get you, I'll get all of you, if it's the last thing I'll ever do!"
> La, la, la, la, la, la, now you know the tune
> La, la, la, la, la, la, you'll be Smurfing soon.[20]

At the end of her Smurfette performance, Sun is honored by the cheers and applause that fill the theater. She proudly yet humbly bows and returns to her onstage dressing area. This lighthearted moment gradually becomes ironic, as Louis Armstrong melancholically sings "(What Did I Do to Be So) Black and Blue," and Sun wipes off her blue paint. She stares at the audience (the mirror), not in triumph, but in dismay. Her face, now black and blue smeared, reveals a painful lingering question about hybridity and racial consciousness—what *did* I do to be so black and blue?

Just as the song "(What Did I Do to Be So) Black and Blue" captures the trauma of racial oppression, this scene in Sun's performance shows how colorism left black-and-blue bruises on her psyche, especially when she attempted to mold her identity to fit the campers' perceptions of Blackness and Latinidad. When Sun witnesses her black-and-blue reflection in the mirror, her postperformance celebration transforms into a daunting moment. Her black-and-blue, bruised-looking face tempers her celebratory finale, as she realizes how tired she is of trying to fit into dominant ethnoracial paradigms.

Sun's appearance as Smurfette also competes with her talented dancing and singing. Although she can execute her movements and lines with passion, she still cannot fully embody Smurfette. As a child, Sun believed that the proper makeup and costumes would easily allow her to transform into Smurfette. As an adult, Sun reveals that this theatrical illusion fails. When Sun applies blue paint to her Black body, the audience witnesses her trying to embody a character to which the young Latinx campers had denied her access. By painting her face blue, Sun allows the audience to see her navigating between the fractures of two communities: African American and Latinx. Her blueface also depicts the social bruising that young Sun experienced when she played the role of Smurfette. Sun has experienced violent acts of internal racism that—although not physical—have definitely bruised her psyche.[21]

Disturbed by internalized racism, Sun displaces the physical attributes signifying ethnic and racial categories of Latinidad and Blackness onto the cartoon character Smurfette. She rejects the white and Black binary and embraces a heterogeneous notion of Latinidad. As Juan Perea states, Americans have conceived of race as "either exclusively or primarily, of only two constituent racial groups, the black and white."[22] Other racial identities are understood from this limiting binary, which does not work for Latinxs or other migrant communities in the same way that it does for African Americans and Caucasians.[23] This paradigm does not reflect the diverse racial identities that are claimed by a growing number of residents of the United States. In exposing this reality, Sun produces a theatrical experience that brings into dialogue Africanity, Latinidad, and Americanity.

FROM LATIN BOMBSHELLS TO ROACHES: NILAJA SUN'S *LA NUBIA LATINA*

La Nubia Latina was Sun's first one-woman show. She created it in a playwriting class at Franklin and Marshall College in Lancaster, Pennsylvania, and the play was produced on April 25 and 26, 1996, at the college's Other Room Theatre. The following year, it was staged at Duo Theater in New York, and later, it was produced at Henry Street Settlement's Experimental Theater, as part of the Women of Color Festival, in spring 1999. In one of the press photographs used for *La Nubia Latina,* Sun lovingly embraces a blue mask (see figure 14).[24] This image captures Sun reconciling her identity as black and blue, negotiating between her African American and Latinx heritages. In another photograph, Sun peeks through one eyehole of the mask, while revealing the other half of her face. Sun's racial visibility and ethnic ambiguity create unrecognizable moments, since viewers cannot easily decipher her cultural background. On one level, the visual materiality and embodiment of the blue mask break away from a white/Black paradigm, revealing the complexities of race and racism. On another level, they signify modernist poses and the fetish of Blackness as figure and form.

While Sun states that there is no relationship between the blue mask in *La Nubia Latina* and the one in *Black and Blue,* reading these two performances in tandem calls attention to how Sun inspires her audience to think more about the performance of racialized identity outside of Black and Latinx paradigms. In *Black and Blue,* Sun dons blueface to perform her diasporic identity, and she reveals the often-tense relationships among diasporic communities. In *La Nubia Latina*, Sun performs a series of characters who are learning to be comfortable in their skins. She embodies her younger self; a Latina interacting with a roach, who asserts his everlasting presence on earth; and a nameless woman wearing a blue mask (who might be representative of Sun), coming to terms with a terrible breakup. In *La Nubia Latina*—similar to in *Black and Blue*—Sun weaves together moments of her life to show how she bridges the gap between her African American and Latinx heritages.

Figure 14. Photograph for *La Nubia Latina* (1997), Nilaja Sun holds a mask, reminiscent of her bluefacing to become Smurfette, to express her Afro-Latina identity.

The title, *La Nubia Latina*, explicitly indicates how Sun attempts to join her Black and Latina identities. The title stresses her Afro-Latina identity and ushers the audience into a Spanish and English worldview. Although the non-Spanish speakers in the audience might feel uncomfortable—or even alienated—because Sun speaks in Spanish, she quickly makes them feel comfortable by asking whether she is using the correct Spanish verb tense. She positions herself as a non-Spanish speaker to make audience members feel included, even though she is fluent in Spanish. Some audience members, however, are not sure whether her uncertainty with Spanish means that she is an African American woman learning to speak Spanish, or perhaps a Latina who is code-switching. By speaking both Spanish and English, Sun demonstrates the complexities of her Afro-Latina identity. In *La Nubia Latina*, the audience cannot easily place Sun into a single racial or ethnic category, since her linguistic maneuvering produces an ambiguous self-imagining. Sun thus challenges "authentic" notions of both Africanity and Latinidad.

Sun continues to explore the concept of authenticity in *La Nubia Latina* through the character of Yolanda, the hyper-Latina blonde bombshell, who reappears in *Black and Blue*. As Sun puts on a long wig, a nicely fitted black skirt, and high-heeled shoes, Yolanda emerges onstage to the song "Bemba colorá," popularized by renowned Afro-Cuban salsa singer Celia Cruz in the 1960s. Yolanda abruptly hollers for Richie, her boyfriend, to explain why he has ignored her phone calls. Obsessed with figuring out Richie's whereabouts, Yolanda relies on his attention for her own self-confidence.

Like the stereotypical images of Latinas, Yolanda focuses on projecting her body more than her mind. She is not an intellectual, but rather a sexy, boy-crazy, materialistic Latina. She is more concerned about the way that she looks to men than about her search for her inner self. From the outset, Yolanda's character is a jarring hyperrepresentation of a Latina. She makes the audience uncomfortable because they are confronted by an image that is fossilized by dominant categorizations of race, sexuality, and gender. When the audience witnesses Sun stepping out of the character of Yolanda, she brings them closer to understanding how women—especially Latina and Black women—function as objects of production and consumption in mass media, and she illustrates how women are also complicit in the reproduction of these stereotypes.

Yolanda often states that she cannot "find the value within myself." In the absence of her boyfriend, however, Sun suggests that Yolanda's inner self can be found within the history of Africa. Yolanda explains that Richie's current history course has taught him that everyone comes from Africa. Flabbergasted by his newly learned theory, Yolanda immediately responds that she is not an "African booty-snatcher." Despite the fact that Richie says that her eyes, nose, lips, hair, and skin can define her racial identity, Yolanda does not admit to any African roots. She explains that she is not Black but rather has a cinnamon complexion, and her hair is not kinky, but long and wavy. What Yolanda does not recognize is how her hypersexuality fits into a stereotypical image of both Latinas and Black women. This moment highlights Yolanda's mistaken understanding of ethnic differences, since she is playing to the stereotypes of Black and brown women, rather than embodying Latina cultural practices.

To "find the value within herself," Yolanda participated in a Miss Piel Canela pageant in Puerto Rico, a beauty contest specifically for women who have cinnamon complexions.[25] In the same way that Yolanda disassociates herself from Nilaja/Nigeria in *Black and Blue*, Yolanda explains that having cinnamon skin is different from being Black. Given that Eurocentrism and whiteness have informed how Latinas construct notions of gendered beauty, it is not surprising that Yolanda dismisses her Blackness, which clearly exists within her ethnic family. This racist ideology explains the absence of positive images of Black people and Latinxs in the mass media, as well as the excess of negative ones. Yolanda propagates this ideology when she advises her girlfriend to use a British accent when she returns some overpriced Nikes. Knowing how difficult it is to return used items, Yolanda's strategy is to mimic a kind of whiteness that is often privileged in the United States. Yolanda's recommendation illustrates how she tries to manipulate a system that is structured by racial categories. She understands that to navigate the system effectively, she must perform identities that, depending on the given moment, can give her instant access to power, even if only temporarily. This strategy is her way of protesting a system that keeps her from gaining mobility, better living conditions, education, and professional development.

Interestingly, Yolanda's dismissal of Blackness does not mean that she prefers whiteness to her own cinnamon complexion. In fact, she is quick to indict Latino men who date white women. Sun complicates notions of race, gender, and sexuality when Yolanda instigates a dispute between Pedro and his white girlfriend. Yolanda believes that she can teach Pedro a lesson: choosing a white woman will cause Pedro to be shunned by the community and treated like a traitor. Yolanda pretends that Pedro is her ex-boyfriend and that he missed his son's second birthday. Yolanda's trick must have worked, because the couple leaves arguing. However, Yolanda is still not dating Pedro. This fact clearly bothers Yolanda, as she clicks her teeth and looks displeased. This behavior contributes to her ongoing effort to protect what it means to be Latina. She continues to perpetuate negative stereotypes. Initially, she convinces herself that breaking up with Richie was the right thing to do. When he finally comes to visit her, however, she falls head over heels for him again and decides, "every girl needs a little loving." Sun leaves the audience with the disturbing idea that Yolanda embraces the hypersexualized, stereotypical notions of Latinidad.

Although Yolanda is a caricature of Latinas and Black women, her character is useful in that she shows us how the dominant culture packages stereotypical images. Sun's performances of these ethnoracial stereotypes create critical sites to analyze how racial hierarchies stem from capitalism. Yolanda lives in a world that feeds her images of who she is, and she is an embodied product of these racial and ethnic stereotypes. In displaying her clothes, she constructs her identity around the performance of material capital.[26] This provocative fashion reinforces her identity as a hypersexualized Latina. She co-opts these material markers as part of her true identity and then reasserts them as authentically Latina. Sun presents the hypersexualized character of Yolanda to mirror the plethora of consumable stereotypical representations of Latinas.

As a Latina, Yolanda—despite her resistance—cannot separate her ethnic identity from her racial and gender identity. Sun, an Afro-Latina, re-signifies Blackness back onto Yolanda by using the song "Bemba Colorá." While it plays when Yolanda enters on stage for only a short time, for an audience member familiar with the story line of the song, the message resonates throughout the entire piece. Similar to how Sun strategically uses Louis Armstrong's "Black and Blue" to underline the emotional trauma of racism, she uses "Bemba colorá" to underline the internal racism within the Latinx community, exemplified by Yolanda. From the outset, the lyrics "bemba colorá, colorá, colorá, colorá (colored lips, colored, colored, colored)" can simply refer to the voluptuous lips of a women wearing red lipstick—like something Celia Cruz would wear. However, the lyrics are about affirming ones "Africanity." The continuous repetition of *bemba colorá*, along with the lyric "esa es colorá (she is colored)" attempts to recover the African history of Latinxs people. This reclamation is crucial because of people like Yolanda, who deny their Black lineage. Yolanda, who remains caught in a web of essentialist notions of Latinidad, loses her sense of self and agency.

Coincidentally, while Yolanda is busy erasing her Black identity, when she sings Cruz "bemba colorá, colorá," she unconsciously reinserts Blackness onto her body. Sun, as a Black bodied women, then affirms not only her Blackness, but also Yolanda's Blackness. The juxtaposition of Sun's Black body, the hypersexualized persona of Yolanda, and inclusive vision of African roots in the song "Bemba colorá" sets the stage for understanding Afro-Latina identity. For individuals who have been marginalized because of their ethnicity, race, and gender, one way to survive this discrimination—as Sun demonstrates—is to create representations that challenge these social norms. In combating Black stereotypes, Yolanda overly asserts her Latinaness by authenticating hypersexualized images created by the media. Sun performs these extreme representations of Latinidad as a survival strategy, to inform others of who she is and who she is not.

Nilaja Sun's *La Nubia Latina* first addresses the racial tensions within the Latinx community and then critiques society's portrayal of the increasing population of Latinxs as a crisis akin to a roach infestation in one's home. In the second vignette of *La Nubia Latina*, she recalls growing up in the tenements of the Lower East Side, living side by side with roach invaders, and she parodies the relative positions of humans and roaches. Mimicking a radio announcer, she reports: "The roach population has increased over one hundred percent." Due to the roach outbreak, she and her mother must clean up dead roaches and roach remains. In her household, this chore was not seasonal, but weekly. Religiously, she and her mother cleaned their apartment, in hopes of controlling the roach invasion. They manically cleaned the entire house—from flowerpots to figurines—that "beckoned *la isla del encanto* [the enchanted island]." They eventually eliminated the roach colony, and they both rejoiced. Sun ends this vignette with a roach's recommendation: "You can kill me, but we, we ain't never going to go. So you just live your life, and let us live ours."

Sun parallels the human-roach relationship with relations of power among minorities and less-marginalized individuals. The use of roaches as a metaphor or as an allegorical stand-in for humans is not uncommon in Latinx plays. In Luis Valdez's *Shrunken Head of Pancho Villa* (1964), a Chicano farmworker family tries to find its place in society, and Mexicans and Mexican Americans are paralleled by an invasion of roaches. *The Red Rose*, produced by Pregones Theater (2005), is based on the life and works of Puerto Rican activist and journalist Jesús Colón. In his short story "Cuentos para niños de uno a ochenta años" (Stories for children one to eighty years old)

(1927), which Pregones dramatizes, Colón writes about encountering a village of roaches that taught him about radicalism and social action.[27] In *With What Ass Does the Cockroach Sit?* (2004), which premiered at INTAR in repertory with Sun's *Blues for Gray Sun*, Cuban American artist Alina Troyano—better known as Carmelita Tropicana—reenvisions the popular children's short story "La Cucarachita Martina" to address the experience of a Cuban exile, the international crisis of Elián González, and anti-immigrant sentiments.[28] Last, in Rubí Theater Company's theatrical adaptation of Martín Espada's *Imagine the Angels of Bread* (2001), the poem "My Cockroach Lover" describes the intimate relationship between roaches and New Yorkers.[29]

While Sun uses the blue mask to show the interwoven systems of racial and gender categorization, she also embodies the roach as a way of looking at the Other. She uses a roach to discuss the issue of race, and then, in turn, she shows how social forces shape notions of identity formation and community building. While the roaches are a real problem in many of New York City's old tenement buildings, Sun's vignette makes the roaches symbolic of the challenging conditions faced by working-class families of color. Although cleaning her roach-infested home is not a pleasant recollection, the event invokes a family memory that teaches the audience about the American social world in which she lives. Sun and her mother bonded as they maintained the family's living quarters, transforming an unpleasant task into one that generates joy and laughter.

Unable to control the roach population, Sun's family turns to the exterminator, whom she associates with the resurrection of Jesus on Easter Day. She rejoices with a "hallelujah" as the exterminator blesses the house with pesticide. Although this moment is quite comedic, the exterminator is emblematic of the ways that people often react with blind violence to others who are different. Sun's portrayal of the exterminator and those inflicted by roach epidemics reminds the audience of the legal forces that attempt to contain and control immigrants and people of color. These legal forces were made quite evident with the 1994 passing of the anti-immigrant Proposition 187 in California. Sun's performance strategy is reminiscent of how Suzan-Lori Parks's *Imperceptible Mutabilities in the Third Kingdom* (1989) uses bugs as a metaphor to represent women of color, and an exterminator to represent a white naturalist, who perceives African American women as a species to be scientifically observed, analyzed, and experimented on.

Despite the extermination, Sun confesses that the roaches returned, especially when the lights were off. One of them approaches Sun and tells her that no matter what humans do, they can never get rid of the roaches. The roach suggests that they must learn to live with the Other. The audience bursts into laughter at the realization that the roach is commenting on Sun's reality as an Afro-Latina. Despite being different species, Sun and the roaches must learn how to coexist in a world that despises roaches. Sun's embodiment of the roach offers her an altered sense of self. As a roach, she affirms that, no matter how many times the exterminator returns, the roaches will survive. Instead of trying to fit in a specific racial or ethnic category, Sun attempts to foment relationships that allow humans and creatures to coexist, communicate, and interact in any temporal or spatial landscape.

In the final scene of *La Nubia*, we meet a nameless young woman who dances with a blue mask to emphasize her emotional state. Unlike Sun's other characters, this young woman offers no indication of her ethnic or racial identity. However, Sun's racialized body reminds spectators that the nameless young woman's gender experience is not separate from her racial or ethnic identity. This young woman has recently lost her virginity to her first love. Like many young adults, she considers sexual intercourse to be a rite of passage into womanhood. Despite confessing to the excruciating pain of her first sexual encounter, she romanticizes the whole experience and convinces herself that she is in love. The audience witnesses this young woman's compulsive behavior over her first romantic relationship, since she incessantly inquires about his lack of communication. The more that she obsesses about him, the more unresponsive he is. As long as this dysfunctional relationship continues, the young woman has lost her sense of self.

The audience witnesses young Sun reconcile with who she has become. She feels powerless. Sun intensifies the emotional toll that the relationship has had on her by dancing with the blue mask to the song "Strength" (1994) by Patricia Cathcart Andress. This song narrates the hardship faced by a woman who waits for the father of her children to return, something that never happens. The interplay of the blue mask and the dancing body is a central component in Sun's work. In *Black and Blue*, she masters the kinetic dynamism of Smurfette to embody Latinidad. In *La Nubia Latina*, her dancing body materializes feelings of love, loss, birth, and rebirth. When Sun dances with the blue mask, she does not speak. Here, silence is not passive but instead fully engaged with the body. The tension between the rigid blue mask and the flowing body demonstrates how ethnic, racial, or gendered identities require a body to be in motion to trouble social constructions of identity. The blueface performance in *Black and Blue*—as well as in *La Nubia*

Latina—is symbolic of the various masks that Sun must wear to cross ethnic, racial, gender, and social divides. As in *Black and Blue*, the young woman takes off the blue mask. There is a sense of empowerment as she gently places it on the floor and walks away. When she discards the blue mask, she metaphorically sets aside the imposed racial, ethnic, and gender constructions that have consumed her to the point of destroying her sense of freedom. The spotlight focuses on the blue mask and gradually dims to black. Cathcart's song remains in the background, noting how women, despite the hardships they face, turn to their inner spirit to find the "strength and courage to dry [their] own tears."

In both *Black and Blue* and *La Nubia Latina*, we witness the ways that Sun physically mutates her body to "feel Latina." By using a Nuyorican and hip hop feminist aesthetic, she either hyperracializes her performance with gestural signifiers of Blackness or Latinaness, or she reinvents herself as Smurfette or a roach. In doing so, she enacts multiple identities to make visible different attitudes toward race, various ethnic/racial/gendered stereotypes, and distinct forms of resistance. Most importantly, she affirms her desire to belong to the Black and Latinx communities and troubles her engagement with her Afro-Latina diasporic lineages. Rather than splintering her racial identity from her ethnic roots, she performs the ebbs and flows of her intertwined diasporic identity to address the traumatic alienation that Afro-Latinas encounter when caught in the social web of identity categorization.

CHAPTER 7

A Hip Hop Feminist Approach to Aya de León's Thieves in the Temple

LIKE MANY OF THE performeras in this book, the artist-activist Aya de León works in a variety of media: poetry, spoken word, hip hop theater, and literary fiction. De León is from the West Coast. She was not born and bred in New York City like Sandra María Esteves, La Bruja (the Witch), Mariposa (Butterfly), or Nilaja Sun. And though she partakes in the spoken word movement and performs at the Nuyorican Poets Café, she does not have the long history or deep connection to the café that the other performeras in this book have. However, as a woman of Puerto Rican, African American, and West Indian roots—a woman shaped by the end of the civil rights era; militarized political movements such as the Black Panthers, the Young Lords, and the Brown Berets; the devastating effects of Reaganomics on urban America; and the age of technology—de León must be placed in dialogue with Nuyorican and hip hop feminist aesthetics.

Nuyorican and hip hop aesthetics emerged almost simultaneously, from the same sociohistorical circumstances. Both Nuyorican and hip hop aesthetics draw from Afrodisaporic performance practices, to which de León brings a feminist perspective. She explores how systems of domination intersect with gender, race, and class oppression. Both Nuyorican and hip hop feminist aesthetics derive from the work of third-wave feminists such as Cherríe Moraga, Gloria Anzaldúa, Patricia Hill Collins, and bell hooks. Following the lead of feminists in addressing the role of race and intersectionality in their work, this chapter closely examines de León's one-woman show *Thieves in the Temple: The Reclaiming of Hip Hop* (2004), and the ways that she engages with hip hop feminism.[1] This chapter seeks to identify the hip hop feminist strategies utilized by de León to centralize bodily experiences in relation to media and

Figure 15. Aya de León as a wigga, a white teenage wannabe hip hop thug, in *Thieves in the Temple* (2002). Photo by Deanne Fitzmaurice. Courtesy of San Francisco Chronicle/Polaris.

popular culture representations. I argue that in her performance, de León stages her female body as a site of political knowledge to disrupt or "wreck," as Gwendolyn D. Pough calls it, the internal and external discourses of Blackness, Latinidad, and hip hop. De León "brings wreck in order to create change," as she firmly politicizes the "I," uses nostalgia, reveals power dynamics, and creates a feminist utopia to expose the grotesque ways that music and politics package hip hop, race, gender, and sexuality.[2]

Using performance as a mode of dissemination in *Thieves in the Temple*, de León offers an illuminating history of hip hop, from its radical origins to its commercial success. She juxtaposes this evolution with her personal journey from a teenage hip hop fanatic to a proactive feminist emcee, taking hip hop beyond the television and onto the stage. As she reveals her love-hate relationship with hip hop, she "turns up the noise," to quote Michael Jeffries's phrase, so that audiences can confront and question the packaging of race and consumption of hip hop.[3] De León portrays a range of characters, including the three I discuss here: the Executive, a stout white businessman representing the hip hop music industry; the Consumer, a white teenager co-opting hip hop; and Lady Triple X, a fictitious porno star. These characters address the ways that hip hop has evolved from a cultural, artistic, and political phenomenon to a machine operated by capitalistic ideals, which include packaging hip hop with drugs, sex, and violence. To this end, de León embodies stereotypical characters to comment on how the music industry packages hip hop and race, including how she, as a Black woman, navigates the media's construction of Blackness. But as Jeffries contends, critiquing is only productive when activists offer alternative visions of hip hop's future. De León's culminating scene, "If Women Ran Hip Hop," challenges conventional representations of race and gender. She transforms hip hop from producer of degrading depictions of women to promoter of strong, agentive women.

STAGING THE PERSONAL AS POLITICAL

Similar to the Nuyorican performeras discussed, de León engages with the foundational feminist idea that "the personal is political." Bringing the personal into de León's work is a vital practice embedded in Nuyorican and hip hop feminist aesthetics. This investment in both public truth telling and the sharing of real experiences are both personal and political because, as Stephanie L. Batiste reminds us, they "call out systemic failures of justice and accountability in our democracy."[4] And that is exactly what Batiste does when she performed her own one-woman hip hop show *Stacks of Obits* (2005) and turned to experiences that are "shared or at least recognizable by Black people."[5] Because staging the personal as political is part of a Nuyorican and Black aesthetic—of which hip hop is a part—it is important to contextualize the relationship between de León's work and her upbringing.

Thieves in the Temple, which is composed of rap songs and spoken word pieces, and which addresses hip hop consumerism and the representation of women in hip hop, is for de León that staging of the personal, the "I," to allow for the public to understand her everyday life experiences in relation to broader political structures of power. De León's work often references her background, her personal history, and the pivotal experiences that shaped her life.[6] In "Hip-Hop Ventriloquism: From Sexism to Corporate Control," de León assertively locates her racial and cultural identity: "I am a Black/Puerto Rican woman from Northwest Berkeley." In another essay, "Hiroshima 70th

Anniversary: Remembering My Teenage Anti-Nuclear Protest Years," she historicizes her background and discloses the trauma of poverty and violence that haunts her family. Her maternal grandfather—a first generation Estonian piano player, photographer, and West Point man—worked as a military officer at Oak Ridge, where the United States was constructing the nuclear bomb.[7] "After he saw the destruction it caused, he proceeded to slowly drink himself to death."[8] He died when de León's mother, Anna de León, was twelve years old. Her widowed maternal Puerto Rican grandmother was forced to look for a job during the 1950s in Los Angeles. Undoubtedly, racism prevented her from attaining one, as she was a Black Puerto Rican with a thick accent.[9] Aya de León's mother grew up poor in Rodger Young Village, the first integrated housing project in Los Angeles. After receiving bachelor's and master's degrees in arts at University of California, Los Angeles, she became a civil rights attorney.[10] When she was in her midtwenties, she married blues and roots musician Taj Mahal, after which she had Aya de León.[11] Mahal was raised in a musical environment, since his father was a West Indian jazz pianist and composer, and his grandmother was an African American gospel singer and teacher.[12] This personal truth telling brings de León's personal history and political fervor into public consciousness.

Aya de León's personal history anchors her and gives her the strength to write and perform about social injustices. Because the personal functions as evidence of social disparities, her positionality is a significant part of her artistry and activism. Her activist history ranges from being a teen leader in the antinuclear movement in Northern California in the early 1980s, to becoming a college feminist activist in the late 1980s, to working as a community organizer for racial justice in Roxbury, Massachusetts, in the early 1990s.[13] A graduate of Harvard College, with an MFA in creative writing from Antioch University, de León gained national attention as a spoken word artist in San Francisco's underground poetry scene in the mid-1990s. De León was reading her poems in the community during a time when poetry slams were taking flight, and she joined the movement.[14] She won poetry slams from San Francisco to New York City, including the 1999 Nuyorican Poets Café Poetry Slam. She also won the 2000 San Francisco Poetry Slam in a four-way tie, and she was on the San Francisco Slam Team when it won Western Region Poetry Slam in 2000.[15]

Performing in a variety of events—from open mics to social justice fundraisers—de León soon found herself connected to hip hop theater. In *Thieves in the Temple*, she recounts the genesis of her one-woman show. She attended the Lyricist Lounge tour to see the political rapper Mos Def perform in 2000, but she was appalled by the sexist acts, both on- and offstage.[16] After enduring an offensive opening act, she sought respite in the ladies' lounge, but there she walked into more misogynistic behavior. A group of guys had entered the lounge to hit on the women. She returned to the concert to find yet another group performing with the same sexual bravado. Frustrated that the hip hop performance was allowing men to disregard women's boundaries, she found herself using her spoken word skills and crafting her own rap to respond to the female objectification in full display.[17] "They would fire off sexual lyrics onstage, and I was firing off to my friend," de León recalled.[18]

Because of this tumultuous experience, de León began to think about her relationship to hip hop. She realized that she had been unconsciously boycotting hip hop since she was fifteen, due to the sexism and violence. She remembers: "I was gonna be an actress, a novelist, a poet, a solo performer, any traditionally female artist role, *anything but a hip-hop artist*."[19] In *Thieves in the Temple*, the audience learns about the social factors that prevented her from pursuing her dream of becoming an emcee. First, hip hop was centered on the East Coast, and de León was from Berkeley. Consequently, it would be difficult for her to tap into the resources that would allow her to thrive.

Second, she was never encouraged to pursue her dream, mostly because emceeing was not typically perceived as a profession. This view was the byproduct of an era that did not perceive hip hop as an art form.[20] Third, since hip hop is a male-dominated culture, de León did not have access to avenues often available to aspiring male emcees. Instead of assuming the role of the passive hip hop consumer, she resolved to continue "the tradition of Lyte and Roxanne and Latifah and so many other strong female emcees," and she grabbed the mic without reservation.[21]

The same year that de León attended the Mos Def concert, Danny Hoch—along with Clyde Valentine and Kamilah Forbes—launched the first New York City Hip-Hop Theater Festival, featuring artists from all over the country. The festival cultivated a blend of hip hop, poetry, and performance, a combination that de León had already explored. Ultimately, the festival furthered the development of de León's one-woman show *Thieves in the Temple*. She performed this show at the third New York City Hip-Hop Theater Festival, in 2002, which I was fortunate enough to attend. Her participation in the Hip-Hop Theater Festival led to tours with the Hip-Hop Theater All Stars, which included Danny Hoch, Will Power, and Jonzi D. *Thieves in the Temple* then debuted at the Hip-Hop Nation Festival at San Francisco's Yerba Buena

Center for the Arts in 2004, among other venues. She then converted *Thieves in the Temple* into a film in 2007.

In 2004, de León put in a bid for the White House in her solo show *Aya de León is Running for President* (2004). Along with these theatrical productions, she published her writings in multiple journals and anthologies, and she released several independent publications: three spoken word CDs, chapbooks, and a video of *Thieves in the Temple* (2007).[22] She has received critical acclaim for her work in the *Village Voice, Washington Post, Oakland Tribune, American Theatre, San Francisco Chronicle, San Francisco Bay Guardian,* and *East Bay Express*. At the University of California, Berkeley, de León has served as the director of June Jordan's Poetry for the People since 2006. She also teaches creative writing, poetry, and spoken word at the university, and she explores her poetry and activism both in and out of the classroom.

De León toured extensively until 2009, when she decided to focus on being a novelist, a choice that aligned with her desire to start a family. She publicly shared her decision to become a mother, and she communicated with her fans about how she balanced her roles as mother, writer, and activist. Motherhood did not seem to slow her down, and she explored online outlets, which allowed her to write from home. Since 2013, she has blogged and tweeted on *xoJane, Bitch, Ebony, Racialicious, Writer's Digest, Fusion, Woman's Day, Movement Strategy Center, Quartz, The Toast,* and *The Feminist Wire*. She self-published the children's book *Puffy: people whose hair defies gravity* (2013) on CreateSpace. The book was dedicated to her daughter, and she worked to portray positive images for children of African heritage and others with "puffy" hair. Her debut novel, *Uptown Thief* (2016), was published by Kensington Books and is one of the few novels that feature a Latina Robin Hood protagonist.[23] Her most recent novels include *The Boss* (2017) and *Accidental Mistress* (2018) and *Side Chick Nation* (2019).

A FEMINIST REMIX OF HIP HOP'S GOOD OLE DAYS

For the generations that grew up during the first two decades of hip hop—from the 1970s to the mid-1990s—there is a tendency to hearken back to the golden age of hip hop, the bygone era of the 1980s and 1990s, a time of political vibrancy and urgency. De León frames the opening of *Thieves in the Temple* with nostalgia for hip hop's past.

Since hip hop is a lucrative global industry, the packaging and commodifying of hip hop elements—such as rap, deejaying, break dancing, graffiti, and fashion—has become part of a global commercial empire. In this context, examining the mood and mode of nostalgia in *Thieves in the Temple* is essential to understanding the piece. I am interested in the ways that de León manipulates nostalgia as feelings of longing for hip hop's past. She produces nostalgia by sampling women-centered hip hop songs for the theatrical stage. She then takes nostalgia to a mode of feminist resistance, one that theatrically celebrates the commercial consumption and branding of hip hop, while simultaneously critiquing its misogynistic practices. The recycling of these women-centered raps excavates hip hop's musical past and reveals the history of women's influence in hip hop and their resistance within the hip hop music industry. De León rescues and recycles women-centered hip hop songs, not solely to demonstrate a sense of dissatisfaction with hip hop's present, but also to revise its canonical past by adding the contributions of women.

Here, I use nostalgia as a mood and a mode, a social emotion and an aesthetic modality.[24] The works of Fred Davis, Fredric Jameson, and Paul Grainge concerning nostalgia are useful tools. Fred Davis's sociological study examines the concept of nostalgia as a collective mood, an emotional response, and a reaction to social change or discontinuity.[25] The collective mood develops a distinct aesthetic that encourages or reinforces the emotion. Nostalgia then is both a collective feeling and cultural manifestation of longing. Fredric Jameson, by contrast, focuses on the capitalistic production of nostalgia as a mode, a form of pastiche, symptomatic of the postmodern crisis of historicity.[26] Nostalgia, in this case, is a style of consumption mirroring economies of taste (likes and dislikes) and textuality (literature, film, music, dance, and performance), rather than feelings of longing and loss. Paul Grainge further expands the concept of nostalgia by focusing on the source of the nostalgia, its developmental trajectory, and its function. He also divorces nostalgia from the master narrative of cultural longing and postmodern forgetting.[27] He contends that consumerism strategically deploys nostalgia through the influence of technologies that rescue, recycle, and reconfigure images, styles, and sounds, all drawn from the past. Digital technologies, for instance, resurrect and reproduce old classical recordings that are often devoid of any feeling of loss.

In the first two scenes of *Thieves in the Temple*—"Prologue" and "Cellulite Monologue"—de León reminisces about the golden age of hip hop, evoking nostalgia for hip hop's past. When the houselights first dim, the audience hears the passing of a gentle breeze interlaced with wind chimes and bells. Behind a dim light, de León appears center stage, evoking a dreamlike feeling, and begins to rap:

> Way back in the '80s
> when hip hop was live
> male MCs respected the ladies
> we wanted black people to thrive
> Then somehow we lost the love
> somewhere along the way
> it's the time for the reclaiming of hip hop.[28]

Using elements of the hip hop tradition of storytelling, de León sets her rap on top of a beatbox track, locating herself in the realm of old-school hip hop. In de León's view, the good old days of hip hop were in the past. Today, hip hop is dead. "Hip hop was all about—Power to the people! But then the nineties came along, and it was all about—The Benjamins? The money?" In conjuring the 1980s, de León sets nostalgia as both a mood and a mode. She situates herself within a memory of hip hop culture, asserts her hip hop identity, and negotiates her social position in the context of global capitalism.[29] Hip hop has sold itself to the music industry, becoming a consumable global good, yet de León continues to use it as an oppositional artistic, cultural, and political tool. De León's performances investigate not only hip hop consumerism, but also the ways in which hip hop represents women. In *Thieves in the Temple*, de León *wrecks* dominant hip hop discourse by rearticulating the context of hip hop's political economy and engaging the tropes of Black gender roles.

To address the packaging of hip hop as a commodity that promotes misogyny, sexism, and violence, de León calls for the return of the political hip hop of the 1980s, and she injects that nostalgia with a strong dose of feminism. Hip hop feminists, as Aisha S. Durham claims, "recognize hip-hop hegemony . . . [and use] its popularity to turn a spotlight on the social conditions of women of color."[30] De León gives airtime to the foundational female rappers of the 1990s, using their popular musical lyrics to counter some of hip hop's misogynistic representations of women of color. Immediately after her call for the golden age of hip hop, we hear a sampling of Queen Latifah's fierce lyrics "who you callin' a bitch?" from her 1993 song "U.N.I.T.Y." The audience immediately recognizes the lyrics and sings along. The act of listening to these lyrics constructs a collective memory and a social cohesiveness. In the song, Queen Latifah questions the unity of the Black community, when men verbally and physically disrespect her and her Black sisters. She urges Black women to challenge men who call them bitches or hoes and to end unhealthy relationships, a point that de León stresses in her opening rap.

Audiences were prepped for Queen Latifah's women-centered rap, since the preshow playlist included Lauryn Hill's "Doo Wop (That Thing)," from her 1998 debut solo CD, *The Miseducation of Lauryn Hill*. As with "U.N.I.T.Y.," the song spotlights the real-life experiences of Black women. Hill warns: "Girls, you know you'd better watch out. Some guys, some guys are only about that thing, that thing, that thing."[31] In the song, Hill confesses that she too lost sight of herself in a relationship, and she advises women not to follow her example. Interestingly, Hill not only advises sisters to seek self-respect, she also encourages men to reflect on their damaging behavior in relationships.[32]

Although the performance of *Thieves in the Temple* had not yet officially begun, the underlying message was already present in the pre-show music: daily modes of empowerment are available for women. When the audience walks into the theater, de León tethers her nostalgia to feminism. The use of well-known songs of the 1990s—by female rappers like Lauryn Hill and Queen Latifah—allows de León to honor the contributions of women in the male-dominated hip hop industry. These songs talk back to men and demand respect for women. The nostalgic framework passes the mic to women, who prompt the audience to consider the damaging representations of sexism, masculinity, and femininity in hip hop.

De León interlaces the nostalgia for political hip hop with her personal journey as an emcee, positioning women as intellectual beings and important contributors to hip hop culture. Although it took her over a decade, she overcame her fear of public speaking and finally became an emcee. She now comfortably picks up the mic and powerfully graces the stage with her words of wisdom. Her contemplative yet high-energy syncopated rap explains how she once believed that she could never be an emcee because she was a girl. She did what most young girls often do—she waited, observed, and stood on the sidelines. Frustrated by the negative representations of Black women in mainstream hip hop, de León started to utilize poetry to distinguish herself from the stereotypes, in hopes of demolishing them. As her rap notes, hip hop is rife with the sensationalism of sex and violence, but "[she is] not a pimp, [she is] not a ho, [she is] not a slanger or a noc."[33] De León defiantly raps against what Tricia Rose calls "the hip hop trinity"—the caricatures of gangstas, pimps, and hos—in commercial hip hop.[34]

Commercial hip hop expects de León, as a woman, to be an object of desire, not a witty poet, adamantly claiming her agency. De León combats these stereotypes by urging women to "keep it real." She proudly raps about fashioning "her real hair, real nails, real tits, real ass, real smart, real age."[35] She exposes the ways that commercial hip hop colonizes the minds, bodies, and souls of its youth. In juxtaposing references to the gangsta-pimp-ho trinity with her own frustrations with hip hop, de Léon shows how hip hop practitioners can powerfully resist these stereotypes in feminist ways. When she proudly embraces her physical assets, she encourages women to question the false representations of women in hip hop and to embrace their own natural beauty. This move disrupts the power dynamic that is deeply rooted in subjugating women. Despite the evolution of hip hop from a political art form to a trendy consumable art form, de León affirms that she is "built to last, built to last." The coupling of de León's nostalgic imagining of old-school hip hop as a purely activist and harmonious cultural art form with her feminist perspective allows de León to face hip hop's packaging of hypersexualized female bodies of color.

As the second scene unfolds, de León continues to revisit the 1980s and 1990s. This time the audience hears an announcer introduce de León as a spoken word and slam poet, a "sista who has been blowing up poetry spots all over the country."[36] Nostalgia also percolates through her sartorial choices. De León enters dressed in a black hoodie tracksuit and Adidas shelltoe sneakers, the classic 1980s hip hop outfit. She then begins to recall LL Cool J's song "Jingling Baby" (1990), another classic. Both her costume and her musical choice help trigger a mood and mode of nostalgia. Since de León does not use a deejay for her performance, she asks the audience to create the musical samplings. She takes the time to orchestrate and rehearse the call-and-response sequence with the audience: "it's jiggling baby. . . . go 'head baby." She sings the first part and then points at the audience, who sings the refrain, "go 'head baby." Since this piece uses the interactive call-and-response style of hip hop music, de León creates an organic, in-house, collective deejay. Thus, audience members not only participate in de León's performance, they also shape the piece itself. She activates a shared feeling and experience (mood), while also hearkening back to what she sees as a more generative time in hip hop history.

Satisfied with the audience's performance of the "go 'head" sampling, de León then delivers "Cellulite." De León specifically dedicates this poem to "the fat girls like [her]." She addresses the way that media obsesses with body image, and she promotes body confidence. She accuses the media of perpetuating an anorexic body image. De León claims, "A sick society / turns women's bodies into problems to be solved," with its "lite" advertisements: "lite beer / lite cake / lite cookies / pepsi lite / 99% fat-free / but who's trying to be fat-free? Certainly, not me," declares de León. "Let me see your thighs jiggle / they're jiggling, baby," she continues, and the audience responds "go 'head, baby."[37] In referencing LL Cool J's lyrics in her poem, de León glorifies old-school hip hop music as an ideal past, but she still does not discredit the present. She uses nostalgia to establish the problem with hip hop culture, revising it to engender a positive version of communal identity. This revision is more than just a feeling or experience; it is a hip hop feminist mode of resistance.

Unbeknown to them, audiences become collaborators in shaping the piece itself. They become advocates for body consciousness, as de León recasts women's bodies from sites of sexual pleasure to sites of pride and honor. Instead of saturating the audience with false ideas of beauty—flawless and skinny bodies—she admires "the big bodacious mujeres de Cuba" or "the big-body women of the West Indies."[38] De León culminates "Cellulite" with a final "go 'head baby" from the audience. She thus turns the theater into what she calls a "body-acceptance zone," and her performance mobilizes this new collective toward body-conscious actions.[39]

Using nostalgia as the opening framework for her performance, de León recognizes the foundational female rappers of the 1980s and 1990s, which emotionally and politically connects fans with hip hop. Her use of nostalgia mobilizes today's generation to scrutinize the representations of women in hip hop. De León communicates that she is not the silent, sexualized dancing body often portrayed in the mass media's version of hip hop. Rather, she is the intellectual body of the rapper, speaking onstage with a microphone. She urges the audience to pay attention to the work of women who politically and artistically contribute to hip hop culture.

UNPACKING WHITENESS AND THE POLITICAL ECONOMY OF HIP HOP

In the first two scenes, de León models how to use hip hop songs to incite nostalgia as the mood and mode for igniting feminist social awareness. In the scene "The Decline and Fall," she unpacks hip hop's extreme commodification to reveal how the labor relations between the music industry and hip hop culture are no different than the relationship between a slave and slave owner.[40] In fact, journalist, author, and former producer of New York City's WBAI radio Norman Kelley argues that Black music operates within a "structure of stealing" that dates back to the antebellum period. This structure serves as the foundation for the contemporary economic relationships between Black musicians and the music industry. "The history of black music has been a continuous replay of the uncontested and lucrative expropriation of black cultural forms by whites."[41] The music industry reduces hip hop artists to Black bodies and their talent to Black labor, no different from the labor of slaves.

De León personifies the music industry's impact on individuals through two characters: the Executive and the Consumer. In slow motion, the audience first witnesses de León transform into the Executive, a white music producer who makes final decisions about the content of hip hop songs. She crouches, picks up a cigar, and takes a couple of puffs. Then, in a nasal voice, she half speaks and half sings:

> I want albums, I want albums
> I want albums with big guns and naked chicks
> sounds good, but throw in a few more "suck my dick"
> kill the part about missing your pops
> and the part about crooked cops
> and I think we'll have a big hit in our hands—heh-heh-heh.
> Sex is selling violence is selling
> it always has, it always will this is no big news
> you people have sung about it ever since the days of the blues
> Just now the profits are much much bigger,
> so get back to work ni—[42]

From the outset, the nasal voice and stout physique of the Executive portrays a nerd-like personality, but the complete authority that he exudes over the content of hip hop contradicts this expected characterization. His demand for more curses, sex, or guns demonstrate how the music industry shapes hip hop. This shaping leads to the treatment of people of color as stereotypes, their identities constructed by the oppressive categories of race, ethnicity, and gender. As Kelley reminds us, "Blacks served as commodities—objects purchased, controlled, and sold by others—while their labor was valued as instrument in the production of cotton and other goods and services."[43] Ultimately, the Executive illustrates how the music industry exploits Black music. The music industry packages hip hop and Blackness into a consumable item, devoid of historical, political, or cultural contexts.

De León further explores the co-option of hip hop by comparing the music industry, in its relationship to Black culture, with an overseer running a plantation. The Executive's last words, "so get back to work ni—," establishes how the Executive is no different from the overseer who ensured the welfare and discipline of slaves, while also maximizing profits for plantation owners. Like the overseer, the Executive is under pressure to ensure that hip hop artists do everything needed to keep increasing the music production yield. The Executive requires hip hop artists to bind Black men and women to stereotypical representations, particularly as criminals or sexual objects. The saturation of these stereotypes normalizes the negative representations that Black people have been battling since Jim Crow.

Additionally, these stereotypes disconnect the violence and poverty from systemic oppression, and they fault Black people for social injustice. Artists are complicit in this system when they agree to meet the music industry's demands. Artists also gain publicity and wealth by embodying these toxic stereotypes. As a Black Latina artist, de León understands this complicity when she embodies the role of the white male Executive, who is responsible for circulating images of Black masculinity, Black female sexualization, and Black-on-Black violence. While de León is a highly skilled Black Latina embodying a white character, we still cannot help but read her race. She is an Afro-Latina performera, testifying to the systematic racism of consumerism that hides our own participation in its vicious economy.

De León further complicates the troubling relationship between the music industry and hip hop when she assumes the role of the Consumer, a white teenage thug. Placing a cap on her head, and taking on a timid yet thuggish demeanor, she transforms into the Consumer. This character understands that the power of hip hop lies in truth telling and narrating the story of the self. Thus, he follows the methodology of gangsta rap by self-identifying and describing his social reality: "I'm a white boy / in a small town / nothing ever nothing ever happens here / my parents work all day, then watch TV or hit each other and drink beer."[44] The Consumer is representative of "wiggas"—white people who appropriate Black music, fashion, and attitude. This character repeatedly strikes the classic hip hop stance—an aggressive stare and a mountain-posed body, with arms crossed. Attempting to rap, he often pauses and trips over his words. Unsure about whether he executes the lyrics and moves properly, he questions himself:

> Cuz it ain't no heart in the heartland fool.
> *(In boyish voice)* or should it be "ain't no heart in the heartland
> motherfucker"?
> And should I grab my dick during or after I say?
> *(In thugged out voice)* "ain't no heart in the heartland motherfucker"?
> *(In boyish voice)* yeah, that's it! that's it![45]

It is clear to the audience that the white thug has not quite mastered the mannerisms and poses from commercial hip hop. There is a self-conscious anxiety in his demeanor—he fidgets and corrects his words, his moves, and his stands—which contrasts with his aggressive physical performance. The inauthenticity of this role-playing of Blackness by this white teenage wannabe thug is made more pronounced because the role is executed by de León, a Black Latina woman.

Once again, as in the performance of the Executive, the legacy of slavery haunts the performance of the Consumer. De León's portrayal of the Consumer is an embodiment of how the structure of stealing plays out in the political economy of Black music. Clearly, the white wannabe thug is a bystander of consumerist hip hop. He raps:

> But last year in sixth grade my best friend got MTV
> and rap music is transforming me
> I want the realness
> I want the realness
> I want the realness
> of slanging and banging
> of thugs and drugs
> of hoes and clothes
> of shorties and forties
> of sagging and do-ragging
> I bought every rap CD that you could get in town[46]

De León portrays the ways that the Consumer has assumed or stolen hip hop fashion, speech, and mannerisms. The audience members laugh, as they clearly perceive de León's performance as a mockery of a wigga, a white boy mimicking hip hop culture.

De León critically notes how hip hop culture is trapped in a dangerous cycle of performing and consuming Blackness. She fiercely accuses hip hop of selling out "our revolution for a gold chain, three rocks of crack, a girly magazine, and a record deal."[47] De León suggests that the record industry's massive production of commercial hip hop music nullifies the grassroots qualities of the art. It also spotlights whatever the dominant culture values as easily consumable. The Consumer admits that he does not care "if this thug life is a fantasy," because gangsta rap offers him an outlet to express himself: "thank God for Tower Records or MTV / I was numb til gangster rap set me free / the rage it expresses is the rage in me / *(Turns hat backwards and assumes thugged out posture)*."[48] By simulating a Black person, the wigga romanticizes his desires to belong to a culturally rich community. However, his misconceptions of hip hop culture are what disconnects him from the hip hop community. He feels that he can relate to being urban, but he does not realize that he does not have to pay the social consequences of being Black in a predominately white society.

When de León takes on the characters of the white entrepreneur and the white thug, she not only performs whiteness but also demonstrates the racial dynamics in hip hop culture. Racism is deeply embedded in our society, in which racist practices misunderstand, misrepresent, and betray hip hop participants. Taking a cue from Faedra Chatard Carpenter's *Coloring Whiteness: Acts of Critique in Black Performance*—in which she examines the enactments of whiteness in the works of African American playwrights, performers, and visual artists—we can see how de León's portrayal of white characters reveals that whiteness is not just a racial category but also "a social, political, and economic construct."[49] By performing the producer (as opposed to the creator) and consumer of hip hop as white, de León underscores how the media packages hip hop as a good that consumers can purchase and use. Ultimately, these consumers are complicit in the commercialization of hip hop. Without engaging the sociopolitical dimensions of hip hop music, the Executive and the Consumer construct the most consumable images—overtly violent Black men and overtly sexualized Black women—as a form of domination and control.

MIRRORING AND SHATTERING BLACK HYPERSEXUAL IMAGES

What happens when the consumer is no longer the young white hip hop fanatic co-opting Blackness, but a woman of color buying into the hyperconstructed images of sex and violence? This question emerges when de

Figure 16. Aya de León as Lady Triple X in *Thieves in the Temple* (2002). De León stages a hypersexualized constructed caricature as a theatrical intervention to shatter the social prescriptions of Black women as hos, bitches, and pimps.

León reenters the stage as Lady Triple X, a female emcee wearing a blonde wig, black spandex boyshorts, a black tube top, and black heels. She holds a forty-ounce bottle of malt liquor, occasionally posing with the bottle near her crotch while she sneers. As with the Executive and the Consumer, here de León offers an embodied narrative to reflect on the dehumanizing stereotypes of women created by commercial hip hop—and then she wrecks these stereotypes. Audiences witness as de León's performance of Lady Triple X transforms the mass media corporate constructions of Black sexuality into a reality that can be understood through the body. De León's performance is theory in the flesh—to use Cherríe Moraga's words—theory in action. Lady Triple X mirrors the stereotypical image of Black women as sexually promiscuous. However, as the performance unfolds, we realize that her mirroring strategy actually shatters this hypersexualized image.

On the day that I attended the performance, after Lady Triple X entered the stage, the audience gasped. (Interestingly, de León's outfit is reminiscent of the clothes that Sun wore when playing Yolanda, and the wig that she used for Smurfette.) This gasp is indicative of how de León both mirrors the trope of Black women as hypersexual and also shatters it. While Lady Triple X attempts to seduce the audience through her behavior, she instead produces tremendous discomfort among the audience members. This moment points to the messy tension between pleasure and misogyny that Joan Morgan establishes within hip hop feminism. Throughout the entire scene, Lady Triple X gesticulates her butt uncontrollably, and she sings, "I be shaking my ass / do you think I am hot? / I be shaking my ass / like what? Nigga what."[50]

Triple X recalls that, even as a young child, she was sexually objectified. From fellatio at the age of twelve to an abortion at thirteen, and to today, when she is generously paid for her services as a gangsta bitch, the video ho, and the porn star. She proclaims this progression as sexual freedom and empowerment. Lady Triple X's sex appeal is the only currency by which the audience values or devalues her.[51] Although Lady Triple X is not subversive by any means, she remains an object for male fantasies. She acknowledges that she and other women are "sexual beings who enjoy sex, and lots of it."[52] Lady Triple X's unapologetic openness about her sexuality shatters the silence and shame around female sexuality and erotic desire in the Black and Latinx communities.[53]

De León makes the audience come face to face with hypersexualized representations of a Black woman in commercial hip hop in order to wreck the stereotypical tropes of Black women. While Lady Triple X acknowledges and performs her sexual prowess, the audience witnesses as she comprehends the grim reality of assuming such a role. Realizing that she has lost the interest of her spectators, she pleads with them to wait a minute, at which point she bends down on all fours and continues to shake her butt. Convinced that the audience is not captivated by her spectacular performance, she more forcefully gyrates her hips and desperately supplicates: "I thought you loved me. Wait a minute. Do you love me now? I am shaking my. . . . Okay, wait don't leave! Do you love me now? I am shaking my . . . wait . . . wait. Do you love me now?"[54]

Her supplication dissolves into a painfully shrieking sob, as she realizes that she is complicit in the reduction of herself to a mere body part. Again, de León mirrors this image of hypersexuality. She uses what Gwendolyn D. Pough calls the "tools of spectacle and representation" to engage with the public sphere, but then she wrecks the trope by directing the audience to bear witness to Lady Triple X's pain. Pough explains that the theory of "bringing wreck" articulates how Black people redirect "the public gaze in such a way to be recognized as human beings—as functioning and worthwhile members of society—and not to be shut out of or pushed away from the public sphere."[55] As such, we must understand Lady Triple X, this hypersexualized constructed caricature, as a theatrical intervention. De León reconfigures the social prescriptions of Black women as hos, bitches, and pimps. She ultimately brings the audience closer to understanding how women—especially Black women—function as objects of consumption to sell new hip hop albums.

IF WOMEN RAN HIP HOP: THE EFFICACY AND LIMITS OF HIP HOP FEMINISM

In this male-dominated arena, women's contributions to hip hop, though significant, have been downplayed. Hip hop has often been a contested space for women. The play's title, *Thieves in the Temple: The Reclaiming of Hip Hop*, speaks to a generation of individuals that not only engage with hip hop culture but also, and more importantly, recognize the power of hip hop as a forum to wreck misogyny and the sexploitation of women of color. So as not to confuse the audience about who she really is, De León speaks back to Lady Triple X, angrily declaring, "Hip hop, I thought you loved me and you betrayed me."[56] While performing Lady Triple X, de León uses the stereotype of Black female hypersexuality so that the audience can comprehend the damaging effects of the media's representation of women. The final scene, "If Women Ran Hip Hop," reclaims the Black female body by creating a hip hop feminist utopia. With a syncopated beat in the background, de León raps, envisioning a hip hop world governed by women:

> If women ran hip hop
> the beats & rhymes would be just as dope,
> but there would never be a bad vibe when you walked in
> the place . . .
>
> If women ran hip hop
> there would never be shootings
> cuz there would be onsite conflict mediators

> to help you work through all that negativity & hostility
> & there would also be free condoms & dental dams
> in pretty baskets throughout the place
> as well as counselors to help you make the decision:
> do I really want to have sex with him or her? . . .
>
> If women ran hip hop
> same gender—loving & transgender emcees
> would be proportionally represented
> & get mad love from everybody
> & females would dress sexy if we wanted to celebrate our bodies
> but it wouldn't be that important because
> everyone would be paying attention to our minds, anyway . . .
>
> but best of all, if women ran hip hop
> we would have the dopest female emcees ever
> because all the young women afraid to bust
> would unleash their brilliance on the world
>
> cause it's the time for the reclaiming of hip hop[57]

De León's prescient words make it possible for the audience to imagine—if only for a moment—what a women-led hip hop world would look like. The repetition of "if women ran hip hop" inspires the audience to envision a world apart from patriarchal society.

The embodiment of these imaginings on the stage produces what Jill Dolan calls a utopian performative:

> Small but profound moments in which performance calls the attention of the audience in a way that lifts everyone slightly above the present, into a hopeful feeling of what the world might be like if every moment of our lives were as emotionally voluminous, generous, aesthetically striking, and inter-subjectively intense.[58]

Ultimately, de León's imaginings create utopian performatives—moments of political agency, hope, and futurity for women. According to de León, if hip hop were left to women, men and women would not be stuck in inequitable gender roles. The world would be less violent and more committed to resolving conflicts peacefully. Her proposal promotes a cashless and uncompetitive society, and it advocates sharing, bartering, and collectivity.

As a reprieve from our decidedly patriarchal society, de León's embodied narrative of "If Women Ran Hip Hop" creates a social space in which she imagines a feminist hip hop world that is radically better. Her world welcomes, includes, and supports women from all walks of life—be they transgender, lesbian, undocumented, or disabled. As a culminating act, de León sits down cross-legged, closes her eyes, and sings meditatively, "Mos Def said hip hop is going where we go. I am going somewhere positive. I will take hip hop with me."[59] She holds her power fist raised as the lights fade to black, leaving the audience with the affirmation that her dreams of "if women ran hip hop" will become a feminist reality. The imagining of a woman-centered hip hop world aims to uplift women and liberate them from sexist oppression. *Thieves in the Temple* unapologetically engages with a hip hop feminist consciousness, transforming hip hop from a site that often produces degrading depictions of women to one that promotes diverse representations of strong women with agency. This shift is an important alternative vision for hip hop's future.

CHAPTER 8

Beyond the Tangible

Performing Spirituality in Nuyorican Performances and Hip Hop Theater

CREATING POETRY IS SO SACRED that Sandra María Esteves opens the anthology of *Yerba Buena* with the poem "Oye me que mi espíritu habla," in which she shares that her spirit told her that everyone is born free. Preceding the poem, she creates an illustration that visually invokes the spirit world. She depicts a godlike figure, with an enlarged head and ears. On top of the head are four ventricular chambers. The eyes are half open, as if the figure is in a meditative state. Contour lines cover the entire torso, creating a corporeal topographic map. In topographic studies the contour lines locate a specific place and identify geological features differentiating the material from the spiritual world. The four ventricles pointed above emphasize the fluid connection between the material body and the spirit word. Similar to the ways that ventricles in the body collect and expel blood, these ventricles—which point above—suggest that this godlike figure in meditation gathers information from above, the spirit world, and then circulates the information through the contour lines on the body. Together, Esteves's poetry and illustration engage with the spiritual world.

In addition to infusing her artistic work with the spiritual, Esteves also publicly brings spirituality to the forefront. "I am a spiritual person, and I am a dreamer," Esteves declared at a public event at Hunter College, sponsored by Sangre Viva Art Alliance and El Centro de estudios puertorriqueños.[1] She continued, "I believe that it is important to imagine the world that we would like to have or would like to see or would like to become because if we cannot imagine it, how can we ever get there?"[2] That Esteves disclosed herself as spir-

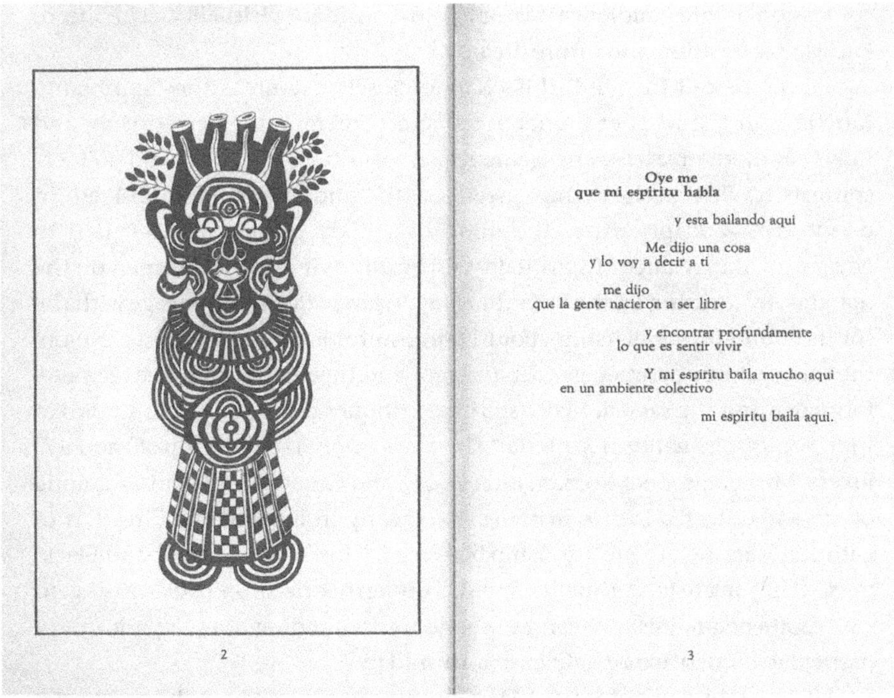

2

Oye me
que mi espiritu habla

y esta bailando aqui

Me dijo una cosa
y lo voy a decir a ti

me dijo
que la gente nacieron a ser libre

y encontrar profundamente
lo que es sentir vivir

Y mi espiritu baila mucho aqui
en un ambiente colectivo

mi espiritu baila aqui.

3

Figure 17. Poem *Oye me que mi espíritu habla* with drawing by Sandra María Esteves.

itual at a public event in an academic setting is significant. To speak about spirituality raises myriad anxieties and misconceptions. As Irene Lara reminds us, "Lamentably, more than seven centuries after the establishment of the Inquisition in the so-called Old World and more than four centuries after its inauguration in the New World, women who exercise spiritual and sexual agency continue to be feared and hence socially judged, ostracized, and punished."[3]

Beliefs and practices that consciously refer to spirituality are often perceived as superstitions, folk beliefs, or New Age delusions. In an academic setting, spirituality does not neatly fit into conventional forms of knowledge. Esteves speaks not of the knowledge sourced by the mind, but rather that sourced from the body-mind-spirit.[4] For Esteves to state that she is spiritual is a political move. She understands that "spirituality," as Gloria Anzaldúa puts forth, "is oppressed people's only weapon and means of protection," and that "changes in society only come after the spiritual."[5] Her confession invites audience members to consider spirituality as a site of knowledge creation and future dreams.

With this call in mind, this chapter closely examines how spirituality functions in the work of foundational and contemporary performeras, and how they dramatize their engagements with spirituality in social and political contexts. When scholarship neglects to understand a non-Western perspective—and prioritizes the mind over body or vice versa—it fails to engage the importance of spirituality, especially as it relates to women on the margins. By focusing on the ways that Nuyorican performeras engage with the spirit, I build on scholarship about Latinx spirituality. I also further explore the intersections between gender and race and the relationship between performance and the sacred. Many spiritual critiques can be found in studies of Indigenous spirituality or Santeria.[6] The foundational scholarship of Raquel Z. Rivera, Miriam Jiménez Román, Juan Flores, and Ginetta Candelario—among others—about Afro-Latinx histories has greatly influenced the direction of Latinx studies. Yet, the relationship between a Nuyorican aesthetic and Blackness as they relate to spirituality remains undertheorized. Spirituality is a generative site of analysis that can be used to understanding how Nuyoricans, in particular women, express their Afro-Latinidad.[7]

I turn to the work of Sandra María Esteves to explore how she practices a Nuyorican feminist aesthetic that pushes spiritual discourse to a different level. Esteves weaves a spiritual dimension in her poetry, mandala series, and handmade jewelry as a way of healing her body-mind-spirit from the trauma of racism. Using Esteves as a model for the Nuyorican feminist aesthetic, I examine the multiple ways that hip hop solo performeras—in this case, La Bruja (the Witch), Mariposa, and Aya de León—express the sacred in performance. They layer their works with spirituality as a strategy of belonging, which firmly situates their Afrodiasporic identities as powerful resources for making change. Esteves's little-known performance piece *La Cura: A Ritual of Healing and Feeling* (1976–78), La Bruja's *Boogie Rican Boulevard* (2001, the focus of chapter 5), Mariposa's *DiaspoRican Dementia* (2001), and Aya de León's annual self-marriage ceremonies (1996–2012) all engage with spirituality to heal individual and communal traumas. I conclude by considering how repositioning spirituality expands the ways we can do theater history and reconstruct theater productions of the past. This methodological shift accentuates the sociopolitical significations of spirituality as an important component of identity making. It also underlines complex relationships among gender, performance, and the sacred.

Drawing from Anzaldúa's theory of spiritual activism, I position Esteves, La Bruja, Mariposa, and de León as spiritual activists. In the works of these performeras, ritual takes on a spiritual dimension that promotes self-reflection, collectivity, and social transformation. Notably, these performeras raise spiritual consciousness and promote political action. As AnaLouise Keating defines it, "spiritual activism posits a metaphysics of interconnectedness and employs relational modes of thinking. At the ethical level, spiritual activism includes specific actions designed to challenge individual and systemic racism, sexism, homophobia, and other forms of social injustice."[8] These performeras include a spiritual discourse in their work—one that is inseparable from questions of social justice in relation to class, gender, sexuality, and race.

Like the Nuyorican aesthetic, spiritual activism begins with the self, and in expressing the self, artists call attention to concerns that affect an entire community. Performeras bring in a feminist aesthetic when they tap into their *conocimientos*, "faculties of knowledge," as Anzaldúa explains, it "encompass[es] all the dimensions of life, both inner—mental, emotional, instinctive, imaginal, spiritual, bodily realms—and outer—social, political, lived experiences," to advance personal and community healing.[9] Implementing these *conocimientos* as a means toward social justice is the work of spiritual activists. In accordance with Anzaldúa's theory of spiritual activism, these performeras "connect the inner life of the mind and spirit to the outer worlds of action."[10] As they move from individual work to public art, they expose, challenge, and transform unjust social structures.

As spiritual activists, these performeras allow their *conocimientos* to engage the personal, while also moving outward and engaging the interconnectedness between the self and the community. Esteves declares her spirituality in a space that typically values knowledge produced by the mind—rather than the body-mind-spirit—a move that positions her as a witch. In the same vein, I see these performeras taking on what Irene Lara calls a *bruja-curandera* (witch-healer) positionality.[11] Lara uses the hyphen to "deconstruct the view that they form an oppositional binary."[12] In a Christian spiritual world, a *bruja*, or witch, is perceived as an evil sorceress: a mad, hysterical woman with malignant supernatural powers, someone who is dangerous to the social order. Despite the negative stigmatization of the word *bruja*, these performeras publicly embrace their spiritual *conocimientos* and implement them as transformative healing powers. As *bruja-curanderas* they make sense of the social chaos of oppression that comes with racism, sexism, elitism, homophobia, and ageism.

READING SPIRITUALITY IN THEATER HISTORY

In *Chicana Art: The Politics of Spiritual and Aesthetic Altarities*, Laura Pérez offers new critical ground with which to read the spirituality within Latinx visual culture. She examines how Chicana practitioners engage the spiritual in addressing questions of social justice. Her study of more than forty artists positions the artworks as *ofrendas* (offerings) that draw on spirituality to protest social injustices. Pérez explains that the spiritual "is meant only to indicate the system of beliefs, institutionalized or not, about the nonmaterial component of human nature and/or the natural world that may encompass what in the Westernized world we describe as the divine, and about the life of the conscious and unconscious mind."[13] Reading art through the lens of spirituality requires an alternative methodological approach. Pérez studies the work of art as a primary object and explores spirituality as a theme that characterizes that work. She urges scholars in the fields of art history, Chicana studies, and feminism to focus on spirituality as a site of inquiry. In making this recommendation, Pérez theorizes how spirituality informs, shapes, and redresses the narration of history.

Using spiritual dimensions in theater is not a new phenomenon. During the 1960s and 1970s, spirituality was a powerful tool used by many marginalized communities. As shown in the Chicano movement and Black Arts movement, theater practitioners imbued their work with both a spiritual and political presence. Take, for instance, the spiritual *mitos* of El Teatro Campesino; the ritual social protest of Amiri Baraka's Black Arts Repertory Theatre and School (BARTS; est. 1965) and Spirit House (est. 1966); and the rituals of liberation at Barbara Ann Teer's National Black Theatre of Harlem (est. 1968). Theater scholars like Yolanda Broyles-González and Harry J. Elam Jr. have explored the ritualistic and spiritual dimensions in El Teatro Campesino and the Black revolutionary theater of the 1960s and early 1970s. As Broyles-González explains, during the Chicano movement, theater practitioners infused spiritual elements into their social protest performances because they offered a space of hope and possibility.[14]

As part of their organizing, members of the United Farm Workers (UFW) permeated their political discourse with spiritual iconography that was important to Mexican Catholic migrant farmworkers. As a result, striking workers, activists, and protestors marched behind religious emblems of the Virgin of Guadalupe and other deities from Indigenous and Christian spiritual belief systems. These images functioned as both protectorates and galvanizing figures, and they marked the workers' resistance to hegemonic forces.[15] UFW members also transformed pickup trucks into impromptu, mobile shrines, reminiscent of altars, that were adorned with sacred images, flowers, candles, and pictures of families to invoke a spiritual dimension in their protest and activist spaces. These nomadic shrines signaled spirituality as a means to politically incite and mobilize Mexican farmworkers—and the entire Chicano community—to resist social injustices.

This "sacroprofane" fusion—a term coined by Broyles-González to denote the deep interconnections between the sacred and secular—also resonated in the cultural production of El Teatro Campesino.[16] While known for its *actos* (short, one-act, agitprop sketches), staged at rallies, fields, and houses, El Teatro Campesino also reenacted miracle plays and practiced Theater of the Sphere, a self-created performance practice inspired by Maya and Aztec philosophy, which incorporated prayers, ritual dances, and other spiritual exercises.[17] A spiritual consciousness (whether intentional or not) permeates cultural productions and theatrical works as vehicles of social activism.

Harry Elam, in turn, argues that the 1970s social protest theater of Baraka and Luis Valdez operated ritualistically to create an aesthetic of opposition.[18] While social protest theater provoked the theater audience to respond to social injustices, it also "functioned as a spiritual celebration, a sacred/secular ceremony." This point of entry allows theater historians to understand that social protest theater included rituals as performative acts. This theater brought the spiritual into the social realm and the personal into the political realm. The protest theater of BARTS and El Teatro invoked spirituality and, thus, fueled the meanings of the social protest performance. Similar to how ritual functions as "symbolic mediation"—negotiating between the sacred and secular spheres—social protest theater mediates two spaces: the current social reality and the struggle for social change.[19]

Implicit in social protest performance is the use of ritual as symbolic act. Using Victor Turner's concept of reading social dramas as rituals, Elam explains that BARTS and El Teatro deployed rituals as the background for staging the social crisis experienced by Blacks and Latinxs. The ritualistic component of social protest theater was meant not to connect participants with gods or powers beyond, but instead to unite spectators and participants in the greater cause of social action.[20] BARTS and El Teatro redressed the order of social power and demanded justice. Elam's study suggests that social protest theater operates ritualistically to address the making of self and community. Together, Broyles-González and Elam center spirituality as an important object of study to understand theater making.

I am interested in recasting spirituality as an agentive site for reclaiming identity and affirming a sense of belonging. Spirituality in Latinx performance is often read as reflective of the culture, rather than as representative of practices that inform identity construction. That is, rather than staging identity, these performeras use spirituality to stage one's sense of identity. The body is a crucial site for accessing spiritual ways of knowing and for revealing the multifaceted dimensionalities of identity. Gloria Anzaldúa and Cherríe Moraga's "theory in the flesh" is of utmost importance, as "the physical realities of our lives—our skin color, the land or concrete we grew up on, our sexual longings—all fuse to create a politics born out of necessity."[21]

Moraga—among other women—creates what Jorge Huerta calls "necessary theater," or theater that is born out of necessity and that contributes to theater traditions in vital ways. In Moraga's *Heroes and Saints* (1994), the irreal, "bodiless" character of Cerezita, born with *only* a head and no body—due to her mother's exposure to pesticides while pregnant—represents the split between the body and the mind, as well as the presumed separation between physical and spiritual agency. Cerezita must be clothed in the regalia of the Virgin Mary, a costume loaded with religious symbolism, for her mother to see her as a political leader. She also wears this costume when she leads the community to burn the fields in protest. She uses the force of her material body, adorned with religious iconography, as a spiritual conduit to provoke change. Just as Moraga writes about bodily experiences through a spiritual consciousness, Esteves, La Bruja, Mariposa, and de León also unite the corporeal with the spiritual. Hence, their bodies become an extraordinary medium for materializing memories, experiences, and feelings encountered in both the material and spiritual worlds. Their bodies carry social meaning as living repositories of knowledge that expose matrices of power.

FINDING *LA CURA*: SPIRITUAL PRACTICES OF HEALING IN ESTEVES'S WORK

As one of the only founding female poets of the Nuyorican Poets Café, Esteves advocated for a feminist consciousness during a time when the Nuyorican poetry scene was predominantly male and masculinist in its aesthetic. Esteves infused her work with spirituality to create a feminist aesthetic, as evidenced in her poetry, visual art, and handmade jewelry. Expanding the performance tradition of Nuyorican poetry from the 1970s into the twenty-first century, Esteves's works stress the connections among the social, political, and spiritual. The relationship between the spiritual and social—whether in her visual, literary, or theatrical productions—guides Esteves's work.

The title of Esteves's book of poetry *Yerba Buena* (Good herb) refers to the mint herb used for medicinal purposes. With her choice of title, she invokes a *bruja-curandera* subjectivity. Esteves sees her poetry as having healing attributes. As a reminder of the political nature of standing up for one's spiritual practices, her poem "The Ignorant Laugh" questions the critical mass of people that refuses to accept multiple modes of existence. She writes: "Don't they believe? / in magic / witchcraft / *brujería* / *la religión* / Santeria / meditation / chanting / astrology / *caracoles* / spirits and other living beings / even the rocks are alive / there are other ways to live."[22] She draws from somatic practices, witchcraft, and religious practices to establish how these modes of being are sources of knowledge. Poems such as "Oye me que mi espíritu habla" (Hear me for my spirit speaks) and "Weaver" reveal the racial and gendered stigma experienced by women of color.[23] These poems suggest that the healing properties of nature and the spirit world both offer disenfranchised communities new ways to envision their futures. Her poems put into practice her *conocimiento* to reveal spiritual traditions that have been marginalized.

In 2005, Esteves added the expressive practice of mandala making to her repertoire. Mandalas are art pieces that follow geometric patterns, in which a symmetrical and often intricate image is produced (see figure 18). They have been used in many cultures throughout history as vehicles to promote meditation, healing, self-awareness, and unconscious expression. In her 2005 mandala series—which includes *Mandala de Elegua*, *Mandala de Oschosi*, *Mandala de Ochun*, and *Mandala de Yemoja*—Esteves pays homage to various *orishas* of Yoruba religion. In doing so, she re-signifies the mandala, which is most often used as a meditative practice in Hinduism and Buddhism, within

Figure 18. *Mandala de Elegua* (2005), 18"x 18" mixed media decoupage mandala on canvas. Courtesy of artist Sandra María Esteves.

an African-based religious and cultural landscape. Similarly, Esteves invokes Yoruba orishas to name her handmade beaded earrings, calling these pieces by such names as *Elegba Portals*, *Elegba Spirals*, *Elegba Dragons*, and *Ochun Egypt* (see figure 19). The reference to orishas illustrates how Esteves draws from an Afrodiasporic religious practice to create her art, thus legitimating spirituality as a source of knowledge. While there is not anything gender specific about the objects, the physical labor and artistry of making them calls attention to the way that she creates sacred curative spaces or spaces to heal from trauma and distress.

Figure 19. Handmade earrings by Sandra María Esteves. Clockwise from top left: "Elegba Portals," "Elegba Spirals," "Ochun Egypt," and "Elegba Dragons."

From 1976 to 1978, Esteves produced *La Cura: A Ritual of Healing and Feeling*, a multimedia, poetic performance with music and dance by flutist Andrea Brachfeld and dancer-choreographer Marilyn Worrell. *La Cura* has a similar aesthetic to Ntozake Shange's choreopoems and evokes elements of spirituality that inspire her work. Esteves showcased *La Cura* at the Nuyorican Poets Café in 1976. The title, *La Cura*, alludes not only to healing, but also to the fix that satisfies cravings for drugs or any other addiction.[24] The performance was a ritual of healing for both individuals and a community that craves a fix for social disparities. *La Cura* is a performance that attempts to cure the Nuyorican Poets Café from the plague of sexism. Esteves recalls the Nuyorican Poets flier incident mentioned in the opening of this book, when Joseph Papp invited the Nuyorican Poets Café artists to perform at the Delacorte Theater in Central Park. Esteves was invited, along with café artists Miguel Algarín, Miguel Piñero, and Lucky CienFuegos; and Pedro Pietri, Willie Pietri, and Jesús Papoleto Melendéz, who made up the Latin Insomniacs Motorcycle Club (Without Motorcycles). Since there were factions in the male Nuyorican camps, the Latin Insomniacs created their own publicity material, and the café poets did the same. Neither rival group included Esteves's name on their fliers. Again, her part of the performance was unacknowledged and "lost" to the performance history of the Nuyorican poetry scene.[25]

Esteves's anecdote shows how the community's unacknowledged sexism creates pain, but her performance shows how she transforms pain into action and knowledge. Doing a *limpieza* (spiritual cleansing) was as much about attending to the trauma of daily oppressions in the community as it was about cleansing the café of patriarchal practices. In *La Cura*, Esteves attempts to reinscribe her life back into history—not through the wounds of sexist acts, but rather through personal and collective healing. Esteves's decision to enact a *limpieza* at the café was about her desire to "heal you from your sea of tears / remove blindfolds that led you away / break shackles that encased your spirit / transcend boundaries of bitter tongues and closed minds."[26]

In guiding the audience through a collective *limpieza*, Esteves, Brachfeld, and Worrell embodied a *bruja-curandera* positionality. They used their spiritual *conocimientos* for personal and community healing. The *limpieza*—both as a performance and as an embodied spirituality—transforms the historical moment and the current social reality. Esteves and her collaborators had to traverse the material world and employ their *conocimientos* to discard and overcome the traumatic aftermath of racism, sexism, and homophobia.

Notably, *La Cura* reveals the intersections between the personal, social, political, and embodied aspects of spirituality.

In preparing for this performance, Esteves acknowledged her ancestors, and she invoked spiritual dimensions, moving beyond the corporeal limits of the material. She considered herself to be a conduit that could convey messages from other realms. Esteves believed that without this sacred gift, her work would not exist. Esteves also paid close attention to how the space facilitated the process of healing. Rather than walking into a theater space, the audience entered an environment that was conducive to the transformative process of healing from painful, destructive, or negative memories, thoughts, and feelings associated with the experience of social oppression. Esteves adorned the space with turquoise chiffon fabric, which contrasted with the café's brick walls. She selected this color and texture symbolically, rather than as an act of beautification. Turquoise symbolizes fluidity and mutability in water and air, essential components of *limpiezas*. Esteves's use of the color turquoise was an attempt to draw out negative vibrations and to encourage creativity, transformation, and communication.

In addition to creating a colorful environment with textured fabric, Esteves, Brachfeld, and Worrell also used objects and scents that promoted spiritual awareness. During the performance, they lit candles, swept the space with rue, smudged it with sage, and sprinkled *agua de florida* (floral-scented cologne) to dispel negativity and to attract positive spiritual forces. While objects, colors, textures, and scents can serve as theatrical devices, Esteves, Brachfeld, and Worrell enacted a collective *limpieza* in the café to underscore the transformative power of a ritual. They included the performative elements needed to heal from the physical, mental, and spiritual trauma induced by systematic oppression.

Performance reviews, prompt scripts, production drawings, and information on costumes, lighting, and sound from this production are lacking in Esteves's archive. However, the theatrical event's publicity flier—which Esteves designed—survived (see figure 20). The flier for *La Cura* helps establish the existence of the production, but if we attend to the component of spiritual agency, it also allows for another narration of theater history. The flier provides information about how Esteves haunts—to employ Marvin Carlson's term—the contemporary moment with a spiritual presence. As Carlson reminds us in *The Haunted Stage: The Theatre as Memory Machine*, ghosts haunt the US theatrical stage, the dramatic text, and the performing body. For Carlson, haunting takes on several generative meanings, linking past to present, memory to culture, and theater to history. Playwrights, directors, actors, designers, and managers recycle words, texts, concepts, sets, and designs. In this way, the past is reiterated in the present, and historical traces continuously hover over the work. The images of performing bodies on the flier for *La Cura* communicate how embodied practices of spirituality act as forms of resistance within the Nuyorican community.

On the one hand, the flier reveals the physical labor required to design the publicity material, and on the other, it highlights the presence of the spirit. Image editing software now allows designers to alter images with ease. The images and text on the *La Cura* flier, however, were carefully cut, laid out, and pasted by hand, creating a black and white photomontage. In using cutouts of the performeras' silhouettes, Esteves removes their bodies from their original context and focuses on the performing body in movement. Esteves makes the body the primary source of discovering spiritual ways of knowing. This departure in design is telling, because it references, disrupts, and moves beyond the realism of photographs.

Drawing from Victor Turner's call to read social dramas as rituals, we can see how the flier's imagery signifies the ways that Esteves, Brachfeld, and Worrell embody the various phases that incite personal and social change.[27] Since Esteves arranges the images on different planes of depth, there is visual interaction between the foreground and background. The image of Esteves in the foreground captures the first phase of change: breaching. Her declamatory posture suggests some separation from Brachfeld and Worrell. While the image of Esteves establishes the emergence of a crisis, the image of Worrell holding her head speaks as if she were in the middle of crisis. The fact that Worrell's image is smaller than Esteves's accentuates the splintering that can arise during moments of conflict. The third and final image, Brachfeld, is on the same plane as Worrell's image, but larger in size. Brachfeld's image portrays a sense of release, letting go of the social traumas that cripple the soul. While the flier does not suggest reintegration—Turner's final phase of social dramas—Esteves suggests that the ritual performance of *La Cura* will cultivate regeneration, a moment where the community will envision and possibly enact ways to enable change.

Esteves's emphasis on spirituality delivers a counternarrative to hegemonic practices imposed on Nuyoricans and inspires activism. She moves away from focusing on a specific leading actor, instead modeling a collective notion of leadership and mobilization. As ritual officiates,

Figure 20. Flier for *La Cura: A Ritual of Healing and Feeling*, Nuyorican Poets Café, 1976. Designed by Sandra María Esteves. Courtesy of artist.

Esteves, Brachfeld, and Worrell enact the roles of cultural healers who connect the body to the soul. In contrast to conventional plays—during which actors remain within the constraints of the stage—in *La Cura*, the audience participates in the healing process and assumes the role of officiate. The performeras smudge members of the audience with *agua de florida*. This show demonstrates the healing power of collective performance.[28] As the title indicates, *La Cura* is intimately tied to a ritual of healing that the theater community enacts. This ritual ushers the spectators into an empathetic position, and audience members promote change by creating a spiritual foundation on which to build a political consciousness.

Unlike Jose Alvarez—who assumes the role of a two-thousand-year-old shamanistic spirit—and Guillermo Gómez-Peña—who also developed a shamanistic persona—Esteves, Brachfeld, and Worrell do not embody *characters* that function as conduits for the spirit to manifest.[29] Rather, they are the *curanderas* (spiritual healers), reclaiming spiritual practices to empower women of color and affirm their strength to the community of spectators. Just as Esteves sees a need to heal the social wounds of trauma, I suggest that her *limpieza* baptizes a new site, particularly for women, as well as for other community members who were left out of previous masculinist articulations of Nuyorican cultural production.

While the flier for *La Cura* is attuned to the spiritual, the collage of black and white photographs of the performeras evokes a ghostly quality. In light of the ways that female artists have been almost erased from this history of the Nuyorican movement, the ghostly aura of this flier suggests that the history of women of color has been invisible. Haunting and ghosting also take on literal qualities through the figures of Esteves, Brachfeld, and Worrell, all of whom demand to be heard, seen, and felt. I turn to this flier of *La Cura* because, unlike the 1975 anthology *Nuyorican Poetry*, women were directing the events and involved in the process; they visibly and audibly participate in making art and inspiring social change. Just as Esteves uses her body to animate her poetry, the performing body on the flier appears to jump off the page. The flier becomes an archive, and it records the embodied spiritual practices of the Nuyorican community during the late 1970s. This flier is an important archival document as it captures the feminist practice of spiritual activism, a performance tradition often forgotten from the Nuyorican poetry and performance scene.

SPIRITUAL DECOLONIZATION IN *BOOGIE RICAN BOULEVARD* AND *DIASPORICAN DEMENTIA*

Esteves's *limpieza* not only sought to heal the wounds of trauma, it also baptized the café as a new site for women and other people who had been previously left out because of masculinist practices. This ritual intervention carved the way for Nuyorican contemporary performeras like La Bruja and Mariposa, who mark their work with a spiritual sensibility. Twenty-five years after the performance of *La Cura*, La Bruja and Mariposa still stage their work at the café—evidence that this venue has provided a nurturing and spiritual space for artists, historically as well as presently. Performed in fall 2001, La Bruja's *Boogie Rican Boulevard* captures the social experiences of the urban Latinx community in America and also explores the healing power of the spirit. The character of Marta, a wannabe Boogie Rican (as described in the program), steps out of the house for a smoke after an argument with her boyfriend because she thinks he has been disloyal. While outside, she has a brief exchange with a Buddhist that brings her a dose of inner peace. We also meet the Espiritista—performed by La Bruja herself—who enacts a semi-*limpieza*.

Clearly, La Bruja's name asserts her witch identity. She calls herself La Bruja because she openly embraces her spiritual history. In *Boogie Rican Boulevard*, she shares that her parents were married on Halloween, and she was named Caridad de la Luz after the patroness of Cuba, La Virgen de la Caridad del Cobre (the Virgin of Charity). This Catholic figure is often associated with the Yoruba goddess of love, Oshun, whom La Bruja frequently invokes on stage. In publicly disclosing her origin story as part of her performance, La Bruja marks herself as inherently spiritual. Her album *For Witch It Stands* (2010) further addresses her *bruja-curandera* positionality. From the top of the title song, she says: "una pregunta: ¿Porque La Bruja?" (a question: Why La Bruja?). Similar to how Esteves opens her poetry with a spiritual stance, La Bruja begins by addressing this question about witches that comes up in many interviews. Rather than allowing misconceptions of *brujas* to drive the lyrical narrative, she publicly asserts a positive take on her name. Rapping to an energetic sound track that harmonizes hip hop beats with salsa rhythms, she responds to the rhetorical question: "My name is La Bruja / For witch it stands."

La Bruja's insertion of the word *witch* instead of *which* into the title of her song and album invokes a spiritual realm. In the music video, when she sings the rhetorical question "¿Por que la bruja?" she puckers her red lips, flirtatiously looks to and away from the spectators, and subtly dances to the music. After seductively fashioning herself, she responds in an astute rapping style:

> *¿Por qué la bruja?*
> *Ooh ¿por qué La Bruja?*
>
> I'm making magic with the mic in my hand
>
> *¿Por qué la bruja?*
> *¿Por qué la bruja?*
> *Ooh ¿por qué La Bruja?*
>
> My magic wand is a pen, understand?

The basic ingredients of La Bruja's "witches' brew" include her pen, the microphone, and the words that she spits into the mic. Her costume—reminiscent of Carmen Miranda—adds some playfulness to the scene. While Miranda's signature was to wear an excessive amount of jewelry and tropical fruit adornments, La Bruja flaunts the classic fruit-topped turban, but she shies away from all the necklaces and rings. In doing this, she exposes the "constructedness" of the iconic image of Miranda. In his pioneering book *José Can You See?* Alberto Sandoval-Sánchez explains that Franklin D. Roosevelt's Good Neighbor Policy of 1933 created a big incentive to establish Pan-American unity.[30] Since it was in the United States' best interest to protect its profitable Latin American investments, Hollywood and Broadway became vehicles for promoting this partnership. Miranda—along with Desi Arnaz—became "the iconic mediators and cultural promoters of the Good Neighbor policy."[31] Miranda's emblematic costume gave her the title Queen of All Banana Republics, and her choral refrains, which were at times reduced to gibberish, reminded spectators that the United States was profiting from Latin America's agricultural production.

Similar to the ways that Esteves manipulated her lawsuit against Papp into a theatrical event, La Bruja manipulates the face of Latin America during the 1930s in the song "For Witch It Stands." She reinscribes Miranda's costumes onto her own body to demonstrate her awareness of how Miranda's image was distorted, her body objectified, her singing reduced to mere noise. In controlling the visual and aural aspects of her work, La Bruja confronts spectators with a persona who performs and sings, but who also engineers her own image, words, and sounds. She is erotic but not objectified, sexual but intelligible, and a masterful wordsmith.

La Bruja disrupts the stereotypes of witches in her rap:

So no! I don't kills chickens or do voodoo pin stick-ins
And my mission isn't wicked
Superstitions are wicked, no Spanish inquisition
Spooky premonitions
No treat and no trickin'
It's just oral tradition
I only spell with words
Verbal incantations
It's old tense so don't ask me again what the name meant

In her music video, she raps and intermittently crouches down to tend to a brewing pot on a flaming fire. Powerfully chanting "Una bruja buena poeta-curandera" (a good witch poet-healer), La Bruja demystifies signifiers of African-influenced religious practices—such as black magic, voodoo pin dolls, and the sacrifice of poultry—by declaring that the only spell that she brews is her performance of poetry. Drawing from the Nuyorican poetry aesthetic, she returns to oration as a strategy to debunk the stereotypes of witches. Just as Esteves understands that healing trauma necessitates performative elements, La Bruja emphasizes that her poetic performances have curative properties. As a *bruja-curandera* spiritual activist, she embodies a spiritual *conocimiento* and creates alternative sources of knowledge for others. She remarked in an interview, "everyone has a *brujo* or *bruja* inside that they can use their own magic to do positive things. . . . I hope to inspire people to find the magic in themselves."[32]

In *Boogie Rican Boulevard,* La Bruja enacts characters who experience spiritual enlightenments to transcend the social barriers of disenfranchised communities like the Bronx. The characters Marta and Espiritsta bring a spiritual presence to this piece. Marta is a young woman who goes to the park to smoke, but she stops when she meets a Buddhist. She enters the scene hoping to smoke a blunt, but she has forgotten her lighter. Frustrated, she asks someone "for a light." Although we neither see nor hear the person from whom Marta requests a light, the audience can speculate about the individual from Marta's comments. Marta coquettishly calls out, "Excuse me.

Excuse me. Come over here please. You have a light for this?" There is a brief pause, and she apologetically continues, "I saw the dreads. I figured you were a Rasta. You're not? I'm sorry." La Bruja plays with the associations made by one's appearance. First, Marta assumes that because this individual has dreadlocks, he smokes weed and would therefore carry a light. Then, when she asks him for his name, Marta does not understand his reply. She asks, "What kind of name is that? A Buddhist name? What is that?" She playfully responds, "I am a Buddhist, too."[33] The audience breaks out in laughter over Marta's mistaking the self-declared Buddhist for a Rastafarian.

Despite her joking demeanor, the Buddhist agrees to give Marta a light, but only if she tells him what stresses cause her to smoke. She explains that her longtime boyfriend is "playing her like a record," but that he denies it and accuses her of being "cuernophobic." This invented Spanglish word—reminiscent of the Nuyorican style of creating a new language—incites great laughter. As a talented wordsmith, La Bruja draws from the Spanish idiom "poner los cuernos" (to be unfaithful, cheat, or to make a cuckold of) and invents the slyly humorous new word.[34] "Cuernophobic" then refers to the insecurity that Marta is feeling about being cheated on, or as La Bruja described in an interview, what is a "a common condition when you are in love with a playboy."[35] At this point, the Buddhist attempts to calm her down and invites her to chant Myōhō Renge Kyō. Marta jokingly responds that she will try the Spanish version, and she sings, "¿Mamí qué será lo que quiere el negro?" (Momma, what is it the Black man wants?), which is the choral refrain of "El Africano" (1983), sung by Dominican merengue singer Wilfrido Vargas. In the song, a girl complains to her mother about an angry Black man who has harassed her, but here, Marta sings about what the Black Buddhist wants from her. La Bruja shatters the hypersexualized image of Black men by placing them in a spiritual realm in relation to her body. After several other humorous detours, the Buddhist asks Marta to close her eyes and repeat the chant Myōhō Renge Kyō, with a focus on world peace. At the end of her recitation, Marta feels so much better that she no longer needs to smoke, at least not until the Buddhist leaves.

The Buddhist is a ghostlike presence that is only fully realized by the audience's imagination. La Bruja expresses the spiritual as unseen, although the references to his hairstyle and race allow the audience to imagine an embodied Buddhist. La Bruja not only racializes spirituality but genders it, as when Marta attempts to identify with a religion about which she knows nothing. La Bruja plays with preconceived constructs of race and religion.

Marta paints an image of a male Black Buddhist with dreadlocks. Although there are irreconcilable racial, religious, and gender differences between the Buddhist and Marta, La Bruja cultivates a consciousness of self and others. La Bruja creates Marta to navigate from the self to the collective, redirecting the quotidian experiences of the heart to global affairs. Marta's concerns about her unfaithful partner are now informed by the Buddhist practice of mindfulness. That is, the suffering caused by the betrayal of her partner is one that she creates and tolerates. Now that she can envision a global perspective, she can create that part of the world in her life. This scene is a journey of enlightenment, in which Marta receives a different light, one that leads her on a different path.

After enacting several other characters, La Bruja takes a ten-minute intermission. Upon her return, she emerges wearing a long white dress instead of her usual sweatshirt and baggy jeans. A red velvet turban covers her head, and a maraca necklace hangs on her neck. She lights several candles and begins to play the drums. The beats of the drums replace the hip hop beat that played during the intermission. Now La Bruja chants about the orishas—such as Shango, Babalú Ayé, and Ogún—who echo in the same space where she rapped before. She sings: "Si los espíritus me oyen, que viva Shango, que viva Shango" (If the spirits can hear me, long live Shango. Long live Shango). This chanting is her way to tap into the spiritual world. She continues jubilantly, asking the audience: "The music feels good, right? Let the spirit fill you. Let it fly all over the room and come back right inside you. Do you know how protected you are? How loved you are? But life has funny choices. You have to find that balance." She leaves the stage and walks into the audience: "Anybody have any questions this evening? Vamos a leer las cartas. ¿Quien quiere saber? ¿Quien tiene una pregunta?" (Let's read the cards. Who wants to know? Who has a question?)[36]

La Bruja, who has enacted a series of everyday common people, now asserts her *bruja-curandera* identity. She embodies the role of Espiritista. There is a sense of confusion among the audience members, since they are not sure whether the performance is an actual spiritual ritual—especially with the ceremonial music, songs, and card reading. These audience members—by the mere fact of their presence—have unknowingly become her clients, looking for advice or guidance. When asking whether members of the audience can feel a spiritual presence, she attempts to materialize what is unseen. She teaches the audience to discuss the experiences related to the body, while also acknowledging that there are experiences that are felt outside the body. She renders everyone in the theatrical space spiritual beings, interrelated and connected. The idea here is to heal the fragmented spirit and flesh—the us and them, the I and it.

If *La Cura* and *Boogie Rican Boulevard* bridge the social with the spiritual, then Mariposa's *DiaspoRican Dementia* (2001) uses the artist's familial history to strengthen this link. *DiaspoRican Dementia* is an autobiographical, one-woman performance of the artist's transformation from María Teresa Fernández—her given name—to Mariposa (Butterfly), the woman that she is today. As Fernández, she is a victim caught in the web of oppression. As Mariposa, she taps into cultural practices to heal from mental, physical, and spiritual ailments caused by the traumatic experiences of racism and sexism. She takes the audience through the stages of her life. Like a butterfly, she undergoes several metamorphoses to break through specific oppressive nets. She plays the role of herself as a Catholic schoolgirl, often punished for expressing her ideas. She reveals how, at a young age, religion piqued her curiosity, as she pleads in prayer, "but why, why can't I say this or do that?" She then reenacts her time in a psychiatric ward, asking God why she has been labeled insane for burning a copy of *Hustler* in a bathtub. She also plays her uncle, a revolutionary figure who was lost in a diagnosis of mental illness, and who eventually died in a mental institution. And she plays her mother, who always interrogated the many unconventional decisions that she made, yet who eventually becomes a source of inspiration. Mariposa explains how the systemic-*isms* in our society literally drove her and other family members insane. In this way, she takes the individual and community through a history of oppression toward a new path of healing.

In the final act, Mariposa states that, for her to transform, she must undergo the process of rebirth. In a voice-over, she shares a letter that she wrote to her family. She says in the letter that she has started practicing alternative medicine to cope with depression. She has become a vegetarian and detoxified her body with homeopathic remedies. She declares that she is not lost, not fragmented, not colonized, but whole and free. She tells her family how she will shave her hair and claim a new name, Mariposa, which many indigenous cultures associate with a warrior. This five-minute voice-over takes on a ghostly aesthetic, expressing the spiritual as a disembodied, aural element. As the stage light dims, the voiceover ends, and two drummers enter. They play bomba, a defining musical sound of the Afro–Puerto Rican population, and Mariposa enters in her white, flowing dress. Her white dress evokes the transience of her spiritual healing process. She dances with enthusiasm, invigorating the audience members as they applaud and welcome her, reborn as Mariposa.

Mariposa centers the body to articulate her transformative, spiritual, and healing journey. As suggested by the shift from a past-present body to an absent body to a reborn-present body, this articulation of the spiritual healing process demands that Mariposa speak from the body, and that the audience learn from the body. She uses her body—in its multiple identities—to illuminate how racism, sexism, elitism, and colonialism manifest in the physical, mental, and spiritual experiences of marginalized people. The spiritual journey that both Esteves and La Bruja advocate is one that audience members witness in Mariposa's performance.

TOWARD A METHODOLOGY OF READING SPIRITUALITY AND SPIRITUAL ACTIVISM IN THEATER AND PERFORMANCE

Drawing from the monumental work of Anzaldúa and Moraga, I have illustrated how Nuyorican performeras are spiritual activists, taking on *bruja-curandera* positions. I put Sandra María Esteves in dialogue with hip hop solo performers La Bruja, Mariposa, and Aya de León to understand how their performances operated as communal cleansing rituals that fused the spiritual, the political, and the intellectual—elements that are fundamental to Nuyorican feminist aesthetic practices. Equally important is the agency of these working-class Latina artists who found individual and collective refuge in bringing the sacred into the fabric of their performances.

To what extent can the spiritual shape the way that theater historians read the past? To read spirituality as a practice of identity requires theater historians to consider alternative methodological approaches. Laura Pérez proposes to theorize spirituality as a form of epistemology, one that recounts and reenacts what artists and spectators intuitively feel or know, rather than what they see, hear, or touch.[37] Only the latter has been the subject of discussion in most essays about theater and spirituality. It is difficult to theorize spirituality and to position it as the object of study because doing so means engaging knowledge beyond the material world. The challenge is to find the vocabulary that best describes the metaphysical dimensions of theatrical works. Since what is familiar is the material world, this materiality becomes the citational reference for understanding spirituality.

In traditional theater studies, scholars have interpreted the spirit world as an opportunity to stage a theatrical spectacle. Take, for instance, the infamous apparition of Banquo's ghost in *Macbeth*. Popular discourse finds Banquo as a staging device that shows how Lady Macbeth has been driven to madness. In a more contemporary context, August Wilson's *The Piano Lesson* features ghosts that haunt Berniece and Boy Willie, reminding them that their beloved family piano carries the legacies of slavery, murder, revenge, and retribution. In both plays, the incorporation of spirituality yields to theatrical spectacle to recall the past.

Dipesh Chakrabarty observes in "The Time of History and the Times of God" that there is a process of assigning people, places, and objects to existing historical frameworks. He argues that history tends to mediate the supernatural in terms of the universal.[38] When theater studies relegate spiritual expressions to staging devices—rather than treating them as systems of experiences and beliefs—it erases "a field of difference" and forces scholars into "a universal language."[39] That is, when gods, spirits, ghosts, and the divine power become mere stage devices, the spiritual dimensions are assimilated into the continuum of theater history. Marvin Carlson's *The Haunted Stage* traces a history of ghosting as a staging device across time. Elinor Fuchs's *The Death of the Character: Perspectives on Theater after Modernism* suggests that the occult overtones in the works of Antonin Artaud, Samuel Beckett, Bertolt Brecht, and Georg Kaiser are part of a tradition in which characters function as signs. Both these texts offer insightful frameworks with which to read dramatic works. Yet, using these frameworks normalizes spirituality into theatrical terms, assimilating it into the continuum of theater history.

How then can spirituality be included in the history of theater, when it has been virtually reduced to signs or ornaments? In conclusion, I want to consider Aya de León's annual self-marriage ceremonies (coincidentally, Mariposa also went through the rite of passage of marrying herself). In 1996, de León married herself, which she wrote about in *Essence* magazine (June 1997). After undergoing the transformative process of committing to unconditionally loving herself, she decided in 2004 to organize public self-marriage ceremonies every Valentine's Day. A flier (figure 21) makes a call for "brides of all genders," and she further elaborates in her email blasts: "Whether you are female, male, trans, other, married, divorced, coupled, singled, or dating, everyone needs self-love and self-care. We are the ones we've always been waiting for." While this event might not be a theatrical performance in the traditional sense of the word, it merits a performance analysis. As part of per-

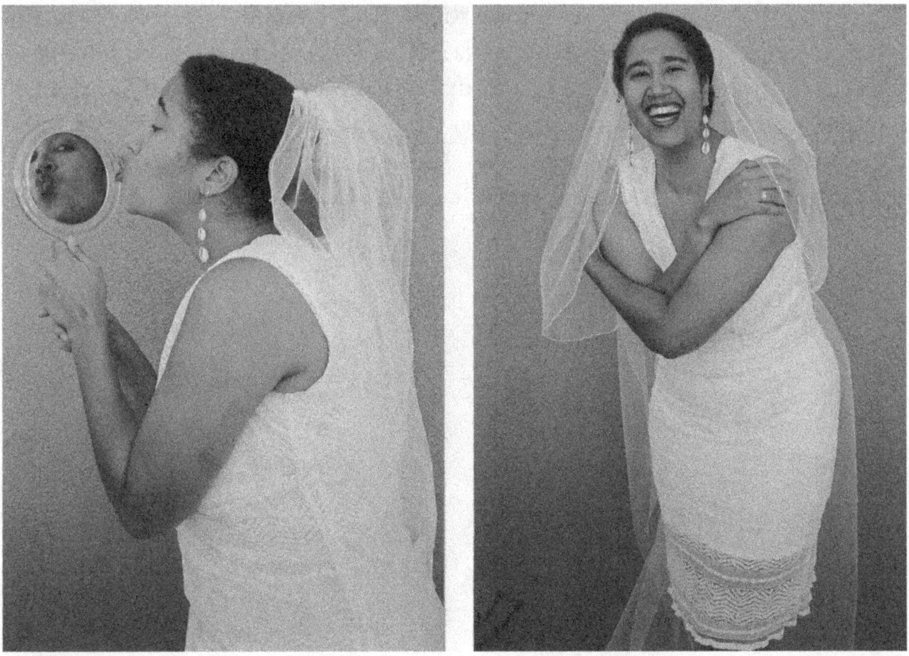

Figure 21. Flier for Aya de León's Self-Marriage Ceremony, February 14, 2004. Photo and courtesy by Anna de León.

forming the wedding ritual, participants write and make their vows, put on rings, take pictures, catch bouquets, eat cake, dance, and celebrate with loved ones.

If we were to read the self-marriage ceremony devoid of its spiritual intent, it could easily be mistaken for a mass spectacle. Considering the dimensions of spirituality offers another lens, one that allows us to understand the profound rite of passage into wholeness, self-liberation, and love sourced from within, as de León advertises in her flier. This ritual of transformation is a proclamation to one's self in a collective setting. As a feminist artist, de León uses theater to subvert one of the most prominent topics in women's lives—marriage—which illuminates the potential for theater to become a nonhegemonic space. That is, her performance of a self-marriage ceremony is indicative of the ways that historians need to reconsider how artists use theater unconventionally and inclusively. We cannot legally marry ourselves, but the very act of performing the wedding rituals puts the possibility of self-marriage in question. The ceremony also reveals how women use spirituality in a theatrical setting to reinsert themselves into history. Furthermore, de León's performance is a warning to theater historians that, if we continue to look at theater through its conventional lens, we will continue to erase some of our most valuable participants—women—just like Esteves experienced with her Nuyorican male counterparts.

Epilogue

AT THE NATIONAL CONVENING of the 2013 Latina/o Theatre Commons—the first *encuentro* (meeting) since 1986—Latinx actors, directors, producers, playwrights, and scholars gathered in Boston to share the past, current, and future state of Latinx theater making in the United States. In one of the sessions, Richard Montoya, a member of theater troupe Culture Clash, vividly recalled a story from his father—the renowned Chicano poet José Montoya—about a similar gathering with Nuyorican poets Miguel Piñero and Miguel Algarín, among others. Montoya recounts this moment as if he were there. This memory becomes part of the fabric of Latinx theater history, as he parallels the significance of the earlier gathering among poets from the East and West Coasts to that of the 2013 Latina/o Theatre Commons *encuentro*. I heard this same anecdote when I saw Culture Clash's *Nuyorican Stories: Culture Clash in the City* (1999). *Nuyorican Stories* captured the vibrancy of the Nuyorican movement, a period of broad cultural, artistic, and political awakening that was led by second-generation Puerto Rican poets, visual artists, musicians, and dancers in New York City during the late 1960s and 1970s.

Precisely because the arts were vital to the expression of oppressive conditions faced by Puerto Ricans living in New York City, artist-activists became central to *Nuyorican Stories*. Among these notable Nuyorican artists were avant-garde poets Miguel Piñero, Miguel Algarín, and Pedro Pietri; salsa singer Héctor Lavoe; and photographer Máximo Colón. *Nuyorican Stories* memorialized a politically charged period in which Latinxs—namely Nuyoricans and Chicanxs—were social agents inspiring and mobilizing people in their respective communities. This theater production was the first to focus exclusively on the Nuyorican movement and to incorporate the words of living people to understand a critical moment in Latinx history.

While Montoya was profoundly moved by the collectivity of the *encuen-*

tro, the narrative that he offered centered on male poets. All I remembered about *Nuyorican Stories* was that, while the Culture Clash celebrated the cultural production of Nuyoricans, heteropatriarchy was infused in the play's interpretation of Nuyorican history, eliding key female figures who were equal partners in this cultural movement.[1] Women played minor roles in *Nuyorican Stories*, and the two female characters that Culture Clash portrayed were either melodramatic or melancholic. An examination of the dramatic placement of female characters in the play highlights the roles that women play in this docudrama. It also demonstrates how women's involvement in the movement always came at the expense of self and family.

By the time that the audience met the two female activists, Becky Boricua and Olguie, Culture Clash had already established some of the key male players in the Nuyorican movement, including Algarín, Piñero, Colón, and Junior. Thus, the female characters did not drive the story. More importantly, their presence was not missed, since Culture Clash engrained a male-centric Puerto Rican nationalist imaginary. In the scene before Becky Boricua and Olguie were introduced, Culture Clash reminded us of the pride and anger that invigorated the Nuyorican movement. Herbert Siguenza portrayed Máximo Colón, a pro-independence photographer. Expressing frustration at the lackadaisical stance of the 1990s generation, Colón remembered how, during the 1970s, the Puerto Rican Parade felt "like a big *familia*," gracing the streets of New York City with *la bandera puertoriqueña*. As he recalled this feeling of pride, he unfurled a curtain—a Puerto Rican flag—across the stage, and then he called out the names of political prisoners who were released in 1999. When he announced each name—as if rehearsed—the audience responded *presente* (present). "Edwin Cortés. Presente! Elizam Escobar. Presente! Ricardo Jiménez. Presente! Adolfo Matos. Presente! Antonio Camacho Négron. Presente! Alejandrina Torres. Presente! Juan Enrique Segarra-Palmer, *presente*. . . . Dylcia Pagán. Presente! Que Viva Puerto Rico Libre. Que Viva!" (Long live free Puerto Rico. Long live!).[2]

The utilization of a flag—which eventually covered the entire back wall of the theater—and the audience's participation in paying homage to those who put their lives at risk corporealized Puerto Rican national belonging. Although these political prisoners were not physically present, the audience's response beckoned their presence. The utterance of *presente* acknowledged their courage to fight for Puerto Rico's independence. This moment was even more salient because just two weeks before the opening of *Nuyori-*

can Stories, President Clinton had granted Dylcia Pagan clemency after an eighteen-year incarceration. Culture Clash further reminded the audience of how Puerto Ricans put their lives in danger in the name of *la bandera* (the flag). The group projected black and white newsreel footage showing Lolita Lebrón and other nationalists being arrested for attacking the US House of Representatives on July 8, 1954. Embodying prominent artist-activists from the Nuyorican movement while unveiling the curtain of *la bandera* conjures the presence of the political prisoners who are clearly not there. Showing archival footage of nationalists being detained served as a catalyst to encourage a Puerto Rican nationalist imaginary, which has extended across oceans and even through prison bars. This helped inscribe the body of Puerto Ricans and Nuyoricans back into history of America.

While this newsreel footage called attention to the nationalist work of women since the 1950s—and also created a continuum with the activist work of Nuyorican women in the 1970s—Culture Clash positioned these women as triggers of both humor and sadness. Unlike most scenes, which usually stayed in the style of realism, with light moments of humor, Culture Clash performed the scene with Becky Boricua in a melodramatic style. A voiceover—evocative of the dramatic narration of Superman—introduced Becky Boricua to the stage: "Faster than a speeding bullet! More powerful than a locomotive!" This superhero, however, is a barrio heroine, who exceeds the likes of her Black or white peers: "Look out Cleopatra Jones, step aside Charlie Angels. There's a new super barrio hero in town. Straight out of the Loisada—it's Becky Bori[c]ua!" She is a "soul sister and defender of the barrio," and "the only thing [she] hates more than junkies and statehooders is honky pigs."[3] The audience laughs at what is clearly a superhero satire. Like her male activist peers, she is committed to improving the living conditions of her neighborhood by creating a drug-free zone; however, to be heard she must act a certain way—over the top.

For every superhero, there is a villain, and in this scene, there are two: O'Hara, the "honky pig" police officer, and Mofongo Man, the Puerto Rican junkie. This scene is full of racial and ethnic jokes, which produce ubiquitous laughter. At the sight of Becky Boricua, O'Hara insists that she needs to go home to cook *platanos* (plantains) and take care of her five mixed kids. O'Hara chides Becky for her activism and relegates her to domesticity. Regardless of O'Hara's misogynist perceptions, Becky Boricua labors to save her neighborhood from drug infestations, so that her community can live in a safe space.

Becky Boricua works to get drug dealers, like Mofongo Man, off the streets, but this task comes with several challenges. Mofongo Man's entrance song, "Pusherman" (1972) by Curtis Mayfield, glorifies his occupation as a drug dealer.[4] As in the song, Culture Clash portrays how Mofongo Man controls the community. When Becky Boricua asks O'Hara for his assistance in getting Mofongo Man off the streets, he responds: "Oh no child, I'm in cahoots with Mofongo Man, I protect him! He does whatever I say. Right? Riverdance for me, negro!"[5] *Nuyorican Stories* alludes to how, even though there were initiatives that served Black and Latinx communities, there was also a larger mechanism in place that proliferated the drug infestation.

This scene suggests that the judicial system is partially responsible for maintaining the drug epidemic of the 1970s. That is, O'Hara, the police officer, uses Mofongo Man as the face of power in the streets. The latter's ethnoracial identity positions him as a trustworthy insider who can successful deal drugs, but all the while, O'Hara controls Mofongo Man, profiting from his drug transactions. While O'Hara represents the police corruption, his thick Irish accent also reminds the audience how the Lower East Side of New York City was populated by Irish immigrants. With the increasing numbers of Puerto Rican migrants moving to the Lower East Side, some Irish immigrants fled elsewhere in the city, while others stayed, stirring tension among Irish and Puerto Rican immigrants. Thus, O'Hara legitimizes his misuse of police power because of his resentment of Puerto Rican migrants, who—he believes—are taking over what used to be "his" territory.

A superhero spoof cannot end without a fight scene with the villain. Of course, O'Hara simply watches while Mofongo Man fights Becky Boricua. Every superhero has their special powers; Mofongo Man squeezes the toxic garlic juices from his high Afro—which is made out of *mofongo* (a Puerto Rican dish of mashed, fried plantains)—as his weapon to blind his enemies. Becky Boricua, on the other hand, carries homemade remedies from the *botánica* (a retail store that sells herbs, charms, and other spiritual items) as her artillery.

The Afros of Mofongo Man and Becky Boricua racially mark them as Black Latinxs, which expands and complicates perceptions of Latinx identity. Culture Clash further codes this scene with cultural signifiers that function as absurd or comical. Mofongo Man, for instance, pokes fun at Becky Boricua by calling her Becky Bacalao (dried salt cod). When he sprays her with *mojo de ajo* (garlic juice) from his *mofongo* Afro, she exclaims that she is blind like José Feliciano, the renowned Puerto Rican guitarist, singer, and composer. Although the fight is close, Becky Boricua rescues the day with her homemade remedy.

Mofongo Man exits the stage exclaiming, "I am melting," and Becky Boricua proclaims: "I am Becky Bori[c]ua, Independentista and righteous soul sister. Defending life, liberty, justice, and the Nuyorican way! And now I have to go clean up the Bronx! Qué viva la mujer. [Long live women.] Damn—I broke a nail!"[6] This tension between the revolutionary woman and the superficial fashionista stirs up a lot of laughter. In addition, Becky's Afro hairstyle and militant sartorial style—reminiscent of the Black Panthers or the Young Lords—is a visual communication to America that, despite what white society feels, she is proud of her cultural and racial identity. However, after a grueling fight with Mofongo Man, the only injury that concerns Becky is her broken nail. As such, Culture Clash's melodramatic spoof of Becky as a superhero fashion queen reduces her desire to end the drug infestation in her neighborhood to petty notions of femininity.

Becky's concerns about breaking her nails, messing up her Afro, and dirtying her army fatigue jacket or bell-bottom jeans undercut her work as a female community activist. Rather than centering on Becky Boricua's efforts to improve her living conditions and advocate for social equity, Culture Clash recasts her revolutionary act as a labor of love that is not taken seriously. The group sees her action as dictated by melodrama, comedy, and notions of beauty and femininity. So, while this scene acknowledges the participation of women in the Nuyorican movement, the melodramatic portrayal of Becky situates the men as doing the "serious" work of social justice and makes the women's labor at most, insignificant—or at worst, a joke.

Culture Clash juxtaposes the exaggerated portrayal of Becky with a melancholic representation of Olguie, performed by Richard Montoya. Sacrifice, loss, and pain all replace the humor invoked by Becky Boricua. In this scene, Olguie shares that her sixteen-year-old son is afraid of being shot by a cop, and he does not want to go to school. She recalls that she joined the Young Lords at this age, and she was involved with the breakfast programs, clothing drives, and TB testing provided to the Bronx community. She was brave enough to confront a gang member on a roof, after he was throwing Molotov cocktails from one building to another, and a crib caught on fire. Her son, on the other hand, fears the authorities. As she expresses her anxiety, a merengue song welcomes Mayor Guiliani. Olguie's son, played by Ric Salinas, enters, wearing a baseball cap, baggy pants, and an oversized sweater. He stares at Mayor Guiliani with disapproval. Then, suddenly, Mayor Guiliani pulls a gun out and shoots Olguie's son.

As with the shooting of Trayvon Martin, Olguie's son's clothing and mannerisms made him a target.[7] The fact that Major Giuliani is the person who shoots Olguie's son complicates this scene. During his time as mayor, Giuliani earned a reputation for cracking down on crime. While criminal activity decreased, young people of color also became easy targets for criminal charges, police harassment, or brutality. On the one hand, Culture Clash reinforces the idea that the life of Olguie's son comes to an end as the cost of cleaning up the neighborhood. On the other, the death of the boy comes as a direct result of Olguie's involvement with social and political work. The mixed message is that, when women participate in political work, there can be tragic consequences.

Ultimately, while this scene acknowledges the political work of women, this work comes at the expense of Olguie's child. For women, being an activist means being always at a loss: Becky Boricua gives up her revolutionary chutzpah for beauty, and for Olguie, she loses a child in the name of activism. If they are activists, their loyalty can only be to the revolution. They cannot be women, mothers, and activists. For mothers, activism can only come at the expense of their families. Like O'Hara proclaims, if a woman is not a mother—as in the case of Becky Boricua—then "[she is] acting like that lesbian Angela Davis."[8] In other words, if she is not a lesbian, her radicalism resorts to superficial beauty (a broken nail). These sexist and homophobic enactments, although skillfully and humorously performed, speak to how the community stigmatized women involved in the Nuyorican movement.

As Culture Clash reveals, even in the act of practicing equity and belonging, members of the Nuyorican movement undermined the participation of women and queers. This elision raises questions about how Nuyorican history is written and performed. There is certainly a scholarly gap in the Nuyorican historical narratives being written, a gap that privileges men and heteronormativity. This book attempts to fill that void. During the Nuyorican movement—and many other movements of the 1960s and 1970s—women were invisible to the poetry and theater scene. The Nuyorican Poets Café developed a performance aesthetic that appealed to people on the cultural frontlines of street politics. By mapping out the performance traditions from the café, this book examines the strategies of belonging, in the Nuyorican arts scene and beyond. This practice marks individuals and communities who create networks based on social kinships; artistic affinities; cultural affiliations; and political ideologies, which invite civic dialogue, propel social action, and incite social change.

Although the café committed itself to social equity, this commitment existed alongside a troubling history of gender politics. The masculinist ethos of the café made it difficult for women to thrive in the 1970s Nuyorican scene. Nuyorican performeras of the 1970s—such as Sandra María Esteves, Amina Muñoz, and Luz Rodriguez—were marginalized. To counter their invisibility, women used feminist practices that have carved avenues for contemporary performeras, such as La Bruja, Mariposa, Nilaja Sun, and Aya de León, who carried on the Nuyorican feminist aesthetic. By privileging these women throughout this book, I examine how a Nuyorican feminist aesthetic works into their literary, visual, and theatrical works. They develop feminist strategies of belonging to counter patriarchal dominance, while also embracing their culture and advocating for cultural difference.

Building on the performance traditions forged by women in the post–civil rights era, I turn to La Bruja, Nilaja Sun, Mariposa, and Aya de León, all of whom expand the practices of a Nuyorican poetry aesthetic by interweaving hip hop, solo performance, and other art forms in which text, movement, and sound do not necessarily begin with a script. These female performers problematize notions of Blackness and Latinidad, and they reflect on their Afro-Latina identity and women's contributions to hip hop.

The performeras interweave multiple artistic modalities to create hybrid performance genres. More importantly, they address the contributions of women to the movement. They bring hip hop, poetry, and theater together; weave the past in the present; blur the political and the personal; and conjure up the spiritual world. These women construct a platform on which they can document, reflect, contest, and reimagine their social roles, both as Latinas and as global citizens. More importantly, this hybrid performance strategy encourages artists to develop female communal networks, in which women—rather than men—establish community.

It is my hope that this book adds to the growing work on the continuum of Nuyorican feminist aesthetics and creates a platform that narrates this collective history. The work of the performeras emphasizes overcoming gender-based obstacles, thus recovering the archive of feminist poetic, theatrical, and performative modes of community and expression. These Nuyoriqueñas dared to speak the unspeakable truths about the history of gender oppression.

Notes

Prologue

1. Rubí produced theatrical adaptations of Martín Espada's book of poetry *Imagine the Angels of Bread* (1999), Nicholasa Mohr's collection of stories El Bronx Remembered (1999), and the bilingual children's book *A Woman Who Outshone the Sun* (2003). The company conducted performances and workshops at Brooklyn Arts Exchange; Pregones; INTAR; Dixon Place; the second Hip-Hop Theater Festival at PS 122; the International Community Theatre Festival in Rotterdam, the Netherlands; New Jersey Performing Arts Center; Nuyorican Poets Café; Puerto Rican Traveling Theater; and New WORLD Theater. Rubí has also appeared on Dan Zanes's *¡Nueva York!* (2008), *Catch that Train!* (2006, Grammy Award for Best Children's Musical Album), *House Party* (2003), and *Night Time!* (2002).

2. bell hooks's words resonate strongly here. She states: "Living as we did—on the edge—we developed a particular way of seeing reality. We looked from both the outside in and the inside out. We focused our attention on the center as well as the margin. We understood both. This mode of seeing reminded us of the existence of a whole universe, a main body made up of both margin and center." *Feminist Theory: From Margin to Center* (Cambridge, MA: South End Press, 2000), xvi.

3. Cherríe Moraga and Gloria E. Anzaldúa, *The Bridge Called My Back: Writings by Radical Women of Color* (New York: Kitchen Table/Women of Color Press, 1983), 23.

4. Spirituality, as C. Alejandra Elenes explains, "is a way of understanding someone's (or a community's) position in the world by trying to make sense of unfair economic conditions and gender inequality, and to do something about it." "Spiritual Roots of Chicana Feminist Borderland Pedagogies: A Spiritual Journey with Tonantzin/Guadalupe," in *Fleshing the Spirit: Spirituality and Activism in Chicana, Latina, and Indigenous Women's Lives*, ed. Elisa Facio and Irene Lara (Tucson: University of Arizona Press, 2014), 44.

5. Inés Hernández-Avila, "In the Presence of Spirit(s): A Meditation on the Politics of Solidarity and Transformation," in *This Bridge We Call Home: Radical Visions for Transformation*, ed. Gloria E. Anzaldúa and AnaLouise Keating (New York: Routledge, 2002), 532.

6. Norma E. Cantú's thinking of spiritual activism as "living a holistic life focused

on issues of social justice" is especially illuminating. As she explains, "Spirituality and activist actions are related. We touch the spirit when we change the world with our actions, and it is spirit that 'inspires' right action, especially our social justice actions." This positive domino effect is at the crux of theater for social change. "Living La Vida Santa: My Chicana Spirituality and Activist Scholarship," in Facio and Lara, *Fleshing the Spirit*, 216.

7. During the civil rights era, organizations like ASPIRA (1961), Real Great Society (1964), the Puerto Rican Traveling Theater (1967), El Museo del Barrio (1969), the Young Lords Party (1969), Taller Boricua (1970), the Nuyorican Poets Café (1973), and New Rican Village (1976) grew out of social activism in the Puerto Rican community. These groups demonstrate the ways that Nuyoricans created forums for Puerto Rican communities to express and affirm their identity. These organizations also fought for Puerto Ricans' rights as citizens who contributed to the American economy, culture, and society.

8. I am joining a cadre of scholars, activists, journalists, and other allies who are using the term Latinx to move beyond gender binaries and underscore the need for a gender nonconforming, genderqueer, genderfluid alternative to Latina/o. For more insight on the significance of this linguistic change, see Catalina (Kathleen) M. De Onís, "What's in an 'X'? An Exchange about the Politics of 'Latinx,'" *Chiricú Journal: Latina/o Literatures, Arts, and Cultures* 1, no. 2 (2017): 78–91. The essay features a conversation with scholars Pilar Melero, Eric César Morales, Roy Pérez, Sandra L. Soto-Santiago, and Stacey K. Sowards about the politics of Latinx. The debate over Latina/o and Latinx has also been covered in the popular press. See Nancy Bird-Soto, "¿Términos apropiados? El potencial latinx," *Cruce: Crítica Socio-cultural Contemporánea*, November 30, 2015, http://revistacruce.com/politica-y-sociedad/item/2255-terminos-apropiados-el-potencial-latinx; Gilbert Guerra and Gilbert Orbea, "The Argument against the Use of 'Latinx,'" *Phoenix* (Swarthmore College), November 19, 2015, http://swarthmorephoenix.com/2015/11/19/the-argument-against-the-use-of-the-term-latinx/; Raquel Reichard, "Why We Say Latinx: Trans & Gender Non-Conforming People Explain," *Latina*, August 29, 2015, https://www.latina.com/lifestyle/our-issues/why-we-say-latinx-trans-gender-non-conforming-people-explain; Lissette Rolón Collazo, "De la @ a la x," *80grados*, April 18, 2014, http://www.80grados.net/de-la-a-la-x/; and María R. Scharrón-del Río and Alan A. Aja, "The Case FOR 'Latinx': Why Intersectionality Is Not a Choice," *Latino Rebels*, December 5, 2015, http://www.latinorebels.com/2015/12/05/the-case-for-latinx-why-intersectionality-is-not-a-choice/

9. The migration of Puerto Ricans to the United States is such a definitive event in Puerto Rican history that many Nuyorican poets address it in their work. Sandra María Esteves, for instance, opens *Yerba Buena* (1980) by establishing how Operation Bootstrap profoundly shaped her identity. Similarly, in an interview—just days before his death—Pedro Pietri recalled the "darker side" of the industrialization plan: "I was born in 1949, because that's the day I went to the first theatre with my grandfather, who felt deceived by Operation Bootstrap and committed hara-kiri, but I don't think it was suicide. He was killed by the system that deceived him, the system that made him

sell his land in Borinquen." Pietri, "There Was Never No Tomorrow, Nuyorican Pedro Pietri in His Own Words," edited by Ramond Beltrán, *La Prensa*, February 6, 2004.

Pietri assumes 1949 as his birth year—instead of 1944, the year he was actually born—to stress how Operation Bootstrap shaped his experiences and identity. Historian Virginia Sánchez Korrol also refers to the detrimental impact of Operation Bootstrap as "the darker side." She notes, "in the early seventies it became clear that the Bootstrap industrialization plan also had its darker side: It never fully incorporated the island's growing population into the workforce; it displaced thousands from agrarian production and reinforced the island's dependency on the United States; and the radical decline of the island's agrarian sector had caused higher unemployment and an escalation in the importation of basic food staples." Sánchez Korrol, *From Colonia to Community: The History of Puerto Ricans in New York City* (Berkeley: University of California Press, 1994), 217.

10. For more on the diversity of Puerto Ricans and their community-building efforts, see Juan Flores, *The Diaspora Strikes Back: Caribeño Tales of Learning and Turning* (New York: Routledge, 2008); Carmen Teresa Whalen and Victor Vázquez-Hernández, eds., *Puerto Rican Diaspora: Historical Perspectives* (Philadelphia: Temple University Press, 2005); Arlene Dávila, *Barrio Dreams: Puerto Ricans, Latinos, and the Neoliberal City* (Berkeley: University of California Press, 2004); and Andrés Torres and José E. Velázquez, eds., *The Puerto Rican Movement: Voices from the Diaspora* (Philadelphia: Temple University Press, 1998).

11. More recently, Myrna Nieves's Spanish-English anthology of poems *Breaking Ground: Anthology of Puerto Rican Women Writers in New York 1980–2012/Abriendo caminos: Antología de escritoras Puertorriqueñas en Nueva York 1980–2012* (New York: Editorial Campana, 2012) included the works of Sandra María Esteves, Mariposa, and La Bruja.

12. James M. Harding's historiographical study of women in the avant-garde movement inspired me to think about the broader effects of gender and sexism and the feminist practices that engage and challenge a male-dominated world and the ways in which these practices change how we understand history. *Cutting Performance: Collage Events, Feminist Artists, and the American Avant-Garde* (Ann Arbor: University of Michigan Press, 2010).

Chapter 1

1. Sandra María Esteves was invited to perform and discuss her work as a part of a diversity initiative at Berkshire Community College. This gathering was entitled "Nuyorican Contrapunto."

2. Feminism as a political movement, tradition, or philosophy represents generational differences, and consequently, it has been categorized in terms of waves. The first wave of feminism took place in the late nineteenth and early twentieth centuries, growing out of the reform movements of the 1840s and 1850s. It formally began at the Seneca Falls Convention in 1848, when Elizabeth Cady Stanton drafted the Seneca Falls Declaration, establishing the ideology and political strategies of the women's

movement. The feminists of this era focused on suffrage and expanding opportunities for women, but they did not give voice to the suffrage rights of Black women. As African American abolitionist Sojourner Truth explained in her famous speech "Ain't I a Woman?" at the 1851 Women's Rights Convention, although the first wave of feminism intersected with the abolitionist movement, activists practiced feminism in a racist fashion.

Betty Friedan's *The Feminist Mystique* (1963) marked the beginning of the second wave of the feminist movement, which advocated for women to forgo housewifery in favor of professional careers in the 1960s and 1970s. This notion was radical for the time, and it struck a chord for many college-educated, middle- and upper-class, married white women. The main problem with the second wave, as bell hooks argued in *Feminist Theory* (1984), was that Friedan's vision of feminism was racist and classist, and it universalized women. It liberated white, upper-middle-class women from their domestic duties, but it neglected to consider who would do the domestic labor of raising children and maintaining house chores. Thus, Friedan's universalization of women actually contributed to the oppression of poor, working-class, women of color, which resulted in the widespread limitation of the second-wave feminist movement.

The feminists of the second-wave era led the campaign to pass the Equal Rights Amendment to the Constitution in 1972, guaranteeing social equality among men and women. But, as Benita Roth reveals in *Separate Roads to Feminism* (2004), although Black and Latina women agreed on basic issues—like reproductive rights, prevention of violence against women, low-cost high-quality child care, and increased educational and employment opportunities for women—the feminist movement lumped these groups of women together and erased their variant social histories. Roth moves away from the dominant historical narrative of a singular second wave of feminism. Instead, she examines the distinct and complex feminist mobilizations of white women, African American women, and Chicanas. See: Friedan, *The Feminist Mystique* (New York: W. W. Norton, 1963); hooks, *Feminist Theory: From Margin to Center*, 2nd ed. (Cambridge, MA: South End Press, 2000); and Roth, *Separate Roads to Feminism: Black, Chicana, and White Feminist Movements in America's Second Wave* (Cambridge: Cambridge University Press, 2004).

3. Kimberlé Crenshaw, "De-Marginalizing the Intersection of Race and Sex: A Black Feminist Critique of Antidiscrimination Doctrine, Feminist Theory, and Antiracist Politics," *University of Chicago Legal Forum* 1989, 139–67.

4. Esteves is not alone in this identification practice. Nuyorican writers—like Piri Thomas, who is Cuban–Puerto Rican—also emphasize their Nuyorican identity.

5. Sandra María Esteves, *Tropical Rain: A Bilingual Downpour* (New York: Caribbean Poetry Theater, 1984), 26.

6. "Poem for Closet Poets" was performed on November 30, 2006, at Berkshire Community College. It may also be found in Esteves's *Undelivered Love Poems* (New York: No Frills, 1997), 46.

7. Esteves, 46.

8. Qtd. in Mark Eleveld and Marc Kelly Smith, *The Spoken Word Revolution: Slam, Hip Hop & the Poetry of a New Generation* (Naperville, IL: Sourcebooks, 2003), 3.

9. Diana Raznovich's cartoon "PerFORwhat Studies?" (2000) contributed to my thinking about Nuyorican performeras. It was printed in Diana Taylor's *The Archive and the Repertoire: Performing Cultural Memory in the Americas* (Durham, NC: Duke University Press, 2003), 2; and in Taylor's article "Translating Performance," *Profession*, 2002, 45.

10. For scholarship on Latinx theater and performance, see Alberto Sandoval-Sánchez and Nancy Saporta Sternbach, *Stages of Life: Transcultural Performance and Identity in U.S. Latina Theater* (Tucson: University of Arizona Press, 2001); Sandoval-Sánchez, *José, Can You See? Latinos On and Off Broadway* (Madison: University of Wisconsin Press, 1999); Alicia Arrizón, *Latina Performance: Traversing the Stage* (Bloomington: Indiana University Press, 1999); Jorge Huerta's *Chicano Drama: Performance, Society and Myth* (Cambridge: Cambridge University Press, 2000); Huerta, *Chicano Theatre: Themes and Forms* (Ypsilanti, MI: Bilingual Press, 1982); David Román, *Performance in America: Contemporary US Culture and the Performing Arts* (Durham, NC: Duke University Press, 2005); and Román, *Acts of Intervention: Performance, Gay Culture, and AIDS* (Bloomington: Indiana University Press, 1998).

11. I am also inspired by Susan Gubar's notion of "feminism inside out." Gubar urges scholars to "consider again the urgency of tackling the tribulations contemporary women encounter daily: domestic and sexual violence; the nonexistence or erosion of civil, reproductive, and educational rights globally; the war-related calamities and casualties suffered by civilians, journalists, philanthropic volunteers, soldiers, and their families." "Feminism Inside Out," *PMLA* 121, no. 5 (2000): 1716.

12. Juan Flores's *Divided Borders: Essays on Puerto Rican Identity* (Houston, TX: Arte Público Press, 1993), *From Bomba to Hip-Hop: Puerto Rican Culture and Latino Identity* (New York: Columbia University Press, 2000), and *The Diaspora Strikes Back: Caribeño Tales of Learning and Turning* (New York: Routledge, 2008) explore a variety of artistic modalities to think about the complexities of how Puerto Ricans from the diaspora express their identity. Eugene Mohr's *The Nuyorican Experience: Literature of the Puerto Rican Minority* (Santa Barbara, CA: Praeger, 1982) and Lisa Sánchez González's *Boricua Literature: A Literary History of the Puerto Rican Diaspora* (New York: New York University Press, 2001) also opened up avenues for theorizing Nuyorican literature.

13. See Frances Negrón-Muntaner, *Boricua Pop: Puerto Ricans and the Latinization of American Culture* (New York: New York University Press, 2004); Arlene Dávila, *Barrio Dreams: Puerto Ricans, Latinos, and the Neoliberal City* (Berkeley: University of California Press, 2004); Dávila, *Latino Spin: Public Image and the Whitewashing of Race* (New York: New York University Press, 2008); and Dávila, *Culture Works: Space, Value, and Mobility across the Neoliberal Americas* (New York: New York University Press, 2012).

14. Urayoán Noel, *In Visible Movement: Nuyorican Poetry from the Sixties to Slam* (Iowa City: University of Iowa Press, 2014).

15. For a queer reading of Nuyorican performance practices see Karen Jaime's forthcoming book, *The Queer Nuyorican: Racialized Sexualities and Aesthetics in Loisaida*.

16. Other scholarship that has greatly influenced my thinking and has equipped me with theoretical frameworks to read the nuanced cultural histories and meanings

of Latina theater and performance includes: Ramón H. Rivera-Servera, *Performing Queer Latinidad: Dance, Sexuality, Politics* (Ann Arbor: University of Michigan Press, 2012); Jacqueline Lazú, "Nuyorican Theater: Prophecies and Monstrosities" (PhD diss., Stanford University, 2002); Alicia Arrizón, *Queering Mestizaje: Transculturation and Performance* (Ann Arbor: University of Michigan Press, 2006); and José Esteban Muñoz, *Disidentifications: Queers of Color and the Performance of Politics* (Minneapolis: University of Minnesota Press, 1999).

17. Noel, *In Visible Movement*, xvii.

18. Whitney A. Peoples explains that a new feminism addressing young women of color in the hip hop generation began as early as the mid-1990s. This genealogy allows for a deeper understanding of the continuities of third-wave, Black, and hip hop feminisms. "'Under Construction': Identifying Foundations of Hip-Hop Feminism and Exploring Bridges between Black Second-Wave and Hip-Hop Feminisms," *Meridians* 8, no. 1 (2008), 20. See also: Treva B. Lindsey, "Let Me Blow Your Mind: Hip Hop Feminist Futures in Theory and Praxis," *Urban Education* 50, no. 1 (2014): 56; Kristal Brent Zooks, "A Manifesto of Sorts for a Black Feminist Movement," *New York Times Magazine*, December 3, 1995; Joan Morgan, *When Chickenheads Come Home to Roost: My Life as a Hip-Hop Feminist* (New York: Simon and Schuster, 1999); and Morgan, "Hip-Hop Feminist," in *That's the Joint: The Hip Hop Studies Reader*, ed. Murray Forman and Mark Anthony Neal (New York: Routledge, 2012), 413–18.

19. Aisha S. Durham, *Home with Hip Hop Feminism: Performances in Communication and Culture* (New York: Peter Lang, 2014), 5; and Bakari Kitwani, *The Hip-Hop Generation: Young Blacks and the Crisis in African American Culture* (New York, New York: Basic Civitas, 2002), 4.

20. Durham, *Home with Hip Hop Feminism*, 5; and Kitwani, *The Hip-Hop Generation*, 37–43.

21. Durham, *Home with Hip Hop Feminism*, 5.

22. Lindsey, "Let Me Blow Your Mind," 56.

23. Joan Morgan, afterword to *Home Girls Make Some Noise: Hip Hop Feminism Anthology*, ed. Gwendolyn D. Pough, Elaine Richardson, Aisha Durham, and Rachel Raimist (Mira Loma, CA: Parker, 2007), 478.

24. Morgan, *When Chickenheads Come Home to Roost*, 58, 59.

25. Shani Jamila, "Can I Get a Witness? Testimony from a Hip-Hop Feminist," in *Colonize This! Young Women of Color on Today's Feminism*, ed. Daisy Hernández and Bushra Rehman (New York: Seal Press, 2002), 392.

26. Durham, *Home with Hip Hop Feminism*, 3. Hip hop feminism has greatly impacted the field of education. See Ruth Nicole Brown and Chamara Jewel Kwakye, eds., *Wish to Live: The Hip Hop Feminist Pedagogy Reader* (New York: Peter Lang, 2012); Bettina L. Love, *Hip Hop's Li'l Sistas Speak: Negotiating Hip Hop Identities and Politics in the New South* (New York: Peter Lang, 2012); and Lindsey, "Let Me Blow Your Mind." These scholars use hip hop feminism to teach audiences how to see, listen to, and read the complexities of women, their embodied knowledge, and the female body politics of representation with the aim of creating more inclusive communities.

27. Tricia Rose, *The Hip Hop Wars: What We Talk about When We Talk about Hip Hop and Why It Matters* (New York: Basic Civitas, 2008), 11.

28. For further discussion of the relationship between hip hop and the diaspora, see George Lipsitz, *Dangerous Crossroads: Popular Music, Postmodernism, and the Poetics of Place* (New York: Verso, 1997).

Chapter 2

1. Miguel "Mickey" Meléndez, *We Took the Streets: Fighting for Latino Rights with the Young Lords* (New York: St. Martin's Press, 2003), 103.

2. For essays and visual materials relating to the Young Lords, see: Young Lords Party, *Palante: Voices and Photographs of the Young Lords, 1969–1971*, photographs by Michael Abramson (New York: Haymarket Books, 1971); and Duane L. Jones, ed., "The Young Lords Party, 1969–1975," photographs by Hiram Maristany, text by Felipe Luciano, double issue, *Caribe* 7, no. 4 (1983).

3. *Caribe* dedicated a double issue to Hiram Maristany's photographic exhibition of the Young Lords Party, which was presented at the Caribbean Cultural Center in 1983. The picture of the Young Lords' headquarters with Martorell's image of Campos can be found in *Caribe* 7, no. 4 (1983): 29. This image was first featured in the Young Lords' newspaper, *Palante* 2, no. 3 (1970). Maristany's photographs were also exhibited in *El Barrio: Puerto Rican New York* at the Museum of the City of New York during spring 2005. This exhibition was organized by Kathleen Benson, curator of community projects, along with the Center for Puerto Rican Studies at Hunter College.

4. *Pedro Albizu Campos* (1969) was created at Taller Alacrán (Scorpion Workshop), a workshop and art school that Martorell established in 1968. Taller Alacrán was devoted to mentoring Puerto Rican and Caribbean artists, teaching graphic arts to youth, and addressing Puerto Rican politics and social conditions.

5. Members of the Nationalist Party and Communist Party, both in Puerto Rico and on the mainland, were placed under surveillance, and a number of their homes were raided by FBI agents.

6. For a historical account of the nationalistic acts led by Albizu Campos, see Antonio Stevens Arroyo, *The Political Philosophy of Pedro Albizu Campos: Its Theory and Practice* (New York: New York University, Ibero-American Language and Area Center, 1974). See also, Juan Rodriguez Cruz, *Pedro Albizu Campos: un asomo a su vida y su época* (San Juan, PR: Centro de Estudios Avanzados de Puerto Rico y el Caribe, 1994); and Nélida Pérez and Amilcar Tirado, eds., *Pedro Albizu Campos, 1891–1965* (New York: Centro de Estudios Puertorriqueños, 1986). José García Torres's film *The Nationalists*, edited by Israel Ortiz, written and narrated by Pablo Cabrera (New York: Realidades, 1973), VHS and DVD, 28 min., is also a useful source.

7. There are numerous sources that document the history of the Young Lords Party. Most recently, Darrel Enck-Wanzer has edited *The Young Lords: A Reader* (New York: New York University Press, 2010), which includes interviews, stories from *Palante*, speeches, and organizational documents. Other primary sources that grounded my research include: the Young Lords' publications *Ideology of the Young*

Lords Party (Bronx, NY: Young Lords Party, 1972) and *Palante: Young Lords Party* (1971); *Caribe*'s 1983 photographic narration of the history of the Young Lords (Jones, "The Young Lords Party, 1969–1975"); Meléndez's memoir, *We Took the Streets* (2003); and two video documentaries, Iris Morales's *¡Palante, Siempre Palante!* (1996) and the Young Lords' *El Pueblo Se Levanta* (1971).

8. The date was no accident. It coincides with the first offensive of the Cuban revolutionary struggle at the Moncada Fort in Santiago de Oriente. On July 26, 1953, exactly sixteen years earlier, Fidel Castro, alongside 150 comrades, assaulted the Moncada Barracks, the main provincial garrison of Fulgencio Batista's armed forces. Although the revolt failed, Castro earned recognition as a leader for opposing the Cuban dictator.

9. For a thorough discussion of the appropriation of *jíbaro* by the elite, see Lillian Guerra, *Popular Expression and National Identity in Puerto Rico: The Struggle for Self, Community, and Nation* (Gainesville: University Press of Florida, 1998). For a detailed study of how Luis Muñoz Marín manipulated the image of *el jíbaro* to fit the campaign discourse of the Popular Democratic Party, see Nathaniel L. Córdova, "In His Image and Likeness: The Puerto Rican Jíbaro as Political Icon," *Centro: Journal of the Center for Puerto Rican Studies* 17, no. 2 (2005): 171–91.

10. Urayoán Noel, *In Visible Movement: Nuyorican Poetry from the Sixties to Slam* (Iowa City: University of Iowa Press, 2014), xxi.

11. Felipe Luciano, "Jíbaro, My Pretty Nigger," in *Puerto Rican Poetry: An Anthology from Aboriginal to Contemporary Times*, ed. Roberto Márquez (Amherst: University of Massachusetts Press, 2006), 410.

12. Young Lords Party, *Palante* 3, no. 13 (1970): 16.

13. A young performer by the name of Augie introduces the children's play by stating "Our people are poor and you know damn real nobody wants to be poor. This play is going to show how the pigs react when the people take control over what belongs to them and liberate." He then assumes the character of a Young Lord and declares, "We want the breakfast program. We do not want to destroy the church." The children playing the role of the cops immediately attack him. Augie ends the scene encouraging the crowd to sing "Power to the People," which echoed in the People's Church, creating an atmosphere of strength, unity, and empowerment.

14. Iris Morales, *Through the Eyes of Rebel Women: The Young Lords, 1969–1976* (New York: Red Sugarcane Press, 2016), 43; see also, Morales and Denise Oliver-Velez, foreword to Enck-Wanzer, *The Young Lords*, ix–xiv.

15. Enck-Wanzer, *The Young Lords*, 163.

16. For more information on Puerto Rican nationalist heroines, see Olga Jiménez de Wagenheim, *Nationalist Heroines: Puerto Rican Women History Forgot, 1930s–1950s* (Princeton, NJ: Markus Wiener, 2016).

17. In *We Took the Streets*, Meléndez vaguely remembers how the Lords came up with the name for this initiative and suggests that they probably got it from the Vietnamese, who identified any type of political or military program action as an "offensive" (101).

18. Morales, *Through the Eyes of Rebel Women*, 16.

19. Morales, 19.

20. Morales, 20.

21. Miguel Algarín, "Introduction: Nuyorican Language," in *Nuyorican Poetry: An Anthology of Puerto Rican Words and Feelings*, ed. Miguel Algarín and Miguel Piñero (New York: William Morrow, 1975), 15.

22. Jaime Carrero, *Jet neorriqueño/Neo-Rican Jetliner* (San Germán, PR: Universidad Inter American, 1964), 49.

23. Robert L. Muckley, introduction to *Notes of Neorican Seminar*, ed. Jaime Carrero (San Germán, PR: Inter American University, 1972), 2.

24. This back-and-forth migration has been widely discussed. Ana Y. Ramos-Zayas states: "This phenomenon is one of the elements that differentiates Puerto Ricans as U.S. citizens, from other migrants from Latin American and Caribbean countries, whose legal status does not allow easy back-and-forth migration." Jorge Duany refers to this social phenomenon as *vaivén*; Alberto Sandoval-Sánchez explores the use of the metaphor of "air bridge" to facilitate the movement between Puerto Rico and the mainland. See: Ramos-Zayas, *National Performances: The Politics of Class, Race, and Space in Puerto Rican Chicago* (Chicago: University of Chicago Press, 2003), 31; Duany, *The Puerto Rican Nation on the Move: Identities on the Island and in the United States* (Chapel Hill: University of North Carolina Press, 2002), 2; Sandoval-Sánchez, "Puerto Rican Identity Up in the Air: Air Migration, Its Cultural Representations, and Me 'Cruzando el Charco,'" in *Puerto Rican Jam: Essays on Culture and Politics*, ed. Frances Negrón-Muntaner and Ramón Grosfoguel (Minneapolis: University of Minnesota Press, 1997), 203.

25. The works of Nuyorican poets have influenced the work of young poets from the island and have therefore redefined notions of Puerto Rican identity. See Guillermo Rebollo-Gil, "The New Boogaloo: Nuyorican Poetry and the Coming Puerto Rican Identities" (Master's thesis, University of Florida, 2004).

26. Efrén Rivera Ramos, for example, argues that US legal discourse produces Puerto Ricans as colonial subjects. See his study *The Legal Construction of Identity: The Judicial and Social Legacy of American Colonialism in Puerto Rico* (Washington, DC: American Psychological Association, 2001).

27. To date Puerto Ricans cannot vote in presidential elections, and do no have voting representatives in the US Congress, which means that the Jones Act amounted to "taxation without representation." For an extended discussion of Puerto Rican citizenship, see Lorrin Thomas, *Puerto Rican Citizen: History and Political Identity in Twentieth-Century New York City* (Chicago: University of Chicago Press, 2010). The question of citizenship is also addressed in Frances Negrón-Muntaner's edited anthology *None of the Above: Puerto Ricans in the Global Era* (New York: Palgrave Macmillan, 2007). The title *None of the Above* gestures at the voting results of the island-wide referendum in 1998. This referendum would decide the island's status in relation to the United States. Included on the ballot were five options: (1) commonwealth, as defined by the United States; (2) associated republic, implying the creation of a somewhat independent nation with protectorate terms; (3) independence, meaning the founding of a separate nation-state; (4) statehood, referring to joining the federal union as a

state with equal rights and responsibilities; and (5) none of the above. The "none of the above" option garnered the highest vote (50.3 percent), and statehood was the second highest (46.5 percent). The commonwealth vote was only 0.1 percent; associated republic received 0.3 percent; and independence received 2.5 percent of the vote (Negrón-Muntaner, 5). The results "helped expose an often, overlooked truth about the current state of the status discussion: not only that most prefer not to resolve the matter as presently articulated but also that the majority of Puerto Ricans will continue to avoid turning their full attention to status resolution until it is perceived less as a juridical question of sovereignty than as a means to ward off a dangerous threat to a way of life [poverty, deteriorated infrastructure, inferior government services, high unemployment, street violence, and low wages]" (Negrón-Muntaner, 6).

28. Muckley, introduction to Carrero, 2.

29. It was quite appropriate to invite Herman Badillo and Juan Manuel García-Passalacqua to the conference. At the time, they were important political figures in New York and Puerto Rico, respectively. Badillo held office as a Bronx borough president, congressman, and deputy mayor of New York City. He became the chairman of the Board of Trustees of the City University of New York during Rudy Giuliani's administration. He later published *One Nation, One Standard: An Ex-Liberal on How Hispanics Can Succeed Just Like Other Immigrant Groups* (New York: Sentinel, 2006). García-Passalacqua is a renowned lawyer, writer, and political analyst who assisted governors Luis Muñoz Marín and Roberto Sánchez Vilella, both of the Popular Democratic Party of Puerto Rico, during the 1970s. Dissatisfied with the political party, he left and became a television producer in Puerto Rico. In a televised interview at the conference, Badillo argued that, despite the differences among generations, migration experiences, and residential status, all Puerto Ricans—whether in the States or on the island—should equally collaborate in the making of their community. Young Lords Juan Ramos Cruz, vice president of the Ministry of Defense from Philadelphia, and Pedro Rodriguez Cosme, from the chapter in Puerto Rico, added that even if culture and generation were significant factors, the social and economic status of a group of people could not be overlooked, especially since this status was a determining factor in the way that the US government treated Puerto Ricans and Neo-Ricans.

30. In spring 1970, the New York Young Lords Organization (YLO) became known as the Young Lords Party. Under the approval of "Cha Cha" Jiménez, the founder of the Young Lords Organization (YLO) in Chicago, Pablo "Yoruba" Guzmán, David Peréz, "Mickey" Miguel Meléndez, and Felipe Luciano started a chapter in New York City. The New York chapter outgrew the central branch and gained so much national attention that members requested to split from the YLO because of the Chicago organization's ties with gangsters. The chapter in New York included people from all walks of life—former college students, mothers, factory and hospital workers, ex-addicts, ex-alcoholics, and ex-convicts, and former gang members who became socially and politically conscious. The Lords' initial central committee included Guzmán and Peréz, who were at the time students from Old Westbury College; Juan González, who was studying at Columbia University; Luciano, who was attending Queens College; and Juan "Fi" Ortiz, a street youth from El Barrio. Committed to the future of the organiza-

tion, most of these Lords decided to dedicate their time solely to the organization and ended their studies.

31. For further discussion of the in-between spaces that Nuyorican poetry generates, see Efraín Barradas, introduction to *Herejes y mitificadores: Muestra de poesía puertoriqueña en los Estados Unidos*, ed. Efraín Barradas and Rafael Rodriguez (Rio Piedras, PR: Ediciones Huracán, 1980), 11–30; and Juan Flores, "Puerto Rican Literature in the United States: Stages and Perspectives," in *Recovering the U.S. Hispanic Literary Heritage*, ed. Ramón Gutierrez and Genaro Padilla (Houston, TX: Arte Público Press, 1993), 31–68.

32. In "Home and the Ruins of Language: Victor Hernández Cruz and Miguel Algarín's Nuyorican Poetry," Carmelo Esterrich offers a psychoanalytical approach to Nuyorican poetry. Using the theory of incorporation—a concept created by post-Freudian psychoanalysts Nicolas Abraham and Maria Torok—he argues that Nuyoricans cope with the loss of their "original" home by inscribing their poems with home-related fantasies. The memories of the island of Puerto Rico are put away, kept a secret, and maintained in a crypt known to us as poetry. However, the ways that a poet uses both Spanish and English can create fractures in a poem that allow the reader/audience to understand the loss of the "original" home and the creation of an alternative home through the processes of acculturation, transculturation, and assimilation. *MELUS* 23, no. 3 (1998): 43–57.

33. Puerto Ricans on the island also faced an English-only experience in public education.

34. With the publication and performances of her signature poem "Ode to the DiaspoRican" (1993), Mariposa has popularized the term DiaspoRican. While she is often credited for the portmanteau, Wilson Valentín-Escobar acknowledges the work of Adam Pagan, who uses the term in an unpublished paper. See Valentín-Escobar, "'Nothing Connects Us All but Imagined Sounds': Performing Trans-Boricua Memories, Identities, and Nationalisms through the Death of Héctor Lavoe," in *Mambo Montage: The Latinization of New York*, ed. Agustín Laó-Montes and Arlene Dávila (New York: Columbia University Press, 2001), 208; and Vanessa Pérez-Rosario, "Affirming an Afro-Latin@ Identity: An Interview with Poet María Teresa (Mariposa) Fernández," *Latino Studies* 12, no. 3 (2014): 468–75.

35. David Colón, "Other Latino Poetic Method," *Cultural Critique* 47 (2001), 268. Colón explains: "In a word, the other or *the other heading*, is a complex amalgam of reason and chaos: a succinct phrase implying that culture and identity are articulations, not *of* language, not belonging *to* language, but language itself: or without "itself": language" (268). For a more detailed discussion of how language functions in Nuyorican poetry, see Juan Flores, "Living Borders/Buscando América: Language of Latino Self-Formation," in *Divided Borders: Essays on Puerto Rican Identity* (Houston, TX: Arte Público Press, 1993), 199–224 and Frances R. Aparicio, "La Vida Es un Spanglish Disparatero: Bilingualism in Nuyorican Poetry," in *European Perspectives on Hispanic Literature of the United States*, ed. Genevië Fabre, (Houston: Arte Público Press, 1988), 147–60.

36. While in La Princesa prison, Albizu Campos repeatedly charged that he was

being subjected to human radiation experiments and that he was being "systematically killed." After his death, his body was examined, and it showed signs of torture by radiation, confirming that he was one of the unfortunate prisoners experimented on without consent. For more details on this story, see Pedro I. Aponte Vázquez, *¡Yo acuso! Tortura y asesinato de Don Pedro Albizu Campos* (Bayamón, PR: Movimiento Ecuménico Nacional de Puerto Rico, 1985); José Benjamín Torres, *El proceso judicial contra Albizu Campos*, 2nd ed. (San Juan, PR: Editorial Jelofe, 1979); and Partido Nacionalista de Puerto Rico, *Tortura de los presos políticos en Puerto Rico: Denuncia elevada a la Organización de los Estados Americanos*, compiled by Secretaría de Relaciones Exteriores (Havana: La Secretaría, 1952).

37. Algarín describes his leadership role of EPRP/AW in Algarín and Louis Griffith, eds., *Action: The Nuyorican Poets Café Theater Festival* (New York: Touchstone, 1997), 538.

38. In the introduction to *Nuevos Pasos: Chicano and Puerto Rican Drama* (Gary, IN: Arte Público Press, 1979), Nicolás Kanellos and Jorge A. Huerta refer to the group as the Nuyorican Writers' and Actors' Workshop (viii). On the other hand, Algarín, in a *New York Newsday* interview conducted on December 5, 1990, and later included in the afterword to his coedited volume *Action*, calls it El Puerto Rican Playwrights'/Actors' Workshop (538). The interchangeable use of the terms Puerto Rican and Nuyorican suggests that the latter term was coming into being. The process of self-identifying as Nuyorican in writing was not public until Algarín and Piñero's 1975 anthology *Nuyorican Poetry*. I imagine that the term was already in use, but that it was not necessarily made public until there was enough cultural output in print to educate the larger public of its political significance.

39. Algarín and Griffith, *Action*, 538.

40. Algarín and Griffith, 540.

41. Barry and Algarín worked together to direct *Apartment 6D* (1974). They started with a fifteen-minute narrative that extended to thirty minutes, which was then translated into symbolic actions for the stage. The script of *Apartment 6D* is less like a traditional drama and more like a collage chronicling a series of quotidian realities.

42. *Short Eyes* won an Obie Award and received the New York Drama Critics Award for Best American Play of the 1973–74 season.

43. "Short eyes" is slang for pedophile or a person who is in jail for child molestation.

44. Papp met Piñero in 1973 when the former became the producer of the Family, the resident theater group at Riverside Church in Upper Manhattan. Marvin Camillo, the director of this group, met Piñero when he conducted a theatrical workshop at Sing Sing, where Piñero was serving time. Camillo inspired Piñero to write the play *Short Eyes* while incarcerated.

45. In EPRP/AW, Piñero partook in the creation of *Apartment 6D*, a compilation of stories gathered from the group, along with poems from Algarín's 1976 translation of *Song of Protest* by Pablo Neruda. *Apartment 6D* featured Hector Rodriguez, an eleven-year-old boy who later wrote his own play, *Hoe Stroll, Lonely Lives*. See John C. Miller, "Hispanic Theatre in New York, 1965–1977," *Revista Chicano-Riqueña* 6, no. 1 (1977), 40–59.

46. The Nuyorican Theater Festival was performed in at the Space for Innovative Development, an unused theater space in one of Samuel Rubin's buildings on Thirty-Sixth Street between Eighth and Ninth Avenues. In *Action*, Algarín refers to Rubin's unused theater space, but he does not mention the given name (540). In the *New York Times* review of *América Conga Mania* (February 19, 1975), the theater is referred to as the Space for Innovative Development.

47. Carlos Morton, "Nuyorican Theatre," *TDR: The Drama Review* 20, no. 1 (1976): 43–49.

48. "Shattering the Silences: Minority Professors Break into the Ivory Tower," PBS.org, updated 1997, accessed August 17, 2019, http://www.pbs.org/shattering/shattering2.html. See especially the page about Algarín, in the section on the scholars. This website was created as the companion to the 1997 documentary film *Shattering the Silences: The Case for Minority Faculty*.

49. There are conflicting accounts of the year that the café opened, ranging from 1973 to 1976. In his essay "Hispanic Theater in New York, 1965–1977," John C. Miller notes that, in 1973, the café produced its first work, *Olu Clemente*, a play written by Miguel Algarín and Tato Laviera (54). However, in the description of *Olu Clemente*, Algarín states that the play was produced by the Public Theater and presented at the Delacorte Theater in Central Park. The café is not mentioned at all. One can infer that by 1973, the café had been founded but did not have a physical location. In addition to Miller's article, see the introduction to Kanellos and Huerta's *Nuevos Pasos* (also found in *Revista Chicana-Riqueña* 7, no. 1 [1979]: 151).

50. By 1981 the collective purchased its building from Ellen Stewart, founder and director of La MaMa Experimental Theatre Club.

51. Miguel Algarín, "Volume and Value of the Breath in Poetry," *Revista Chicana-Riqueña* 6, no. 3 (1978): 52.

52. Martín Espada, "Documentaries and Declamadores: Puerto Rican Poetry in the United States," in *A Gift of Tongues: Critical Challenges in Contemporary American Poetry*, ed. Marie Harris and Kathleen Aguero (Athens: University of Georgia Press, 1987), 257–66.

53. Algarín, "Volume and Value of the Breath in Poetry," 53.

54. For work on the significance of the body politic as it relates to Latinx expression, see Urayoán Noel, "Bodies That Antimatter: Locating U.S. Latino/a Poetry, 2000–2009," *Contemporary Literature* 52, no. 4 (2011): 852–82; and Lázaro Lima, *The Latino Body: Crisis Identities in American Literary and Cultural Memory* (New York: New York University Press, 2007).

55. Miguel Algarín, "Nuyorican Literature," *MELUS* 8, no. 2 (1981): 90.

56. Espada, "Documentaries and Declamadores," 260.

57. Algarín, "Introduction: Nuyorican Language," 11.

58. "For more discussion on bomba and its diasporic origins see Ángel G. Quintero Rivera's, *Cuerpo y Cultura: Las Músicas Mulatas y La Subversión Del Baile*, Colección Nexos y Diferencias 24, (Madrid: Iberoamericana/ Frankfurt am Main: Vervuert, 2009) and "El tambor oculto en el cuatro: la melodización de ritmos y la etnicidad cimarroneada en la caribeña cultura de la contraplantación." *BOLETÍN AMERICANISTA*,

vol. 42–43, 1992: 87–106 as well as Raquel Z. Rivera, "New York Afro-Puerto Rican and Afro-Dominican Roots Music: Liberation Mythologies and Overlapping Diasporas." *Black Music Research Journal*, vol. 32, no. 2, 2012: 3–24. *JSTOR*, www.jstor.org/stable/10.5406/blacmusiresej.32.2.0003.

59. Chögyam Trungpa, the founder of Naropa Institute, invited Allen Ginsberg, Diane di Prima, and Anne Waldman to share and teach poetry in 1974. From that moment, the Jack Kerouac School of Disembodied Poetics was created. Among the many poets invited to read in 1978, the year of the documentary, were Peter Orlovsky (Ginsberg's long-time companion), Meredith Monk, Diane di Prima, and Amiri Baraka, as well as Piñero and Algarín. Their presence demonstrates the exchange and interconnection between the Nuyorican, Black, and Beat poets. Constanzo Allione, dir., *Fried Shoes, Cooked Diamonds*, 1979 film (Montauk, NY: Mystic Fire Video, 1989), DVD, 55 min.

60. "Seekin' the Cause" appears in Miguel Piñero, *Outlaw: The Collected Works of Miguel Piñero*, introduction by Nicolás Kanellos and Jorge Iglesias (Houston, TX: Arte Público Press, 2010), 19–21.

61. In an interview conducted by Martín Espada, Louis Reyes Rivera states, "there is no distinction between the reader and the writer. Without someone to clean streets and sew garments, there would not be someone with time to write poetry." In Espada, "Documentaries and Declamadores," 259.

62. For a discussion of the historical trajectory of Nuyorican poetry and its function as a form of documentation, see Espada, 257.

63. I am reminded of Daniel Kane's *All Poets Welcome: The Lower East Side Poetry Scene in the 1960s* (Berkeley: University of California Press, 2003), where he considers the readings as events that problematized the state of poetry. "Readings," he writes, "were not just public presentations of texts, but events that defined a contemporary avant-garde as they redefined the way poetry was used in contemporary American culture" (27).

64. The poetry scene of the 1970s on the Lower East Side also played an important role. In an interview with Bruce Allen Dick, Algarín discusses the influence of Allen Ginsberg. The Beats' style of live poetry readings—seemingly spontaneous word-making—their use of breath, and their incantations are all elements that resonate in Algarín's repertoire. In his book of poetry *Love is Hard Work: Memorias de Loisaida* (1997), Algarín calls a section of his book "Nuyorican Kaddish" to underline the intersections between himself as a Nuyorican poet and Ginsberg as a Jewish poet. These moments of artistic encounter are crucial, as they demonstrate how the period's poetry traversed race, ethnicity, and economic class and created dialogue among various communities. See Bruce Allen Dick, *A Poet's Truth: Conversations with Latino/Latina Poets* (Tucson: University of Arizona Press, 2003), 17–18.

Chapter 3

1. Naturally, some women had poetic styles that were in sharp contrast to the conversational style of the female authors featured in the anthology.

2. Jill Dolan, *The Feminist Spectator in Action: Feminist Criticism for the Stage and Screen* (Basingstoke, UK: Palgrave Macmillan, 2013), 1. See also Charlotte Canning, "Feminist Performance as Feminist Historiography," *Theatre Survey* 45, no. 2 (November 2002): 227–28.

3. Miguel Algarín and Miguel Piñero, eds., *Nuyorican Poetry: An Anthology of Puerto Rican Words and Feelings* (New York: William Morrow, 1975), 181–82.

4. Amina Muñoz, pers. comm., March 16, 2013.

5. Yvonne Yarbro-Bejarano, "The Female Subject in Chicano Theatre: Sexuality, 'Race,' and Class," in *Performing Feminisms: Feminist Critical Theory and Theatre*, ed. Sue-Ellen Case (Baltimore: Johns Hopkins University Press, 1990), 132. Yarbro-Bejarano specifically refers to the Chicano movement, but I extend her argument to the Nuyorican movement because the gender dynamics played out in similar ways.

6. Ortega compares the female poets to Anacaona—one of the Taíno Caciques (chiefs) who fought off the Spanish conquerors—to root the Nuyorican poetic tradition in the Taíno tradition of the *areítos* (performances of music and dance) and to underscore the performeras' subversive poetry in the anthology. Eliana Ortega, "Poetic Discourse of the Puerto Rican Woman in the U.S.: New Voices of Anacaonian Liberation," in *Breaking Boundaries: Latina Writing and Critical Readings*, ed. Asunción Horno-Delgado, Eliana Ortega, Nina M. Scott, and Nancy Saporta Sternbach (Amherst: University of Massachusetts Press, 1989), 122–35.

7. Sandra María Esteves, pers. comm., March 14, 2013; and Amina Muñoz, pers. comm., March 16, 2013.

8. Cherríe Moraga and Gloria Anzaldúa's *This Bridge Called My Back: Writings by Radical Women of Color* (New York: Kitchen Table/Women of Color Press, 1981) and the Latina Feminist Group's *Telling to Live: Latina Feminist Testimonios* (Durham, NC: Duke University Press, 2001) are powerful models that illustrate how Latinas use testimonio to theorize lived experience.

9. Tiffany Ana López, "Critical Witnessing in Latina/o and African American Prison Narratives," in *Prose and Cons: Essays on Prison Literature in the United States*, ed. D. Quentin Miller (Jefferson, NC: McFarland, 2005), 64.

10. Bruce Allen Dick, *A Poet's Truth: Conversations with Latino/Latina Poets* (Tucson: University of Arizona Press, 2003), 45.

11. Amina Muñoz, pers. comm., March 16, 2013.

12. Miguel Algarín, "Volume and Value of the Breath in Poetry," *Revista Chicana-Riqueña* 6, no. 3 (1978): 56.

13. The concept of *pláticas* has been heavily theorized in the field of education studies. The edited volume *Chicana/Latina Education in Everyday Life: Feminista Perspectives on Pedagogy and Epistemology* by Dolores Delgado Bernal, C. Alejandra Elenes, Francisca E. Godinez, and Sofia Villenas (Albany: State University of New York Press, 2006) offers insightful examples of how scholars have created informal yet intimate conversations among youths, educators, families, mothers, and activists where they share their thoughts, feelings, and testimonies about their experiences with the educational system. More than collecting data, these *pláticas* offer a method of understanding experiences in educational institutions and broader society. In this volume,

see Jennifer Ayala, Patricia Herrera, Laura Jiménez, and Irene Lara, "Fiera, Guambra y Karichina! Transgressing the Borders of Community and Academy," 261–80.

14. David Vidal, "'Nuyoricans' Express Pain and Joy in Poetry," *New York Times*, May 14, 1976.

15. In a personal interview, Esteves confirmed that she was the poet publicly shamed. Sandra María Esteves, pers. comm., March 14, 2013.

16. Lawrence La Fountain-Stokes, *Queer Ricans: Cultures and Sexualities in the Diaspora* (Minneapolis: University of Minnesota Press, 2009), 82.

17. La Fountain-Stokes, 82.

18. Algarín and Piñero, *Nuyorican Poetry*, 59.

19. Algarín, "Volume and Value," 53.

20. Miriam DeCosta-Willis compares CienFuegos's poem about Lebrón to Esteves's. She describes Esteves's poem as "more personal, almost lyrical, but just as powerful," and suggests that Esteves is "talking to the activist in a quiet, conversational voice (almost woman-to-woman)." "Sandra María Esteves's Nuyorican Poetics: The Signifying Difference," *Afro-Hispanic Review* 23, no. 2 (2004): 5.

21. Sandra María Esteves, *Yerba Buena: Dibujos y poemas* (Greenfield Center, NY: Greenfield Review Press, 1980), 33.

22. Esteves, 33.

23. Dolan, *The Feminist Spectator in Action*, 4.

24. Algarín and Piñero, *Nuyorican Poetry*, 109.

25. Dolan, *The Feminist Spectator in Action*, 4.

26. Algarín and Piñero, *Nuyorican Poetry*, 110.

27. For more information on the troubled relationship between the US military and Puerto Rico, see Katherine McCaffrey, *Military Power and Popular Protest: The US Navy in Vieques, Puerto Rico* (New Brunswick, NJ: Rutgers University Press, 2002).

28. Algarín and Piñero, *Nuyorican Poetry*, 35.

29. Algarín, "Volume and Value," 54.

30. Algarín and Piñero, *Nuyorican Poetry*, 91.

31. Algarín and Piñero, 113.

32. Algarín and Piñero, 113.

33. Algarín and Piñero, 91.

34. Algarín and Piñero, 49.

35. Algarín and Piñero, 50.

36. Algarín and Piñero, 51.

37. Algarín and Piñero, 51.

38. For a discussion of the feminist activities around reproductive health, see chapter 5, "Our Bodies, Ourselves," in bell hooks, *Feminism Is for Everybody: Passionate Politics* (Cambridge, MA: South End Press, 2000).

39. Algarín and Piñero, *Nuyorican Poetry*, 136.

40. Algarín and Piñero, 148.

41. Algarín and Piñero, 150.

42. For a study of menstrual activism from the 1970s to the twenty-first century,

see Chris Bobel's *The New Blood: Third-Wave Feminism and the Politics of Menstruation* (New Brunswick, NJ: Rutgers University Press, 2010).

43. Luz Rodriguez, interview by Joyce Follet, 2006, Sophia Smith Collection, Smith College, Northampton, MA.

44. Esteves, *Undelivered Love Poems* (New York: No Frills, 1997), 40–41.

45. Esteves, 44.

46. Esteves, *Yerba Buena*, 42.

47. Esteves, 41.

48. Algarín and Piñero, *Nuyorican Poetry*, 130.

49. Algarín and Piñero, 133.

50. Algarín and Piñero, 133.

51. Algarín and Piñero, 133.

52. Darrel Enck-Wanzer, ed., *The Young Lords: A Reader* (New York: New York University Press, 2010), 35.

53. Sandra María Esteves, pers. comm., March 14, 2013.

54. The flyer is part of Sandra María Esteves's personal collection.

55. The flyer states, "Este no es un incidente aislado dentro de la comunidad Puertorriqueña. Nosotros, el Comité del Primero de Diciembre, creemos que Tito fué asesinado y dejado ahorcado en las barras de la celda para crear un ambiente de suicidio" (This is not an isolated incident within the Puerto Rican community. We, the December First Committee, believe that Tito was killed and left hanging in the bars of the cell to create an impression of suicide).

56. Armando Andre, "Entrenados en Cuba: El Terrorismo de la FALN [Fuerzas Armadas de Liberación Nacional Puertoriqueña/Armed Forces of National Liberation] en EE.UU.," *La Crónica Gráfica*, San Juan, 1987. As reported by Andre,

> El 11 de diciembre de 1974, la FALN colocó una bomba trampa detrás de la puerta de un edificio abandonado en el 336 E. 110 Street, en el barrio hispano, a ocho cuadras de donde vivió el dirigente del MIRA Carlos Feliciano Vásquez, y una mujer llamó a las autoridades reportando que allí había un cadáver. El policía puertorriqueño Angel Felipe Poggi, de 22 años, perdió un ojo y recibió graves lesiones en la explosión, al abrir la puerta de entrada. El segundo comunicado de la FALN señaló que esa era "la respuesta del pueblo puertorriqueño al asesinato brutal de Martín (Tito) Pérez por los animales sadistas del Precinto 25 el domingo, Dic. 1, 1974." Pérez, un músico boricua de 31 años, fue arrestado junto con otras dos personas por conducta desordenada, y se ahorcó con un cinturón al ser dejado olvidado en una celda. Después de una investigación de un mes, donde fueron interrogados 18 testigos, un gran jurado determinó que la muerte de Pérez fue suicidio.

> On December 11, 1974, the FALN placed a bomb trap behind the door of an abandoned building at 336 E. 110 Street, in the Hispanic neighborhood, eight blocks from where the leader of the MIRA Carlos Feliciano Vásquez lived, and a woman called the authorities reporting that there was a corpse. The Puerto Rican police

Angel Felipe Poggi, 22 years, lost an eye and received serious injuries from the blast, when he opened the entrance door. The second statement from the FALN members noted that this was "a response from the Puerto Rican people regarding the brutal murder of Martín (Tito) Pérez by the sadistic animals of Precinct 25 on Sunday, Dec. 1, 1974." Pérez, a 31-year-old Puerto Rican musician, was arrested along with two other people for disorderly conduct, and he hung himself with a belt when he was left alone forgotten in a cell. After a month's investigation, where they interrogated 18 witnesses, a grand jury determined that Pérez's death was suicide.

57. Esteves, *Yerba Buena*, 28.

58. In 2004, Boricua College moved into the former building of the American Geographical Society. Located in Upper Manhattan's Washington Heights in the Audubon Terrace Historic District, this building is situated in a complex of eight early twentieth-century beaux arts buildings that sit around a plaza. The architectural grandeur drastically differs from the surrounding apartment towers, bodegas, shops, and restaurants.

59. Patricia Hill Collins, "Is the Personal Still Political? The Women's Movement, Feminism, and Black Women in the Hip-Hop Generation," in *From Black Power to Hip Hop: Racism, Nationalism, and Feminism* (Philadelphia, PA: Temple University Press, 2006), 164. Inspired by the civil rights movement, which began in the late 1950s, many second-wavers had a heightened feminist consciousness. Feminist organizations like the New York Radical Feminists and the Black feminist group Combahee River Collective in Boston adopted the slogan "the personal is political," arguing that women's personal experiences were not just individual problems but were, rather, intrinsically connected to the structures of power that enforce patriarchy. This slogan points to a shift in the women's movement, away from valuing women's individual experiences and toward a group consciousness-raising. The mantra "the personal is political" brought about intensive, group discussions that heightened women's awareness of their lived gender oppression, both as individuals and as a collective. What was once something personal was now understood as part of a collective experience. As a result, groups worked to design and implement action strategies to resist women's oppression.

60. The New Rican Village opened in October 1976, three years after the Nuyorican Poets Café officially established its own space. Located on Avenue A between Sixth and Seventh Streets, three blocks away from the café, the New Rican Village is another historic space that produced Nuyorican music, art, poetry, theater, and dance. For an ethnographic approach to the history of musicians and the music produced in the New Rican Village, see Marina Roseman, "The New Rican Village: Artists in Control of the Image-Making Machinery," *Latin American Music Review/Revista de Musica Latinoamericana* 4, no. 1 (1983): 132–67.

61. New Rican Village called the performance *Conjunto Libre* (Free Set) because it showcased an array of works. The evening included live music with Mario Rivera, the Salsa Refugees, and Brenda Feliciano on vocals; a poetry reading from Esteves, Pedro Pietri, Lou Pérez, and Américo Casiano; and an exhibition of Jorge Soto's and Néstor

Otero's artwork. Otero designed the set. His work has been part of exhibitions throughout the United States, the Americas, and beyond, in places such as Bienal de São Paulo in Brazil, Cuenca in Ecuador, Documenta in Basel, Switzerland, and many other international venues. For a history of the New Rican Village, see Wilson Valentín-Escobar's forthcoming book project *Bodega Surrealism: New York City Latina/o/x Activists* (New York University Press).

62. Sandra María Esteves, pers. comm., December 10, 2006.

63. Sandra María Esteves, pers. comm., December 10, 2006.

64. Conjunto Libre was one of the key New York–based salsa bands. After breaking away from Eddie Palmieri's La Perfecta Orchestra, Puerto Rican percussionist Manny Oquendo and bassist Andy González founded Conjunto Libre. It was created under the premise that the band would be "free" of commercial exploitation, a direct stance against the commercialized formula of salsa music that was exploding during the 1970s. As Wilson Valentín-Escobar argues in "*Bodega Surrealism*," Conjunto Libre was more than just the name of a band. More importantly, it was a philosophy of creating and performing salsa. New Rican Village was known as a musician's refuge, encouraging musical exploration and cultivating musical innovation.

Chapter 4

1. José Esteban Muñoz's notion of minoritarian performance is useful here; he uses the term "to index citizen-subjects who, due to antagonism within the social such as race, class, and sex, are debased within the majoritarian public sphere." *Cruising Utopia, The Then and There of Queer Futurity* (New York: New York University Press, 2009), 56.

2. Suzanne Bost, "'Be deceived if ya wanna be foolish': (Re)Constructing Body, Genre, and Gender in Feminist Rap," *Postmodern Culture* 12, no. 1 (2001), https://doi.org/10.1353/pmc.2001.0017

3. For more on this musical ferment, see Ray Allen and Lois Wilcken, eds., *Island Sounds in the Global City: Caribbean Popular Music and Identity in New York* (Champaign: University of Illinois Press, 2001); Juan Flores, *From Bomba to Hip-Hop: Puerto Rican Culture and Latino Identity* (New York: Columbia University Press, 2000); Will Hermes, *Love Goes to Buildings on Fire: Five Years in New York That Changed Music Forever* (New York: Faber and Faber, 2012); and Raquel Z. Rivera, *New York Ricans from the Hip Hop Zone* (New York: Palgrave Macmillan, 2003).

4. For a discussion of the transethnic relationships in hip hop music, see Flores, *From Bomba to Hip Hop*; and Rivera, *New York Ricans from the Hip Hop Zone*.

5. For further examination of feminist strategies that counter masculinist practices, see Murray Forman, "'Movin' Closer to an Independent Funk': Black Feminist Theory, Standpoint, and Women in Rap," *Women's Studies* 23 (1994): 35–55; Nancy Guevara, "Women Writin' Rappin' Breakin'," in *Droppin' Science: Critical Essays on Rap Music and Hip Hop Culture*, ed. William Eric Perkins (Philadelphia: Temple University Press, 1995), 49–62; Cheryl L. Keyes, "'We're More Than a Novelty, Boys': Strategies of Female Rappers in the Rap Music Tradition," in *Feminist Messages: Coding in Women's*

Folk Culture, ed. Joan Newlon Radner (Urbana: University of Illinois Press, 1993), 203–19; Joan Morgan, *When Chickenheads Come Home to Roost: My Life as a Hip-Hop Feminist* (New York: Simon and Schuster, 1999); and Bost, "Be deceived if ya wanna be foolish."

6. Walter Robinson and Carlo McCormick, "Slouching toward Avenue D," *Art in America* 72, no. 6 (1993): 135.

7. For an overview of the history of slam poetry, see Cristin O'Keefe Aptowicz's *Words in Your Face: A Guided Tour Through Twenty Years of the New York Poetry Slam* (New York: Soft Skull Press, 2008).

8. Aptowicz, *Words in Your Face*, 24.

9. For a discussion on the potentiality of spoken word and slam poetry, see: Javon Johnson, *Killing Poetry: Blackness and the Making of Slam and Spoken Word Communities* (New Brunswick, NJ: Rutgers University Press, 2017); Susan B. A. Somers-Willett, "From Slam to Def Poetry Jam: Spoken Word Poetry and Its Counterpublics," *Liminalities: A Journal of Performance Studies* 10, no. 3–4 (2014): 1–23; and Somers-Willett, *The Cultural Politics of Slam Poetry: Race, Identity, and the Performance of Popular Verse* (Ann Arbor: University of Michigan Press, 2009).

10. Somers-Willett, *The Cultural Politics of Slam Poetry*, 16.

11. O'Keefe Aptowitcz, *Words in Your Face*, 151. Holman's success eventually eclipsed the history of the Nuyorican Poets Café and its original founders, so much so that tensions between Holman and Algarín were exacerbated until their split in 1996. Six years later, Holman, with O'Keefe Aptowicz, would establish the Bowery Poetry Club as a new home to slam poetry.

12. Maria Damon, "Avant-Garde or Borderguard: (Latino) Identity in Poetry," *American Literary History* 10, no. 3 (1998): 487. In the epilogue to his *All Poets Welcome: The Lower East Side Poetry Scene in the 1960s* (Berkeley: University of California Press, 2003), Daniel Kane points to the drastic differences between Nuyorican Poets Café and other Lower East Side spaces: "Most Wednesday-night readings [at the Poetry Project] are comparatively staid events where the poet for the most part reads as the audience quietly (with perhaps the occasional shout, giggle, or yell) listens. Friday nights at the Nuyorican are entirely different. Audience and performer call-and-response are the norm, alcohol flows, cigarette smoke fills the air, and so on. Additionally, the crowd is more heterogeneous in terms of age and race at the Nuyorican than at St. Mark's. If one's standards rest solely on promoting the idea of poetry to a diverse group of people, the Nuyorican is clearly ahead of other reading series—including the series at the Poetry Project" (207).

13. For a brilliant examination of work influenced by the café after its second birth, look out for Karen Jaime's book project *The Queer Nuyorican: Racialized Sexualities and Aesthetics in Loisaida*.

14. Qtd. in J. Johnson, *Killing Poetry*, 37; also qtd. in Johnson, "Manning Up: Race, Gender, and Sexuality in Los Angeles' Slam and Spoken Word Poetry Communities," *Text and Performance Quarterly* 30, no. 4 (2010): 405.

15. Frederick Bernas, "The Nuyorican Revolution," *Narratively*, February 21, 2014, http://www.frederickbernas.com/2014/02/the-nuyorican-revolution.html

16. J. Johnson, *Killing Poetry*, 74–78.

17. Qtd. in O'Keefe Aptowitcz, *Words in Your Face*, 51.

18. Joe Coscarelli and Melena Ryzik, "Music Mogul Russell Simmons Is Accused of Rape by 3 Women," *New York Times*, December 13, 2017.

19. "Who's Who in the Cast: Def Poetry Jam," *Playbill Theater Edition*, November 2002. For more on the commercialization of spoken word poetry and the packaging of race, see Somers-Willett, *The Cultural Politics of Slam Poetry*. On the commodification of hip hop, poetry slam, and hip hop theater, she claims: "It seems that for better or worse the *Def Poetry Jam on Broadway* hopes to promote and capitalize on the 'hipness' of the voices of people of color proclaiming their identities against the status quo" (124).

20. *Def Poetry Jam on Broadway*, xii.

21. Harold Bloom, interviewed in "The Man in the Back Row Has a Question VI," by David Barber, *Paris Review* 42, no. 154 (Spring 2000).

22. Danny Hoch's pertinent question comes to mind: "What happens to hip-hop's aesthetics when they are mixed with the aesthetics of 'recognized' art, or when hip-hop's venue changes from the street to the stage, from the subway car to the gallery, from the school yard to the screen?" Hoch, "Toward A Hip Hop Aesthetic: A Manifesto for the Hip Hop Arts Movement," in *Total Chaos: The Art and Aesthetic of Hip-Hop*, ed. Jeff Chang (New York: Basic Civitas, 2007), 350.

23. Dolan, *Utopia in Performance*, 103.

24. Dolan, 112.

25. Many credit *So! What Happens Now?* as the first hip hop musical. The website of Rock Steady Crew member "Crazy Legs" explains, "In 1991 Mr. Wiggles approached Crazy Legs about an idea he and Fable (Magnificent Force) had for a Hip-Hop musical. Crazy Legs (with the help of Mr. Wiggles) then needed to persuade Ken Swift to start dancing again in order to have Ken involved as well. The musical was called 'So, What Happens Now?.' Rock Steady member Buck 4 (R.I.P) provided the perfect scenario to base the musical on. He said, 'You don't know what it feels like to go fill out a job application . . . where it says, 'what do you do?' what do I write? I spin on my head?' 'So, What Happens Now?' was the critics' choice in the *New York Times* and received rave reviews in *The Village Voice*, *The Daily News* and *El Diario*. In 1992, they received a standing ovation lead by Gregory Hines at the Kennedy Center Honors where Gregory Peck and the Nicholas Brothers were all in attendance." "Rock Steady Crew," Crazy Legs Workshop, accessed May 9, 2013, http://crazylegsworkshop.com/rock-steady-crew/about-rsc

26. As a way of democratizing the arts, Roberta Uno has edited anthologies that spotlight the voices of women and people of color, including *Unbroken Thread: An Anthology of Plays by Asian American Women* (Amherst: University of Massachusetts Press, 1993) and, with Lucy Mae San Pablo Burns, *The Color Of Theater: Race, Culture, and Contemporary Performance* (London: Continuum, 2002). She also recently edited second editions of several volume for Routledge: *Monologues for Actors of Color: Men* (2015), *Monologues for Actors of Color: Women* (2015), and *Contemporary Plays by Women of Color* (2018).

27. Roberta Uno, "Democratizing the Arts, Aesthetic Practice, and the Relationship to Community Change: A Conversation with Roberto Uno," interview by P. Carl,

HowlRound, April 14, 2016, http://howlround.com/democratizing-the-arts-aesthetic-practice-and-the-relationship-to-community-change-a-conversation

28. On April 12–13, 2000 New WORLD Theater organized the third Intersections Conference, focusing on hip hop theater as the future aesthetic. In the theater's fall 2002 newsletter, editor Irma Mayorga describes the conference as a gathering where "a coast-to-coast, cross-section of artists and presenters put their viewpoints in dialogue with other artists and map the territories of new aesthetic" (7). The event featured numerous solo writers, performers, and ensembles, including Luis Alfaro, Tracie Morris, Suheir Hammad, Martín Espada, Jessica Hagedorn, I Was Born With Two Tongues, Rha Goddess, and UNIVERSES.

29. These articles in *American Theatre* include Holly Bass, "Blowing Up the Set: What Happens When the Pulse of Hip-Hop Shakes Up the Traditional Stage," November 1999; Kim Euell, "Tha Playz tha Thang: A New York City Festival Confirms That Hip-Hop Is a Theatre Genre to Contend With," September 2002; Martha Hostetter "Sarah Jones: Wrestling Her Way Out," September 2003; Randy Gener, "Bling, or Revolution: A Roundtable Discussion with Daniel Banks, Chadwick Boseman, Gamal Abdel Chasten, Gwendolen Hardwick, Danny Hoch, Baraka Sele, Marla Teyolia, Clyde Valentin and Raphael Xavier," July/August 2004; Jorge Ignacio Cortiñas, "Are We Dancing to Our Own Beat?," May/June 2004; and Roberta Uno, "The 5th Element: Hip-Hop Culture Confronts the Theatre and Asks, 'Where to Go, Beyond the Borders of Outreach and Audience Development?,'" April 2004.

30. Bass, "Blowing Up the Set," 18.

31. Qtd. in Euell, "The Playz tha Thang," 37.

32. Chang, *Total Chaos*, 86.

33. Cortiñas, qtd. in Chang, *Total Chaos*, 56.

34. Ruiz, qtd. in Uno, "The 5th Element," 30.

35. Uno, 30.

Chapter 5

1. Dan Zanes is a renowned children's musician and the former lead singer of the Del Fuegos. Brooklyn Information and Culture, Brooklyn Independent Network, *Caught in the Act*, episode 8, aired September 23, 2009, YouTube, 8 min., http://www.youtube.com/watch?v=KWTMqHhU1kM

2. Maxine Baca Zinn, "Feminist Rethinking from Racial-Ethnic Families," in *Women of Color in U.S. Society*, ed. Maxine Baca Zinn and Bonnie Thornton Dill (Philadelphia, PA: Temple University Press, 1994), 18–26.

3. In Spanish, baseball is *béisbol*. La Bruja writes the word as *basebol* to stress how Don José inflects Spanish in English.

4. For more on Puerto Rican women authors challenging the family trope, see Marisel C. Moreno, *Family Matters: Puerto Rican Women Authors on the Island and the Mainland* (Charlottesville: University of Virginia Press, 2012).

5. See Stephanie Coontz, *The Way We Never Were: American Families and the Nostalgia Trap* (New York: Basic Books, 1993). Coontz argues that the nuclear family of the

1950s was relatively new and did not reflect most white, middle-class families. She exposes the myth of the American family by revealing that cohabitation, out-of-wedlock births, and nonmarital sex were all widespread.

6. Caridad de La Luz, *Boogie Rican Boulevard* (2001), unpublished manuscript.

7. I am drawing from Leigh Gilmore, who argues, "nowhere is the reliance on naïve autobiographical realism more evident than in the conflation of 'book' and 'man' on the ground that they share the same proper name" (35). Gilmore, *Autobiographics: A Feminist Theory of Women's Self Representation* (Ithaca, NY: Cornell University Press, 1994), 35.

8. Ellen McCracken acknowledges that autobiography can lead the reader to essentialize certain individuals. She challenges the essentialized self at the center of the autobiography and recognizes multiple subjects within the self. McCracken, *New Latina Narrative: The Feminine Space of Postmodern Ethnicity* (Tucson: Arizona University Press, 1999), 74.

9. McCracken, 74.

10. Gilmore, *Autobiographics*, 185–86.

11. Caridad de La Luz, pers. comm., November 19, 2000.

12. Afarin Majioi, "At Home with Caridad de la Luz," *Urban Latino* 21, no. 1 (1999):95. Also see interview with Caridad de la Luz by Oneka LaBennett, October 23, 2007, the Bronx African American History Project, BAAHP Digital Archive, Fordham University.

13. Since 2005, the South Bronx has been undergoing what Ralph da Costa Nuñez, president of the Institute for Children, Poverty, and Homelessness, calls "gentrification on a lower level." His office reports that the average income in the Highbridge and Grand Concourse neighborhoods in the South Bronx rose 15 percent between 2005 and 2010. This increase was due to relocation, since many people who lived in the gentrifying areas of upper Manhattan were searching for affordable apartments in the South Bronx. This influx triggered a 10 percent increase in rents. The number of families from Highbridge and Grand Concourse living in shelters rose by one-third. Joe Anuta, "High Rents Have Bronx Locals Packing Up: Gentrification Starts to Hit Highbridge and Grand Concourse," *Crain's New York Business* (March 31, 2014).

14. Juan Flores's concept of the Latino imaginary identifies three ways in which Latinxs have been interpreted: demographic (an instrumental, homogenizing method that produces alarming truisms about the number of Latinxs in the United States); analytic (a method that uses socially constructed statistical evidence to capture the diversity of Latinx groups and experiences); and imaginary. The "imaginary" rendition of Latinxs—one that the literature I examine performs—consists of an aggregate of lived experiences and historical memory, and it foregrounds the country of origin's history and presence. This imaginary produces Latinx identity as productive, and it ultimately creates a new map of the Americas. Juan Flores, *From Bomba to Hip-Hop: Puerto Rican Culture and Latino Identity* (New York: Columbia University Press, 2000), 203.

15. Flores, 199.

16. La Bruja performed *Brujalicious* at the Bronx Academy of Arts and Dance as part

of its BAAD!Ass Women Festival, which was held on March 18, 2006. This seventy-seat performance space—founded by dancer and choreographer Arthur Avilés and writer and activist Charles Rice-González—"creates, produces, presents, and supports the development of cutting-edge and challenging works in contemporary dance and all creative disciplines that are empowering to women, Latinos and people of color, and the LGBTQ+ (lesbian, gay, bisexual, transgender, and queer) community." Bronx Academy of Arts and Dance, "Mission and Values," accessed September 18, 2019, http://www.baadbronx.org/.

17. Lawrence La Fountain-Stokes, *Queer Ricans: Cultures and Sexualities in the Diaspora* (Minneapolis: University of Minnesota Press, 2009), 132.

18. While Nuyorican Bronx-based dance performers Arthur Avilés and Elizabeth Marrero envision Nuyorico as an intrinsically queer space that embraces queer experiences, La Bruja specifically conceptualizes Nuyorico using race, ethnicity, and gender as her central axes of identification. La Fountain-Stokes, 133.

19. E. Machado Sáez Dalleo and Elena Machado Sáez, *The Latino/a Canon and the Emergence of Post-Sixties Literature* (New York: Palgrave Macmillan, 2007), 36.

20. La Fountain-Stokes, *Queer Ricans*, 133.

21. "It ain't New York and it ain't Puerto Rico" comes from La Bruja's song "Nuyorico," included on the album *Brujalicious* (2005).

22. Caridad de La Luz, *Boogie Rican Boulevard* (2001), unpublished manuscript, 8–9.

23. Teresa Wiltz, "Racial and Ethnic Disparities Persist in Teen Pregnancy Rates," Pew Charitable Trusts Stateline (blog), March 3, 2015, http://www.pewtrusts.org/en/research-and-analysis/blogs/stateline/2015/3/03/racial-and-ethnic-disparities-persist-in-teen-pregnancy-rates. Compare this rate with the report from the National Campaign to Prevent Teen and Unplanned Pregnancy, which stated, "53 percent of Latinas get pregnant in their teens, about twice the national average." Moni Basu, "Survey Delves into High Rate for Young Latinas," CNN, May 19, 2009, http://www.cnn.com/2009/HEALTH/05/19/latinas.pregnancy.rate/index.html, accessed September 18, 2019.

24. Moreno, *Family Matters*, 9.

25. In 2013, Miriam Colón, the founder and producer, announced the merger of the Puerto Rican Traveling Theater and Pregones, another leading Latinx theater, known for incorporating Puerto Rican art, music, and literature in their works since 1979. For more on these companies, see Elisa De la Roche, *Teatro Hispano! Three Major New York Companies* (New York: Garland, 1995); and Eva C. Vásquez, *Pregones Theatre: A Theatre for Social Change in the South Bronx* (London: Routledge, 1998).

26. Nelson Vásquez is best known for the cinematic roles of Tito Goya in *Piñero* (2001) and Johnny Pacheco in *El Cantante* (2006), both directed by León Ichaso. Onstage, Vásquez performed in Oliver Mayer's *Blade to the Heat* at the Public Theater (1994), which was directed by George C. Wolfe. Vásquez has also been in productions of Nuyorican playwright Edwin Sanchez's plays, including *Clean*, *Icarus*, and *Barefoot Boy with Shoes*.

27. Qtd. in Raquel Z. Rivera, *New York Ricans from the Hip Hop Zone* (New York: Palgrave Macmillan, 2003), 227.

28. Maite Junco, "'Boogie Rican Blvd.' Joins the Chorus," *New York Daily News*, July 1, 2009.

29. Brooklyn Information and Culture, "Caught in the Act."

30. Amílcar Antonio Barreto, *The Politics of Language in Puerto Rico* (Gainesville: University Press of Florida, 2001), 5–6; Henry K. Carroll, *Report on the Island of Porto Rico: Its Population, Civil Government, Productions, Roads, Traffic and Currency* (Washington, DC: Government Printing Office, 1899), 59; and Bonnie Urciuoli, *Exposing Prejudice: Puerto Rican Experiences of Language, Race, and Class* (Boulder, CO: Westview, 1998), 42.

31. Carroll, *Report on the Island*, 65.

32. Barreto, *The Politics of Language in Puerto Rico*, 6–18.

33. For a close reading of the protagonist Suzie Bermiúdez, see: Suzanne Bost, "Transgressing Borders: Puerto Rican and Latina Mestizaje," *MELUS* 25, no. 2 (2000): 187–211; and Diana L. Vélez, "*Pollito Chicken*: Split Subjectivity, National Identity and the Articulation of Female Sexuality in a Narrative by Ana Lydia Vega," *Americas Review* (formally *Revista Chicana-Riqueña*) 14, no. 2 (1986): 68–76.

34. William Burgos, "Puerto Rican Literature in a New Clave: Notes on the Emergence of DiaspoRican," in *Writing Off the Hyphen: New Critical Perspectives on the Literature of the Puerto Rican Diaspora*, ed. José L. Torres-Padilla and Carmen Haydée Rivera (Seattle: University of Washington Press, 2008), 133.

35. I am gesturing here to a debate between Vega and fellow writer Nicholasa Mohr about Vega's short story "Pollito Chicken." See the following articles by Mohr in response to Vega's story: Mohr, "Puerto Ricans in New York: Cultural Evolution and Identity," in *Images and Identities: The Puerto Rican in Two World Contexts*, ed. Asela Rodriguez de Laguna (New Brunswick, NJ: Transaction Books, 1987), 157–60; and "Puerto Rican Writers in the U.S., Puerto Rican Writers in Puerto Rico: A Separation beyond Language (Testimonio)," in *Breaking Boundaries: Latina Writings and Critical Readings*, ed. Asunción Horno-Delgado, Eliana Ortega, Nina M. Scott, and Nancy Saporta Sternbach (Amherst: University of Massachusetts Press, 1989), 111–16.

36. Several scholars agree with Mohr. For instance, in *The Diaspora Strikes Back: Caribeño Tales of Learning and Turning* (New York, NY: Routledge, 2008), Juan Flores discusses how Vega's "Pollito Chicken" perpetuates a disparagement of Nuyorican writing and any claims to Puerto Rican culture by Puerto Ricans from the mainland (180). For a detailed investigation of Vega's "Pollito Chicken," see: Burgos, "Puerto Rican Literature in a New Clave," 132–34; Yolanda Martínez-San Miguel, *Coloniality of Diasporas: Rethinking Intra-Colonial Migrations in a Pan-Caribbean Context* (New York: Palgrave Macmillan, 2014), 147–58; and Mary Green, "The Representation of Puerto Rican Women in Two Short Stories by Ana Lydia Vega: 'Letra Para Salsa y Res Soneros' (1979) and 'Pollito Chicken' (1977)," *Journal of Iberian and Latin American Studies* 8, no. 2 (2002): 127–41.

37. Green, "The Representation of Puerto Rican Women," 137.

38. Burgos, "Puerto Rican Literature in a New Clave," 134.

39. The Puerto Rican diaspora, as Jorge Duany argues, "occupies an ambiguous space between colonial and postcolonial population movements. This ambiguity is

the long-term historical consequence of the oxymoronic legal doctrine declaring that Puerto Rico 'belongs to but is not a part of the United States.'" "Puerto Rican Diaspora to the United States: A Postcolonial Migration?" (presentation, El Centro Center for Puerto Rican Studies, Hunter College, New York, February 13, 2009).

40. Dan Zanes and Caridad de la Luz, "Pollito Chicken," *¡Nueva York!* (Brooklyn, NY: Festival Five Records, 2008), compact disc.

41. Raquel Z. Rivera's *New York Ricans From the Hip Hop Zone* explores the integral role of Puerto Ricans in creating hip hop culture.

42. Miguel Algarín and Miguel Piñero, eds., *Nuyorican Poetry: An Anthology of Puerto Rican Words and Feelings* (New York: William Morrow, 1975), 9; and Tricia Rose, *The Hip Hop Wars: What We Talk about When We Talk about Hip Hop and Why It Matters* (New York: Basic Civitas, 2008), 11.

Chapter 6

1. Sun's most acclaimed one-woman show, *No Child . . .* (2006), was first performed off-Broadway May 10 to June 18, 2006, at Theatre Row's Beckett Theatre. It then transferred at the Barrow Street Theatre, on July 8, 2006. It had an open-ended run and also toured nationally, stopping at venues such as the Lookingglass Theatre Company and American Repertory Theater. *No Child . . .* received many awards, including a 2007 Obie Award and a 2007 Lucille Lortel Award. Here, though, I focus on Sun's earlier pieces *La Nubia Latina* (1996, 1999) and *Black and Blue* (2001) because they offer a palette of scenarios in which the social dimensions of ethnicity, gender, and race are foregrounded. In *No Child. . .*, Sun signals to these social factors, but her focus is in portraying the state of New York City's public education through the eyes of teachers, parents, administrators, janitors, security guards, and students with whom she worked as a drama instructor at Malcolm X High School in the Bronx, addressing the lack of resources available to New York City's public schools. She primarily deals with the experiences, interactions, and relationships of various characters, mapping out the complex cultural, generational, and economic differences confronted by students and teachers.

2. Her work is reminiscent of the style of novelist and playwright Charles Rice-González, who is also the son of an African American father and a Puerto Rican mother. Rice-González incorporates this aesthetic in works like *Chulito* (2011).

3. See Danny Hoch, "Toward A Hip Hop Aesthetic: A Manifesto for the Hip Hop Arts Movement," in *Total Chaos: The Art and Aesthetic of Hip-Hop*, ed. Jeff Chang (New York: Basic Civitas, 2007), 349–64.

4. Several anthologies feature a critical perspective on hip hop theater, among them: Daniel Banks, ed., *Say Word! Voices from Hip Hop Theater* (Ann Arbor: University of Michigan Press, 2011); Kim Euell and Robert Alexander, eds., *Plays from the Boom Box Galaxy: Theater from the Hip-Hop Generation* (New York: Theatre Communications Group, 2009); and Harry J. Elam Jr. and Robert Alexander, eds., *The Fire This Time: African American Plays for the 21st Century* (New York: Theatre Communications Group, 2004). For more insight on hip hop theater, see Hoch, "Toward a Hip Hop Aesthetic";

Holly Bass, "Blowing Up the Set: What Happens When the Pulse of Hip-Hop Shakes Up the Traditional Stage?" *American Theatre*, November 1999; Eisa Davis, "Found in Translation: The Emergence of Hip-Hop Theatre," *American Theatre*, July/August 2004; Davis, "Hip Hop Theater: The New Underground," *Source*, March 2000, 172–76; and Roberta Uno, "The 5th Element: Hip-Hop Culture Confronts the Theatre and Asks, 'Where to Go, Beyond the Borders of Outreach and Audience Development?,'" *American Theatre*, April 2004.

5. Suzanne Oboler and Anani Dzidzienyo, "Flows and Counterflows: Latinas/os, Blackness, and Racialization in Hemispheric Perspective," in *Neither Enemies nor Friends: Latinos, Blacks, Afro-Latinos*, ed. Suzanne Oboler and Anani Dzidzienyo (New York: Palgrave Macmillan, 2005), 3, 16.

6. On the diasporic histories of Afro-Latinos, see Miriam Jiménez Román and Juan Flores, eds., *The Afro-Latin@ Reader: History and Culture in the United States* (Durham, NC: Duke University Press, 2010); Augustín Laó-Montes, "Decolonial Moves: Trans-Locating African Diaspora Spaces," *Cultural Studies* 21, no. 2 (2007): 309–38; and Kathryn Joy McKnight and Leo J. Garofalo, eds., *Afro-Latino Voices: Narratives from the Early Modern Ibero-Atlantic World, 1550–1812* (Cambridge, MA: Hackett, 2009).

7. Laó-Montes, "Decolonial Moves," 320.

8. José Esteban Muñoz, "Feeling Brown: Ethnicity and Affect in Ricardo Bracho's *The Sweetest Hangover (and Other STDs)*," *Theatre Journal* 52, no. 1 (2000): 70.

9. Laó-Montes, "Decolonial Moves," 320.

10. Laó-Montes, 310.

11. In my essay "She Wears the Masks: Bluefacing in Nilaja Sun's *Black and Blue* and *La Nubia Latina*" (*African American Review* 45, no. 3 [2012]: 403–18), I argue that Sun's physical mutation of her body is a strategy of belonging. I coin the term *blueface* to illustrate how Sun works within the traditions of blackface by African Americans.

12. *Black and Blue* was featured in the second annual New York City Hip-Hop Theater Festival at Performance Space 122 (PS 122) in summer 2001, and it was recorded at New York City Center Stage. Originally a public school in Manhattan's Lower East Side, PS 122 has been a hub of contemporary performance since 1985. It housed the first and second Hip-Hop Theater Festivals in 2000 and 2001. My attendance at this show and the video recording both informed my analysis. A complete manuscript of *Black and Blue* is not available. Sun reported that the original manuscript was lost in a computer malfunction. Quotes were transcribed from the video recording.

13. The Belgian cartoonist Pierre "Peyo" Culliford created *The Smurfs*, which debuted in 1958, as part of the comic series "Johan et Pirouit," which was featured in the magazine *Le Journal de Spirou*. Smurfs are fantastical blue creatures that live deep in the forest in a village full of mushroom-shaped cottages. There is only one female Smurf, and her name is Smurfette. See: Cynthia Rose,"Behind the Blue: The Story of Peyo," *The Comics Journal*, August 28, 2018, http://www.tcj.com/behind-the-blue-the-story-of-peyo/

14. For a close reading of the works of Avilés and Marrero, see Ramón H. Rivera-

Servera, *Performing Queer Latinidad: Dance, Sexuality, Politics* (Ann Arbor: University of Michigan Press), 72; and Lawrence La Fountain-Stokes, *Queer Ricans: Cultures and Sexualities in the Diaspora* (Minneapolis: University of Minnesota Press, 2009), 148.

15. See Antoine Bueno *Le Petit Livre Bleu—Analyse Critique et Politique de la Société des Schtroumpfs* (France: Hors Collection, 2011), and Marc Schmidt, "The Socio-Political Themes in the Smurfs," June 2, 2011, http://www.pop-cultured.net/socio-political-themes-in-the-smurfs/, accessed June 13, 2015. Schmidt argues that the Smurf society resembles the basic principles of Communism; however, French sociologist Bueno accuses the Smurfs of being racist and anti-Semitic.

16. Linda Martín Alcoff, *Visible Identities: Race, Gender, and the Self* (Oxford: Oxford University Press, 2006), 242.

17. Nicolás Corona Vaca examines the tensions between Black and Latinx people, using case studies from New York, Los Angeles, Miami, Washington, DC, Compton, and Houston. He argues that language barriers, competition over affirmative action, and the overlooked contributions of Hispanics during the American civil rights movement are factors that have aggravated the relationship between these populations. *The Presumed Alliance: The Unspoken Conflict between Latinos and Blacks and What It Means for America* (New York: HarperCollins, 2004).

18. Keeshaw and Tyrell's comments also suggest that in addition to hierarchies of race and colorism, a gendered structure is at work here. Smurfette is the only girl in the village, and she was magically transformed from a "bad" brunette to a "good" blonde. She is also the only Smurf defined neither by her occupation nor by her personality, but by her gender. Although she solves many of the community's crises, her primary occupation often appears to be standing around and looking pretty. Just as the male gaze objectifies Smurfette, Keeshaw and Tyrell objectify Sun and Yolanda.

19. In a personal interview, Sun recalled that in the opening scene, she intended to show how she, as an adult, was remembering the dance movement. This choreography was intended to signal to the audience a distinction between the young Sun as someone trying to understand who she is and the older Sun as a racially conscious adult.

20. Joseph Barbera, William Hanna, and Hoyt Curtin, "Smurfs," Warner-Tamerlane Publishing Corp., 1982.

21. In the essay "Letter to a Friend," Sun shares her experiences of alienation as an Afro-Latina. She writes:

> Dear _____,
>
> I spent a good deal of last night after my show thinking about whether I should write something about my family, re-create in print the monologue I performed from my first one-woman show, or write something from my heart. Needless to say, I spent a good deal of that time crying.
>
> When I think about being Afrolatina all of the above rings true indeed; but even truer in my heart is such a deep sense of rejection that I have felt from so many of my Latinx brothers and sisters; especially growing up—not from my family but from neighbors and classmates and boys and friends. I knew one day I would have

to confront this deep hurt but I don't know if I can give it the time it needs. (Jiménez Román and Flores, *The Afro-Latin@ Reader*, 296)

22. Juan Perea, "The Black/White Binary Paradigm of Race," in *The Latino Condition*, ed. Richard Delgado and Jean Stefani (New York: New York University Press, 1998), 361.

23. Other theorists who reject a strict white/Black paradigm include Elaine Kim, Gary Okihiro, Elizabeth Martínez, and Richard Delgado.

24. My analysis of this performance is based on my attendance and the video recording at Duo Theater and Henry Street Settlement. A complete manuscript of *La Nubia Latina* is not available. Sun reported that the original manuscript was lost in a computer malfunction. Quotes were transcribed from the recording.

25. Deracializing Puerto Rican identity is an institutional project, as evidenced by Miss Piel Canela Pageants, annual beauty contests originated in Puerto Rico since 1976.

26. Annette J. Saddik discusses how rappers understand their role in the system of commodity capitalism, which is a theatrical mode of performing, playing, and socially critiquing dominant worldviews. She looks to an interview that Ice Cube did with Charlie Rose where the rapper/producer/actor explains what it means to be American by "locat[ing] the foundation of American identity not only in what is conventionally seen as natural and healthy competition within the system of commodity capitalism, but in the proud *display* of one's capital—the flaunting or performance of ownership, wealth, and material success." "Rap's Unruly Body: The Postmodern Performance of Black Male Identity on the American Stage," *TDR: The Drama Review* 47, no. 4 (2003): 110.

27. Jesús Colón's "Cuentos para niños de uno a ochenta años" (1927) can be found in his *"Lo que el pueblo me dice . . .": Crónicas de la colonia puertoriqueña en Nueva York* (Houston, TX: Arte Público Press, 2001).

28. On Thanksgiving Day 1999, six-year-old Elián González was found clinging to an inner tube in the raging waters off Florida, after his mother and ten other Cubans drowned. Elián's great-uncle, who was based in Miami, petitioned for asylum and gained temporary custody. When Elián's father, Juan Miguel, learned of the incident, he began proceedings to get his son back. The US government ruled that the boy must return to his father in Cuba, but the great-uncle made it clear that he would not surrender the boy and defied the order by the attorney general. The saga ended abruptly on April 22, 2000—Easter Saturday—when Elián was removed by the marshals during a raid and then reunited with his father. As the asylum and custody battle sparked an international media and political frenzy, the Elián González case became a symbol of troubled relations between the United States and Cuba.

29. Other Latinx literary works utilize a roach metaphor to signify social realities. Oscar Zeta Acosta's *The Revolt of the Cockroach People* (1972) is a semiautobiographical novel that recalls the Chicano Moratorium on August 29, 1970, a mass protest against the Vietnam War. This historic act of resistance often remains unacknowledged because, as the title of the novel indicates, society perceives minorities as undesirables.

In *Puerto Rican Obituary* (1973), Pedro Pietri's anticonsumerism poem "Suicide Note from a Cockroach in a Low Income Housing Project" recounts the integration of the ghetto into the consumer society of late capitalism through a suicide note from an irate cockroach, protesting the genocide of his people. Despite the denigratory connotations of roaches, Lalo Alcaraz calls his syndicated comic strip and radical comic protagonist *La Cucaracha* (2002–). Aware of the many stereotypical images that the song "La Cucaracha" connotes—from the image of the Mexican with a wide-brimmed sombrero to Speedy González—Alcaraz names the protagonist Cuco Roach. With this character, Alcaraz addresses the issues of ethnicity, race, immigration, and current events.

Chapter 7

1. In her second solo work, *Aya de León Is Running for President: A Campaign Speech Remix in Poetry and Spoken* (2004), de León shares her pro-choice, pro-gay rights, pro-reparations, and antiwar agenda in a campaign speech remix, performed in hip hop theater style. As with *Thieves in the Temple*, *Aya de León Is Running for President* should be examined with a hip hop feminist lens.

2. Gwendolyn D. Pough, *Check It While I Wreck It*, 83.

3. Michael Jeffries, "Re: Definitions: The Name and Game of Hip-Hop Feminism," in *Home Girls Make Some Noise! Hip Hop Feminism Anthology*, ed. Gwendolyn D. Pough, Elaine Richardson, Aisha Durham, and Rachel Raimist (Mira Loma, CA: Parker, 2007), 217.

4. Stephanie L. Batiste, "Hip-Hop and This One-Woman Show," in Pough, Richardson, Durham, and Raimist, *Home Girls Make Some Noise*, 420.

5. Batiste, 420–21.

6. Here I am also thinking about Aisha Durham, who emphasizes the importance of the personal in Black feminist thought and hip hop feminism. She claims, "Other than black feminist social theory, hip-hop feminism builds off of the literary tradition of black and self-identified third-world feminism. We use the 'I' to allow others to see us. Like black feminists scholars, we write testimonials, life stories and poetics that draw from our alternative ways of knowing and understanding the world. We speak from the self outward." "Using [Living Hip-Hop] Feminism: Redefining an Answer to Rap," in Pough, Richardson, Durham, and Raimist, *Home Girls Make Some Noise*, 307.

7. Aya de León, "Hip-Hop Ventriloquism: From Sexism to Corporate Control," in Pough, Richardson, Durham, and Raimist, *Home Girls Make Some Noise*, 439–43; Anna de León, "Biography: Born into War," updated February 14, 2011, http://www.annadeleon.com/bio.html

8. Aya de León, "Hiroshima 70th Anniversary: Remembering My Teenage Anti-Nuclear Protest Years," August 6, 2015, https://ayadeleon.wordpress.com/. In this blog entry, de León reflects on her teenage activism. She has posted a photo of the antinuclear protest that she organized, recalling that she was the only Black teen involved in the 1980s antinuclear protests. At an early age, she used performance as a political vehicle, organizing a die-in on the lawn at University of California, Berkeley.

The performance protest included the characters of Death and the Bomb-maker. She wore a black vintage dress and a Mexican-style *calavera* face to portray Death. She kills the Bomb-maker, who profits from escalating the arms race.

9. Aya de León, "Report from the Field: My MFA Career as a Recovering Prestige Fiend," *VIDA Women in Literary Arts*, March 16, 2016, http://www.vidaweb.org/report-from-the-field-my-mfa-career-as-a-recovering-prestige-fiend/

10. De León, "Report from the Field."

11. Aya de León, "Hiroshima 70th Anniversary."

12. Taj Mahal, "Biography: The Early Years," updated 2019, http://www.tajblues.com/biography/

13. De León, "Report from the Field."

14. Joshunda Sanders, "Taking the Rap / Poet Aya de León Tackles Sexism and Reclaims Hip-Hop in Her New Play," *San Francisco Chronicle*, March 14, 2004.

15. Aya de León, "About Aya," accessed September 18, 2019, https://ayadeleon.wordpress.com

16. Reyhan Harmanci, "Responding in Kind / 'Thieves in the Temple' / Aya de León Took a Stand When Hip-Hop Culture's Sexism Went Too Far," *San Francisco Chronicle*, March 15, 2007.

17. Adrianna Dinolfo, "Finding Power in Poetry: The Many Voices of Aya de León," *Daily Californian* (Berkeley), November 6, 2014.

18. Harmanci, "Responding in Kind."

19. Aya de León, "Lyrical Self-Defense and the Reluctant Female Rapper," in *Word Warriors: 35 Women Leaders in the Spoken Word Revolution*, ed. Alix Olson (Emeryville, CA: Seal Press), 63 (emphasis added).

20. Danny Hoch, artistic director of the New York Hip-Hop Theater Festival, addresses the challenges in "defin[ing] not what Hip Hop means as a culture, but what Hip Hop means as art—in fact, to make the case that Hip Hop is art." See his "Toward A Hip-Hop Aesthetic: A Manifesto for the Hip-Hop Arts Movement," in *Total Chaos: The Art and Aesthetic of Hip-Hop*, ed. Jeff Chang (New York: Basic Civitas, 2007), 349.

21. De León, "Lyrical Self-Defense, 67.

22. Aya de León's publications are extensive and diverse, including CDs, poems, short stories, and essays: "Tell Me Moore," in *Spooks, Spies, and Private Eyes: Black Mystery, Crime, and Suspense Fiction*, ed. Paula L. Woods (New York: Doubleday, 1995), 356–73; "Hitting Dante," in *Dreaming in Color, Living in Black and White: Our Own Stories of Growing Up in Black America*, ed. Laurel Holliday (New York: Simon Pulse, 2003), 99–112; "Sixteen," in *Shout Out: Women of Color Respond to Violence*, ed. María Ochoa and Barbara K. Ige (Emeryville, CA: Seal Press, 2007), 26–29; "Grito de Vieques," in *Fire and Ink: An Anthology of Social Action*, ed. Frances Payne Adler, Debra Busman, and Diana García (Tucson: University of Arizona Press, 2009), 229–31; and "Lyrical Self-Defense and the Reluctant Female Rapper," "Cellulite," and "Grito de Vieques," in *Word Warriors*, 63–72.

23. Kensington Books was one of the first companies to publish African American mysteries, Westerns, and romance novels.

24. As Paul Grainge notes, although the relationship between mode and modality

is vital, this relationship should not be assumed. Nostalgia modes do not necessarily trigger nostalgic moods, nor vice versa. Some styles of nostalgia do not connect with feelings of loss. See his *Monochrome Memories: Nostalgia and Style in Retro America* (Westport, CT: Praeger, 2002).

25. Fred Davis, *Yearning for Yesterday: A Sociology of Nostalgia* (New York: Free Press, 1979).

26. Fredric Jameson, *Postmodernism, or The Cultural Logic of Late Capitalism* (London: Verso, 1991), 331.

27. Grainge, *Monochrome Memories*, 23.

28. Aya de León, *Thieves in the Temple*, in *Plays from the Boom Box Galaxy: Theater from the Hip Hop Generation*, ed. Kim Euell and Robert Alexander (New York: Theater Communications Group, 2009), 309. The basis of my reading of *Thieves in the Temple* relies on my attendance at this piece, which was featured as part of the third New York City Hip-Hop Theater Festival at New York City's PS 122, during summer 2002. I also used the video of this piece, which was performed at the AfroSolo Theater Festival in San Francisco, California, during summer 2001.

29. De León, 314. For more on the relationship between hip hop and global capitalism, see Jeffries, "Re: Definitions." Jeffries argues, "hip-hop forces us to deal with crucial questions about modern capitalism as we see themes of capitalist hegemony clearly reflected in American hip-hop music. From the Horatio Algiers narrative of hustling drug dealers, to the exploitative relationship between pimp and hoe, to the militaristic zero-sum empire fantasies of gangster rappers, the virtues and vices of capitalist logic write themselves large on popular hip-hop's canvas. These themes, the structural starting points of their narrators, and the dog-eat-dog ethos of hip-hop battles force listeners to recognize that modern capitalism creates winners and losers, and fosters ideology that pervades both the material and non-material spheres of life. Hip-hop identity, therefore, implies an awareness of one's social position in the context of global capitalism" (213).

30. Durham, "Using [Living Hip-Hop] Feminism," 306.

31. In the stage directions, Aya de León specifically mentions that Hill's "Doo Wop (That Thing)" or songs of a similar nature should be part of the preshow music.

32. For discussion of the feminist work of rappers—including a reading of the feminism in Lauryn Hill's "Doo Wop (That Thing)"—see Layli Phillips, Kerri Reddick-Morgan, and Dionne Patricia Stephens, "Oppositional Realm: The Case of Feminism and Womanism in Rap and Hip Hop, 1976–2004," *Journal of African American History* 90, no. 3 (2005): 253–77.

33. De León, *Thieves in the Temple*, 372. A *slanger* is a drug dealer, and *noc* refers to a non-official cover without diplomatic status, like a secret agent.

34. Tricia Rose, *The Hip Hop Wars: What We Talk about When We Talk about Hip Hop and Why It Matters* (New York: Basic Civitas, 2008), 11.

35. De León, *Thieves in the Temple*, 310.

36. De León, 311.

37. De León, 312.

38. De León, 312.

39. De León, 307.

40. *Thieves in the Temple* has undergone many changes. The scene "The Decline and Fall" was performed at the 2002 Hip-Hop Theater Festival and is included in the 2002 unpublished script, provided by Aya de León. It does not appear in the published version of the text in the 2009 anthology *Plays from the Boom Box Galaxy*. In the published version, a scene with the character of Set-Style—a male rapper with a strange condition that forces him to reveal personal thoughts instead of the usual macho pattern—replaces this scene.

41. Norman Kelley, ed., *Rhythm and Business: The Political Economy of Black Music* (New York: Akashic Books, 2002), 12.

42. Aya de León, "Thieves in the Temple: The Reclaiming of Hip Hop" (2002), unpublished manuscript, 2. This character was performed at the 2002 Hip-Hop Theater Festival but was not included in the published manuscript of *Thieves in the Temple*.

43. Kelley, *Rhythm and Business*, 7.

44. De León, video recording, Afro Solo Theater Festival, San Francisco, CA, 2001.

45. De León, "Thieves in the Temple" (2002), unpublished manuscript, 3.

46. De León, 3.

47. De León, *Thieves in the Temple* (2009), 314.

48. De León, "Thieves in the Temple" (2002), unpublished manuscript, 3.

49. Faedra Chatard Carpenter, *Coloring Whiteness: Acts of Critique in Black Performance* (Ann Arbor: University of Michigan Press, 2014), 3. Carpenter suggests that in unfolding the social, political, and economic construct of whiteness, performers are using a dramaturgical strategy of making whiteness "strange."

50. De León, *Thieves in the Temple* (2009), 321

51. Margeaux Watson, "When Size 6 Ain't Small Enough," *Honey*, September 2003, 144.

52. De León, *Thieves in the Temple* (2009), 322 and Gwendolyn D. Pough, *Check It While I Wreck It: Black Womanhood, Hip-Hop Culture, and the Public Sphere* (Lebanon, NH: Northeastern University Press, 2004), 188.

53. In *Check It While I Wreck It*, Pough argues that even though female rappers such as Foxy Brown and Lil' Kim draw on the trope of Black women as sexually promiscuous, they disrupt the silence around female sexuality and shame in the Black community (188).

54. De León, video recording, AfroSolo Theater Festival, San Francisco, California, 2001, and "Thieves in the Temple" (2002), unpublished manuscript, 5. I use the video and original script here because this is the version that was included in the performance at the New York Hip-Hop Theater Festival. Furthermore, in the video and original script, de León emphasizes the role of the audience and stresses how Lady Triple X tries but ultimately fails to meet the audience's expectations of Black promiscuous women. The stage directions indicate that there is a recorded applause and that the audience leaves, and thus her comprehension of her own disempowerment is emotionally impactful. By contrast, in the published version, there is no indication of the audience. Instead, the absence of recorded applause indicates her failure to seduce the audience members. De León, *Thieves in the Temple*, 322–23.

55. Pough, *Check It While I Wreck It*, 17.

56. De León, video recording, AfroSolo Theater Festival; and De León, "Thieves in the Temple" (2002), unpublished manuscript, 5.

57. De León, video recording, AfroSolo Theater Festival; and De León, "Thieves in the Temple" (2002), unpublished manuscript, 7.

58. Jill Dolan, *Utopia in Performance: Finding Hope at the Theater* (Ann Arbor: University of Michigan Press, 2005), 5.

59. De León, video recording, AfroSolo Theater Festival; and De León, (2002), unpublished manuscript, 10

Chapter 8

1. On April 1, 2011, El Centro de estudios puertorriqueños (the Center for Puerto Rican Studies) and Sangre Viva Art Alliance, a grassroots collaborative of prominent Latinx art associations functioning in New York City, held a conference entitled, "Boricua Diaspora Poets: An Intergenerational Conversation" at Hunter College in New York City. Since 1974, Centro has been pivotal in disseminating Puerto Rican scholarship and conversation throughout the United States. Sangre Viva Art Alliance was founded in 2007, with the mission of "promoting a grassroots, international vision of Latinidad in the arts . . . [but also] uniting *[their]* family, the artists, poets, musicians, graphic designers, performance and visual artists that *they* work with consistently . . . to change lives." (Jani Rose, founding member of Sangre Viva, http://angelrtalk.com/sangre-viva-presents-historias-a-conversation-on-latino-literature/). This event was moderated by Pedro López Adorno and Juan "PaPo" Santiago, and it included a panel by Sandra María Esteves, Willie Perdomo, Rich Villar, and Jani Bomba Rose.

2. Sandra María Esteves, "Boricua Diaspora Poets: An Intergenerational Conversation," Hunter College, New York City, April 1, 2011.

3. Irene Lara, "Bruja Positionalities: Toward a Chicana/Latina Spiritual Activism," *Chicana/Latina Studies* 4, no. 2 (2005): 11.

4. Because modern Western thought has constructed divisions between the body, mind, and spirit, Irene Lara created this compound to acknowledge one's being as holistically connected. See Lara, "Bruja Positionalities," 11; and Lara, "Healing Sueños for Academia," in *This Bridge We Call Home: Radical Visions of Transformation*, ed. Gloria Anzaldúa and AnaLouise Keating (New York: Routledge, 2002), 435.

5. Gloria E. Anzaldúa, *Interviews/Entrevistas*, ed. AnaLouise Keating (New York: Routledge, 2000), 98.

6. Elisa Facio and Irene Lara's groundbreaking anthology *Fleshing the Spirit: Spirituality and Activism in Chicana, Latina, and Indigenous Women's Lives* (Tucson: University of Arizona Press, 2014) draws from an interdisciplinary framework and uses different genres of writing to theorize the connections among spirituality, women of color, and social activism.

7. For more information on how Nuyorican theater practitioners express their Afro-Latinx identity through music and performance, see Patricia Herrera, "Listening to Afro-Latinidad: The Sonic Archive of *Olú Clemente*," in *Afro-Latin@s in Movement:*

Critical Approaches to Blackness and Transnationalism in the Americas, ed. Petra R. River-Rideau, Jennifer A. Jones, and Tianna Paschel (New York: Palgrave, 2016), 171–94.

8. Anzaldúa and Keating, *This Bridge We Call Home*, 24.

9. Anzaldúa, *Interviews/Entrevistas*, 177.

10. Anzaldúa, 178.

11. Lara, "Bruja Positionalities," 26. For other examples of witch-healers, see Rudolfo Anaya, *Bless Me, Ultima* (1972; New York: Grand Central, 2013; made into a film in 2013); Marta Moreno Vega, *The Altar of My Soul: The Living Traditions of Santería* (New York: One World, 2000); and Louie The Foot González, "Doña Toña of Nineteenth Street," in *Growing Up Chicana/o: An Anthology*, ed. Tiffany Ana López (New York: William Morrow, 1993), 59–68.

12. While Irene Lara uses a hyhen, Tey Diana Rebolledo uses a backslash between *bruja* and *curandera*. "Bruja Positionalities," 38.

13. Laura Pérez, *Chicana Art: The Politics of Spiritual and Aesthetic Altarities* (Durham, NC: Duke University Press Books, 2007), 7. For more discussion on the intersections of art and spirituality, see Perez's essay, "Spirit Glyphs: Reimagining Arts and Artist in the Work of Chicana Tlamatinime," *Modern Fiction Studies* 44, no. 1 (1998): 36–76.

14. I am invoking Harry J. Elam Jr.'s definition of social protest performance to denote how theatrical events during the Chicano and Black Arts movements explicitly countered the dominant social order and incited the audience to change their current situation. This objective, as Elam points out, is drastically different from that of radical theater, which focuses on using nontraditional conventions for performances. Elam, *Taking It to the Streets: The Social Protest Theater of Luis Valdez and Amiri Baraka* (Ann Arbor: University of Michigan, 1997), 142. See also Yolanda Broyles-González, *El Teatro Campesino: Theater in the Chicano Movement* (Austin: University of Texas Press, 1994).

15. La Virgin de Guadalupe became the spiritual and political symbol for the United Farm Workers and the whole Chicano movement. The image of Guadalupe is a reminder of the colonial history of Mexico. While some scholars argue that Guadalupe was invented by the Spaniards to seduce the Aztec into Catholicism, others read Guadalupe as a manifestation of the Indian deity Tonatzin. She continues to be prominently featured in the work of contemporary Chicana artists such as Alma López, Ester Hernández, and Yolanda M. López, though now with an explicit feminist consciousness. Thus, Guadalupe can be seen as a spiritual and political figure that protests Catholicism, colonialism, and patriarchy. For an analysis of the strategic use of La Virgin de Guadalupe by the UFW and El Teatro Campesino, see Broyles-González, *El Teatro Campesino*, especially 58–74. For additional discussion of Guadalupe art by Chicana feminist artists, see Pérez, *Chicana Art*, especially 258–86; and Alicia Arrizón, *Queering Mestizaje: Transculturation and Performance* (Ann Arbor: University of Michigan Press, 2006), 49–82.

16. El Teatro Campesino was mainly involved with two sacred pageants: *Las cuatro apariciones* (The Four Apparitions) and *Pastorelas* (Shepherd's Play). Similar to the way UFW utilized the Virgin of Guadalupe in its demonstrations, Gudalupe in *Las cuatro apariciones* is a symbol of resistance, hope, and survival. Guadalupe mi-

raculously appears, always in the context of saving Native people from colonial violence and annihilation. In the *Pastorelas*, the birth of Jesus frames the story, but El Teatro Campesino emphasizes the struggle between San Miguel (the angel) and Lucifer (the devil). El Teatro Campesino embeds this religious performance with *relajo*, a subversive form of humor, allowing the struggle for self-determination among Native people to become relevant to Chicanos. Broyles-González, *El Teatro Campesino*, 58–60.

17. While Broyles-González encourages scholars to further research the performance theory and practice of Teatro Campesino's Theatre of the Sphere, she emphasizes that the archive is based on oral history, collective memory, and the reclaiming of Indigenous ancestry and tradition. To reconstruct the daily practices of Theater of the Sphere, she interviews members of El Teatro Campesino and engages with the Maya and Aztec teachings of Domingo Martínez Paredez and Andrés Segura, scholars who shaped and informed the troupe. See Broyles-González, 79–127.

18. Elam, *Taking It to the Streets*, 14.

19. Elam, 14.

20. Elam, 14.

21. Cherríe Moraga and Gloria Anzaldúa, *The Bridge Called My Back: Writings by Radicals of Color* (New York: Kitchen Table/Women of Color Press, 1981), 23.

22. Sandra María Esteves, *Yerba Buena: Dibujos y poemas* (Greenfield Center, NY: Greenfield Review Press, 1980), 38.

23. Esteves, 1 and 22.

24. Many thanks to Ramón H. Rivera-Servera for reminding me about the double meaning of this word.

25. Esteves, "Boricua Diaspora Poets," Hunter College, New York City, April 1, 2011.

26. Sandra María Esteves, "I Wish I Could," *Contrapunto in the Open Field* (New York: No Frills, 1998), 89–91.

27. Victor Turner, *Dramas, Fields, and Metaphors: Symbolic Action in Human Society* (Ithaca, NY: Cornell University Press, 1974), 39.

28. See José Antonia Burciaga's pivotal book *Drink Cultura: Chicanismo* (Santa Barbara, CA: Capra Press, 1993), which addresses the healing properties of art and performance. Burciaga was a founding mentor of the Chicano performance troupe Culture Clash, a topic of discussion in the Epilogue.

29. Jose Alvarez is known for his live channeling performances of the two-thousand-year-old spirit of a shaman named Carlos. He has performed at the NASA Johnson Space Center, as well at the Parkes Observatory in Australia. Many people around the world have, through media broadcasts, viewed his performances. These performances were the subject of a video work presented in the 2004 Whitney Biennial, curated by Lawrence Rinder. His solo exhibit *The Visitors* (2008), held at the Kitchen in New York and curated by Debra Singer, also dealt with shamanism. While detained in Krome Detention Center in Miami for identity theft for two months in 2012, he created a series of portraits of his fellow detainees, which is the focus of his most recent exhibition, *Jose Alvarez (D.O.P.A.), Krome* (2016) at the Boca Raton Mu-

seum of Art. Guillermo Gómez Peña has also created his own shamanic persona wearing sometimes a wrestling mask or other times a feathered headdress experimenting with sounds and different languages he harnesses the power of ritual to collectively grapple with the violence of capitalism, racism, gentrification, immigration, and globalization. Combining digital art, videos, and photo performance, Gómez Peña pushes the boundaries of the body, art, and politics to develop a different type of relationship with the public, one full of discomfort.

30. Alberto Sandoval-Sánchez, *José Can You See? Latinos On and Off Broadway* (Madison: University of Wisconsin Press, 1999), 29–31.

31. Sandoval-Sánchez, 33.

32. Claudia Soto, "La Bruja Rocks Quepasa to the Rhythm of Reggaeton," *Quepasa News*, August 14, 2006.

33. Caridad de la Luz, *Boogie Rican Boulevard* (2001), unpublished manuscript, 16.

34. This idiom makes more sense in the context of the proverb "El amor es como tener un toro en frente, te descuidas y te mete los cuernos" (love is like having a bull in front of you; you neglect it and he will be unfaithful).

35. Clarisel González, "Q&A: Caridad De La Luz of Boogie Rican Blvd: The Musical," *Urban Lifestyle Media*, July 3, 2009, accessed June 20, 2012, http://www.examiner.com/ (at time of printing, this article is no longer available online).

36. Caridad de la Luz, *Boogie Rican Boulevard* (2001), unpublished manuscript, 26.

37. Pérez, *Chicana Art: The Politics of Spiritual and Aesthetic Altarities* (Durham: Duke University Press Books, 2007).

38. Dipesh Chakrabarty, "The Time of History and the Times of Gods," in *The Politics of Culture in the Shadow of Capital*, ed. Lisa Lowe and David Lloyd (Durham, NC: Duke University Press, 1997), 36.

39. Chakrabarty, 39. Here I am reminded of Roland Barthes's claim that, "Foam can even be the sign of a certain spirituality, inasmuch as the spirit has the reputation of being able to make something out of nothing, a large surface of effects out of a small volume of causes." He is speaking here of the way in which the advertisement for Omo, a detergent, hinges on a play of meanings with the words *deep* and *foam*; the deep cleanliness and the luxurious foam lure consumers to buy this product. Barthes normalizes spirituality with foam. He does not distinguish it from the divine. Instead, he naturalizes the metaphysical as part of the material world—as if they are one and the same—eventually erasing the ineffable presence of spiritual dimensions. Barthes, *Mythologies* (New York: The Noonday Press, 1972), 36.

Epilogue

1. See my essay "Culture Clash's *Nuyorican Stories*: Building Latinidad, Silencing Queerness," *Theatre Topics* 27, no. 1 (2017): 71–82, for a discussion of the erasure of queer voices.

2. Culture Clash, *Nuyorican Stories*, in *Culture Clash in AmeriCCa* (New York: Theatre Communications Group, 2003), 85.

3. Culture Clash, 85, 86.

4. This song was first released on the sound track of the classic blaxploitation film *Super Fly* (1972).

5. Culture Clash, 88.

6. Culture Clash, 89.

7. On February 26, 2012, Trayvon Martin, a seventeen-year-old African American young man was fatally shot by aspiring police officer and community watch coordinator George Zimmerman. He believed that Martin's clothing and behavior were suspicious. Given Martin's death, the delay in charging Zimmerman, and the debates around stand-your-ground laws in some states, this event has received national and international attention.

8. Culture Clash, *Nuyorican Stories*, 87.

Bibliography

Alarcón, Norma. "Conjugating Subjects in the Age of Multiculturalism." In *Mapping Multiculturalism*, edited by Avery F. Gordon and Christopher Newfield, 127–48. Minneapolis: University of Minnesota Press, 1996.

Alarcón, Norma, Ana Castillo, and Cherríe Moraga, eds. *The Sexuality of Latinas*. Berkeley, CA: Third Woman Press, 1989.

Alcoff, Linda Martín. *Visible Identities: Race, Gender, and the Self*. Oxford: Oxford University Press, 2006.

Algarín, Miguel. "Introduction: Nuyorican Language." In Algarín and Piñero, *Nuyorican Poetry*, 9–20.

Algarín, Miguel. *Mongo Affairs*. New York: East Village Press, 1978.

Algarín, Miguel. "Nuyorican Literature." *MELUS* 8, no. 2 (1981): 89–92.

Algarín, Miguel. "Volume and Value of the Breath in Poetry." *Revista Chicana-Riqueña* 6, no. 3 (1978): 52–69.

Algarín, Miguel, and Louis Griffith, eds. *Action: The Nuyorican Poets Café Theater Festival*. New York: Touchstone, 1997.

Algarín, Miguel, and Bob Holman, eds. *Aloud: Voices from the Nuyorican Poets Café*. New York: Henry Holt, 1994.

Algarín, Miguel, and Tato Laviera. "Olu Clemente." *Revista Chicano-Riqueña* 6, no. 1 (1977): 151–71.

Algarín, Miguel, and Miguel Piñero, eds. *Nuyorican Poetry: An Anthology of Puerto Rican Words and Feelings*. New York: William Morrow, 1975.

Allen, Ray, and Lois Wilcken, eds. *Island Sounds in the Global City: Caribbean Popular Music and Identity in New York*. Champaign: University of Illinois Press, 2001.

Allione, Constanzo, dir. *Fried Shoes, Cooked Diamonds*. 1979 film. Montauk, NY: Mystic Fire Video, 1989. DVD, 55 min.

Anaya, Rudolfo. *Bless Me, Ultima*. 1972. New York: Grand Central, 2013.

Andre, Armando. "Entrenados en Cuba: El Terrorismo de la FALN [Fuerzas Armadas de Liberación Nacional Puertoriqueña/Armed Forces of National Liberation] en EE. UU." *La Crónica Gráfica*, San Juan, 1987.

Anuta, Joe. "High Rents Have Bronx Locals Packing Up: Gentrification Starts to Hit Highbridge and Grand Concourse." *Crain's New York Business*. March 31, 2014.

Anzaldúa, Gloria E. *Interviews/Entrevistas*. Edited by AnaLouise Keating. New York: Routledge, 2000.

Anzaldúa, Gloria E., and AnaLouise Keating, eds. *This Bridge We Call Home: Radical Visions for Transformation*. New York: Routledge, 2002.

Aparicio, Frances R. "From Ethnicity to Multiculturalism: An Historical Overview of Puerto Rican Literature in the United States." In *Handbook of Hispanic Cultures*, edited by Francisco Lomeli, 26–28. Houston, TX: Arte Público Press, 1993.

Aparicio, Frances R. "La Vida Es un Spanglish Disparatero: Bilingualism in Nuyorican Poetry." In *European Perspectives on Hispanic Literature of the United States,* edited by Geneviè Fabre, 147–60 (Houston: Arte Público Press, 1988).

Apontes, Luis. "Lessons from El Barrio: The East Harlem Real Great Society/Urban Planning Studio: A Puerto Rican Chapter in the Fight for Urban Self Determination." In *Latino Social Movements: Historical and Theoretical Perspectives*, edited by Rodolfo D. Torres and George Katsiaficas, 43–78. New York: Routledge, 1999.

Aponte Vázquez, Pedro I. *¡Yo acuso! Tortura y asesinato de Don Pedro Albizu Campos*. Bayamón, PR: Movimiento Ecuménico Nacional de Puerto Rico, 1985.

Arrizón, Alicia. *Latina Performance: Traversing the Stage*. Bloomington: Indiana University Press, 1999.

Arrizón, Alicia. *Queering Mestizaje: Transculturation and Performance*. Ann Arbor: University of Michigan Press, 2006.

Arrizón, Alicia, and Lillian Manzor, eds. *Latinas on Stage: Practice and Theory*. Berkeley, CA: Third Woman, 2000.

Arroyo, Antonio Stevens. *The Political Philosophy of Pedro Albizu Campos: Its Theory and Practice*. New York: New York University, Ibero-American Language and Area Center, 1974.

Ayala, César J., and Rafael Bernabe. *Puerto Rico in the American Century: A History since 1898*. Chapel Hill: University of North Carolina Press, 2007.

Ayala, Jennifer, Patricia Herrera, Laura Jiménez, and Irene Lara. "Fiera, Guambra y Karichina! Transgressing the Borders of Community and Academy." In Bernal, Elenes, Godinez, and Villenas, *Chicana/Latina Education in Everyday Life*, 261–80.

Azize Varga, Yamila. "A Commentary on the Work of Three Puerto Rican Women Poets in New York." In Horno-Delgado, Ortega, Scott, and Sternbach, *Breaking Boundaries*, 146–65.

Badillo, Herman. *One Nation, One Standard: An Ex-Liberal on How Hispanics Can Succeed Just Like Other Immigrant Groups*. New York: Sentinel, 2006.

Banks, Daniel, ed. *Say Word! Voices from Hip Hop Theater*. Ann Arbor: University of Michigan Press, 2011.

Barradas, Efraín. Introduction to Barradas and Rodriguez, *Herejes y mitificadores*, 11–30.

Barradas, Efraín. *Parte de un todo: Ensayos y notas sobre literatura Puertorriqueña en los Estados Unidos*. San Juan, PR: Editorial de la Universidad de Puerto Rico, 1998.

Barradas, Efraín, and Rafael Rodriguez, eds. *Herejes y mitificadores: Muestra de poesía Puertoriqueña en los Estados Unidos*. Rio Piedras, PR: Ediciones Huracán, 1980.

Barreto, Amílcar Antonio. *The Politics of Language in Puerto Rico*. Gainesville: University Press of Florida, 2001.

Barthes, Roland. *Mythologies*. New York: Noonday Press, 1972.

Bass, Holly. "Blowing Up the Set: What Happens When the Pulse of Hip-Hop Shakes Up the Traditional Stage." *American Theatre*, November 1999.

Batiste, Stephanie L. "Hip-Hop and This One-Woman Show," in Pough, Richardson, Durham, and Raimist, *Home Girls Make Some Noise*, 413–32.

Bernal, Dolores Delgado, C. Alejandra Elenes, Francisca E. Godinez, and Sofia Villenas, eds. *Chicana/Latina Education in Everyday Life: Feminista Perspectives on Pedagogy and Epistemology*. Albany: State University of New York Press, 2006.

Bernas, Frederick. "The Nuyorican Revolution." *Narratively*. February 21, 2014. http://www.frederickbernas.com/2014/02/the-nuyorican-revolution.html

Bernstein, Charles, ed. *Close Listening: Poetry and the Performed Word*. New York: Oxford University Press, 1998.

Bernstein, Charles, ed. "Introduction." In Bernstein, *Close Listening*, 3–26.

Bird-Soto, Nancy. "¿Términos apropiados? El potencial latinx." *Cruce: Crítica Socio-cultural Contemporánea*. November 30, 2015. http://revistacruce.com/politica-y-sociedad/item/2255-terminos-apropiados-el-potencial-latinx

Bloom, Harold. Interviewed in "The Man in the Back Row Has a Question VI." By David Barber. *Paris Review* 42, no. 154 (Spring 2000).

Bobel, Chris. *The New Blood: Third-Wave Feminism and the Politics of Menstruation*. New Brunswick, NJ: Rutgers University Press, 2010.

Bost, Suzanne. "'Be deceived if ya wanna be foolish': (Re)Constructing Body, Genre, and Gender in Feminist Rap." *Postmodern Culture* 12, no. 1 (2001). https://doi.org/10.1353/pmc.2001.0017

Bost, Suzanne. "Transgressing Borders: Puerto Rican and Latina Mestizaje." *MELUS* 25, no. 2 (2000): 187–211.

Brooklyn Information and Culture, Brooklyn Independent Network. *Caught in the Act*. Episode 8. Aired September 23, 2009. YouTube. 8 min. http://www.youtube.com/watch?v=KWTMqHhU1kM

Brown, Ruth Nicole, and Chamara Jewel Kwakye, eds. *Wish to Live: The Hip Hop Feminist Pedagogy Reader*. New York: Peter Lang, 2012.

Broyles-González, Yolanda. *El Teatro Campesino: Theater in the Chicano Movement*. Austin: University of Texas Press, 1994.

Burciaga, José Antonia. *Drink Cultura: Chicanismo*. Santa Barbara, CA: Capra Press, 1993.

Burgos, William. "Puerto Rican Literature in a New Clave: Notes on the Emergence of DiaspoRican." In *Writing Off the Hyphen: New Critical Perspectives on the Literature of the Puerto Rican Diaspora*, edited by José L. Torres-Padilla and Carmen Haydée Rivera, 125–42. Seattle: University of Washington Press, 2008.

Canning, Charlotte. "Feminist Performance as Feminist Historiography." *Theatre Survey* 45, no. 2 (November 2002): 227–33.

Canning, Charlotte. "Performance as Feminist Historiography." *Theatre Survey* 45, no. 2 (2004): 227–33.

Canning, Charlotte, and Thomas Postlewait. *Representing the Past: Essays in Performance Historiography*. Iowa City: University of Iowa Press, 2010.

Cantú, Norma E. "Living La Vida Santa: My Chicana Spirituality and Activist Scholarship." In Facio and Lara, *Fleshing the Spirit*, 202–17.

Carlson, Marvin. *The Haunted Stage: The Theatre as Memory Machine*. Ann Arbor: University of Michigan Press, 2003.

Carlson, Marvin. *Performance: A Critical Introduction*. London: Routledge, 1996.

Carpenter, Faedra Chatard. *Coloring Whiteness: Acts of Critique in Black Performance*. Ann Arbor: University of Michigan Press, 2014.

Carrero, Jaime. *Jet Neorriqueño/Neo-Rican Jetliner*. San Germán, PR: Universidad Inter American, 1964.

Carrero, Jaime, ed. *Notes of Neorican Seminar*. San Germán, PR: Inter American University, 1972.

Carroll, Henry K. *Report on the Island of Porto Rico: Its Population, Civil Government, Productions, Roads, Traffic and Currency*. Washington, DC: Government Printing Office, 1899.

Case, Sue-Ellen. *Feminism and Theatre*. New York: Palgrave Macmillan, 2008.

Case, Sue-Ellen, ed. *Performing Feminisms: Feminist Critical Theory and Theatre*. Baltimore: Johns Hopkins University Press, 1990.

Case, Sue-Ellen, ed. *Split Britches: Lesbian Practice/Feminist Performance*. London: Routledge, 1996.

Chang, Jeff. *Can't Stop, Won't Stop*. New York: St. Martin's Press, 2003.

Chakrabarty, Dipesh. "The Time of History and the Times of God." In *The Politics of Culture in the Shadow of Capital*, edited by Lisa Lowe and David Lloyd, 35–60. Durham, NC: Duke University Press, 1997.

Collazo, Lissette Rolón. "De la @ a la x." *80grados*. April 18, 2014. http://www.80grados.net/de-la-a-la-x/

Collins, Patricia Hill. *Black Feminist Thought: Knowledge, Consciousness, and the Politics of Empowerment*. Boston: Unwin Hyman, 1990.

Collins, Patricia Hill. "Is the Personal Still Political? The Women's Movement, Feminism, and Black Women in the Hip-Hop Generation." In *From Black Power to Hip Hop: Racism, Nationalism, and Feminism*, 161–96. Philadelphia, PA: Temple University Press, 2006.

Colón, David. "Other Latino Poetic Method." *Cultural Critique* 47 (2001): 265–86.

Colón, Jesús. *"Lo que el pueblo me dice . . .": Crónicas de la colonia puertoriqueña en Nueva York*. Houston, TX: Arte Público Press, 2001.

Coontz, Stephanie. *The Way We Never Were: American Families and the Nostalgia Trap*. New York: Basic Books, 1993.

Córdova, Nathaniel L. "In His Image and Likeness: The Puerto Rican Jíbaro as Political Icon." *Centro: Journal of the Center for Puerto Rican Studies* 17, no. 2 (2005): 171–91.

Cortes, Felix, Angel Falcón, and Juan Flores. "The Cultural Expression of Puerto Ricans in New York: A Theoretical Perspective and Critical Review." *Latin American Perspective* 3, no. 3 (1976): 117–52.

Cortiñas, Jorge Ignacio. "Are We Dancing to Our Own Beat?" *American Theatre*. May/June 2004.

Coscarelli, Joe, and Melena Ryzik, "Music Mogul Russell Simmons Is Accused of Rape by 3 Women." *New York Times*. December 13, 2017.

Crenshaw, Kimberlé. "De-Marginalizing the Intersection of Race and Sex: A Black

Feminist Critique of Antidiscrimination Doctrine, Feminist Theory, and Antiracist Politics." *University of Chicago Legal Forum*, 1989, 139–67.

Culture Clash. *Nuyorican Stories*. In *Culture Clash in AmeriCCa*, 65–102. New York: Theatre Communications Group, 2003.

Dalleo, E. Machado Sáez, and Elena Machado Sáez. *The Latino/a Canon and the Emergence of Post-Sixties Literature*. New York: Palgrave Macmillan, 2007.

Damon, Maria. "Avant-Garde or Borderguard: (Latino) Identity in Poetry." *American Literary History* 10, no. 3 (1998): 478–96.

Damon, Maria. "Was That 'Different,' 'Dissident' or 'Dissonant?': Poetry (n) the Public Spear: Slams, Open Readings, and Dissident Traditions." In Bernstein, *Close Listening*, 324–42.

Dávila, Arlene. *Barrio Dreams: Puerto Ricans, Latinos, and the Neoliberal City*. Berkeley: University of California Press, 2004.

Dávila, Arlene. *Culture Works: Space, Value, and Mobility across the Neoliberal Americas*. New York: New York University Press, 2012.

Dávila, Arlene. *Latino Spin: Public Image and the Whitewashing of Race*. New York: New York University Press, 2008.

Davis, Eisa. "Found in Translation: The Emergence of Hip-Hop Theatre." *American Theatre*. July/August 2004.

Davis, Eisa. "Hip Hop Theater: The New Underground." *Source*, March 2000, 172–76.

Davis, Fred. *Yearning for Yesterday: A Sociology of Nostalgia*. New York: Free Press, 1979.

DeCosta-Willis, Miriam. "Sandra María Esteves's Nuyorican Poetics: The Signifying Difference." *Afro-Hispanic Review* 23, no. 2 (2004): 3–12.

De la Roche, Elisa. *Teatro Hispano! Three Major New York Companies*. New York: Garland, 1995.

De León, Anna. "Biography: Born into War." Updated February 14, 2011. http://www.annadeleon.com/bio.html

De León, Aya. "Grito de Vieques." In *Fire and Ink: An Anthology of Social Action*, edited by Frances Payne Adler, Debra Busman, and Dian García, 229–31. Tucson: University of Arizona Press, 2009.

De León, Aya. "Hip-Hop Ventriloquism: From Sexism to Corporate Control." In Pough, Richardson, Durham, and Raimist, *Home Girls Make Some Noise*, 439–43.

De León, Aya. "Hiroshima 70th Anniversary: Remembering My Teenage Anti-Nuclear Protest Years." August 6, 2015. https://ayadeleon.wordpress.com/

De León, Aya. "Hitting Dante." In *Dreaming in Color, Living in Black and White: Our Own Stories of Growing Up in Black America*, edited by Laurel Holliday, 99–112. New York: Simon Pulse, 2003.

De León, Aya. "Lyrical Self-Defense and the Reluctant Female Rapper." In *Word Warriors: 35 Women Leaders in the Spoken Word Revolution*, edited by Alix Olson, 63–72. Emeryville, CA: Seal Press.

De León, Aya. "Report from the Field: My MFA Career as a Recovering Prestige Fiend." *VIDA Women in Literary Arts*. March 16, 2016. http://www.vidaweb.org/report-from-the-field-my-mfa-career-as-a-recovering-prestige-fiend/

De León, Aya. "Sixteen." In *Shout Out: Women of Color Respond to Violence*, edited by María Ochoa and Barbara K. Ige, 26–29. Emeryville, CA: Seal Press, 2007.

De León, Aya. "Tell Me Moore." In *Spooks, Spies, and Private Eyes: Black Mystery, Crime, and Suspense Fiction*, edited by Paula L. Woods, 356–73. New York: Doubleday, 1995.

De León, Aya. *Thieves in the Temple*. In Euell and Alexander, *Plays from the Boom Box Galaxy*.

De León, Aya. *Thieves in the Temple: The Reclaiming of Hip Hop*. Afro Solo Theater Festival in San Francisco, CA, Summer 2001. VHS.

De Onís, Catalina (Kathleen) M. "What's in an 'X'? An Exchange about the Politics of 'Latinx.'" *Chiricú Journal: Latina/o Literatures, Arts, and Cultures* 1, no. 2 (2007): 78–91.

Devlin, Paul, dir. *Slam Nation: The Sport of Spoken Word*. New York: Cinema Guild, 1998. VHS, 92 min.

Díaz-Quiñones, Arcadio. *El arte de bregar ensayos*. San Juan, PR: Ediciones Callejón, 2000.

Dick, Bruce Allen. *A Poet's Truth: Conversations with Latino/Latina Poets*. Tucson: University of Arizona Press, 2003.

Dinolfo, Adrianna. "Finding Power in Poetry: The Many Voices of Aya de León." *Daily Californian* (Berkeley), November 6, 2014.

Dolan, Jill. *The Feminist Spectator as Critic*. Ann Arbor: University of Michigan Press, 2012.

Dolan, Jill. *The Feminist Spectator in Action: Feminist Criticism for the Stage and Screen*. Basingstoke, UK: Palgrave Macmillan, 2013.

Dolan, Jill. *Geographies of Learning: Theory and Practice, Activism and Performance*. Middletown, CT: Wesleyan University Press, 2001.

Dolan, Jill. "In Defense of the Discourse: Materialist Feminism, Postmodernism, Poststructuralism . . . and Theory." *TDR: The Drama Review* 33, no. 3 (1989): 58–71.

Dolan, Jill. *Utopia in Performance: Finding Hope at the Theater*. Ann Arbor: University of Michigan Press, 2005.

Duany, Jorge. "Puerto Rican Diaspora to the United States: A Postcolonial Migration?" Paper presented at El Centro Center for Puerto Rican Studies, Hunter College, New York, February 13, 2009.

Duany, Jorge. *The Puerto Rican Nation on the Move: Identities on the Island and in the United States*. Chapel Hill: University of North Carolina Press, 2002.

Durham, Aisha S. *Home with Hip Hop Feminism: Performances in Communication and Culture*. New York: Peter Lang, 2014.

Durham, Aisha S. "Using [Living Hip-Hop] Feminism: Redefining an Answer to Rap," in Pough, Richardson, Durham, and Raimist, *Home Girls Make Some Noise*, 304–12.

Elam, Harry J., Jr. *Taking It to the Streets: The Social Protest Theater of Luis Valdez and Amiri Baraka*. Ann Arbor: University of Michigan Press, 1997.

Elam, Harry J., Jr., and Robert Alexander, ed. *The Fire This Time: African American Plays for the 21st Century*. New York: Theatre Communications Group, 2004.

Elam, Harry J., Jr., and Kennell Jackson, ed. *Black Cultural Traffic: Crossroads in Global Performance and Popular Culture*. Ann Arbor: University of Michigan Press, 2005.

Elenes, C. Alejandra. "Spiritual Roots of Chicana Feminist Borderland Pedagogies: A Spiritual Journey with Tonantzin/Guadalupe." In Facio and Lara, *Fleshing the Spirit*, 43–58.

Eleveld, Mark, and Marc Kelly Smith. *The Spoken Word Revolution: Slam, Hip Hop & the Poetry of a New Generation*. Naperville, IL: Sourcebooks, 2003.

Enck-Wanzer, Darrel, ed. *The Young Lords: A Reader*. New York: New York University Press, 2010.

Espada, Martín. "Documentaries and Declamadores: Puerto Rican Poetry in the United States." In *A Gift of Tongues: Critical Challenges in Contemporary American Poetry*, edited by Marie Harris and Kathleen Aguero, 257–66. Athens: University of Georgia Press, 1987.

Esterrich, Carmelo. "Home and the Ruins of Language: Victor Hernández Cruz and Miguel Algarín's Nuyorican Poetry." *MELUS* 23, no. 3 (1998): 43–57.

Esteves, Sandra María. "Blanket Weaver." In Algarín and Piñero, *Nuyorican Poetry*, 134–35.

Esteves, Sandra María. *Bluestown Mockingbird Mambo*. Houston, TX: Arte Público Press, 1990.

Esteves, Sandra María. "I Wish I Could." In *Contrapunto in the Open Field*, 89–91. New York: No Frills, 1998.

Esteves, Sandra María. *Tropical Rain: A Bilingual Downpour*. New York: Caribbean Poetry Theater, 1984.

Esteves, Sandra María. *Undelivered Love Poems*. New York: No Frills, 1997.

Esteves, Sandra María. *Yerba Buena: Dibujos y poemas*. Greenfield Center, NY: Greenfield Review Press, 1980.

Euell, Kim. "Tha Playz tha Thang: A New York City Festival Confirms That Hip-Hop Is a Theatre Genre to Contend With." *American Theatre*, September 2002.

Euell, Kim, and Robert Alexander, ed. *Plays from the Boom Box Galaxy: Theater from the Hip Hop Generation*. New York: Theatre Communications Group, 2009.

Facio, Elisa, and Irene Lara, eds. *Fleshing the Spirit: Spirituality and Activism in Chicana, Latina, and Indigenous Women's Lives*. Tucson: University of Arizona Press, 2014.

Flores, Juan. *The Diaspora Strikes Back: Caribeño Tales of Learning and Turning*. New York: Routledge, 2008.

Flores, Juan. *Divided Borders: Essays on Puerto Rican Identity*. Houston, TX: Arte Público Press, 1993.

Flores, Juan. *From Bomba to Hip-Hop: Puerto Rican Culture and Latino Identity*. New York: Columbia University Press, 2000.

Flores, Juan. "Living Borders/Buscando América: Language of Latino Self-Formation." In Flores, *Divided Borders*, 199–224.

Flores, Juan. "Puerto Rican Literature in the United States: Stages and Perspectives." In *Recovering the U.S. Hispanic Literary Heritage*, edited by Ramón Gutierrez and Genaro Padilla, 31–68. Houston, TX: Arte Público Press, 1993.

Flores, Juan. "Reclaiming Left Baggage: Some Early Sources for Minority Studies." *Cultural Critique* 59 (2005): 187–206.

Forman, Murray. *The 'Hood Comes First: Race, Space, and Place in Rap and Hip-Hop*. Middletown, CT: Wesleyan University Press, 2002.

Forman, Murray. "'Movin' Closer to an Independent Funk': Black Feminist Theory, Standpoint, and Women in Rap." *Women's Studies* 23 (1994): 35–55.

Forman, Murray, and Mark Anthony Neal, eds. *That's the Joint: The Hip Hop Studies Reader.* New York: Routledge, 2012.

Friedan, Betty. *The Feminist Mystique.* New York: W. W. Norton, 1963.

Fuchs, Elinor. *The Death of the Character: Perspectives on Theater after Modernism.* Bloomington: Indiana University Press, 1996.

Gatell, Frank Otto. "Independence Rejected: Puerto Rico and the Tydings Bill of 1936." *Hispanic American Historical Review* 38, no. 1 (1958): 25–44.

Gener, Randy. "Bling, or Revolution: A Roundtable Discussion with Daniel Banks, Chadwick Boseman, Gamal Abdel Chasten, Gwendolen Hardwick, Danny Hoch, Baraka Sele, Marla Teyolia, Clyde Valentin and Raphael Xavier." *American Theatre.* July/August 2004.

George, Nelson. *Hip Hop America.* New York: Viking, 1998.

Gilmore, Leigh. *Autobiographics: A Feminist Theory of Women's Self Representation.* Ithaca, NY: Cornell University Press, 1994.

González, Louie The Foot. "Doña Toña of Nineteenth Street." In *Growing Up Chicana/o: An Anthology*, edited by Tiffany Ana López, 59–68. New York: William Morrow, 1993.

Grainge, Paul. *Monochrome Memories: Nostalgia and Style in Retro America.* Westport, CT: Praeger, 2002.

Grand Slam! Best of the National Poetry Slam. Vol. 1. New York: Mouth Almighty, 1996. VHS.

Green, Mary. "The Representation of Puerto Rican Women in Two Short Stories by Ana Lydia Vega: 'Letra para salsa y tres soneos por encargo' (1979) and 'Pollito Chicken' (1977)." *Journal of Iberian and Latin American Studies* 8, no. 2 (2002): 127–41.

Gubar, Susan. "Feminism Inside Out." *PMLA* 121, no. 5 (2000): 1711–16.

Guerra, Gilbert, and Gilbert Orbea. "The Argument against the Use of 'Latinx.'" *Phoenix* (Swarthmore College). November 19, 2015. http://swarthmorephoenix.com/2015/11/19/the-argument-against-the-use-of-the-term-latinx/

Guerra, Lillian. *Popular Expression and National Identity in Puerto Rico: The Struggle for Self, Community, and Nation.* Gainesville: University Press of Florida, 1998.

Guevara, Nancy. "Women Writin' Rappin' Breakin'." In *Droppin' Science: Critical Essays on Rap Music and Hip Hop Culture*, edited by William Eric Perkins, 49–62. Philadelphia: Temple University Press, 1995.

Guevara Rodriguez, Nancy. "Hip-Hop: Women in New York's Street Culture." PhD diss., Queens College, 1985.

Guzmán, Pablo. *Pablo "Yoruba" Guzmán on the Young Lords Legacy: A Personal Account: Proceedings from the April 8, 1995 IPR Community Forum.* Edited by Joseph Luppens. New York: Institute for Puerto Rican Policy, 1995.

Habell-Pallán, Michelle, and Mary Romero, eds. *Latino/a Popular Culture.* New York: New York University Press, 2002.

Harding, James M. *Cutting Performance: Collage Events, Feminist Artists, and the American Avant-Garde.* Ann Arbor: University of Michigan Press, 2010.

Harmanci, Reyhan. "Responding in Kind / 'Thieves in the Temple' / Aya de León Took a Stand When Hip-Hop Culture's Sexism Went Too Far." *San Francisco Chronicle*, March 15, 2007.

Hernández, Carmen Dolores. "Miguel Algarín." In *Puerto Rican Voices: Interview with Writers*, 33–48. Westport, CT: Prager, 1997.

Hernández-Avila, Inés. "In the Presence of Spirit(s): A Meditation on the Politics of Solidarity and Transformation." In Anzaldúa and Keating, *This Bridge We Call Home*, 530–38.

Herrera, Patricia. "Culture Clash's *Nuyorican Stories*: Building Latinidad, Silencing Queerness." *Theatre Topics* 27, no. 1 (2017): 71–82.

Herrera, Patricia. "Listening to Afro-Latinidad: The Sonic Archive of *Olú Clemente*." In *Afro-Latin@s in Movement: Critical Approaches to Blackness and Transnationalism in the Americas*, edited by Petra R. River-Rideau, Jennifer A. Jones, and Tianna Paschel, 171–94. New York: Palgrave, 2016.

Herrera, Patricia. "She Wears the Masks: Bluefacing in Nilaja Sun's *Black and Blue* and *La Nubia Latina*." *African American Review* 45, no. 3 (2012): 403–18.

Hoch, Danny. "Toward A Hip-Hop Aesthetic: A Manifesto for the Hip-Hop Arts Movement." In *Total Chaos: The Art and Aesthetic of Hip-Hop*, edited by Jeff Chang, 349–64. New York: Basic Civitas, 2007.

hooks, bell. *Ain't I a Woman: Black Women and Feminism*. New York: Routledge, 2014.

hooks, bell. *Black Looks: Race and Representation*. Boston: South End Press, 1992.

hooks, bell. *Feminism Is for Everybody: Passionate Politics*. Cambridge, MA: South End Press, 2000.

hooks, bell. *Feminist Theory: From Margin to Center*. 2nd ed. Cambridge, MA: South End Press, 2000.

hooks, bell. *Yearning: Race, Gender, and Cultural Politics*. Boston: South End Press, 1990.

Horno-Delgado, Asunción, Eliana Ortega, Nina M. Scott, and Nancy Saporta Sternbach, eds. *Breaking Boundaries: Latina Writing and Critical Readings*. Amherst: University of Massachusetts Press, 1989.

Huerta, Jorge. *Chicano Drama: Performance, Society and Myth*. Cambridge: Cambridge University Press, 2000.

Huerta, Jorge. *Chicano Theatre: Themes and Forms*. Ypsilanti, MI: Bilingual Press, 1982.

Israel, Baba. *Remixing the Ritual: Hip Hop Theatre Aesthetics and Practice*. New York: Baba Israel, 2008.

Jameson, Fredric. *Postmodernism, or The Cultural Logic of Late Capitalism*. London: Verso, 1991.

Jamila, Shani. "Can I Get a Witness? Testimony from a Hip-Hop Feminist." In *Colonize This! Young Women of Color on Today's Feminism*, edited by Daisy Hernández and Bushra Rehman, 382–94. New York: Seal Press, 2002.

Jeffries, Michael. "Re: Definitions: The Name and Game of Hip-Hop Feminism." In Pough, Richardson, Durham, and Raimist, *Home Girls Make Some Noise*, 208–27.

Jiménez Román, Miriam, and Juan Flores, eds. *The Afro-Latin@ Reader: History and Culture in the United States*. Durham, NC: Duke University Press, 2010.

Johnson, Javon. *Killing Poetry: Blackness and the Making of Slam and Spoken Word Communities*. New Brunswick, NJ: Rutgers University Press, 2017.

Johnson, Javon. "Manning Up: Race, Gender, and Sexuality in Los Angeles' Slam and

Spoken Word Poetry Communities." *Text and Performance Quarterly* 30, no. 4 (2010): 396–419.

Jones, Amelia, and Andrew Stephenson. *Performing the Body/Performing the Text*. Abingdon, UK: Routledge, 1999.

Jones, Duane L., ed. "The Young Lords Party, 1969–1975." Photographs by Hiram Maristany. Text by Felipe Luciano. Double issue, *Caribe* 7, no. 4 (1983).

Junco, Maite. "'Boogie Rican Blvd.' Joins the Chorus," *New York Daily News*. July 1, 2009.

Kane, Daniel. *Welcome All Poets*. Berkeley: University of California Press, 2003.

Kanellos, Nicolás. *A History of Hispanic Theatre in the United States: Origins to 1940*. Austin: University of Texas Press, 1990.

Kanellos, Nicolás. "Orality and Hispanic Literature of the United States." In *Redefining American Literary History*, edited by La Vonne Brown Ruoff and Jerry W. Ward Jr., 115–23. New York: Modern Language Association, 1990.

Kanellos, Nicolás, and Jorge A. Huerta. *Nuevos Pasos: Chicano and Puerto Rican Drama*. Gary, IN: Arte Público Press, 1979.

Keith, Michael, and Steve Pile. *Place and the Politics of Identity*. New York: Routledge, 1993.

Kelley, Robin. *Race Rebels: Culture, Politics, and the Black Working Class*. New York: Free Press, 1994.

Kelley, Norman, ed. *Rhythm and Business: The Political Economy of Black Music*. New York: Akashic Books, 2002.

Keyes, Cheryl L. "'We're More Than a Novelty, Boys': Strategies of Female Rappers in the Rap Music Tradition." In *Feminist Messages: Coding in Women's Folk Culture*, edited by Joan Newlon Radner, 203–19. Urbana: University of Illinois Press, 1993.

Kitwani, Bakari. *The Hip-Hop Generation: Young Blacks and the Crisis in African American Culture*. New York: Basic Civitas, 2002.

La Fountain-Stokes, Lawrence. *Queer Ricans: Cultures and Sexualities in the Diaspora*. Minneapolis: University of Minnesota Press, 2009.

Laó, Agustin. "Resources of Hope: Imagining the Young Lords and the Politics of Memory." *Centro: Journal of the Center for Puerto Rican Studies* 8, no. 1 (1995): 34–49.

Laó-Montes, Augustín. "Decolonial Moves: Trans-Locating African Diaspora Spaces." *Cultural Studies* 21, no. 2 (2007): 309–38.

Laó-Montes, Augustin, and Arlene Dávila, eds. *Mambo Montage: The Latinization of New York*. New York: Columbia University Press, 2001.

Lara, Irene. "Bruja Positionalities: Toward a Chicana/Latina Spiritual Activism." *Chicana/Latina Studies* 4, no. 2 (2005): 10–45.

Lara, Irene. "Healing Sueños for Academia." In Anzaldúa and Keating, *This Bridge We Call Home*, 433–38.

Latina Feminist Group. *Telling to Live: Latina Feminist Testimonios*. Durham, NC: Duke University Press, 2001.

Laviera, Tato. "Don luis muñoz marin." In *AmerRícan*, 87. Houston, TX: Arte Público Press, 1985.

Lazú, Jacqueline. "Nuyorican Theater: Prophecies and Monstrosities." PhD diss., Stanford University, 2002.

Levin, Marc, dir. *Slam*. Trimark Home Video, 1998. VHS, 103 min.

Lima, Lázaro. *The Latino Body: Crisis Identities in American Literary and Cultural Memory*. New York: New York University Press, 2007.

Lindsey, Treva B. "Let Me Blow Your Mind: Hip Hop Feminist Futures in Theory and Praxis." *Urban Education* 50, no. 1 (2014): 52–77.

Lipsitz, George. *Dangerous Crossroads: Popular Music, Postmodernism, and the Poetics of Place*. New York: Verso, 1997.

López, Edrik. "Nuyorican Space: Mapping Identity in a Poetic Geography." *Centro: Journal of the Center for Puerto Rican Studies* 17, no. 1 (2005): 203–19.

López, Tiffany Ana. "Critical Witnessing in Latina/o and African American Prison Narratives." In *Prose and Cons: Essays on Prison Literature in the United States*, edited by D. Quentin Miller, 62–80. Jefferson, NC: McFarland, 2005.

Love, Bettina L. *Hip Hop's Li'l Sistas Speak: Negotiating Hip Hop Identities and Politics in the New South*. New York: Peter Lang, 2012.

Luciano, Felipe. "Jíbaro, My Pretty Nigger." In *Puerto Rican Poetry: An Anthology from Aboriginal to Contemporary Times*, edited by Roberto Márquez, 410. Amherst: University of Massachusetts Press, 2006.

Luciano, Felipe. "Jíbaro, My Pretty Nigger." *Right On! The Original Last Poets*. Juggernaut, 1969. Collectables Records, 1994, compact disc.

Luz, Caridad de la. *Boogie Rican Boulevard*. 2001. Unpublished manuscript.

Luz, Caridad de la. Interview with Oneka LaBennett, October 23, 2007. Bronx African American History Project, BAAHP Digital Archive, Fordham University, New York.

Mahal, Taj. "Biography: The Early Years." Updated 2019. http://www.tajblues.com/biography/

Majioi, Afarin. "At Home with Caridad de la Luz." *Urban Latino* 21, no. 1 (1999): 95.

Mariposa. *Born Bronxeña: Poems on Identity, Survival, Love and Freedom*. Bronx, NY: Bronxeña Books, 2000.

Martínez-San Miguel, Yolanda. *Coloniality of Diasporas: Rethinking Intra-Colonial Migrations in a Pan-Caribbean Context*. New York: Palgrave Macmillan, 2014.

McCaffrey, Katherine. *Military Power and Popular Protest: The US Navy in Vieques, Puerto Rico*. New Brunswick, NJ: Rutgers University Press, 2002.

McCracken, Ellen. *New Latina Narrative: The Feminine Space of Postmodern Ethnicity*. Tucson: Arizona University Press, 1999.

McKnight, Kathryn Joy, and Leo J. Garofalo, eds. *Afro-Latino Voices: Narratives from the Early Modern Ibero-Atlantic World, 1550–1812*. Cambridge, MA: Hackett, 2009.

Meléndez, Miguel "Mickey." *We Took the Streets: Fighting for Latino Rights with the Young Lords*. New York: St. Martin's Press, 2003.

Miller, John C. "Hispanic Theatre in New York, 1965–1977." *Revista Chicano-Riqueña* 6, no. 1 (1977): 40–59.

Miller, Marilyn. *Grace Rise and Fall of the Cosmic Race: The Cult of* Mestizaje *in Latin America*. Austin: University of Texas Press, 2004.

Miranda Archilla, Graciany. "Que fue y que es el atalayismo." Graciany Miranda Archilla Papers, 1916–1991, box 5, folder 1, Center for Puerto Rican Studies, Hunter College, City University of New York.

Mohr, Eugene. *The Nuyorican Experience: Literature of the Puerto Rican Minority*. Santa Barbara, CA: Praeger, 1982.

Mohr, Nicholas. "Puerto Ricans in New York: Cultural Evolution and Identity." In *Images and Identities: The Puerto Rican in Two World Contexts*, edited by Asela Rodriguez de Laguna, 157–60. New Brunswick, NJ: Transaction Books, 1987.

Mohr, Nicholas. "Puerto Rican Writers in the U.S., Puerto Rican Writers in Puerto Rico: A Separation Beyond Language (Testimonio)." In Horno-Delgado, Ortega, Scott, and Sternbach, *Breaking Boundaries*, 111–16.

Moraga, Cherríe. "Giving Up the Ghost." In Moraga, *Heroes and Saints and Other Plays*, 1–35.

Moraga, Cherríe. *Heroes and Saints and Other Plays*. Albuquerque, NM: West End Press, 1994.

Moraga, Cherríe, and Gloria Anzaldúa, eds. *This Bridge Called My Back: Writings by Radical Women of Color*. New York: Kitchen Table/Women of Color Press, 1983.

Morales, Iris. "*¡Palante, Siempre Palante!* The Young Lords." In Torres and Velázquez, *The Puerto Rican Movement*, 210–27.

Morales, Iris, dir. *¡Palante, Siempre Palante! The Young Lords*. New York: Columbia University Station, 1996. VHS.

Morales, Iris. *Through the Eyes of Rebel Women: The Young Lords, 1969–1976*. New York: Red Sugarcane Press, 2016.

Morales, Iris, and Denise Oliver-Velez. Foreword to Enck-Wanzer, *The Young Lords*, ix–xiv.

Morales, Martita. "Teatro." In Algarín and Piñero, *Nuyorican Poetry*, 102–4.

Moreno, Marisel C. *Family Matters: Puerto Rican Women Authors on the Island and the Mainland*. Charlottesville: University of Virginia Press, 2012.

Morgan, Joan. Afterword to Pough, Richardson, Durham, and Raimist, *Home Girls Make Some Noise*, 475–80.

Morgan, Joan. "Hip-Hop Feminist." In Forman and Neal, *That's the Joint*, 413–18.

Morgan, Joan. *When Chickenheads Come Home to Roost: My Life as a Hip-Hop Feminist*. New York: Simon and Schuster, 1999.

Morton, Carlos. "Nuyorican Theatre." *TDR: The Drama Review* 20, no. 1 (1976): 43–49.

Muckley, Robert L. "Introduction to Carrero." In *Notes on Neorican Seminar*. San Germán: Inter American University, 1972.

Muñoz, Amina. "Puerto Rican Graffiti." In Algarín and Piñero, *Nuyorican Poetry*, 107.

Muñoz, José Esteban. *Cruising Utopia, The Then and There of Queer Futurity*. New York: New York University Press, 2009.

Muñoz, José Esteban. *Disidentification: Queers of Color and the Performance of Politics*. Minneapolis: University of Minnesota Press, 1999.

Muñoz, José Esteban. "Feeling Brown: Ethnicity and Affect in Ricardo Bracho's *The Sweetest Hangover (and Other STDs)*." *Theatre Journal* 52, no. 1 (2000): 67–80.

Negrón-Muntaner, Frances. *Boricua Pop: Puerto Ricans and the Latinization of American Culture*. New York: New York University Press, 2004.

Negrón-Muntaner, Frances. "The Look of Sovereignty: Style and Politics in the Young

Lords." *Centro: Journal of the Center for Puerto Rican Studies* 27, no. 1 (2015): 4–33.

Negrón-Muntaner, Frances, ed. *None of the Above: Puerto Ricans in the Global Era*. New York: Palgrave Macmillan, 2007.

Nieves, Myrna, ed. *Breaking Ground: Anthology of Puerto Rican Women Writers in New York 1980–2012/Abriendo caminos: Antología de escritoras puertorriqueñas en Nueva York 1980–2012*. New York: Editorial Campana, 2012.

Noel, Urayoán. "Bodies That Antimatter: Locating U.S. Latino/a Poetry, 2000–2009." *Contemporary Literature* 52, no. 4 (2011): 852–82.

Noel, Urayoán. "Counter/Public Address: Nuyorican Poetries in the Slam Era." *Latino Studies* 9, no. 1 (2001): 38–61.

Noel, Urayoán. *In Visible Movement: Nuyorican Poetry from the Sixties to Slam*. Iowa City: University of Iowa Press, 2014.

Noel, Urayoán. "NYPR Blues: Experimentalism, Performance, and the Articulation of Diaspora in Nuyorican Poetry." PhD diss., New York University, 2008.

Oboler, Suzanne. *Ethnic Labels, Latino Lives: Identity and the Politics of (Re)Presentation in the United States*. Minneapolis: University of Minnesota Press, 1995.

Oboler, Suzanne, and Anani Dzidzienyo. "Flows and Counterflows: Latinas/os, Blackness, and Racialization in Hemispheric Perspective." In *Neither Enemies nor Friends: Latinos, Blacks, Afro-Latinos*, edited by Suzanne Oboler and Anani Dzidzienyo, 3–36. New York: Palgrave Macmillan, 2005.

O'Keefe Aptowicz, Cristin. *Words in Your Face: A Guided Tour through Twenty Years of the New York Poetry Slam*. New York: Soft Skull Press, 2008.

Ortega, Eliana. "Poetic Discourse of the Puerto Rican Woman in the U.S.: New Voices of Anacaonian Liberation." In Horno-Delgado, Ortega, Scott, and Sternbach, *Breaking Boundaries*, 122–35.

Ortega, Eliana, and Nancy Saporta Sternbach. "At the Threshold of the Unnamed: Latina Literary Discourse in the Eighties." In Horno-Delgado, Ortega, Scott, and Sternbach, *Breaking Boundaries*, 2–23.

Ortega, Eliana, and Nancy Saporta Sternbach. "Poetic Discourse of the Puerto Rican Women in the U.S.: New Voices of Anaconian Liberation." In Horno-Delgado, Ortega, Scott, and Sternbach, *Breaking Boundaries*, 203–19.

Ortiz, Fernández. *Cuban Counterpoint: Tobacco and Sugar*. New York: Alfred A. Knopf, 1947.

Partido Nacionalista de Puerto Rico. *Tortura de los presos políticos en Puerto Rico: Denuncia elevada a la Organización de los Estados Americanos*. Compiled by Secretaría de Relaciones Exteriores. Havana: La Secretaría, 1952.

Peoples, Whitney A. "'Under Construction': Identifying Foundations of Hip-Hop Feminism and Exploring Bridges between Black Second-Wave and Hip-Hop Feminisms." *Meridians* 8, no. 1 (2008): 19–52.

Perea, Juan. "The Black/White Binary Paradigm of Race." In *The Latino Condition*, edited by Richard Delgado and Jean Stefanic, 359–68. New York: New York University Press, 1998.

Pérez, Emma. *The Decolonial Imaginary: Writing Chicanas into History*. Bloomington: Indiana University Press, 1999.

Pérez, Laura. *Chicana Art: The Politics of Spiritual and Aesthetic Altarities*. Durham, NC: Duke University Press, 2007.

Pérez, Laura. "Spirit Glyphs: Reimagining Art and Artist in the Work of Chicana Tlamatinime." *Modern Fiction Studies* 44, no. 1 (1998): 36–76.

Pérez, Nélida, and Amilcar Tirado, eds. *Pedro Albizu Campos, 1891–1965*. New York: Centro de Estudios Puertorriqueños, 1986.

Pérez-Rosario, Vanessa. "Affirming an Afro-Latin@ Identity: An Interview with Poet María Teresa (Mariposa) Fernández." *Latino Studies* 12, no. 3 (2014): 468–75.

Perkins, William Eric. *Droppin' Science: Critical Essay on Rap Music and Hip Hop Culture*. Philadelphia: Temple University Press, 1996.

Phillips, Layli, Kerri Reddick-Morgan, and Dionne Patricia Stephens. "Oppositional Realm: The Case of Feminism and Womanism in Rap and Hip Hop, 1976–2004." *Journal of African American History* 90, no. 3 (2005): 253–77.

Pietri, Pedro. *Loose Joints*. Folkways Records, FL 9722, 1979, LP.

Pietri, Pedro. "There Was Never No Tomorrow: Nuyorican Pedro Pietri in His Own Words." Edited by Raymond Beltrán. *La Prensa San Diego*, February 6, 2004.

Pietri, Pedro. "Traffic Misdirector." In *Traffic Violations*, 103–5. Washington, DC: Waterfront Press, 1983.

Piñero, Miguel. *Outlaw: The Collected Works by Miguel Piñero*. Introduction by Nicolás Kanellos and Jorge Iglesias. Houston, TX: Arte Público Press, 2010.

Pough, Gwendolyn D. *Check It While I Wreck It: Black Womanhood, Hip-Hop Culture, and the Public Sphere*. Lebanon, NH: Northeastern University Press, 2004.

Pough, Gwendolyn D., Elaine Richardson, Aisha Durham, and Rachel Raimist, eds. *Home Girls Make Some Noise! Hip Hop Feminism Anthology*. Mira Loma, CA: Parker, 2007.

Ramírez, Elizabeth C., and Cather Casiano, eds. *La Voz Latina: Contemporary Plays and Performance Pieces by Latinas*. Champaign: University of Illinois Press, 2011.

Ramos, Efrén Rivera. *The Legal Construction of Identity: The Judicial and Social Legacy of American Colonialism in Puerto Rico*. Washington, DC: American Psychological Association, 2001.

Ramos-Zayas, Ana Y. *National Performances: The Politics of Class, Race, and Space in Puerto Rican Chicago*. Chicago: University of Chicago Press, 2003.

Rebollo-Gil, Guillermo. "The New Boogaloo: Nuyorican Poetry and the Coming Puerto Rican Identities." Master's thesis, University of Florida, 2004.

Reichard, Raquel. "Why We Say Latinx: Trans & Gender Non-Conforming People Explain." *Latina*. August 29, 2015. http://www.latina.com/lifestyle/our-issues/why-we-say-latinx-trans-gender-non-conforming-people-explain

Reinelt, Janelle. "Approaching the Sixties: Between Nostalgia and Critique." *Theatre Survey* 43, no. 1 (2002): 37–56.

Reinelt, Janelle. "The Politics of Discourse: Performativity Meets Theatricality." *SubStance* 31, no. 2/3 (2002): 201–15.

Rivas, Bimbo. "Loisada." In Algarín and Holman, *Aloud*, 361–62.

Rivera, Louis Reyes. "Within the Context of a Nuyorican Element: Sandra María Esteves." *Centro: Journal of the Center for Puerto Rican Studies* 2, no. 3 (1988): 51–59.

Rivera, Raquel Z. *New York Ricans from the Hip Hop Zone*. New York: Palgrave Macmillan, 2003.

Rivera-Servera, Ramón H. *Performing Queer Latinidad: Dance, Sexuality, Politics*. Ann Arbor: University of Michigan Press, 2012.

Robinson, Walter, and Carlo McCormick, "Slouching toward Avenue D." *Art in America* 72, no. 6 (1993): 135–61.

"Rock Steady Crew." Crazy Legs Workshop. Accessed May 9, 2013. http://crazylegsworkshop.com/rock-steady-crew/about-rsc

Rodriguez, Abraham, Jr. "Boy without a Flag." In *Tales of the South Bronx: Boy without a Flag*, 11–30. Minneapolis, MN: Milkweed Editions, 1999.

Rodriguez Cruz, Juan. *Pedro Albizu Campos: Un asomo a su vida y su época*. San Juan, PR: Centro de Estudios Avanzados de Puerto Rico y el Caribe, 1994.

Rodriguez-Morazzani, Roberto P. "Political Cultures of the Puerto Rican Left in the United States." In Torres and Velázquez, *The Puerto Rican Movement*, 25–47.

Román, David. *Acts of Intervention: Performance, Gay Culture, and AIDS*. Bloomington: Indiana University Press, 1998.

Román, David. *Performance in America: Contemporary US Culture and the Performing Arts*. Durham, NC: Duke University Press, 2005.

Rose, Tricia. *The Hip Hop Wars: What We Talk about When We Talk about Hip Hop and Why It Matters*. New York: Basic Civitas, 2008.

Roseman, Marina. "The New Rican Village: Artists in Control of the Image-Making Machinery." *Latin American Music Review/Revista de Musica Latinoamericana* 4, no. 1 (1983): 132–67.

Roth, Benita. *Separate Roads to Feminism: Black, Chicana, and White Feminist Movements in America's Second Wave*. Cambridge: Cambridge University Press, 2004.

Saddik, Annette J. "Rap's Unruly Body: The Postmodern Performance of Black Male Identity on the American Stage." *TDR: The Drama Review* 47, no. 4 (2003): 110–27.

Sánchez, Juan. *Puerto Rican Equation: Puerto Rican Artists Ponder 100 Years since the 1898 Invasion*. New York: Bertha and Karl Leubsdorf Art Gallery, 1998.

Sánchez González, Lisa. *Boricua Literature: A Literary History of the Puerto Rican Diaspora*. New York: New York University Press, 2001.

Sánchez Korrol, Virginia. *From Colonia to Community: The History of Puerto Ricans in New York City*. Berkeley: University of California Press, 1994.

Sanders, Joshunda. "Taking the Rap/Poet Aya de León Tackles Sexism and Reclaims Hip-Hop in Her New Play." *San Francisco Chronicle*, March 14, 2004.

Sandoval-Sánchez, Alberto. *José Can You See? Latinos On and Off Broadway*. Madison: University of Wisconsin Press, 1999.

Sandoval-Sánchez, Alberto, and Nancy Saporta Sternbach, eds. "Puerto Rican Identity Up in the Air: Air Migration, Its Cultural Representations, and Me 'Cruzando el Charco." In *Puerto Rican Jam: Essays on Culture and Politics*, ed. Frances Negrón-Muntaner and Ramón Grosfoguel, 189–208. Minneapolis: University of Minnesota Press, 1997.

Sandoval-Sánchez, Alberto, and Nancy Saporta Sternbach, eds. *Puro Teatro: A Latina Anthology*. Tucson: University of Arizona Press, 2000.

Sandoval-Sánchez, Alberto, and Nancy Saporta Sternbach, eds. *Stages of Life: Transcultural Performance and Identity in U.S. Latina Theater*. Tucson: University of Arizona Press, 2001.

Scharrón-del Río, María R., and Alan A. Aja. "The Case FOR 'Latinx': Why Intersectionality Is Not a Choice." *Latino Rebels*. December 5, 2015. http://www.latinorebels.com/2015/12/05/the-case-for-latinx-why-intersectionality-is-not-a-choice/

Sevcenko, Liz. "Making Loisaida: Placing Puertorriqueñidad in Lower Manhattan." In Laó-Montes and Dávila, *Mambo Montage*, 293–318.

"Shattering the Silences: Minority Professors Break into the Ivory Tower." PBS.org. Updated 1997. Accessed August 17, 2019. http://www.pbs.org/shattering/shattering2.html

Simmon, Russel. *Def Poetry Jam*. Seasons 1–5. Directed by Stan Lathan. HBO Series, 2002–5. DVD.

Smith, Sidonie. *Subjectivity, Identity, and the Body: Women's Autobiographical Practices in the Twentieth Century*. Bloomington: Indiana University Press, 1999.

Somers-Willett, Susan B. A. *The Cultural Politics of Slam Poetry: Race, Identity, and the Performance of Popular Verse*. Ann Arbor: University of Michigan Press, 2009.

Somers-Willett, Susan B. A. "From Slam to Def Poetry Jam: Spoken Word Poetry and Its Counterpublics." *Liminalities: A Journal of Performance Studies* 10, no. 3–4 (2014): 1–23.

Soto, Claudia. "La Bruja Rocks Quepasa to the Rhythm of Reggaeton." *Quepasa News*, August 14, 2006.

Sun, Nilaja. *La Nubia Latina*. Performance, Henry Street Settlement, NY, April 19, 1999. VHS.

Taylor, Diana. *The Archive and the Repertoire: Performing Cultural Memory in the Americas*. Durham, NC: Duke University Press, 2003.

Taylor, Diana. *Disappearing Acts: Spectacles of Gender and Nationalism in Argentina's "Dirty War."* Durham, NC: Duke University Press, 1997.

Taylor, Diana. "Translating Performance." *Profession*, 2002, 44–50.

Tenant/Inquilino: Housing for People, Not Profit 32, no. 1 (January 2002): 1–7.

Thomas, Lorrin. *Puerto Rican Citizen: History and Political Identity in Twentieth-Century New York City*. Chicago: University of Chicago Press, 2010.

Torres, Andrés. "Political Radicalism in the Diaspora—The Puerto Rican Experience." In Torres and Velázquez, *The Puerto Rican Movement*, 1–24.

Torres, Andrés, and José E. Velázquez, eds. *The Puerto Rican Movement: Voices from the Diaspora*. Philadelphia: Temple University Press, 1998.

Torres, José Benjamín. *El proceso judicial contra Albizu Campos*. 2nd ed. San Juan, PR: Editorial Jelofe, 1979.

Torres, José García, dir. *The Nationalists*. Edited by Israel Ortiz. Written and narrated by Pablo Cabrera. New York: Realidades, 1973. VHS and DVD, 28 min.

Turner, Victor. *Dramas, Fields, and Metaphors: Symbolic Action in Human Society*. Ithaca, NY: Cornell University Press, 1974.

Uno, Roberta, ed. *Contemporary Plays by Women of Color*. 2nd ed. New York: Routledge, 2018.

Uno, Roberta, ed. “Democratizing the Arts, Aesthetic Practice, and the Relationship to Community Change: A Conversation with Roberto Uno.” Interview by P. Carl. *HowlRound*. April 14, 2016. http://howlround.com/democratizing-the-arts-aesthetic-practice-and-the-relationship-to-community-change-a-conversation

Uno, Roberta, ed. “The 5th Element: Hip-Hop Culture Confronts the Theatre and Asks, ‘Where to Go, Beyond the Borders of Outreach and Audience Development?’” *American Theatre*. April 2004.

Uno, Roberta, ed, ed. *Monologues for Actors of Color: Men*. 2nd ed. New York: Routledge, 2015.

Uno, Roberta, ed, ed. *Monologues for Actors of Color: Women*. 2nd ed. New York: Routledge, 2015.

Uno, Roberta, ed. *Unbroken Thread: An Anthology of Plays by Asian American Women*. Amherst: University of Massachusetts Press, 1993.

Uno, Roberta, and Lucy Mae San Pablo Burns, eds. *The Color Of Theater: Race, Culture, and Contemporary Performance*. London: Continuum, 2002.

Urciuoli, Bonnie. *Exposing Prejudice: Puerto Rican Experiences of Language, Race, and Class*. Boulder, CO: Westview, 1998.

Vaca, Nicolás Corona. *The Presumed Alliance: The Unspoken Conflict between Latinos and Blacks and What It Means for America*. New York: HarperCollins, 2004.

Valentín-Escobar, Wilson. “‘Nothing Connects Us All but Imagined Sounds’: Performing Trans-Boricua Memories, Identities, and Nationalisms through the Death of Héctor Lavoe.” In Laó-Montes and Dávila, *Mambo Montage: The Latinization of New York*, 207–34.

Vásquez, Eva C. *Pregones Theatre: A Theatre for Social Change in the South Bronx*. London: Routledge, 1998.

Vega, Marta Moreno. *The Altar of My Soul: The Living Traditions of Santería*. New York: One World, 2000.

Velázquez, José. “Another West Side Story: An Interview with Members of El Comité-MINP.” In Torres and Velázquez, *The Puerto Rican Movement*, 88–106.

Vélez, Diana L. “*Pollito Chicken*: Split Subjectivity, National Identity and the Articulation of Female Sexuality in a Narrative by Ana Lydia Vega.” *Americas Review* 14, no. 2 (1986): 68–76.

Vidal, David, “‘Nuyoricans’ Express Pain and Joy in Poetry.” *New York Times*, May 14, 1976.

Wagenheim, Olga Jiménez de. *Nationalist Heroines: Puerto Rican Women History Forgot, 1930s–1950s*. Princeton, NJ: Markus Wiener, 2016.

Whalen, Carmen Teresa, and Víctor Vázquez-Hernández, eds. *Puerto Rican Diaspora: Historical Perspectives*. Philadelphia: Temple University Press, 2005.

Williams, Raymond. *Marxism and Literature*. New York: Oxford University Press, 1978.

Wiltz, Teresa. “Racial and Ethnic Disparities Persist in Teen Pregnancy Rates.” Pew Charitable Trusts Stateline (blog). March 3, 2015. http://www.pewtrusts.org/en/research-and-analysis/blogs/stateline/2015/3/03/racial-and-ethnic-disparities-persist-in-teen-pregnancy-rates

Yarbro-Bejarano, Yvonne. “The Female Subject in Chicano Theatre: Sexuality, ‘Race,’ and Class.” In Case, *Performing Feminisms*, 131–49.

Yarbro-Bejarano, Yvonne. "*Teatropoesía* by Chicanas in the Bay Area: *Tongues of Fire.*" *Revista Chicano-Riqueña* 11, no. 1 (1983): 78–94.

Young Lords Party. *El Pueblo Se Levanta*. New York: Third World Newsreel, 1971. VHS, 42 min.

Young Lords Party. *Ideology of the Young Lords Party*. Bronx, NY: Young Lords Party, 1972.

Young Lords Party. *Palante: Voices and Photographs of the Young Lords, 1969–1971*. Photographs by Michael Abramson. New York: Haymarket Books, 1971.

Zanes, Dan, and Caridad de la Luz. "Pollito Chicken." *¡Nueva York!* Brooklyn, NY: Festival Five Records, 2008, compact disc.

Zinn, Maxine Baca. "Feminist Rethinking from Racial-Ethnic Families." In *Women of Color in U.S. Society*, edited by Maxine Baca Zinn and Bonnie Thornton Dill, 18–26. Philadelphia, PA: Temple University Press, 1994.

Zooks, Kristal Brent. "A Manifesto of Sorts for a Black Feminist Movement." *New York Times Magazine*, December 3, 1995.

Index

abortion, 57, 94, 134
Afrodiasporic: aesthetics, 26; histories, 18; identities 140; linguistic practices, 100; performance practices, 2, 13–14, 61, 91, 118; performance traditions, 2, 49, 86–87; religious practices, 146
Afro-Latinidad, 3, 14, 18, 56, 101–18, 130, 140, 169, 198n21
"Agua que va caer," 58–59
Albizu Campos, Pedro, 20–23, 27, 37–39, 59, 63, 181n36
Alcoff, Linda Martín, 105
Algarín, Miguel, 3–5, 39–46, 55, 60–61, 75, 87–88, 99, 148, 163–64, 183nn48–49; *Apartment 6D*, 182n41, 182n45; and the Beats, 184n59, 184n64; El Puerto Rican Playwrights'/Actors' workshop, 39-40; and *Nuyorican* (term), 30, 182n38; and *Nuyorican Poetry*, 29–30, 49, 68, 76; and oral expression, 43-46, 49, 51, 53, 76
Aloud (anthology), 42–43, 76
Alvarez, Jose, 152, 206n29
América Conga Mania, 41, 87
Andersen, Lemon, 78, 80
Anzaldúa, Gloria, 2, 9, 18–19, 118, 141, 159
Aparicio, Frances R., 12–13
Aptowicz, Cristin O'Keefe, 76
Arrizón, Alicia, 13
autobiographics, 89
Aya de León is Running for President (de León), 123, 200n1

Baker, Houston, 14
Banks, Daniel, 14
Baraka, Amiri, 142–43
Barradas, Efraín, 12–13
Bass, Holly, 79. *See also* hip hop theater
Batiste, Stephanie L., 120
Beats, the, 44, 47, 184n64
"Bemba colorá," 111, 113–14
Berkshire Community College, 8, 47
Black and Blue (Nilaja Sun), 18, 80, 101–9, 111–12, 116–17, 196n1, 197n11, 197n12
Black Arts Repertory Theatre and School (BARTS), 142–44
Blackness, 15, 18, 101–03, 106–09, 112–14, 117, 119–20, 130–32, 140, 169
Black Panther Party, 21, 24, 118, 167
"Blanket Weaver" (Esteves), 51
blueface, 103–9, 116
bomba, 1, 2, 44–45, 46, 59, 158
Boogie Down Bronx, 86, 88–92
Boogie Rican, 88–91
Boogie Rican Boulevard, 18, 80, 84–100, 140, 153–59
Boricua College, 65
Bost, Suzanne, 73–74
Boyd, Todd, 14
"Boy without a Flag" (Abraham Rodríguez, Jr.), 56
Brachfeld, Andrea, 148–52
Braschi, Giannina, 52
Browne, Mahogany L., 77
Broyles-González, Yolanda, 19, 142–44, 205n16, 206n17
bruja-curandera, 141–42, 145, 148–49, 153, 155, 157–59
Burgos, William, 99

call and response, 44–45, 127, 190n12
Canales, Blanca, 21, 22, 23, 28, 56
Canning, Charlotte, 48, 58

Carlson, Marvin, 149–50, 160
Carpenter, Faedra Chatard, 132, 203n49
Carrero, Jaime, 17, 20, 28, 30–38. See also *Notes of Neorican Seminar*
Casiano, Américo, 55–56
Caught in the Act, 86, 192, 195
Chakrabarty, Dipesh, 160
Chang, Jeff, 82
Chin, Staceyann, 80–81
CienFuegos, Lucky, 4, 5, 41, 51, 53, 148
civil rights, 6, 15–17, 20, 46, 65, 118, 121, 169, 172n7, 188n59
Civil Rights Act of 1964, 15
Collins, Patricia Hill, 118, 188n59
Colón, Máximo, 163–64
colonialism, 14, 19, 21-23, 27, 33, 49, 53–56, 59–60, 159; and El Teatro Campesino, 205nn15–16; histories of, 10, 30–31; and language, 43, 98–99; and the Virgin of Guadalupe, 195–96n39. *See also* decolonization, spiritual
Conjunto Libre (Free Set), 66, 71, 188n61
conocimientos, 141–42, 145, 148, 155
consumerism, 54–55, 120, 122–25 130–33, 207n39
Cortiñas, Jorge Ignacio, 82, 192
Crenshaw, Kimberlé, 8, 174
critical witnessing, 50, 185
Cross Bronx Expressway, 73–74
cuernophobic, 156
Culture Clash, 163–69
curandera(s), 141, 152, 155. See also *bruja-curandera*

Daughters of Freedom, 21
Dávila, Angelamaría, 52
Dávila, Arlene, 13
de Burgos, Julia, 52–53
declamatory style, 43, 51, 52
decolonization, spiritual, 153–59
Def Poetry Jam, 77–79, 190; *on Broadway* 78–79, 191n19
Delacorte Theater, 6, 66, 69, 71, 148, 183n49
de la Luz, Caridad. *See* La Bruja
de León, Aya, 11, 14–19, 72, 73, 77, 80, 83, 118–37, 169, 200n8, 201n22; *Aya de Léon Is Running for President*, 123, 200n1; masculinist hip hop aesthetic, 73, 75; self-marriage ceremonies, 140–41, 159–62. *See also* feminist aesthetics, hip hop, *Thieves in the Temple*; *and individual works by the author*

del Valle, Mayda, 78, 80
DiaspoRican, 34, 181n34
DiaspoRican Dementia (Mariposa), 81, 140–41, 153, 158–59
Díaz-Quiñones, Arcadio, 12–13
Dolan, Jill, 49, 54, 79, 136, 185
Durham, Aisha S., 15–16, 125, 175, 200n6

Elam, Harry J., Jr., 14, 142–44, 205n14
El Bronx Remembered, 3
El Comité del primero de diciembre (the December First Committee), 63, 187
El Grito de Jayuya, 21, 22, 56
El Nuevo Despertar, 6
El Partido Nacionalista. *See* Puerto Rican Nationalist Party
El Pueblo Se Levanta, 26, 178
El Puerto Rican Embassy Project, 91–92
El Puerto Rican Playwrights'/Actors' Workshop (EPRP/AW), 39–42
El Teatro Campesino, 19, 142–44, 205nn15–16
embodied counterpolitics, 24–26, 39–40
Espada, Martín, 1, 3, 43, 115, 171n1, 184n61, 192n28
Esteves, Sandra María, 3–7, 14–15, 17–19, 48–72, 76, 89, 92, 96, 100, 162, 169; influence on other performeras, 72, 84, 86, 89; performance at Berkshire Community College, 8–11, 47; and spirituality, 138–41, 144–55, 159; *and individual works by the author*
Euell, Kim, 14
"Eulogy for Martín Pérez" (Esteves), 62

Facio, Elisa, 2, 204n8
familia, 86–88, 90, 164
feminism: first wave 8, 16, 173n2; intersectional, 8–14, 28–29, 50, 58; second wave, 8–9, 16, 173n2, 188n59; third wave, 9, 15, 118, 176n18. *See also* hip hop, feminist
feminist aesthetic(s), 7, 8–19, 48, 68–71, 75, 159, 169; in Aya de Léon's work, 118, 120; in La Bruja's work, 84–87, 89, 100; in Nilaja Sun's work, 101, 117; spiritual dimensions of, 138, 140–41, 145. *See also* hip hop, feminist; Nuyorican aesthetic
feminist historiographical moments, 48–49, 58–61, 65, 71. *See also* Pérez, Martín
Fernández, María Theresa. *See* Mariposa
Figueroa, Eduardo (Eddie), 66–68, 91

First Spanish Methodist Church, 58. *See also* Hispanic Methodist Church
Flores, Juan, 13, 14, 90, 140, 193n14, 195n36
"For Lolita Lebron" (Esteves), 53
"for tito" (Esteves), 60, 63. *See also* Pérez, Martín
For Witch It Stands (La Bruja), 18, 84, 87, 97–98, 153–55
founding mothers, 17–19, 48–72, 76
"fuck with the grays," 15–16, 18
Fuerzas Armadas de Liberación Puertoriqueña (Armed Forces of National Liberation), 63, 187–88

Gómez-Peña, Guillermo, 152
Green, Mary, 99, 195
Guajana, 52

Hammad, Suheir, 80, 81
hip hop, 1–3, 12–19, 73–83, 169, 191n25; commercialization of, 18, 119, 123–24, 126–34, 191n22, 202n29; feminist, 13–16, 18, 75, 101, 117, 118–37, 176n18, 176n26, 200n6; in Aya de Léon's work, 118–37; in La Bruja's work, 84–88, 91, 96, 98, 100; in Nilaja Sun's work, 101, 103, 117; origin of, 73–75; and spirituality, 138, 140, 153, 157, 159
hip hop theater, 1–3, 7, 12–14, 73, 84, 118, 121–22, 201n20; definition of, 82–83; emergence of, 72, 79–82
Hip-Hop Theater All Stars, 122
Hip-Hop Theater Festival (HHTF, Hi-ARTS), 1, 81, 84, 122, 197n12, 201n20, 202n28, 203n40, 203n54
"Hip-Hop Ventriloquism" (de León), 120
"Hiroshima 70th Anniversary" (de León), 120–21
Hispanic Methodist Church takeover, 26–28, 39, 45, 178n13
historiographical moments, 48–49, 58–61, 65, 71. *See also* Pérez, Martín
Hoch, Danny, 80, 81, 82, 122, 191n22, 201n20
"Holding you" (Rodriguez), 58
Holman, Bob, 75–77, 190n11
"Homicidio, No Suicidio," 63
hooks, bell, 1, 9, 118, 171n2, 174n2
Huerta, Jorge, 2, 13, 144
hypersexualized representations, 16, 36, 112–14, 127, 132–35, 133, 134, 135, 156

"i feel the eve," 57
"If Women Ran Hip Hop" (de León), 120, 135–37
"The Ignorant Laugh" (Esteves), 145
"i look for peace great graveyard" (Estevez), 57
Imagine the Angels of Bread, 1, 3, 81, 115
Independentistas, Puerto Rican, 55
intersectionality, 37, 58, 92, 101–2, 105–6, 118, 140, 148–49, 172n8, 173n2. *See also* feminism, intersectional
Israel, Baba, 14

Jackson, Elam and Kennell, 14
Jaime, Karen, 77, 190n13
Jamila, Shani, 16
"Jet Neorriqueño/Neo-Rican Jetliner" (Carrero), 30–31
"Jíbaro, My Pretty Nigger," 24–25
Johnson, Javon, 77
Jones, Amelia, 12
Jones, Sarah, 77, 82
Jones Act, 30–31, 34, 179n27

Keating, AnaLouise, 141
Kelley, Robin D. G., 14
Kelley, Norman, 129
Kingston, Maxine Hong, 9
Kitwani, Bakari, 15

La Bruja, 11, 14–18, 34, 73–78, 80–83, 84–100, 118, 140–41, 144, 153–59, 193n16; *and individual works by the author*
La Cura (Esteves), 140, 145–52
La Fountain-Stokes, Lawrence, 13, 52, 91, 103, 194n18
La Ley de la Mordaza (Gag Law of 1949), 23
La Luchadora, 28
La Nubia Latina (Nilaja Sun), 18, 101–2, 109–17, 196n1, 197n11, 199n24
Lara, Irene, 2, 139, 141
Lathan, Stan, 78–79
Latina/o Theatre Commons, 163
Latinidad, 13, 18, 101–3, 106–14, 116, 119, 169, 204n1. *See also* Afro-Latinidad
Latinx (term), 90–91, 172n8
Laviera, Tato, 51, 183n49
Lavoe, Héctor, 163
The Lawsuit, 65–71, 154
Lebrón, Lolita, 21–23, 27–28, 51–53, 56, 59, 165, 186n20; and 1954 attack on US Congress, 21, 22, 53, 56, 165, 178n8

limpieza, 148–49, 152, 153
"Lolita Lebrón, Recuerdo Te Mandamos" (CienFuegos), 53
López, Tiffany Ana, 13, 50–51
Longacre Theater, 78
Lorde, Audre, 9
Lower East Side, 24, 41–42, 56, 68, 75, 101, 104, 106, 114, 166, 190n12
Luciano, Felipe, 24–26, 27, 180–81n30

Maldonado, Adál, 91
mandala series (Esteves), 140, 145–46
Mariposa, 11, 14, 16–18, 73, 81, 140–41, 144, 153, 158–60, 169; DiaspoRican, 34, 181n34
Martínez, Antonia, 54–55
Martorell, Antonio, 21–23, 27, 177n3
masculinist: aesthetic, 20, 39, 73–75, 145; ethos, 17, 20, 29, 169; narrative, 23, 28, 33, 50; perspectives, 3, 12, 15, 23–25, 28, 36, 79, 152; practices, 16, 29, 41, 48, 59, 71, 74–75, 77, 83, 153
McCarran Act of 1950, 23
McCracken, Ellen, 89, 193n8
McMahon, Marci, 13
Meléndez, Jesús "Papoleto," 51, 55–56, 148
Meléndez, Miguel "Mickey, " 20–21, 180n30
menstruation, 57–58
Miranda, Carmen, 154–55
Mohr, Eugene, 13
Mohr, Nicholasa, 3, 99, 104, 171n1, 195n35
Montoya, Richard, 163, 167
Moraga, Cherríe, 2, 9, 18, 118, 133, 144, 159
Morales, Iris, 27–28
Morales, Martita, 17, 50–52, 55–57, 71, 76
Moreno, Marisel C., 94
Morgan, Joan, 15–16
Muckley, Robert L., 31
Muñoz, Amina, 17, 48–51, 54–55, 71, 76, 169
Muñoz, José Esteban, 13, 189n1
Muñoz Marín, Luis, 3–4, 178n9, 180n9

Naropa Institute, 44, 184n59
National Black Theater Festival, 80
National Black Theatre of Harlem, 142
necessary theater, 2, 144
Negrón-Muntaner, Frances, 13, 179n27
"Neo-Rican Lesson" (Carrera), 37–39
Neorican Seminar, 17, 20, 28–29, 31–38
New Rican Village, 66–71, 188n60, 188n61, 189n64
New WORLD Theater, 81, 171n1, 192n28
New York Hip-Hop Theater Festival. See *Hip Hop Theater Festival*
New York Shakespeare Festival, 6; Summer Mobile Theater, 66, 71. *See also* Joseph Papp: *Conjunto Libre*
Nilda (Mohr), 104
Noel, Urayoán, 13, 24
nostalgia, 119, 123–28, 201n24
Notes of Neorican Seminar, 17, 20, 28–38; cover of, 34–36
Nueva York! (Esteves and Zanes), 84, 86
Nuyorican aesthetic, 3, 6–7, 13, 17–19, 26–27, 40–47, 73–77, 80
Nuyorican feminism, 14–15, 48, 57
Nuyorican feminist aesthetic, 7–11, 18–19, 48, 56–57, 71, 84–87, 120, 138, 140–41, 169
Nuyorican identity, 6–7, 8–10, 29, 33–36, 39, 46, 97–99
Nuyorican movement, 6, 19, 27–29, 41, 46, 65, 71, 152, 163–68
Nuyorican poetry, 3, 6–7, 13, 39, 42, 46, 48, 50–52, 61, 66, 71, 84, 86, 145, 155, 169, 181n32, 185n6
Nuyorican Poetry, 29, 42, 43–44, 46, 48–49, 50–52, 55, 57, 60, 65, 68, 76, 94, 152
Nuyorican Poets, 6–7, 34, 43, 51–52, 87, 148, 163, 172n9
Nuyorican Poets Café, 3, 6–7, 27, 29, 39–49, 51–52, 66, 75–78, 84–89, 145–49, 153, 168–69, 183n49; founding mothers 48–72
Nuyorican(s), 3, 6–7, 8–9, 24, 29, 89–91, 93, 150, 152, 164–65
Nuyorican Stories, 163–69
Nuyorican theater, 3, 6–7, 14, 41, 42, 66
"Nuyorico" (La Bruja), 87, 91–92, 194n18
Nuyoriqueña(s), 7, 8–13, 17, 20, 29, 50, 72, 73, 169

"Ode to a Tequila Head" (Esteves), 59
ofrendas (offerings), 142
Open Theatre, 39–40, 47
Operation Bootstrap, 3–4, 99, 172n9
orisha(s), 44, 145–46, 157
Ortega, Eliana, 50, 185
Otero, Néstor, 69, 71, 189
"Oye me que mi espíritu habla" (Esteves), 138–39, 145

Papp, Joseph, 6, 39–40, 47, 66–67, 148, 154, 182

People's Church. *See* Hispanic Methodist Church
Pérez, Laura, 18, 142, 159, 187n56
Pérez, Martín, "Tito" 60–65, 187
performeras, 7, 10–19, 48–52, 71–73, 140–42, 150–53, 159, 169, 185n6
Pietri, Pedro, 3, 27, 51, 55–56, 91, 148, 163, 172–73n9, 188, 199n29
Pietri, Willie, 148
Piñero, Miguel, 3–5, 29–30, 40–46, 49–51, 75, 87–88, 148, 163–64, 182n38, 184n59
Pláticas / platicando(s), 48, 50–54, 58–65, 71–72, 76, 185n13
"Poem for Closet Poets" (Esteves), 10–11
poetry slam. *See* slam poetry
Poets Café. *See* Nuyorican Poets Café
The Poets of the City, 5–7
"Pollito Chicken" (La Bruja), 18, 84, 87, 97–100, 195nn33–36
Pough, Gwendolyn D., 16, 50, 119, 134–35
Power, Will, 82, 122
prison theater, 47
Psalmayene 24, 82
Public Theater (Papp), 47, 66–67, 80, 183n49
"Puerto Rican Discovery #3 Not Neither" (Esteves), 9–10
Puerto Rican Nationalist Party, 17, 20, 21, 23, 37, 46

Queen Latifah, 122, 126
queer performers, 77, 103, 168
queer studies, 13, 90–91, 103, 172n6

race 76, 79, 91, 101–20, 129–30,140–41, 156; and intersectionality, 46, 49, 58. *See also* Afro-Latinidad
racism, 15, 24–27, 60, 91, 103–9, 113, 121, 130–32, 140–42, 158–59; internalized 56
Reserve Officers Training Corps (ROTC), 55
revolts, women-led, 20–23
Rivera, Raquel Z., 14, 140
Rivera-Servera, Ramón H., 13, 103
roach as metaphor, 27, 102, 109, 114–17, 199n29
Rodriguez, Abraham, Jr., 56
Rodriguez, Héctor, 41
Rodriguez, Luz, 17, 50–53, 57–58, 71, 76, 169
Roldan, Julio, 62
Román, David, 13
Rose, Tricia, 14, 126–27
Rossini, Jon D., 13
Rubí Theater Company, Inc., 1–2, 81, 86, 115, 171n1
Ruiz, Mildred, 83

sacroprofane, 143
Sánchez González, Lisa, 13
Sandoval, Chela, 9
Sandoval-Sánchez, Alberto, 13, 154, 179n24
self-marriage ceremonies (de León), 140, 160–62
Short Eyes, 40
Sideshow, 41, 87
Simmons, Russell, 77–78
"sister, *para nuestras hermanas*," 55–56
slam poetry, 73, 75–79, 82–83, 91, 121, 127, 190, 191
Smith, Marc, 75–77
Smurf(s), 102–8, 198n15
Smurfette, 102–10, 116, 134, 197n13, 198n18
"The Sounds of Sixth Street" (Morales), 56
South Bronx, 18, 73–74, 89–90, 93, 193n13
Spanglish, 34, 36, 44, 49, 91–92, 156
Spanish language, 10, 29–31, 34–37, 44, 49, 104, 106, 111, 156, 181n32. *See also* "Pollito Chicken"
spiritual activism, 1, 2, 141, 152, 159, 171, 204
spiritual discourse, 18–19
spirituality, 3, 16, 138–62; and theater history, 142–44
spoken word, 7, 12, 72, 73, 75–79, 81–82, 118, 120–23, 127
Stephenson, Andrew, 12
"Strength" (Andress), 116–17
Sun, Nilaja, 14–18, 80, 81, 101–18, 134, 169, 197nn11–12, 198nn18–19, 199n24; "Letter to a Friend," 198–99n21; *No Child . . .*, 196n1; *and individual works by the author*

taboos, cultural, 57–58
testimoniando, 50–53, 60
Thieves in the Temple (de León), 18, 80, 118–37, 202n28, 203n40, 203n54
Tropical Rain (Esteves), 92
Turner, Victor, 143–44, 150
"Twice a Month Is Mother's Day" (Pietri), 55

Umpierre, Luz María, 52
United Farm Workers (UFW), 143, 205n15
UNIVERSES, 81, 83

Valdez, Luis, 114, 141
Vásquez, Nelson, 95–96, 194n26
Vega, Ana Lydia, 98–99, 195nn35–36
violence: against women, 59–60; police, 27, 60–65
Virgin of Guadalupe, 143, 171, 205n15, 205n16

"Weaver" (Esteves), 145
"welcome to san juan, oldest city in the u.s." (Muñoz), 54
"When was the last time you saw mami smile?" (Casiano), 55
Whiteness, 106–7, 112, 128–32
Worrell, Marilyn, 148–52
wreck(ing), 16, 50, 65, 119, 125, 133–35. *See also* Pough, Gwendolyn D.

Yarbro-Bejarano, Yvonne 49
Ybarra, Patricia, 13
Yerba Buena, 53, 61–62, 92, 138, 145, 173n9
Young Family, 39–42
Young Lords, 17, 20–29, 31, 45–47, 52, 58–60, 118, 167, 180n30; herstory of, 27–29; Women's Caucus of, 28

Zanes, Dan, 84, 86, 97, 171n1